THIS CAGED WOLF

SOUL BITTEN SHIFTER 3

EVERLY FROST

Copyright © 2021 by Everly Frost
All rights reserved.

No part of this book may be reproduced or used in any manner whatsoever without the express written permission of the author, except for the use of brief quotations in a book review.

This book is a work of fiction. Names, characters, places, and incidents either are the product of the author's imagination or are used fictitiously. Any resemblance to actual persons, living or dead, is purely coincidental.

Frost, Everly
This Caged Wolf

Cover design by Luminescence Covers

For information on reproducing sections of this book or sales of this book, go to
www.EverlyFrost.com
everlyfrost@gmail.com

Anyone can be pack.

CHAPTER ONE

My mother stands across the moonlit forest clearing holding a crossbow pointed at my heart.

"Hello, Natalia," I say, addressing her by name.

She doesn't flinch. Moments ago, she told me that she's here to kill me.

Even a day ago, her intentions would have shocked and hurt me, but my heart is harder now. I gave up my human soul the same way that Cody Griffin gave up his wolf—in the name of survival. I am the daughter of Fenrir, the monstrous wolf. That mere fact makes me a target. Not only a target of my father himself, but of others as well.

Anyone I care about will be used as leverage against me. Never again will I be caged and forced to align my strength with those who want to dominate and control me.

I learned my lesson the hard way.

Now, the only supernatural I will allow to stand beside me is the Killer. He was once Tristan Masters in the same way that I was once a wolf shifter with a human soul.

He hunches beside me, dressed only in black jeans, his chest slicked with sweat and remnant blood from the fight we left behind tonight. Minutes ago, we swam in a clear creek, but it seems that violence and death doesn't wash off us so easily. The Killer's black hair is wild and long enough to cover his green eyes, but the amber flecks in his irises glint in the dark. I learned to distinguish the Killer's mind by the way his muscles cord and his biceps bulge, perpetually pumped, but it's becoming harder and harder to tell Tristan's minds apart. They can manifest in any combination: Deceiver, Coward, Killer... and Tristan.

He is as hard to kill as I am.

I tip my head to the side, considering my mother carefully as I remain directly in her line of fire. "If you're here to end me, you should take your chance right now," I say to her. "I may not give you another."

The crossbow she's holding had better have some sort of magic to it. My father has survived through the ages despite what I'm sure have been many attempts to kill him. He and I—and Tristan, for that matter—are creatures of old magic. We are not immune to each other but are highly resistant to all other forms of magic. I also suspect that it would take more than killing my human form to end me. My wolf's energy must also die. Otherwise, no matter how badly I'm hurt, I will heal.

My mother's weapon doesn't waver, but I sense the heaviness of her sigh as she exhales. "It isn't easy to kill what you love."

"Love?" I scoff. "What love could you possibly have for me?"

My lips draw back into a snarl as I take a step closer to her, daring her to pull the trigger.

My voice is cold. "When I thought you were dead, there was a chance you didn't leave me willingly. Now that you're here, it's clear you must have abandoned me. Rejected me. You gave me to a wolf shifter who tried—but couldn't—protect me from a pack that tormented me. Where is the love in that?"

It's a guess on my part that she voluntarily handed me over to Andreas Dean—the wolf shifter who raised me. Since my mother's alive, it's more likely that she gave me up willingly than that I was stolen from her. Otherwise, she would have come for me.

My mother might appear to be made of stone right now, but I can sense nearly every flicker of her emotions beneath the impassive mask she's wearing. Her breathing caught when I accused her of rejecting me, and her pulse started hammering when I said that my former pack tormented me.

She is not as emotionally guarded as I am—despite being an assassin, and apparently a very good one.

She's dressed in a black, fitted bodysuit that, combined with her boots, covers her body from her feet all the way up to her chin. Her features resemble an older version of me, although the more I look at her, the more I realize she's a mirror image of what I used to look like. Before my true nature was revealed.

She has long, wavy, red hair, high cheekbones, and bright, sapphire eyes. She carries multiple weapons in a harness around her hips, but the ring on her left hand draws my attention more sharply than anything else she's wearing. The silver band is crafted into a sequence of leaves with a single diamond set deep into the top. It looks like an engagement ring, except that it's sitting on the forefinger of her left hand.

"What I did to you was unforgivable," Natalia says, surprising me with her admission. "I was faced with a jagged maze of dead ends and only one way out that would keep you alive and safe from your father."

"So your intention was to save my life?" My voice drips with cynicism as I shrug off the sincerity in her declaration. "Despite that, you're here to end me, after all."

A muscle clenches in Natalia's jaw. "I have no choice, Tessa. The pure magic that preserved your human soul and caged your darker nature has been broken. Someone has to stop you before you walk your father's path. This world can't survive two war wolves."

My lips part. Then close. My eyes narrow. It's not her threat that makes me pause, but what she said about my human soul.

I take another step toward her but stop myself as soon as her grip on the crossbow tightens. I'm not afraid of her—not at all—but I want answers while I can get them. The minute she fires, I will be forced to fight her, and then the opportunity for information will be gone.

"What pure magic?" I ask, a sharp demand for the truth.

Natalia's lips press into a hard line, as if she's regretting speaking about it, but she doesn't deny me answers. "Only the purest of old magic could hide your existence from your father. There was always a risk that you might destroy its protective essence around your soul. As soon as that happened, you would become a monster like him. The moment he captured you, I knew I had no choice but to find you and end you."

I want to tell her to do it. *Get the fuck on with it. Try to end me.*

But I'm not finished seeking answers. The first time I met my father in his white wolf form, he ranted about someone hiding me from him, that it was a nearly impossible feat and could only have been achieved using old magic. He promised to find the person responsible and end them. Now my mother has confirmed that the purest of old magic kept me hidden from him all of these years.

"*Whose* pure magic?" I ask.

Who would have that kind of power? Helen is the most powerful witch I know, but, even as strong as she is, Helen was genuinely confused when she first met me. She didn't know who or what I was.

"A woman who gave me hope," my mother says. She takes a shaky breath, her voice wobbling. "She convinced me that you wouldn't follow your father's path. She made me believe you would choose light over dark. She persuaded Andreas to protect you from your father—and from yourself. He and his mate had lost their own cub that very night, born too soon, and nobody else knew about it." My mother's lips press together. "This woman... She even convinced Cora, Andreas's mate, that Cora could find healing by raising you as her own. We were three people struggling and in pain and she gave us answers..."

My mother's lips twist, her voice becoming bitter. "Reality is so much harder to navigate than a fairytale. Andreas was the only one of us who stayed true to his promise to her."

Andreas had protected me until his death, but Cora had rejected me within a day. Despite that, she didn't tell anyone that I wasn't her daughter. I'll never know for sure, but maybe she didn't say anything because it would have involved revealing the pain of losing her cub. Or... maybe she used her knowledge about me as leverage to force Andreas to lose the fight with Peter Nash. I always wondered why Andreas didn't beat Peter that day.

"What promise did *you* break, mother?" I ask.

"I'm breaking it now," she says. "I wasn't supposed to see you again. Not even if I thought you'd turned to darkness."

As unafraid of her as I am, I'm chilled that she's being so candid with me right now, especially in front of the Killer.

She must be very confident that we won't walk away alive tonight to repeat what she has said. All assassins are human, but Cody warned me that they derive their power from old magic—the magic of the gods somehow bestowed on them.

For a second, I allow my crimson vision to rise, harnessing its power to try to detect whether or not Natalia carries any magical objects on her body.

A flash of power from her ring nearly blinds me.

Within a blink, I shut down my crimson vision, fast enough that she might believe she imagined the color change in my eyes.

Or not.

Her expression hardens as she takes a steady step toward me. Step by step, we've decreased the gap between us as we were speaking, and now we are within striking distance of each other.

"Whose blood is on your body, Tessa?"

I'm dressed in a cobalt blue dress with thin straps and a plunging neckline. The skirt is tight and short, sitting beneath a diaphanous overskirt that joins at the center of the waist and splits to either side.

My dress is stained with blood. Smears of it still cling to my arms where I will need to scrub at my body to remove the signs of battle.

"I destroyed Mother Lavinia's coven tonight," I say, giving my mother the same honesty she gave me.

A crease appears in Natalia's forehead. "What of Mother Lavinia herself?"

"Dead."

My mother's eyes narrow even further. "And Cody Griffin? What about him?"

A sharp sensation pierces my heart.

Within the space of a breath, a wash of rage threatens to overcome my reason. Cody had tried to stop the warlock, Silas, during the battle tonight. Painful images flash through my mind of Cody leaping at Silas with a makeshift dagger while Silas struck back with a blast of lightning too strong for Cody's weakened body. I can't shake the last moment of Cody's life when his heart burned with a fire that stunned me, a last surge of strength that allowed him to fight.

Cody's death was the final crack in my heart that set me on this path.

Cody didn't succeed in killing Silas, but I did.

Snarls rise to my lips as I close the distance between me and my mother, not caring that her hand now tightens on the trigger.

I reach her so fast that she takes a step out of the direct beam of moonlight, her upper body disappearing into the shadows.

My night vision allows me to discern her features in the shadows, but my crimson vision rises with my anger, seeking the shape of my mother's true impulses and emotions—avoiding focusing directly on her ring. I'm frustrated to discover that her real feelings are now hidden by the surging power that streams from the ring. The ebb and flow from it is like sudden armor around her mind.

Before she can retract the crossbow, I bump right up against the front of it. I want her to pull the trigger because it will give me an excuse to lash out.

All I need is a reason.

Give me a fucking reason.

"Cody Griffin was my friend," I say. "My father's warlock—Silas—killed him. So I killed Silas. If you hurt anyone I care about, I will kill you, too."

I'm still gripping the magical orb that Silas used to store the dark magic that kept him alive if he suffered a mortal wound. I have nowhere to put it, which means I'll have to fight my mother one-handed.

"Cody Griffin is dead?" she asks.

"Anyone who cares about me dies," I say. My voice lowers. Threatening. "I won't let that happen again."

The tension rises between us as I continue to press against the front of the crossbow and my mother remains steadfast and quiet in the shadows.

Why the fuck hasn't she pulled the trigger already?

My free hand is loose at my side, but my bare feet are planted in the moist forest floor. I'm ready to move as soon as she twitches. I've caught a bullet midair. I'm sure I'll be able to deflect the crossbow bolt as soon as it releases. Then I will let out my wolf, knock Natalia to her knees, and remove her ring. Without her power, she'll be helpless.

The moonlight is so bright where I'm standing that her knuckles appear to be turning white as she clutches her weapon tighter and tighter.

"Make your move, mother," I whisper. "Will you try to end me or not?"

A muscle in her jaw ticks. A confident smile.

Her finger squeezes the trigger.

The mechanism releases, the force behind it strong enough to drive the bolt into my heart.

My free hand snaps out, my fingers closing around the bolt faster than blinking. I rip the bolt right off the mechanism before it can fly toward me. The force of my attack tears the entire crossbow from my mother's hands while leaving the arrow in my hand.

She jolts back with a shout when the weapon sails to the side.

It clatters along the mossy ground while I take a quick look at the bolt.

The tip of the arrow looks normal. So does the top, but when I turn it over, I discover that it has a transparent strip along its bottom side, revealing silver liquid contained within it.

It looks like the same liquid that Cody used to tranquilize my father and the ice jotunn on the night I was captured. He took them down with darts filled with fluid that looked just like this. There's enough liquid in the bolt I'm holding now to equal four darts' worth. It only took two to knock out my father. Three for the ice jotunn. My mother is definitely not taking any chances with me.

Natalia stiffens, her shoulders tense, her gaze suddenly wild as she glances at the fallen crossbow. She doesn't appear to have another bolt, so the weapon is useless to her unless she wants to use it as a bludgeon. Her only other options are her gun and knives.

I'm strong enough to snap the bolt in my fist, but I can't risk any of the tranquilizer fluid coming into contact with my skin. I don't know whether the liquid is strong enough to take me down on mere contact.

"You're not here to kill me," I say, hot anger rising inside me. "You're here to capture me."

With a furious scream, I spin and pitch the bolt into the nearest tree trunk so hard that it vibrates where it impales the wood.

My father caged me, broke me, and continued to break me, piece by piece over the course of days.

Never again will I be chained. *Never.*

Tears of rage fill my eyes as I scream. "I would rather die than be caged!"

While I grip the warlock's orb, my free fist snaps out, aimed at Natalia's face. She blocks the blow, but I've already positioned myself for another hit, my fist jabbing low at her ribs, then high at her shoulder, then at her neck, all rapid punches.

Her reflexes are impressive. She blocks each blow, leaping back with every step I take toward her.

The Killer jumps clear of our fight, but the flash of violence in his eyes, the descent of his incisors, and the intensity with which his gaze follows my mother's movements tells me he considers her to be easy prey. I'm sure he would have killed her already, but he won't cross me. He and I have an uneasy truce that I doubt he'll break. Possibly. His increasingly unhappy growls tell me he might not care.

"What were you going to do with me, Mother?" I ask, my voice raw with hatred, rising with a pain that is so cold, it makes me want to rip the earth apart beneath her feet. "Chain me? Beat me? Hurt the people I love?"

"Tessa!" she shouts. "I have to take you in."

"Take me in?" My fist flies in another sequence of one-handed jabs that she blocks. I force her to backstep around the clearing as I snarl at her. "How long did you imagine you could cage me?"

"As long as it takes to convince the Master Assassin to end you."

I don't know much about the assassin hierarchy, but I have to assume the Master Assassin—whoever they are—holds the highest position.

As I prowl after my mother, I quickly run through every detail Cody told me about their organization. He tried to convince me to flee to their stronghold. He told me to find the boxing gym where Andreas Dean had once trained because nobody would come after me there—not even my father.

Everyone is afraid of the assassins. Apparently.

Everyone except me.

I extend the claws of my free hand. "Only two creatures have the power to end me."

One of them is standing behind me—the Killer. The other is my father.

"Wrong!" my mother shouts. "The Master Assassin of the Dominion can finish you!" Her hands are raised defensively, but I catch the flicker of her gaze back to the bolt stuck in the nearby tree trunk. She must still hope she can use it against me. "He's the most powerful Master we've ever had."

I take her claim with a healthy dose of distrust. Even Helen, the witch who controls Hidden House, can't kill me, and she's possibly the strongest supernatural I've met who wasn't born of old magic.

The moment my mother darts toward the bolt, I step into her path, my claws snapping out and cutting the weapon belt from her waist. Her guns and daggers clatter to the earth. She reacts swiftly, snatching the handles of two of the falling daggers before they drop, lunging toward me in a fluid movement.

The blades flash.

I twist to the side just in time to avoid the cut across my ribs, but—*damn*—I don't quite avoid the nick to my shoulder, positioned right above the spot where my father drew my deep blood.

As she attempts to strike at my neck, her ring glints directly in my vision and I finally get a sense of its power. There is death in its intricate pieces. Death and unnatural physical strength.

With a scream, I retaliate, knocking her arms to the side, jabbing at her jaw—a trick throw to distract her before I follow up with my real move. A kick to her stomach knocks her into the nearest tree. I kick again to relieve her of one dagger and grab her wrist and twist to force her to drop the other.

Pushing my free hand against her heart as she presses against the tree, I threaten to cut through her chest with my claws.

She smirks at me as she tries to catch her breath. "You can't cut through my protective suit—"

My claws slice right through the material, making her gasp when they prick her skin.

"It looks like I can," I say. "You should remain very still, Mother, while I decide whether or not to end you."

I could cut out her heart. I could release my wolf and send my energy tearing through her body. I could kill her as easily as I killed Mother Lavinia's witches. The only unknown for me is the power of the ring she wears—what exactly it allows her to do.

Her cheeks are flushed. "You're as dangerous as your father," she cries. "*More* dangerous! You're volatile! Fenrir has learned to live within the boundaries of the natural and supernatural world, to manipulate the course of events from the shadows, but you…" She attempts to strike out at me, her fist flying toward my cheek before I deflect it. "You will start new wars."

"I will *finish* the old wars!" I shout. "I will finish my father."

Shallow lines of blood bloom across her cheekbones. I must have nicked her with my claws when I disarmed her.

Making a decision, I lower my voice. "Your choices after I was born had nothing to do with keeping me safe. I am my father's daughter and that makes me unworthy of your love or your protection."

She blanches and stops fighting me for a moment. "I never believed that." Her eyes glisten with tears, but she blinks them away. "I couldn't keep you safe back then. I had no other choice. It's different now. Our new Master Assassin has changed everything. *He* is the reason your father is afraid of us."

"Well," I whisper, "be sure to thank your new master for the offer of captivity. But I decline."

I retract my claws and shove her away from me before I leap back from her.

My shoulders hunch like the Killer's as I take one last look at her.

"I see now why my father loved you," I say.

I thought my heart had broken in all the places that mattered, that it was misshapen and cold already, but now I discover that I still have a vulnerable spot reserved for my mother.

She jumps away from the tree and spins to the side of the clearing, shocking me when she screams. "Kill her! For fuck's sake, do it now!"

What the…?

I whirl in the direction she's facing because it's clear she isn't speaking to me. I back into the Killer's chest as he steps up behind me, his growls low and threatening, his claws extended at the edge of my vision.

The back of my neck prickles and it's not because the Killer's breathing down it. My mother's presence was impossible to pinpoint until she chose to reveal herself. Until then, all I had was a heightened awareness of danger.

The same creeping sensation makes all of the hairs on my arms stand on end now.

"She isn't alone," the Killer says.

"How many are there?" I ask in a low whisper.

How long have they been here?

And how many fucking tranquilizers do I have pointed at me now?

CHAPTER TWO

"Show yourselves!" I call, turning in a circle.

Stepping toward the center of the clearing, Natalia clutches her side where I'm sure I bruised her ribs with my kick. Her ruby red hair falls across her face. Between the strands, I make out the unhappy way the corners of her mouth are turned down.

Her focus shifts around the clearing, as if she's watching the path of someone—or many people—whom I can't see. Her gaze stops at a point halfway between herself and us.

It's the brightest part of the clearing, where the moonlight spears through the canopy overhead.

A male figure appears in the rays of light. He's naked from the waist up, wearing only black jeans and boots, his broad chest and enormous arms a chiseled mass of muscles on muscles... on muscles...

My head tips back—*and back*—as I look up to meet the stormy gray eyes of the largest mountain of muscles I've ever seen—and that includes Brynjar, the ice jotunn.

The newcomer is easily seven feet tall with dark hair and a nose that looks like it's been broken a few too many times. Possibly in the supernatural boxing ring I've heard so much about.

He doesn't carry any weapons. Certainly no tranquilizers that I can see. Instead, his fists rest at his sides, his posture terrifying in the way that he's so relaxed, appearing completely in control of his emotions and body.

Like my mother, he wears a ring on the forefinger of his left hand. It's jet-black with three chunky rubies set in the top of it—eerily similar to the color of my hair. The stones catch the moonlight and flash crimson beams across the clearing.

This is a man who doesn't need any fucking weapons. He could snap my neck with his bare hands and not break a sweat.

He's as dangerous as Tristan.

The Killer growls behind me, hunching even further where he stands at the corner of my view as he takes in the new threat.

"Master." My mother drops to her knees in front of the man with the stormy gray eyes. "I ask that you end my daughter."

His jaw clenches as he looks down at her.

"No," he says.

Her head snaps up, her eyes wide. "What? But—"

He turns his back on her and strides toward me.

Stopping a few paces away, he positions himself far enough from me that I can't take a swipe at him with my claws. I stand my ground even when he blocks out most of the light with his big body.

"My name is Alexei Mason," he says, his expression betraying not a shred of emotion—not anger, not hatred, not loathing, nothing that allows me to get a handle on his intentions. "I'm the Master Assassin of the Dominion." His lips press together, possibly his first hint of anger. "This is not how I wanted to meet you."

"What do you know of me?" I ask, my defenses high.

Alexei exhales a heavy sigh. "I know you've had a tough night, Tessa. I'm not here to make it worse."

I glance around the clearing, wary of whom else I can't see.

"There's nobody else with me," he says, apparently perceptive enough to read my actions. "I'm here for the sole purpose of stopping my aunt from making a fatal mistake."

I take a quick step back. "Your aunt?"

"Natalia Mason—your mother—is my father's sister." Once more, his expression is unreadable; he doesn't betray any emotion as he speaks. "I first became aware of your existence when Cody Griffin walked into my father's boxing gym two months ago. After

13

that, I called my aunt back from her self-imposed exile to discover that I have a cousin. However, she refused to reveal the identity of your father."

I allow an angry growl to escape my lips. "You wouldn't be here now if you didn't know who I am," I say.

He nods. "I have another source, who confirmed your parentage for me tonight. Daughter of Fenrir. Daughter of war."

Another source? I guess the assassins must have spies everywhere —especially if they can disappear into the shadows and I can't detect their presence.

I decide to cut to the chase. "Then you know I'm dangerous," I say. "My own mother wants me dead. Do you really expect me to believe that you don't?"

"My feelings are irrelevant," Alexei says, leveling his stormy eyes with mine, and now I sense the true violence that lurks within his mind, apparent in the hard edges of his jaw and the cold light in his eyes. Yet, he also appears completely in control. "My feelings will never get in my way."

My breath hitches.

If I were to harness my crimson vision right now, I have no doubt I would see that he has attained a perfect balance between compassion and rage. The ability to coldly kill what has to be killed while protecting what needs to be protected.

A balance I'm afraid I will never achieve.

I allow an icy smile to touch my lips, my incisors peeking out and my wolf form glimmering around my chest like a ghost. "Then why don't we get on with it, Alexei Mason, Master Assassin of the Dominion?"

To my surprise, he takes a step back, his actions affirming his decision not to end me.

"I follow the Assassin's Code," he says. "Your name is not written in my ledger. Your death has not been sanctioned." He turns a hard, cold stare on Natalia. "My aunt has broken the Code by coming here tonight, and for that she will be dealt with as the Code requires."

My mother's stare is rebellious, stubborn, but a shiver runs down my spine. Cody said the assassins were not what he expected. When he asked them to end him, he found out they didn't operate that way. Whatever their Code is, the tension in Alexei's jaw tells me my mother is in for a world of pain—despite her indignant attitude and her familial relationship with the Master Assassin.

"What about my father?" I demand to know. "Why haven't you killed *him*?"

Alexei's jaw tightens. His fists clench, his lips twist, and a dangerous light enters his eyes. "A failed assassination can't be attempted again. Every faction of assassins has tried to kill your father at some time or another and failed. We are all barred from trying again."

My eyes widen. My father himself pointed to the spot on the map of Oregon that is controlled by the assassins and told me he doesn't control that area. He is genuinely afraid of the assassins, but now I'm hearing that they won't kill him. "*You* tried and failed?"

"Not me," Alexei says. "It was my predecessor. Soon after Natalia went into exile twenty-three years ago, the former Master attempted to end Fenrir. The mission failed." The storm grows in Alexei's eyes. "Your father would not survive *me*."

Alexei takes a step toward me and my senses buzz. He's human—I'm as sure as I can be about that—but there's an undefinable power around him that isn't stemming from his ring, a darkness that I can't quite pinpoint. He carries shadows that seem to be caused by an absence of light around him, even though he has chosen to remain in the brightest part of the clearing.

His voice is low as he continues. "If the War Wolf comes anywhere near the people I love, I will kill him and damn the Code. I believe he understands this."

Behind him, my mother edges forward. "Tessa is worse than her father," she says. "Alexei, you have to listen to me! She's a threat. You have to end her now—*before* she hurts anyone else."

I snap a quick response to her allegation. "I haven't hurt anyone who didn't deserve it," I say to my mother. "Unlike you."

She casts me a look of outrage. "I haven't—"

"Me!" I shout. "You were alive all of this time. You left me with people who hated me and hurt me. *You.* Hurt. Me."

"Stop lying to me about your life," she says. Her ring suddenly glints, a flash of power, as if she's using it to test the truth of my statements. "Andreas's pack would have adored you. You had the power to make them love you—"

"They didn't." Alexei's voice is quiet, but it breaks through my mother's rant.

She blinks at him.

He continues. "Tessa's body carries the proof that her former pack treated her very badly."

I draw back into the shadows. *How would he know about my past wounds, my broken bones?* I shudder at the thought that maybe he can see more of my body and my mind than I want him to.

He turns to me. "I believe we were born in the same year, Tessa. We both grew up without our mothers. My father is human and he raised me on his own. He would not have been able to protect you, although he would have fought to the death for you if he'd known about you." Alexei's voice hardens. "Had *I* known about you, I would have come for you years ago. Nothing would have stood in the way of me protecting you as a member of my family."

He casts a glare at Natalia that forces her onto her back foot, the blood draining from her face.

Alexei takes a deep breath. "I'm offering you the chance to come with me now, Tessa."

I try to process the vehemence in his declaration that he would have fought for me, try to reconcile it with the gentleness of his request that I come with him now. I'm shell-shocked. The notion that this fierce stranger would have protected me is so unexpected. I want to believe him, to take his speech at face value. I want to feel the warmth that his claim should make me feel, but I can't remove the protective barbs I've placed around my heart.

Sadness stabs inside my chest.

Fuck, I'm discovering all of my heart's remaining fragile places tonight.

I glance at the Killer to gauge his response to Alexei's request. The Killer has remained remarkably quiet, other than his soft and unhappy growls. I'm startled to find that his shoulders are impossibly hunched, his biceps pumped, and a vein throbs in his neck.

He is focused on my mother.

"Killer?" I say.

"She hurt you." The Killer's incisors gleam in the moonlight. "I need to end her."

My lips part in surprise. The more time I spend with the Killer, the more the lines between his minds are blurring. Right now, I hear Tristan's voice in his declaration and it plucks at my heart—right at the spot that Alexei's declaration has warmed.

My mother came here to try to convince the Master Assassin to kill me. She won't give up on her task, but deep in the darkest part of his heart, the Killer knows what it means to end a parent.

Tristan was forced to kill his father, who succumbed to the three minds of Cerberus and caused irreparable damage to his pack. Tristan thought I would be the answer to his own battle against the minds of Cerberus—that I would be strong enough to kill him before he hurt the people he loved. I am, but I'm determined that I won't need to be. My father revealed that a book of old magic is hidden in the library in Tristan's territory. It contains everything I need to know about Cerberus and how to end him. In the meantime, as long as the Killer stays at my side, I will do everything I can to curb his impulses.

I'm resolved that we will only kill what should be killed.

I quickly consider Alexei and Natalia—and then the Killer. If the Killer makes a move, I have no doubt that Tristan will become a sanctioned target of the assassins.

"No." I keep my voice low as I take hold of the Killer's arm. "You won't hurt her. Not today."

The Killer doesn't pay me any attention, edging toward my mother and pulling against my hold.

"Look at me," I say to the Killer, my voice becoming firmer. He shakes me off, but I reach for his face, forcing him to meet my eyes. "*No.*"

My mother said I would start new wars.

I won't start one with the assassins.

The Killer lowers his face to mine, glaring at me. "Your mother should die for what she did to you."

Should she? I honestly don't know. She abandoned me. Left me behind. I believe she was afraid of me when I was born. She's still afraid of me. But does fear deserve death? She can't kill me herself, so she'll never pose a mortal threat to me that could justify killing her in self-defense. What, then, are my choices?

"Her own people will deal with her," I say, drawing another growl from the Killer.

I press my lips together, a resolute line, showing him that I won't be swayed.

Before the Killer can make another move, I turn to Alexei.

"I'm sorry," I say to him. "We can't come with you. My purpose is to end my father. You've revealed that you can't help me with that."

He gives me a single nod, his emotions hidden again. "I understand, but when you have walked your path, come find me, Tessa. You have a family waiting for you if you want us."

Us? I guess he means him and his father. He can't be including my mother.

Backing away from Alexei, I reach for the Killer's hand, carefully squeezing his big palm without touching his claws. I incline my head toward the forest, a suggestion, not an order. "We need to go."

He pauses, his claws still extended before he slowly retracts them. His gaze flashes across me before he turns without another word and lopes ahead of me, aiming for the dark patch between the thickest trees.

I pause before I break into a run.

I glance back once to see Alexei stride to Natalia and place his hand on her shoulder, but it's not a consoling gesture. His grip is visibly firm, his voice hard. "You know the consequences of your actions."

They disappear in a blink, and I can't sense their presence any longer.

I don't look back again.

With every step I take, my footfalls on the damp forest floor seem to drum to a constant beat.

My mother is alive.

She's alive.

And she wants me dead.

Well… she can fucking get in line.

CHAPTER THREE

Following the Killer's trail, I dart between the trees, rapidly leaving my mother and my cousin behind.

"We will find a place to sleep," the Killer says. "Not here. Farther north, there is a neutral zone between territories. The witches in Mother Zala's coven won't go there. I will show you."

He speeds up again, and I follow him for the next half an hour. Along the way, I'm increasingly conscious of the dark magic orb I carry in my hand. I can fight one-handed, but it's an impediment I don't need. When the overskirt attached to my dress flies out at the corner of my vision, it gives me an idea.

Stopping beside a large tree and keeping the Killer's path within my sights, I quickly use a single claw to cut the overskirt off at the waist on the right-hand side, leaving the left side intact in case I need it later. Wrapping the orb tightly in the material and tying it off like a bag in the middle, I wrap the rest of the material around my waist.

Bursting into a sprint again, I follow the Killer's scent until I see him up ahead. He glances back with a cunning smile as if he were waiting for me to catch up. Hitting my stride, I run alongside him for another hour, leaping over debris and darting between the trees.

When the sound of rushing water reaches us, the Killer slows his pace to a quick walk.

"There's a water source up ahead," he says, a crease forming in his forehead. "It sounds louder than a creek, but there shouldn't be any larger rivers in these parts."

The sound of rushing water is increasingly loud, different to the sound of the bubbling creek we swam in earlier tonight.

I decelerate quickly while he also slows down. I gauge that we must be very close to the neutral zone he spoke of—if not within it.

"How do we reach Mother Zala's coven from here?" I ask. I want to destroy it, but I don't want to run into it tonight. Not without some sort of plan.

"A few miles farther north," the Killer says, peering into the shadows ahead of us. "This is the neutral territory—a mile-wide gap between the southern and northern territories."

While the water sounds have grown louder, the light has decreased. The forest is even thicker here, the moonlight barely touching the ground.

It doesn't seem to be in the Killer's nature to be cautious, but his footfalls become more hesitant. "I don't like this," he says, his voice much softer than before. Changed. "The terrain isn't right. There shouldn't be a water source here at all."

I scrutinize his features as best I can in the darkness, anticipating the reappearance of the Coward. It's no use trying to use my crimson vision on him to discern which mind is dominant at any given point in time. All I'd see would be deeply confusing impulses, a mire of conflicting emotions.

His physical appearance is a more reliable indicator of which mind is dominant. The Killer is hunched with muscles that cord. The Coward has soft green eyes, nearly human in appearance. The Deceiver is harder to spot, a subtle change that I'm still trying to pinpoint.

I feel like I have a handle on how to deal with the Killer, but I'm wary of the Coward. The Killer may be brutal, but the Coward is cruel.

His face is turned away from me as he suddenly drops back. I peer at him, increasingly wary as I step through the narrowing gap between two trees ahead of us.

I step out into nothing.

I scream as my front foot drops through space, pulling me downward.

At the same time, the air around me scratches across my skin, tearing at my face, chest, arms, and legs. My mind whirls, trying to catch up with the sensations ripping at my body, trying to catch up with what I'm seeing and feeling.

I teeter on the edge of a ravine that wasn't there a second ago.

Water rushes along the bottom, hundreds of feet below me, so far that it looks like a sparkling silver rope snaking along the ground. A waterfall crashes about fifty feet to my right. A gray stone bridge stretches from one side of the ravine to the other in front of the waterfall, so close to the waterfall that the spray splashes across the stone.

I register my sudden surroundings in the smallest space of time —the interval it takes me to realize I stepped through a magical barrier. It's a barrier that must be—*terrifyingly*—a safety mechanism that nobody should ever break through because on the other side of it is nothing but air and a drop down the side of a cliff.

Damn my ability to tear through magic!

My reflexes fire, but I'm already falling.

I have just enough momentum to twist and throw my arm back through the magical barrier, reaching for the nearest tree, desperate to grab a branch, a vine, anything to stop my fall. My claws shoot out, dragging along the side of the tree trunk, scraping across it without finding purchase.

The tree's silhouette is blurred behind the barrier.

So is the Killer's form.

"Tessa Dean!" He leaps through the magical shield with a roar, his big hand clamping around mine.

My arm wrenches, nearly dislocating as I jolt to a stop, hitting the side of the cliff. At the same time, the Killer's momentum and my falling weight pulls him over the edge with me.

The claws of his free hand shoot out, dragging through the rocky cliff's edge. There's another sickening drop before his claws wedge between the rocks at the top of the cliff.

Desperately, I hold on to his hand as I dangle in the air.

The muscles in his arms and chest bulge. His claws have wedged into the ground far enough over the edge that his elbow bends at the lip of the cliff, giving him a small amount of leverage.

He roars with effort, trying to pull me up.

I attempt to help, try to use the claws of my own free hand to scratch at the cliff face, attempting to puncture the rock so I can reduce my weight, maybe climb back up on my own.

The Killer's roar cuts short and his voice becomes suddenly soft. "Tessa."

Still trying to wedge myself against the rock to ease my weight, I look up to find that his eyes have changed and his biceps are no longer pumped.

"Tessa, I can't pull you up," he says.

His eyes are soft. Green. Nearly human.

The Coward's eyes.

"If I don't let you go, we'll both fall," the Coward says.

His grip on my hand eases. Loosens.

I exhale my fear. My father convinced me that my end will only happen if my wolf's power is destroyed. I concluded that my human body can't die unless my power also dies.

It's time to find out if I'm right.

Squeezing my eyes shut, I force myself to unfurl my fingers from the Coward's, releasing him before he releases me.

"*No!*"

Tristan's hand closes around mine again, his roar suddenly filled with fear. "No, Tessa!"

My eyes fly open.

Angry, amber-flecked eyes meet mine.

Tristan.

"I'm not letting you fall," he says.

"The Coward is right!" I cry. "We'll both go down. You have to let me go!"

"Fuck the Coward." Tristan's muscles shake with effort. Sweat drips down his face and chest. My own muscles are trembling, my shoulder nearly tearing, and no matter how hard I harness my power, it isn't enough to defy gravity.

I can't fly.

"Tessa." Tristan lowers his voice. "I'd rather fucking crash with you than let you fall alone."

My lips part. My heart hurts. He knows what it means to fall. He fell from the helipad when my father threw him off the edge. Nobody took the fall with him. Or came to help him.

I try once more to find a handhold on the cliff face.

Just as I move, Tristan's claws slip through the stone above us and we both jolt downward, stopping abruptly when his claws catch again. Right at the edge of the cliff.

He's hanging on by nearly nothing now.

"I'll survive!" I cry. "I'll find my way back to you."

He shakes his head. "No."

I open my hand, preparing to fall, hoping that I'll land in the water and not on the rocks. "Tristan—"

"No." His eyes are still on me, his determination unrelenting.

The rocks at the edge of the cliff shift, a pebble falls past my shoulder, I take a final breath, and then—

We drop.

CHAPTER FOUR

The air rushes around us. My back remains to the river and so does Tristan's, but his body weight pulls him down faster than me so that we're quickly level with each other.

I take a moment to look upward, surrounded by a rushing quiet while a sky full of stars glistens above us. For a second, I think that some of the stars move closer, little streaks of light washing across the air above me, swirling and dancing beyond my reach.

Tristan's grip is firm as he pulls me toward him, rapidly bringing me closer. Without releasing his hand, I turn in the air, facing downward so that—for the briefest moment—we're looking at each other.

His hair flies up around his face, but between the strands, his eyes are crisp and green, flecked with amber. The hint of an incisor peeks between his lips.

He is himself.

Fully Tristan.

Startlingly, he looks more peaceful than I've ever seen him. Well, perhaps, one time, the morning after we melded, I saw him like this. I wonder if, in that moment, there was nothing but truth between us. No other minds. No darkness intruding on who we really are. Only the connection of two heartbeats.

It's impossible to speak as we fall, but he cups the back of my head, pulling me onto his chest, wrapping his arms around me, seeming determined to keep me there. A roar rises inside his chest as he fights gravity to hold me close.

Before my view is obscured by his body, I catch sight of the river rising up beneath us. It's a long fall, but we're only a few seconds away from hitting the surface of the water now—water that is broken by sharp gray rocks jutting upward.

Fuck! Panic rushes through me. Positioned like this, Tristan will take the full force of the impact and I can't let him, not when his spine will break on the peaks of stone.

My lips press together while Tristan's body buffers me from the worst of the wind. I calculate our momentum, speed, and the way the air rushes around us.

In a quick move, I wrap my arms and legs around him before I lean sharply to the right, tipping us around. My move is so fierce that I nearly spin us too far, but for the space of time that matters, I'm positioned beneath him.

His shocked roar meets my ears, garbled in the wind. "No, Tessa!"

He tries to shift us again, but I've timed my move for the last possible moment.

I hold tight.

Exhale the shortest breath.

The impact explodes across my back.

Water. Rocks. Every surface beneath me is a hard force that tears me apart.

Pain... Too much pain.

Followed quickly by a numb sensation that invades my arms and legs. My back must be broken. I can't feel anything below my neck.

Tristan's weight drops onto me and then lifts as we're knocked to the side. He plunges at a sharp angle through the rapids. I try to keep hold of him, but my arms won't respond, and we're pulled apart.

I glimpse his form through the white wash, dragged away from me. Blood swirls in the water, but the river is rushing so fast that it quickly washes away.

The swill of water sucks me down beneath the surface before I can take a breath. I'm thrust against another boulder, my body failing to answer my commands as I wrap helplessly around the large rock, hugging it, pinned by the strength of the river beating at my back.

Reaching deep for my power, I drag at the energy inside me, sensing the deep rage, the heat of anger that sustains the dangerous creature I could become. *Have* become.

Closing my eyes, I ease my power out through my broken limbs, fighting the press of water, sensing every shift of bone and muscle as I fill the shape of a wolf.

Slowly, excruciatingly, I complete a full shift into a wolf that is as volatile as the river crashing around me. Power flows through my arms and legs—seeping into my wolf's legs and paws. Energy fills my head and chest, transforming my broken and bleeding body into the shape of an animal whose only purpose is survival.

My tattered dress and bra are caught, wrapped tightly around my wolf's hips while my underpants disappear through the water. I quickly make my wolf smaller so that the material doesn't strangle any part of my body, although the overskirt tugs and pulls in the wash.

Finally, I can lift my head, poking my nose up to gasp for air before submerging again. I control my exhale, forcing myself to be calm despite the panic-inducing force of rushing water.

My brief glance told me that the riverbank is only a few feet away on my right—the bank opposite to the one we fell from.

I need to get to it and locate Tristan.

If he's drowning, every second counts.

I'm afraid to shift back into my human form in case the transformation into my wolf form hasn't completely healed my human body, but I fight my fear, taking another beat to test the feeling in my wolf's legs and chest. I feel strong again. Ready to move.

Not giving myself another second to succumb to anxiety, I draw on my power.

An involuntary scream wrenches from me, filling my mouth with water as I shift back into my human form and experience the pain from which my wolf form was shielding me. I'm aware of my freshly healed human bones and skin—all down my back, my ribs, my right leg, and right arm. Still healing. Still fragile.

Fuck that. I don't have time to waste.

I tell myself that if I'm hurt getting out of the water, I'll shift into my wolf again to accelerate the healing process.

Right now, I need to get to Tristan.

I grit my teeth as I brace against the boulder, easing my body upward, preparing for the water to toss me past the rock. I need to land on top of the stone. Once I'm released from the water's pull, I can leap across to the riverbank.

I'm not prepared for the immense force.

The moment I succeed in dragging myself upward, the water tosses me like a damn leaf. My claws dart out, scraping across the rock's surface, slowing me down enough that I can hold on, finally wrenching myself up onto the small, uneven platform.

My chest heaves as I carefully draw my legs under me, scraping my knees and calves across the rock. My dress is tangled around my waist and I'm grateful to discover the dark magic orb safely secured in my makeshift belt. I was sure it would have been dragged downstream.

Crouching precariously, half-naked, I scan the water as well as the riverbank, but I don't see Tristan.

The bank appears sandy, about thirty feet deep before it meets the cliff face, and stretches far to my left. It's littered with twigs and the occasional fallen branch from the forest that sits far above. The waterfall crashes much farther upstream to my right, while the river appears rockier downstream.

My heart rises into my throat. I know Tristan was able to survive the fall from the helipad, but he was hurt badly enough for Mother Zala to take control of him. I need to believe that he survived this fall too, that my body was a buffer for his. Even if he wasn't injured in the fall, the water would have hurled him against the rocks like it did to me.

The riverbank is within leaping distance now—assuming my right leg can take the impact of a jump. I would shift into my wolf's form right away, but the rocky platform is too narrow for my wolf's four legs. I need to remain human while I'm crouching on it, but I also need to shift into my wolf's form as soon as I take the jump. That way, my injured leg will be protected.

Gripping the base of my dress and gathering up my bra with it, I carefully ease my clothing up over my shoulders and head to remove it. I balance myself carefully before I twine my clothing and the belt containing the dark magic orb into a bundle and pitch it onto the riverbank. It lands safely on the sand with a wet thud.

Rising upward, aware of the dangerously slippery rock I'm balancing on, I take a deep breath, harness my energy, and throw myself across the space.

At the same time, I shift.

My wolf's powerful hind legs push off the rock. My energy floods me and gives me height and speed, healing me at the same time as I fly across the raging river and land on dry ground.

I dig my paws into the sandy riverbank with a cry of relief, but when I return to my human form, my right leg twinges, making me stumble.

"Fuck! Damn!" I take a deep breath, calm myself, before I put weight on my leg again.

It's okay. I tell myself I'm fine as I hobble toward my clothing.

Scooping up the bundle, I don't waste time putting anything on, breaking into a sprint along the riverbank, the sand scrunching between my toes. "Tristan!"

The water rushes along beside me, a lulling sound now that I'm not threatened by its flow, but I won't be fucking lulled.

"Tristan!" I scream his name again, desperately seeking his location in the water... near the boulders... on the riverbank...

A gathering of large gray rocks rises up out of the water ahead. Rounding it, I skid to a stop.

Tristan lies at the water's edge, his claws dug into the sand, his shoulders and upper arms straining while his chest and lower body remain submerged and in danger of being pulled downstream.

Every visible part of his body is cut and bleeding.

Throwing my clothing to the side, I drop to Tristan's left shoulder so that I can brace against the direction that the water is flowing. Digging my heels into the ground, I wrap my arm across his back, barely able to reach all the way across his broad shoulders.

"Tristan, I'm getting you out."

A quiet groan is his only response.

Heaving with all of my might, pushing against my heels, screaming with effort and calling on my power, I drag his torso out of the wash. Then his hips. Holding tightly, I finally pull him completely out onto the sand, collapsing beneath him.

Forcing myself to rise, I fold my legs under his upper chest so that his head can rest on my thigh, his face turned inward, his hair falling across his cheek.

I try to calm my pounding heart when he barely moves and doesn't speak.

I can't tell what bones in his body could be broken or if the wounds I see are only the obvious ones. His left cheekbone has a cut across it. There's some swelling around the wound already but not enough to close up his eye. The nicks across his shoulders and chest are also flesh wounds, presumably from being thrown against the rocks. I can't immediately see beneath his long pants, but there aren't any obvious rips to indicate a wound.

Leaning over him, I carefully brush the strands of his hair away from his neck.

A cut extends from beneath his ear to his collarbone. It's superficial. A skin wound. But it makes my heart stop.

Suddenly, I'm back on the helipad.

I'm watching my father pitch a knife that slices across Tristan's throat. I'm listening to Tristan fall and my heart is breaking all over again.

"Tristan!" My fingers race across his face and neck, down his back as far as I can reach, desperate for him to respond.

I can't lose another person I care about. *I can't...*

"Tristan!"

With a groan, he plants his fists against the sandy ground, attempting to leverage himself upward, to raise his eyes to mine. I'm trying so hard to pull him closer that, as soon as he gets a knee under himself, I lift him upward, only to slip completely beneath his weight.

I land on my back beneath him, my breathing rapid and panicked, my hands curling into fists against his sides.

He's unfocused as he hovers over me. "Tessa, it's okay."

My fists rattle against his sides, shaking hard. "It's not fucking okay!" Tears burn behind my eyes. I swallow. Try to breathe. "I... let you fall."

I let him fall from the helipad.

Tears spill down my cheeks, and I can't stop them.

It doesn't matter that I was paralyzed at the time. It doesn't matter that I was breaking apart, full of rage and uncertainty and fear. I should have found a way... *somehow*... to stop my father from dragging Tristan off that roof. It was the fight and the fall that triggered the Killer to take over his mind. It was my actions that freed the Coward and the Killer from the cage Tristan was trying to keep them in.

Tristan is quiet. His chest rises above mine as he takes a breath. A slow, even movement.

"I fall every time I see you, Tessa," he says. "I fall hard."

A sob releases from my lips, a deep cry.

He scoops me up—another slow, even movement, the kind he couldn't make if he were badly hurt. His hands are careful, gentle across my back, as he gathers me up to himself. I let him fold me against his chest, my knees curled up, my head pressed to his shoulder.

"It's okay," he whispers, over and over, his forehead brushing mine, his arms tight around me. "We'll be okay. We'll make it through this."

He's lying to me, and I don't know whether the Deceiver is making him do it or if Tristan is trying to convince himself. We won't be okay until I've walked the path I need to walk, until I end my father, and even then...

I grip Tristan's chest, holding tightly, aware of his regular breathing, the way he tips his head toward me so that I'm cocooned in his arms.

Adjusting his hold, he takes my hand and presses it across his heart. Then he slips his own hand over my breast on top of my heart.

"I don't need a true mate bond to love you, Tessa," he says.

My heart fills with pain at his words. The Killer broke the true mate bond Tristan had formed with me—a bond I can't return. The Killer broke it at some point over the last day while Tristan was held captive by Mother Zala. I try to breathe against the hurt filling my chest—hurt that he's talking about love—but Tristan presses his palm more firmly against my heart, as if he can sense that I need the pressure, the certainty.

He brushes my cheek with his. "Breathe with me, Tessa."

I gasp a breath. Close my eyes. Sense his chest rising and falling beneath my palm. I drag in the warmth of his open hand pressing to my breast as if he's holding my heart in his hand and he's being so careful with it.

"This," Tristan says, nudging a kiss against my cheek, trailing kisses to my lips. "This is how you'll know it's really me—how you'll know it's only me. If you can't breathe with me, then I'm not myself."

I return his kiss, tasting salty tears on our lips. His or mine, I don't know, and I don't care. I let them fall.

"I promise you, Tristan…" The vehemence in my voice grows. "I promise you, I won't give up on you."

I don't know how much I can tell him about my plans, how many promises I can make him. So much is still unknown to me. My father was determined to find the book of old magic—he insisted that it contained the secrets of Cerberus's power, but for some reason, my father didn't seize the book when he had the chance. I assume this is because the book is surrounded by magical protections and he doesn't want to risk his life trying to retrieve it. I can only guess that he planned to manipulate me into risking my own life to get the book.

"I asked you about the book of old magic," I say to Tristan. "You couldn't tell me if you knew about it."

The first time I mentioned the book to Tristan, the Deceiver had threatened to take over his mind. Now, he flinches, and I know I'm heading into dangerous territory again.

"I don't want you to tell me anything," I continue quickly. "But I want you to know that I'll find all of the answers we need."

I press my free palm to Tristan's cheek, cupping his face, my voice lowering as I allow my rage to rise, filling my convictions with the darkness that is now my friend.

"I don't care how many enemies I have to burn or tear apart," I say. "I won't stop until I free you from this cage."

CHAPTER FIVE

Tristan presses his lips to mine, his hands rising to tangle in my hair. I'm exhausted and starving, but I want his scent and nearness, to snatch these true moments with him while I can.

My hand remains pressed against his heart and his against mine as I slip my right leg across his hips to straddle him, settling down onto his growing hardness.

He nudges a kiss to my cheek, my neck, trailing kisses to the top of my breasts, turning my skin to fire.

"Tessa?"

"Yes?" I say.

He responds by lifting me one-handed so that he can ease himself back up against the protrusion of rocks at the edge of the rushing river. The largest stone sits high enough to support his back and shelter us from the breeze.

I kiss him the whole time he repositions us. I taste river water on his lips, jaw, and neck, cool and fresh as my kisses descend to his chest, tracing around the cuts on his skin, wary of hurting him.

Gentle kisses. Needy kisses.

Following the curve of his muscles down his torso, I trace the hard planes with my lips, tasting the skin across his stomach, while at the same time I stretch up to brush the fingers of my free hand against his mouth, feeling the vibration of his groan against my fingertips.

He abandons the press of his own hand against my heart, gripping and stroking my naked back, kneading my aching muscles, caressing my shoulders.

When he dips his head toward mine, I read his need to kiss me, to pull me all of the way up against him. I want his kisses too. So badly. To feel his closeness and the way it both heats and soothes me.

Wrapping my fingers around the waistband of his jeans, I sense his stomach muscles clench as I unzip and tug the jeans down his hips. He quickly lifts himself to push his pants to the tops of his thighs, but I'm in the way of him removing them completely, and I refuse to remove my hand from his chest.

I need to know that it's him. That this is Tristan.

When I don't budge, he slides his hands to my hips and across my lower stomach, pressing for a moment before his fingertips brush toward my center. I know he wants to make sure that my body is ready. He's never rushed me. He's always taken the time to make sure I enjoy sex. But this time, I intend to take matters into my own hands.

Sinking lower, I drop my head to his hardness and swirl my tongue across his skin, making him tense and groan. "Tessa. Fuck."

He grips my shoulders as I continue to taste his body, taking him as far into my mouth as I can. I sense his heart beat harder against my palm, sense the growing tension in the muscles across his chest and stomach.

My actions are purely selfish. Well, somewhat.

Rising back up into a straddling position, I join our bodies in one smooth motion, aided by the extra moisture on his skin. The intense pleasure that washes through me is almost unbearable as I draw him completely inside me.

Intense need fills his eyes as he reaches for me, pulling me close, taking control of our movements. He grips my hips and moves me against him, slowly at first and then faster. Then slowly again. As if he doesn't want it to end.

His gaze never leaves my face, and my hand never leaves his torso. The connection between our bodies is so perfect, so powerful, our breathing united, our hearts beating fast, that the crash nearly tears me apart. Ripple after ripple of pleasure flows through me, shaking me to my core.

As the force between us fades, a powerful warmth replaces it.

"Tessa." Tristan murmurs my name, pulling me close, his breathing easing, the tension gone from his shoulders. His amber-flecked eyes are warm, still heated, but the smile on his lips is completely satisfied.

His tongue swirls across my neck and up to my earlobe as I reposition myself in the crook of his arm, taking my time to nestle against him where we stay for the longest time.

The silence is only broken by the rushing water, a lull that I could succumb to now.

When Tristan speaks, it's quiet, barely audible above the river.

"I only have snatches of the last few hours," he says. "I need to know what's true and what isn't." He pauses, an edge of tension rising in his posture again. "Cody?"

I can't put voice to my feelings. I can only shake my head against Tristan's chest.

"Fuck." Tristan holds me close. "I'm sorry, Tessa."

"I won't lose anyone else I care about," I say, not fighting the tears that fill my eyes. Crying doesn't feel like weakness right now.

Tristan strokes my back, brushes my cheeks, giving me time.

Finally, he asks, "Your mother? You saw her." His forehead creases as if he's second-guessing himself already. "That's right, isn't it?"

"She wants me dead." I don't try to push away the hurt I feel about her intentions toward me—or my conflicted feelings about the Master Assassin, who offered me the chance to join his family.

"I know what it means to fight family," Tristan says.

I tip my head back to search his eyes, checking that our breathing is still in sync, hoping I might receive answers. "Will you tell me about your mother?"

On the helipad, Tristan said that my father was complicit in his mother's death. I've pieced together parts of what happened the night his mother died from what Tristan told me, what Cody told me, and finally what I discovered about Cody's sister, Ella.

Tristan's forehead creases. "I want to, but I can't risk the Deceiver taking control and twisting my words. An untruth about what happened that night could cause you to take action you shouldn't take." He closes his eyes and when he opens them, anger resonates in his voice. "I would rather you had questions than deceptive information."

Carefully, I nudge my cheek against his. I feel his frustration deep in my bones, but there's nothing either of us can do about it right now. "I understand."

I squeeze my eyes closed and shiver against him. The moonlight is waning. The first rays of daylight must only be an hour away, which makes these midnight hours the coldest time of the night. I press against Tristan, skin on skin, stealing his body heat.

"We need food and a safe place to sleep," he says.

I draw back far enough to scan the base of the cliffs for some sort of shelter. The sandy riverbank is exposed, but large boulders are situated against the cliff face farther along. I point at them. "We could shelter behind those."

"Okay." He kisses me, a lingering kiss, as if he's grasping the last of this moment before he releases me.

Scooping up my clothing, I hurry to put it on while goosebumps rise along my skin. The dress won't keep me warm, but it's better than walking around naked. My hair is full of sand and still damp. I try to brush the grit off my back and sides without scraping my skin raw as I pull on the flimsy material. Once again, I tuck the dark magic orb into the sash around my waist.

Tristan is quiet behind me and when I turn, my defenses fly up like a wall.

The Killer stands beside me, one corner of his mouth raised in a smile that makes my blood run cold.

"Tessa Dean," he says, giving me a nod. "You need food. I will bring it."

Fuck...

Fuck this hell I'm in.

I swipe at my cheeks, brushing away the remains of my tears.

Every time Tristan's mind is overcome, it feels like he dies. Over and over and over again.

I'm not sure how much more I can take.

Burying my grief, I give the sandy riverbank an exhausted glance. "I'm not sure where you're going to find any food—"

The Killer jogs away from me along the riverside, bending at intervals to peer intently into the water rushing along the edge. My breath catches when he leaps toward a rock jutting up through the wash.

I allow myself to breathe again when he lands safely on top of it.

Dammit, I just got him out of the river!

Blood still drips from his chest and arms, but he doesn't seem to care. My shoulders slump a little. In some ways, the Killer is a protective mechanism for Tristan. There were always hints of his aggression in Tristan's actions when Tristan was in deep pain or afraid for the lives of members of his pack.

It makes me wonder who Tristan will be if—*when*—I find a way to help him overcome his minds.

I shake off my unease as the Killer crouches on the rock, his focus remaining on the rushing water for several moments before his hand plunges into the foam.

With a triumphant snarl, he rises, holding not one, but two fish skewered on his claws. I look away quickly when he bends to dispatch them both on the sharp edge of the rock at his feet.

He leaps across the distance again, landing safely on the sand before his hunched figure towers over me.

I shiver in his shadow.

"I've brought you food," he says, holding the fish out to me like an offering. His eyes are narrowed as he assesses my reaction to his gift.

I'm hungry enough to ignore the fact that we might need to eat the fish raw. I take both fish from him, extending my claws so they don't slip right out of my hands, after which the Killer draws himself upright with a pleased expression.

He tips his head to the side, his gaze running to my toes.

I already inadvertently gave him an eyeful of my body when I retrieved my dress. I return his gaze without blinking, trying to decide whether or not I need to assert some clear boundaries. My body is off limits to the Killer. Sex is out of the question—with any of Tristan's minds, except with Tristan himself.

"You're shivering, Tessa Dean," the Killer says without making any further move toward me. "I will make a fire."

He prowls away to my right, heading downstream. My hands are full with the two fish, but I need to keep moving to stay warm. Heading in the same direction as the Killer, I juggle the fish to one hand and hold them to my chest while I cut off the remaining portion of the overskirt that's hanging by threads to my dress. I wrap the fish in it, tie the ends, and sling it across my shoulder before I set about gathering slender twigs and some dry brush that will be useful as tinder for starting a fire.

Finally, I retrieve a thicker log, juggling it awkwardly in my arms. It won't burn very well without being cut, but it will have to do.

Damn, I miss my axe right now.

Looking for the Killer again, I find the riverbank bare.

I freeze as I search for him farther along, but there's no sign of him.

My heart rises to my throat. *Where is he?*

He can't have fallen into the water. I didn't hear a splash.

Racing along the riverbank while everything I'm carrying bangs against my chest and legs, I run past a lip of rock protruding from the cliff, only to skid to a stop.

I'm astonished to see an opening—a cave of sorts—hidden from view by the angle of the rocks surrounding it. It's only about seven paces wide, but it darkens toward the back in a way that indicates it's deep enough to shelter inside.

The Killer sits a few paces inside the opening, where the moonlight still reaches. He leans over a skillfully placed bundle of twigs, dry brush, and some thicker logs. Blowing gently on a tiny flame growing in the dry brush beneath the twigs, he patiently coaxes a fire into existence.

I want to ask him how he lit the fire, but I hold my tongue, allowing him to concentrate while I circle around its growing warmth. Placing the spare tinder I gathered at the side of the cave's inner wall, I keep the fish with me as I kneel close enough to the flame to feel some of its warmth spread across my outstretched hands.

When the Killer finally rises, I catch sight of the flat rock and leftover tinder he must have used to create the spark that started the fire.

Circling the campfire without speaking, he unties the fish from my makeshift sling and skewers them on two of the twigs I brought with me.

He gives them to me to hold over the fire.

"Cook," he says. "Eat."

The rings around his eyes are dark, and I suspect that he is as desperately in need of food and sleep as I am now.

Without another word, he leaves the cave and disappears from view. When he returns, he's carrying five more fish, which he promptly skewers and holds over the fire all at once, hunching on the other side of the fire.

The moment I'm sure my fish are cooked, I break them apart with my claws, trying not to burn my hands as well as avoid the bones.

As soon as the cooked fish touches my tongue, a moan of appreciation leaves my lips. I don't try to hide it.

The Killer grins at me across the fire as he devours his meal. It's a disconcerting sight to see him smile. His shoulders are just as hunched, his muscles just as corded, but the intensity in his hard green eyes lifts, a gleam entering them.

The cave is deep enough to retain the heat from the fire, but it's shallow enough that the wind doesn't whistle through it. As the warmth touches my skin, my clothing and hair finally dry and the ache in my arms and legs eases. So does the empty pit in my stomach.

We continue to eat in silence. The Killer finishes faster than me but doesn't rise again, settling himself beside the fire. As I lick the final crumbs of food from my fingers, I return his scrutiny across the flames.

The Killer's intentions are becoming more difficult to define. First he caught fish to feed me. Then he made a fire to keep me warm. Every time I look at him, Tristan is closer and closer to the surface.

Tristan said that the Killer and the Coward take over his mind completely, but that he's lived with the Deceiver all his life. He knows when he's lying. Hope rises inside me that maybe—

somehow—he's figuring out how to exist within the boundaries of the Killer's mind now, too.

Rising to my feet, aware of his constant study, I crouch beside the extra tinder I brought with me, choosing the thick log and positioning it across the fire, along with a few of the thinner branches. Now, the fire should burn all night.

I round the fire, approaching the Killer slowly, unsure of my reception and prepared to back off if I'm not welcome. He peers up at me, his incisors peeking between his lips, the only hint of aggression, but I understand it. We are still wary around each other. As we should be.

Taking a deep breath and exhaling it quietly, I kneel beside him, lean against his side, and nudge my head against his shoulder. A simple gesture. I hold my breath as I wait for him to respond.

Quietly, he reaches out so that his arm encircles my waist. He pulls me closer, moving as slowly as I did, his arms firm but not so tight that I can't pull away. One hand glides up to cup the back of my head as he presses me against his chest.

I relax against his shoulder, using my body weight to nudge him in the direction I want him to go. He answers my unspoken command by lowering himself back onto the sandy ground beside the fire.

He keeps me pressed against him so that I'm lying on his chest, one of my knees between his legs, the other beside his outer thigh, not quite straddling him. Even though I'm on top, any proximity to the Killer carries danger. He could reverse our positions in a heartbeat.

I tip my head back to meet his gleaming eyes.

"This is how we'll sleep," I say. A command.

I wait for him to protest, but his lips are relaxed, his eyelids slightly lowered. "My body will be your bed."

I hear Tristan in the timber of his voice, a deep growl. I fight the urge to search his expression, hoping to see more signs of Tristan, but the Killer is already closing his eyes, his breathing deepening as he starts to knead the muscles of my back from my sore shoulders to my lumbar, the same way Tristan did earlier tonight.

His body heat is calming and within seconds, I'm on the verge of falling asleep.

His question comes out of the blue. It's quiet, but it drags me back to the surface. "Why do you want to lie this way?"

"Because this is how I sleep with Tristan," I say, answering him honestly.

I'm not sure how he'll react, given that my answer has everything to do with Tristan and nothing to do with the Killer. I brace once again in case he retaliates.

His eyes are closed, his hands continuing to soothe my aching muscles. He makes a low, rumbling sound in his chest. "I want what Tristan wants."

Only hours ago, all four of Tristan's minds merged for a few moments and he told me they all want the same thing, no matter what it takes: *me*.

I press my palm against the Killer's chest, right over the location of his heart. "It's difficult for me to believe you after you broke Tristan's true mate bond with me."

The Killer's gaze is suddenly intense. "A bond is a cage unworthy of me. I must be free to kill what needs to be killed."

"Including me," I say.

His eyes gleam. "You are a new kind of hell that I must conquer, Tessa Dean. That is my nature."

My forehead creases. "A new hell?"

"You already know that I'm a child of the old gods—like you. But while you were created for war, I was created to guard the gates of the underworld," the Killer says. "I was given the ability to kill, lie, and value my own safety above others. These are necessary traits to protect the world of the living from the souls of the dead who would try all sorts of devious tricks to leave the underworld. My minds had a purpose for which I was uniquely suited."

As he speaks, the Killer's arms tighten around me. "I was not meant to be brought to the world of the living," he says. "My minds have no purpose here."

"Who brought you?" I ask, curious.

"The new gods," he says. "They stole me from the underworld. Because of them, I was cast into the world of the living, where I didn't belong."

Brynjar—the ice jotunn who stands at my father's right hand—said a similar thing to me. He told me that his people were once giants of the Earth, feared and respected, but the new gods took away his purpose. My father had given him purpose again.

The Killer's claws prick my back. "My only purpose since then has been to conquer the mind of the one whose body I am born into." His voice becomes harsh. "Over and over again."

"Not anymore," I say, leveling my gaze with his.

He makes a satisfied sound. "Tristan has given me a worthy new purpose."

I arch an eyebrow at him. "Which is?"

"To kill Fenrir and conquer his daughter."

I lower my chin to the Killer's chest, but my head is tipped a little to the side, challenging him. "Two impossible tasks."

The gleam returns to his eyes. "You will help me with both."

I let out a laugh. "Oh?" But I quickly become somber. "We *will* kill my father, but as for conquering me..." I dare to ease upward and nudge his jaw with my lips, planting a soft kiss against his stubble. "Nobody will."

"We will see." The Killer's hands harden against my spine, the prick of his sharp claws making me tense, but not in fear. There is nothing my inner darkness craves so much as this beast's anger.

"You want to test your strength against me," I say, calling out his thoughts.

His voice is the deepest growl. Animal. Barely human. "Very much."

My lips whisper along his jaw as I slowly shake my head. "Not tonight." I draw back, relaxing against him, daring him to contradict me as I close my eyes. "Tonight, we're too tired to have a worthy fight."

"You may be too tired," he says. He curls his hand into my hair, startling me when he rolls us to the side. I suddenly find myself on my back, staring up at him.

I let out a threatening growl as he rears up over me, warning him not to make any further sudden moves. He startles me even more when he dips his head and nudges my shoulder, his rough tongue grazing one of my healing bruises. It doesn't hurt me. Instead, a warm sensation invades my chest.

His tongue feathers the skin across the top of my breasts before settling on another bruise, every stroke soothing. I relax under his ministrations, struggling not to close my eyes. I sense Tristan in each brush of his tongue, an echo of the moments after Tristan formed a true mate bond with me.

"A cage can protect the beast inside it, as well as contain it," the Killer murmurs. "A cage can keep others out." He shakes his head at me. "There will be no cages between us, Tessa Dean."

He tangles his fingers in my hair again, supporting my head as he rolls and pulls me back on top of himself.

"Now we will sleep like you want," he says. "Tomorrow we will hunt Mother Zala's witches. Then we will hunt your father."

I lower my head to the Killer's chest, relaxing into him, absorbing his body heat and his dark threats, content in the knowledge that he wants to end Fenrir as badly as I do.

CHAPTER SIX

A breeze sighs through the cave's opening, coaxing me awake. It smells like a warm summer afternoon, a scent that is both calming and disorienting after the cold last night. I'm aware that the fire has died down to glowing coals and the light outside the cave has changed drastically. We must have slept for a long time. Maybe into the afternoon.

The Killer's chest rises and falls deeply beneath me. One of his arms is slung across my back, the other tossed out at the side. The tension with which he holds his shoulders, even in his sleep, tells me he isn't Tristan. My inability to match my breathing with his confirms it.

I rest my head down onto his upper body again.

We need to get out of this place. We need supplies and new clothing. Hunting the witches could provide us with both. After that, my goal is to get to the book of old magic. My dilemma is the extent to which I can tell the Killer my plans.

My hope is that the book of old magic will tell me how to put an end to the three-headed wolf without hurting Tristan in the process. My goal is to kill the Killer. I can't exactly tell him that.

I'm about to ease myself away from him when a shadow passes across the cave's entrance, the quickest flicker.

I jolt upright, jostling the Killer awake. He crouches beside me,

43

tipping his head back and inhaling the air while I poise, half-crouched, my feet planted firmly in case I need to fight.

"What is it, Tessa Dean?" he asks. Despite being woken so suddenly, he is clear-eyed, his claws descending in a heartbeat.

"I saw something out there." I prowl toward the cave's entrance, expanding my senses.

The riverbank is empty in both directions.

A splash sounds to my left, making me jolt in that direction, but there's nothing there.

I suppress my shiver of unease.

The sound could just as easily have been made by water rushing over stones. Still, my stomach swirls and my senses prickle. It's not the same sensation that creeps across my skin when assassins are near, but it puts me equally on edge.

This place is surrounded on both sides by cliffs that are hundreds of feet high, at the top of which is a magical barrier that dragged across my skin when I broke through it. The barrier was powerful enough to make me suspect it wasn't created by a modern day witch. Some other form of magic—some sort of ancient magic—is at play here.

The Killer's declaration last night repeats on me. A cage works both ways. For all I know, the magical barrier around this place could have been created to keep something in as much as to keep others out.

"We should leave this place," I say. "Right away."

The Killer looms beside me. "Agreed."

We don't have much to gather. I scoop up my overskirt in case the material will come in handy, but when my hand closes over the folded portion that should contain the dark magic orb, the material squishes between my fingers.

Empty.

"It's gone," I say, curling my hand into a fist, dangerous rage thrumming through me. "Silas's eye is gone."

"We'll get it back." The Killer inclines his head toward the opening, and I follow him out, my senses expanded fully.

"Which way?" he asks.

I consider the river to my right, the way it appears to stretch forever toward the horizon, possibly some sort of illusion since I know for a fact that there are miles and miles of forest in that direction. Turning to the left, I study the waterfall in the distance. It doesn't make a lot of logical sense for someone to swim upstream. It would be impossible, given the strength of the water flow, but that's the direction in which I thought I heard the splash.

"Toward the waterfall," I say. "If nothing else, we might be able to drink from it."

I'm parched and hungry again. The height of the sun tells me that we slept most of the day, but I can't begrudge the sleep and rest for my body. I feel stronger and healed now from the fall.

My feet crunch lightly in the sand as I prowl along the riverbank with the Killer on my heels. We're both on our guard, scanning the opposite bank as well as the space behind and in front of us as we move.

The waterfall glistens up ahead and I'm drawn to the gray stone bridge that passes from one side of the cliff to the other high above us. The bridge is a strange sight because enormous trees rise up on the cliff's edge at either end of it. The trees would block anyone from stepping foot onto the bridge from the cliff.

The cliff face at this end of the river is made of glittering quartz. The river itself is maybe sixty feet wide and the waterfall stretches that same distance across, but when I tip my head back to follow the waterfall to its top, I can't see past the thick covering of mist across it. The water could be falling from the sky, for all I know.

I slow my steps as we approach the side of the waterfall to stand below the location of the bridge far above us. The rock wall behind the waterfall is shadowed.

It's too loud here to be heard over the crashing water, so I reach for the Killer's arm and draw him close. "There's a cave hidden behind the fall," I shout into his ear when he bends his head to mine.

"Let's see what's hiding in it," he says, inclining his head for me to go first.

Although he seems content to follow me, his claws descend, ready for any attack. Edging around the side of the waterfall, I press carefully against the slippery rock at my back while keeping careful watch on the stone ledge at my feet.

Several paces in, I stretch my arm out into the gentle spray at the back of the waterfall, my thirst overcoming my sense of danger. Angling my hand and arm, I press my lips to my forearm and direct the flow of water toward my mouth. I get more on my face than past my lips, but it's worth it—especially when I see the Killer doing the same.

He grins at me as the water overflows down his neck and upper body. His gaze follows the little streams pooling at the top of my dress. For a second, his pupils dilate and his claws retract, an unexpected heat filling his eyes. It looks like he's about to reach for me, but he gives his head a quick shake.

Warily, I continue stepping to the left, edging my way to the opening of the cave behind the waterfall.

Finally at the side of the opening, I try to sense anything alive beyond our position. The smells inside the cave are far from murky; rather, the air is crisp and fresh. I have a sense of depth, as if the cave stretches far away into the distance, but I don't detect anything more than water. Water everywhere.

Confident in my ability to defend myself against any unexpected encounter, I step into the cave.

I pull up short.

A crystal spear with a hard-as-diamond tip presses against my sternum, sharp enough to cut right through my chest.

CHAPTER SEVEN

I take a sharp breath, instinctively leaning backward before the spear cuts me open.

The woman holding the weapon has arctic blue hair braided back from her face and blue-gray eyes. Her skin is the color of frost and her body is covered in indigo armor.

"You will stop!" she says, her voice carrying across the air directly into my ears. I'm startled when I can hear her clearly over the roaring waterfall.

I tip my head to the side while a soft breeze plays around my face. It carries the same disconcerting scent as the breeze that whispered through the cave when I woke up.

The Killer steps from the shadows beside me, his incisors fully descended. I expect the woman to flinch at his appearance, but she stands her ground.

Impressive.

I lower my voice to a whisper, testing a theory that she's using her magic—whatever kind of magic it is—to project her voice so that we can converse over the waterfall's roar. "You don't want to challenge me," I say, allowing my crimson vision to rise, knowing it will turn my eyes from sapphire blue to startling red.

Again, she stands her ground, although her eyes narrow slightly at the change in mine. The breeze snatches at my lips and rushes away from me with a pulling sensation. The woman tips her head to the side. Her expression hardens as, no doubt, my message is delivered to her ears.

"Your confidence is misplaced," she says.

Once again, the breeze plays around my face, bringing her voice to me.

Before I can respond, other figures emerge from the shadows of the deep cave behind the woman. At least thirty women, all carrying crystal spears and dressed in indigo armor, take up formation like a trained army.

Now that I'm standing inside the cave, I can see that it extends into the distance behind the women, giving me the impression of a vast tunnel through the rock that becomes increasingly dark and shadowy.

The women all have different-colored hair: some coral, others dark blue, some with dark brown hair shot through with forest green highlights.

It occurs to me that maybe I can't sense them because they could be controlling the air around us, preventing me from sensing their scents or movements, a different sort of magical camouflage than what the assassins were using.

The woman at the front told me my confidence was misplaced, but I shake my head at her.

"My confidence is perfectly placed," I say, releasing my wolf from my body.

My wolf form appears sleek with sapphire fur this time, her eyes as arctic blue as the first woman's hair, deliberately designed to unsettle her. My wolf's sudden appearance has the desired effect on all of the women. The women in the back jolt while the first woman leaps away from me, continuing to point her spear, but she switches her weight and extends her hand at my wolf.

Icy wind blasts from her palm at my wolf's form. The whirlwind she creates is forceful enough to knock any other animal off its feet, but it merely whistles through my wolf.

My wolf lowers her head, her lips drawn back, snarling as she prowls forward, making the women clamber farther backward.

"Your magic won't work on me," my wolf and I say, speaking in unison.

The first woman casts wild glances between me and my wolf.

"What dark magic is this?" she asks.

"I want my possession back," I say. Not an answer. A demand. "One of your people took it. I don't care what you are or what you can do, I want the orb returned to me."

The first woman pulls to a stop, her head held high. Determined. "That orb is dark magic and must be destroyed before it corrupts the hearts of others."

Ordinarily, I would agree with her, but the orb is a reminder of my past and my purpose. Holding on to it stops me from forgetting what it cost for me to become... *me*. Cody's life. The women from Hidden House whom I now have to push away. My chance to be part of a pack. All of the things I've lost.

"There is no corrupting me," I say. "I am what I am."

"And what is that?" she asks.

"War," I say.

Her nostrils flare as she inhales, and I know she's a breath away from ordering her people to let their power loose.

My claws snap down, my incisors appear, and my wolf form gnashes her teeth in the air. Beside me, the Killer's lips are drawn back in a bloodthirsty snarl. He thought he'd have to wait to hunt anyone. The gleam in his eyes tells me he's happy with this change in events.

I glare him down. A crease appears in his forehead, and a wary light enters his eyes. I can't exactly tell him not to kill them, so instead, I mouth clearly: *"They're mine."*

As much as I want the orb back, these supernaturals seem determined to keep and destroy its dark magic. They may be my enemies right now, but only creatures of the light would want to destroy dark magic.

I don't want to kill these women.

"I'll give you one more chance," I say, casting my gaze across the gathering within the cave. "Hand over the orb and I'll leave you in peace."

The woman with the arctic-blue hair lifts her chin, her lips pressed together. I'm once again impressed at the way she stands her ground—and the speed and skill with which she throws her spear directly at my heart.

My reflexes are instant.

I've caught bullets and snatched crossbow bolts midair. Sidestepping the spear, I snatch the weapon from the air, spin with its momentum, and fling it into the cavern ceiling so hard that it *twangs*, a vibration that sounds above the waterfall's roar.

While the back row of women spin a whirling tornado into existence that plucks at my clothing but doesn't displace me like they must hope, three female warriors from the front of the group somersault toward me. I duck their hits and kicks, spinning between them, knocking each one away from the Killer's reach. Despite my order to leave them to me, I have no doubt that he will crush their skulls if given the chance.

Just as I deflect the third warrior's attack, a woman's voice roars from the back of the cave.

"*Stop!*"

The sound echoes around me as the waterfall suddenly slows, each drop glistening and halting midair, its powerful force brought to a standstill. My eyes widen when even the spray halts, miniscule droplets of moisture misting the air in front of me as if they're frozen.

The sudden silence makes my ears ring.

I brace as the armored women retract their spears and step apart, holding their weapons straight up to allow another woman to pass safely through.

The newcomer has dark brown hair with green streaks in it. She wears a dress that drags through the water on the cave floor, but each droplet rises upward from the ground as she passes like rain in reverse.

"You're a witch," I say.

She has ash-gray eyes and strong eyebrows that draw down with such disapproval that I'm sure I'd quail if I were one of her people.

"I am not," she says, her lips pressing together.

My eyes narrow with distrust. "Then what are you?"

"I am fae. My name is Calanthe of the Springtime. I'm a descendant of Crispin of the Dawn, one of the greatest healers of our people." She levels her stern glare on me. "We are the last of our kind and this is our shelter, protected by the oldest of magic, which you have invaded and threatened."

As she speaks, a stream of water splits from the waterfall at the edge of my vision and curls in my direction.

My lips part in surprise when I see the dark magic orb held within it. I consider plucking the orb from the water, but I rethink that course of action. I'm fast, but she's clearly powerful. She could cast the orb into the river before my hand closes over it. I'd never find it again.

"Why do you carry this vile object with you?" Calanthe asks, eyeing my wolf form.

I lower my voice, although I remain ready to deflect an attack. "It belonged to a warlock who…" Flashes return to me. Silas's dark magic washing across the air on the helipad, his voice inside my mind, telling me to let my darkness out. The oily, acidic wash of his magic across the clearing in front of Mother Lavinia's coven. Cody running through the darkness and leaping at Silas. The blast of Silas's lightning…

I shake my head, gritting my teeth.

"A warlock who killed my friend and damaged my heart," I finish.

Calanthe's hands lower, a slight crease forming in her forehead. "Then why do you want it back? Why haven't you destroyed it?"

"Because I need the pain," I say. "So I don't forget why I've become what I am." *So I can feel the anger, let the darkness rise, but not lose myself completely.*

Calanthe's lips purse, the crease in her forehead deepening. "You seek revenge on others."

I grit my teeth. "*One* other."

She nods. "I understand loss and the need for justice." Her eyebrows draw down fiercely. "But you will not bring danger to my people."

"Give me the orb and let me leave," I say, once again contemplating snatching it from the water. "I won't harm you."

She exhales a heavy sigh. "Can you fly?"

I blink at her. "No."

"Then you can't get back up the cliffs on your own." She folds her arms across her chest, tapping her fingers on her bicep silently

51

for a long moment. "Clearly, Essandra's power over the air can't lift you up." She gestures to the woman with the arctic-blue hair who tried to blast me and my wolf from the cave. "That leaves only one way back the way you came—but you won't like it."

I narrow my eyes at Calanthe, waiting for her to make a decision.

She spins to her people. "Essandra and Myra, you will assist me to escort the invaders back to the riverbank."

Both Essandra and a woman with coral hair step forward. The coral-haired woman must be Myra.

The spool of water nudges up to me and, as soon as I open my hand, it drops the dark magic orb into my palm. I quickly tie it up into the strip of overskirt around my waist. Calanthe isn't wrong about it—touching it makes me shudder, but not with fear, with anger and strengthened resolve about my path.

The Killer growls his discontent as the three fae women pass by. I deliberately step between him and the women, giving him a stern, unspoken command to *behave*, as we follow Calanthe back out to the riverbank.

"We need to move farther downstream," Calanthe says. "You have to be a sufficient distance from the waterfall for this to work."

"For what to work?"

"Please," she says. "You must see them for yourself."

As we return the way we came along the riverbank, I consider the distance between the waterfall and the cave I slept in, along with the strength of the rushing water.

A thought occurs to me.

"You didn't sneak into the cave to take the orb, did you?" I say to Essandra, who has fallen back to walk level with me. "You took the orb with your power over the air."

Essandra gives me a nod. "I am blessed to be a Frost fae. I control wind and ice. It was easy enough to use my power to snatch the orb without coming anywhere near you. Then Queen Calanthe brought it upstream through the water." She shudders as she continues. "That way, none of us had to touch it."

Well, that explains the splash in the absence of a visible thief.

I turn back to Calanthe. "Why do you hide here?" I ask her. "You appear human. You could live among them."

"Do you not see the color of our hair and eyes?" she asks, aghast. "We would be hunted and killed, just as we were centuries ago."

"Many humans color their hair these days," I say. "They even have things called 'contacts' if they want to make their eyes appear a different color." I remember the woman with the pointed ears at Hidden House over whom Helen placed a glamor so her supernatural status was concealed. "If you're really worried, you could wear a glamor."

Calanthe jolts as if she's insulted. "Then we would not be our real selves. We can hide here where we can use our magic openly— or we could hide out there, living in a wide open cage of human expectations."

I'm quiet. I have no answer to that.

She sighs heavily. "My daughter thought the same as you. She said we should venture out and try." Calanthe gestures to the cliffs. "I refused to send out a scouting party, so she left on her own. That was a year ago. We haven't heard from her since."

Calanthe's expression is closed, but I sense her pain. She's afraid for her daughter and so she should be. This sanctuary is located within a forest that is controlled by witches who took prisoners for their games. The chances that Calanthe's daughter is still alive are slim.

The Queen stops and turns to face the way we came. We've now traveled all of the way to the cave's opening and I'm beginning to feel uneasy about Calanthe's intentions.

Calanthe points at the bridge but speaks to Myra, the coral-haired woman. "Please call them."

Myra worries at her lip. "They might not answer me. Not while strangers are present."

Calanthe gives her a reassuring nod. "All you can do is try."

A look of concentration passes across Myra's face as she puts her fingers to her lips and gives two short, sharp whistles, followed by a longer whistle.

As the silence grows, I study the bridge, the waterfall behind it, and the thick mist above it that obscures everything beyond, wondering to what extent the fae have built a home behind it.

A *crack* like booming thunder echoes from the distant mist.

The breath catches in my chest and my senses buzz.

I take a step forward in anticipation, drawn to the lights suddenly swirling in the distant mist. The lights are as sapphire as my fear and as crimson as my rage, gorgeous streaks like electricity that ripple through the fog.

A powerful presence grows in the distance, rapidly approaching.

CHAPTER EIGHT

The mist parts and an enormous bird soars into the open air. Its wingspan is easily thirty feet, its feathers a brilliant blue. Its torso glows and lightning curls around its body, clearly visible in the fading sunlight.

I hold my breath as it soars upward in a majestic arc. It cracks its wings and the sound booms across the distance, making the hairs on my arms rise straight up.

This creature is wild and beautiful.

A second bird soars from the mist, this one even larger with glittering ruby-colored wings. It sails across the air before circling back, both birds soaring toward the bridge and landing gracefully on its surface.

I let out a gasp of surprise. It's not a bridge. It's a perch.

I can't tear my eyes away from the birds. "What are they?"

"Thunderbirds." A smile plays around Calanthe's mouth when I can't seem to pick up my jaw. "Both female. They look beautiful, but beware—a thunderbird only bonds with one rider. The one with the blue feathers bonded with my daughter. The ruby bird has never bonded. Neither of them will want to carry you."

She casts an increasingly wary glance at the Killer. "Especially not him. They will sense his violence and be repelled by it."

I can see now why Calanthe wanted us farther downstream,

though—the birds will need this distance to swoop, fold their wings, and land safely on the riverbank.

"Myra will call them down to you and calm them with her mind," Calanthe says. "Essandra will make sure the wind is beneath their wings to assist them to rise as quickly as possible once you are on their backs. They won't tolerate you for longer than a minute. Possibly not even that long. You must be prepared to climb on as soon as they land."

She steps away from me, as if that's all she has to say, but I'm suddenly filled with an urgent need for knowledge. "Wait. How long have your people been hiding here?"

"Hundreds of years," she says. "Ever since we were driven from our last sanctuary." She gives me a hard stare. "By a wolf very much like you."

I tip my head to the side, my lips pursed and my eyes narrowed in thought. "You've met my father?"

She's suddenly even more wary of me, taking glances between me and the Killer. "The white wolf?" she asks. "He is your father?"

A growl leaves my lips. "What did he do to your people?"

"He drove us from the tower we guarded—"

I jolt. "The Spire? He told me he saved it from being plundered."

Calanthe draws an angry breath. "*He* was the plunderer! He demanded the four books of magic, but we managed to hide them from him. I was only a girl, but I watched my mother…" Her hands clench. "My mother died to protect them."

Ford told me that the magical objects in the Spire had been stolen over the years. *Fucking liar.* He's a destroyer, not a protector. But I'm the fool who believed his story.

"Can you tell me anything about how the books were hidden?" I ask.

She shakes her head. "I'm sorry. I was only a young girl then." She purses her lips in thought. "But I remember my mother saying that she sought help from other supernaturals, who agreed to guard the books. My mother claimed it would be impossible to retrieve them. That's all I know."

Damn. I grit my teeth. I'm determined to tackle the impossible if I have to.

"Maybe one day you'll be able to go back to the Spire," I murmur. "Once I kill my father."

A curious light enters her eyes. "He is the one on whom you seek revenge."

I nod. "I will end him—and anyone who stands with him."

Her expression softens. "After that?" she asks, gently. "What of you?"

I stiffen. She sounds too much like Helen, speaking the wisdom of a woman who has seen both life and death, who has loved and lost, who still fights for truth and purpose in this world.

I find myself turning away—turning toward the Killer.

I know the answer to Calanthe's question; I just won't speak it aloud because it's too fragile and too painful, because it involves seeking forgiveness from the ones I've pushed away and mending wounds that might not be able to mend. Iyana, Danika, Helen... my friends at Hidden House... I need them in my life, but only once it's safe.

"Thank you for your help," I say to Calanthe, burying my pain in formality. "I've asked you too many questions already. We should leave now."

Across the distance, the Killer returns my gaze and for a moment, the tension in his shoulders eases. I catch a glimpse of Tristan in the approaching twilight, can suddenly sense his impulses, am aware of his breathing.

He takes a step toward me, his arms rising.

Myra whistles beside me, I flinch, and when I turn back to Tristan, the Killer has returned, his shoulders hunched, his growls aimed at the approaching birds.

They drop from their distant perch, soaring toward the water, the crimson bird out front while the sapphire bird follows this time.

My forehead creases when they don't veer far enough toward the bank to land, gliding above the river instead.

"They refuse to land!" Myra cries, her arms outstretched and her expression strained. "They sense the violence. I can't calm them!"

I meet the Killer's eyes across the distance.

"Then we'll jump," I say.

He bares his teeth. "You take the red bird," he says. "To match your hair."

"I don't think jumping is a good idea—" Calanthe's shout is lost on me as I focus on the ruby bird, rapidly assessing her speed and wingspan and how close she's flying to the riverbank.

Her gleaming eyes challenge me across the distance, crimson lightning flickering around her body, her wings cracking as she picks up speed, the *boom* pounding across my hearing. Her head is lowered as aggressively as my wolf's would be when facing an attacker. The bird must be preparing to sweep straight past me, possibly even knock me off my feet with the tip of her wing.

A grin spreads across my face as I recognize the challenge in the eyes of this wild creature who refuses to be tamed.

Her and me both.

Instead of waiting for the bird to reach me, I run straight for her, approaching head on, my feet flying across the sand. Her eyes widen. The rapid thud of her heart is startlingly visible in the flickers of lightning pulsing from her body along her wings. She prepares to bank upward to evade me, but I throw myself across the air with a roar.

My jump is nearly too strong, too fast.

I almost fly right over her. At the last moment, I throw my arm out, barely managing to hook it around the joint where her wing meets her body.

My other arm shoots around her neck, my legs across her back, and I hold on as tightly as I can.

I can't risk looking back to see if the Killer has succeeded in leaping onto the sapphire bird. All I can do is cling and bury my face in the ruby thunderbird's feathered neck, inhaling the intoxicating scent of her untamed lightning. She smells like ice-capped mountains. It's unsettlingly similar to the scent I inhaled the first time I set foot in the Near-Apart Room at the Spire.

The thunderbird banks left, tipping so steeply that I can only assume she's trying to rid herself of my unwanted weight.

Leaning over her neck, I cling on desperately with my knees.

I don't know if she'll understand me, but my voice becomes guttural. Deep. *Animal.* As untamed as *she* is. "I respect your right to freedom," I say. "I only ask your help. Will you carry me to the top of the cliffs so that I might leave your people in peace?"

I don't expect her to be able to answer me—and I'm not sure if she understood me—but her feathers ruffle and her head turns slightly as if she's giving thought to my request.

For a scary second, she banks toward the cliff face, and I picture her tipping her wings sharply enough that she could bash me against the rocks. Behind me, I catch sight of the sapphire bird tipping wildly and cracking her wings, sending violent streaks of lightning across the air.

She clearly does not like that the Killer is riding on her back.

Fuck, I don't blame her.

"Please," I say to my bird. "It's a short flight and then you can be rid of us."

The ruby bird gives a loud shriek that echoes across the space between the cliffs. She rises so sharply that I'm in danger of tipping off her back, but behind me, I'm aware that the sapphire bird is now doing the same, both birds sweeping their wings and rising steeply up the cliff.

I hold my breath and cling.

The moment the top of the cliff comes into view, I prepare to leap from the bird's back, intending to make good on my promise.

"Thank you," I whisper, drawing my knees under myself, my heart in my throat as I try not to look down. I've taken this fall and survived it, but there's nothing like a sheer drop and nothing but air beneath me to get my heart pumping.

The magical barrier rises up right at the cliff's edge, a shimmering shield that blurs the shape of the trees behind it. The thunderbird soars up beside it, sweeping her wings to lift me level with the top of the cliff, the closest she seems willing to fly to bring me safely to the side.

Ridding my mind of fear, I leap from her back toward the gap between the trees. The barrier rips across my skin as I pass through it, making my senses scream.

Landing at a crouch, I spin back to the bird.

She coasts beside the cliff for a moment, her gleaming eyes piercing mine.

I rise slowly to my feet, releasing my wolf on instinct so that I stand in front of the thunderbird in both of my forms. I turn my wolf's fur as gleaming ruby red as my hair and allow my crimson vision to dominate both of our eyes.

The thunderbird tosses her head, a fierce nod, as lightning flickers across her chest and neck, a fiery acknowledgement of my presence.

With a crack of her wings, she tips to the side and dives from view.

Farther to my right, the sapphire bird rises level with the cliff's edge. She tips savagely to the side and tosses the Killer from her back. He dives toward the barrier, narrowly missing a tree, and spears through the shield with a shout.

The bird promptly disappears from view with a disgruntled crack of her wings.

I dart around the nearest tree to see him roll through the leafy forest floor and come to a stop on his side.

He flops onto his back and stares up at the trees. "Fuck, that bird hated me."

"Tristan?" I run to him, propelling myself across the distance to land on my knees, straddling his hips. I pull my wolf back to me in a rush as I plant my palm across his heart, seeking the beat and the rhythm of his breathing that tells me he is himself.

"Tessa." He reaches up to pull me down toward him. "We made it out of there."

I rest my head against his torso, matching my breathing to his, grateful for the silence around us and that we're alive. I want to stay right where I am, but... "Damn, I really need to pee."

His upper body rumbles beneath mine and I glance up, startled to find him grinning at me. "Me too," he says.

Laughter bursts out of me. *Here we are, fucking fierce monsters, still troubled by human needs.*

He gestures to his left. "There's a private spot over there."

My laughter fades as I contemplate separating from him again. "Every time I turn my back on you... you disappear."

He strokes my cheek, pushing my unruly hair behind my ear. "I'm fighting it, Tessa. With everything I have."

I lower my voice to a whisper. "I believe you."

Resolved to accept the possibility that he'll change again, I head to the private spot he pointed out, noting the darkness falling around us. Dusk has well and truly fallen and night is coming.

Five minutes later, I return to find the Killer standing hunched beside the nearest tree. I smother my sigh, telling myself I'll see Tristan again soon.

"Tessa Dean," the Killer says, peering at me with a curious expression. "You didn't leave me behind with the fae."

I'm taken aback. "Why would I leave you behind?"

He glances back at the edge of the cliff—or at least, where I know the edge of the cliff is located. From this side, the trees and foliage are so thick that the magic in the barrier is creating an illusion of forest beyond this point.

"That place was the perfect cage for me, but you didn't leave me trapped in it."

He was a danger to the fae, but even so… "No," I say, my vehemence rising. "You don't belong in a cage any more than I do."

He peels himself away from the tree, but his steps are less certain as he walks toward me. I narrow my eyes at him, unsure if the Coward is about to make an appearance. The Killer's hunched shoulders remain visible, his muscles bunching as he suddenly pulls to a stop in front of me.

"The Deceiver plays tricks on my mind too," he says quietly.

I give him a quizzical glance. "What trick could the Deceiver try to play on *you*—the Killer?"

"The Deceiver tries to convince me that you care about me." He hunches his shoulders over even further, a snarl on his lips. "I am not for caring. I am for violence, blood, and death."

I can't respond to his statement about caring. I care about Tristan. I want Tristan back, and I want him to be safe. The Killer is another facet of Tristan's mind—even if he's an uncontrollable one.

Again, I whisper, "I believe you."

Slowly inclining my head to the left, I say, "I want you to take me to Mother Zala's coven—the place where she held you. Her witches are bound to have gathered back there by now. I want to destroy them before they choose a new leader."

He nods, his expression quickly shuttered. "We can take their food, supplies, and clothing."

I nearly moan at the possibility of new clothing. Mother Zala's attire was nothing short of practical—pants, shirt, jacket. It gives me hope that they might have jeans. Even if I'm basically going to steal them...

Striding away from the Killer, I've barely taken three steps when an object bites the ground in front of me.

Leaves and dirt kick up across my bare calves, making me flinch and forcing me to freeze.

Another projectile flies to my left, hitting the ground on that side before two more thud into the earth on my right.

Fucking bullets!

CHAPTER NINE

I remain where I am, following the bullets' path as they pluck around my feet in a rapid arch but don't come closer to my body.

They're warning shots.

My gaze flicks to the Killer, who has frozen, crouched slightly on my right. Judging by the clear space around him, the bullets are only intended for me.

The barrage stops and silence falls.

I expand my senses and allow my crimson vision to rise in a violent rush as I mentally retrace the bullets' trajectory all the way up into the branches of a tree placed fifty paces away that is significantly obscured by trees in front of and on either side of it. Whoever fired the shots is beyond talented to have hit the ground around my feet so accurately without shooting any of the trees on either side of the bullets' paths.

The distant boughs rustle, a figure jumps lithely to the ground, and I shut down my heightened vision.

Danika rises from her landing, her sniper rifle slung over her shoulder. The last time I saw her—only a night ago—she was butt-naked. Now, she's wearing dark denim jeans and a black T-shirt that's dusted with dirt, the sleeves of which are long enough to partially conceal the bird's wing tattoo across her left bicep. Several leaves rest in her light brown hair.

She spins her rifle off her shoulder and into her hands as she strides directly toward me, stopping only a few paces away. She aims the weapon at my heart. Her lips are pressed together into a hard, determined line.

"I didn't have to miss," she says.

"You can't kill me with bullets," I reply, subdued but certain.

Her expression doesn't change. "It would hurt you enough to satisfy my anger with you right now."

"Then do it," I whisper.

She takes three steps forward and presses the barrel against my heart.

I don't flinch.

I wait for her to pull the trigger while the Killer paces an angry arc behind me, his snarls growing louder.

"Stay out of this, Killer," I call without moving or looking away from Danika.

Her hands are steady, but the corners of her mouth turn down. "You won't push us away, Tessa."

Us? I expand my senses again, rapidly trying to locate the other person—or persons. "To keep you safe, I would—"

"Bullshit!" Her shout echoes around us. "*I'll* choose whether or not I put myself in danger."

I'm quiet. "I won't be responsible for another person losing their life."

"Then don't be." She searches my eyes. "I'm here because I'm your friend, Tessa. I *choose* to be here, and I'll take responsibility for my own choices."

I take a step back, away from the rifle. My chest hurts, my stomach hurts, and the hard, misshapen shell around my heart is in danger of cracking.

In the last day, I've encountered unexpected declarations of kindness. A fierce stranger—an assassin, no less—told me he would have come for me if he'd known about me; a fae woman asked me what will happen to me once my path is over; and even the Killer has shown me care. I could almost… maybe… believe that there is still goodness in my life.

"You saw what happened to Cody." I shake my head at Danika.

No. "I can't—*won't*—go through that again. I can't lose another friend. I need you to stay away from me. Let me do what I have to do and then... when it's safe..."

She lowers the rifle. Pauses. Slips it into the harness across her shoulder. "No."

I stare at her. *"No?"*

She tips her chin up, defiant. "You're not pushing me away." She takes a step forward. "Your power doesn't scare me, Tessa. Your path doesn't scare me. I knew I was in for some serious shit the moment I left Hidden House with you. I knew there were risks then and I know there are risks now—"

"But you're risking my heart, too!" I cry. "*My* heart!" I swallow, trying to speak. I remind myself: *I don't have a heart anymore.*

No.

I don't.

I can't.

The darkness inside me can't co-exist with a heart that is fragile, vulnerable, or open.

"Your heart is in pieces, Tessa," Danika says quietly. "It's been torn apart and you don't know how to put it back together."

She reaches for me. Very carefully.

I let her get close enough that her hand hovers above my shoulder. The darkness inside me—the rage—tells me to grab her hand, break every bone in it, and show her what happens to people who get too close to me.

I push it down, fight the volatile anger.

Danika's expression softens and the tension leaves her shoulders.

"You just need a little glue," she says, quietly lowering her hand.

Her touch is light, gentle, warm, and powerful in a way I wasn't expecting. Cody wanted to join my den. He needed to be a part of my life and in the end, he gave his life for that wish. Danika's touch... asks for nothing in return. It's giving without taking.

She bites her lip. "You forget that I'm a survivor, too. It will take a fuck sight more than a war wolf father and a fierce new look to scare me away. I'm in this with you, Tessa."

The pain in my chest burns hot. Someone has pushed a smoldering coal in there and is gently blowing on it to coax it into flames.

"I'm here with you," she says.

Another voice sounds from my right. "*We're* here with you."

Iyana strides through the trees. Her clothing is as dirty as Danika's, her long, black hair is loose, and her blue-gray eyes are fierce with determination. She carries two guns and two daggers, along with what appears to be a compactly folded umbrella at her hip.

The Killer snarls at her as soon as she appears, but she veers directly toward him, forcing him onto his back foot when she pokes her finger against his shoulder.

Her fangs descend and her lips pull back. "You. Killer. I'm not afraid of you. Now back the fuck off."

She stares him down as his scowl grows more ferocious before it eases and a gleam enters his eyes. "Iyana Ballinger. You would make a worthy opponent."

With a dismissive snarl, she swings away from him. Her knee-high black boots are quiet in the underbrush as she draws to a stop in front of me.

Her rose-bud lips soften. "Hello, fierce new Tessa."

She reaches out just like Danika did to place her hand on my other shoulder.

"I'm Iyana Ballinger," she says, speaking carefully. "Twenty-five years old. Mercury-drinking vampire. I used to be a bounty hunter."

Danika steps up beside her. "I'm Danika Eckhart. Twenty-four years old. Hawk shifter. It's okay to tell us as much or as little as you want."

Those are the rules of Hidden House. Rules of acceptance.

The coal inside my chest burns hotter.

I'm Tessa Dean. Twenty-three. Daughter of a monstrous wolf. The man I love is currently under the sway of a killer. My chosen beta—a man who was my enemy and became my friend—was killed by a warlock.

I'm on a path to death.

"No," I whisper. "You can't possibly accept me for who I am. I'm a danger to you now."

"We choose to accept you for exactly who you are," Iyana says, unblinking in the face of my assertion. "Fenrir's daughter—darkness and all."

Her forehead creases, then eases, her mouth forming the smallest smile. "We know that you can kill us where we stand, but we also know you won't. We're your pack." Her hold on my shoulder remains light despite the certainty in her voice. "You're stuck with us."

It's difficult for me to accept what they're saying, to push past my resolution to keep them safe. I've made too many mistakes in the past week. My mistakes repeat on me in waves—each of my flawed decisions from the moment I stepped into Baxter Griffin's home until now. My stomach twists with the fear of how many more mistakes I'll make and who will pay the price when my own life won't be the one at stake.

But I can't deny that there are also moments of truth in the darkness. Meeting Cody without his wolf—he was a different person. Seeking Tristan and connecting with him, even if only for brief moments, but each of those moments has been honest. All of it has forced me to peel back the layers of distrust around my heart. I've torn down walls and rebuilt them over and over.

My head lowers, my shoulders hunching. I close my eyes tightly. "The path I'm walking now has only one purpose," I say. "My father must not prevail."

When I raise my head, they both return my gaze.

"Tell us what you need," Danika says.

"I need to destroy what remains of my father's empire—starting with Mother Zala's coven."

"Then we're coming with you," Iyana says.

I consider them warily. "You should know that I don't plan on leaving the witches alive."

Iyana and Danika don't blink.

"Did those fuckers have anything to do with what happened to Ella?" Iyana asks.

"They were instrumental in the series of vicious fights she was forced to take part in," I say.

Danika grits her teeth. "Sweet Ella."

"We don't have a problem with ending the witches," Iyana

announces firmly. Her cool gaze flicks to the Killer, who has stepped forward, muscles bunched, his focus raking across each of us, an air of anticipation growing around him.

Iyana turns back to me with a gleam in her eyes that matches the Killer's. "Why the fuck are we still standing here?"

CHAPTER TEN

Before we leave the cliffs, Danika and Iyana both retrieve backpacks from hiding spots between the trees. The bags are filled with weapons and supplies. I'm grateful for the fruit and bread they hand me, but I'm especially humbled when Iyana pulls a pair of jeans and a flannel shirt from her backpack, along with clean underwear and my comfortable ankle-high boots.

"I thought you might need these," she says.

I hug the clothing to my chest before I change, ripping the dress off my body as fast as I can. The Killer has already seen me naked so there's no point in trying to find a private place to change, not when I'm desperate for new clothing.

I catch Iyana's surprised look when I strip in front of him—especially when he doesn't make any effort to avert his eyes.

"He's seen it all," I say, pulling on the clean underwear and jeans with a sigh of relief.

The flannel shirt floats over my shoulders like a soft cloud and extends past my butt. After I pull on my boots, I take a moment to appreciate the simple act of wearing clothing that is mine, feeling a thousand times more comfortable now.

When I retrieve the dark magic orb from the layers of the dress I discarded on the ground, Iyana and Danika both step away from it.

I understand their disquiet. The glass orb swirls with wisps of silver, charcoal, and electric blue. I'm accustomed to the bite of dark magic that I feel when I'm near it, but I'm wary of hurting them.

I don't expect them to carry it in their bags, so I quickly push the orb deep into my jeans pocket, where it forms a bump.

By the time I'm ready to keep moving, evening has settled across the forest and the Killer is twitchy. He's still dressed in black jeans and will need new clothing, too, but my immediate concern is his violence. If I don't keep him busy, he's bound to take a swipe at anything living—including my friends.

"Lead the way to Mother Zala's coven," I say to him.

With a snarl, he lopes ahead of us and we jog after him.

I draw level with Iyana while Danika keeps pace behind us, her duffel bag slung across her back, the barrel of a second rifle peeking from it.

I have questions, but I'm not sure where to start or how to ask them. In the end, I leap right in. "Are the shifters safe?"

Before I left Mother Lavinia's, I asked Helen to take care of the female shifters who'd been hurt by Silas's dark magic during the fight.

Iyana's response is matter-of-fact, and I appreciate her lack of emotion as she speaks. "Helen took the shifters back to Hidden House. She's treating them there. We went with her to get supplies and then we came back to the forest to look for you."

"Thank you," I say. "It's all I could have asked for." I lower my voice, even though the Killer will be able to hear us if he wishes. "What about Tristan's pack?"

"Baxter Griffin has left them in peace—so far, at least. Jace has been holding them together." Iyana's gaze flicks to the Killer and back to me. "Whatever you did at Baxter's home that night, it worked. Baxter's pack hasn't launched any further assaults on Tristan's pack."

There's a question in Iyana's voice. She wasn't there that night. She doesn't know about the deal I made or what happened after.

She continues carefully. "When you didn't come back that night, I went after Baxter Griffin's pack myself."

I give her a startled look that makes her flinch.

"Danika and I went on a hunting spree in Baxter's territory," she says with a grimace. "We may have roughed up a few of his men, but none of them could tell us what happened to you. Only that Baxter handed you over to Ford Vanguard. Nobody knew where Ford took you." She clears her throat. "Luckily, Helen located you at Mother Lavinia's coven before Danika and I killed anyone."

I swallow. "What about Jace?"

Iyana exhales heavily as she jogs. "I don't want to say that he's losing it, but without Tristan… and all the history with Ella… He's staying away from Hidden House, he's keeping Tristan's pack calm, but he's fucking angry beneath the surface."

A weight settles on my shoulders. I survived my father, I'm surviving the Killer, but I might not survive the heavy responsibility that rests on my shoulders. Freeing Tristan from Cerberus's three minds means more than saving Tristan from his fate. It means sending him back to his pack—where I'm not sure I can go. I won't ever belong there. I belong in this wild forest, diving into creeks, falling into ravines, flying on thunderbirds. Hell, I even belonged at the Spire, the old magic welcoming me. Returning to the city would feel like another cage.

I can't speak my thoughts aloud, so I quickly change the subject, gesturing to the folded-up umbrella that rests at Iyana's hip. "What is that?"

"It's my cloak." She gestures at the increasingly dark canopy of branches above us. "As long as I stay within the forest, I'm unlikely to be exposed to direct sunlight, but Helen created it for me in case I get stuck." She grins at me. "She was working on it while you were at Hidden House and just completed it. It also transforms into a protective suit that covers my entire body so that I can walk around in sunlight if I need to. It's invisible around my face, without letting the sun in, so I can wear it anywhere. Even in front of humans. And, folded up, it looks like an umbrella. Given how often it rains in Portland, it won't stand out."

I relax a little. Iyana's safety during the day was preying on my mind. "That's good. We don't know what might happen."

Ahead of us, the Killer slows his pace as he reaches an archway formed between the bending boughs of two trees on either side of the path.

The entrance to Mother Lavinia's coven was marked out with

stone pillars while the pathway into Mother Zala's appears to be heralded by a series of leafy archways all set apart about ten paces and curving to the right in the distance.

The forest thickens with each one, until the final visible archway is wedged between dense greenery.

As soon as I pause beneath the first archway, it begins to rain. It's only a soft drizzle, but it makes me flinch. Mother Zala had an obsession with rain and the timing of the shower right now feels too abrupt to be coincidental.

Ahead of me, the Killer tips his head back, raindrops dripping down his cheeks. He bares his teeth at the moist air around him.

I gesture for Iyana and Danika to stop beside me. "The Killer and I will be able to walk through any protective magical barriers unharmed, but you won't. I won't know where the barriers are located until I either sense them or step through them. I don't want to take any chances that you'll be harmed."

Danika glances at Iyana. "If you're trying to tell us to stay here, forget it." She softens her declaration with a smile. "I'll locate the barrier for you."

I'm not sure what she's about to do when her lips part softly. She exhales and her hawk's keening cry emits from her mouth. When I first met her, she nearly shattered glass with her scream. Unlike most hawk shifters, she can access her hawk's voice in her human form.

I prepare to cover my ears, but the vibration in her voice is so high-pitched that it ripples through me soundlessly, more of a sensation across my torso, face, and legs than a sound within my hearing.

Up ahead, the Killer flinches when Danika's cry reaches him but relaxes as it washes over him.

A glimmering barrier appears far ahead, located in front of the final archway. The archway sits between a thick wall of trees and foliage, so it's impossible to see what lies behind it from this viewpoint, but the barrier resonates visibly with the vibration from Danika's voice.

I quickly count five archways between us and the barrier, so I can remember where it is before the glimmer disappears.

"There," Danika says with a satisfied gleam in her hazel eyes.

"Iyana and I won't proceed past that point." She pats her duffel bag. "I'll fly into the trees closest to the barrier and cover you from a distance."

I take her arm. She has always used warning shots, but today could require more. "It's up to you to decide what you can live with," I say. "I won't order you to kill the witches. But I don't intend to leave any of them alive."

"I understand," she says, squeezing my hand. "We each have to choose our own path."

Quickly stripping off, she pushes her clothing into her bag and shifts rapidly, her honey-colored hawk rising up in a gust of wind. Her bronze-tipped feathers catch the rain as she scoops up the duffel bag in her talons, beats her wings, and disappears into the treetops.

Iyana touches my shoulder. "Danika will cover the coven from the air. I'll cover your backs from the ground." She points to a spot on the far right between the trees. "I'll take up position over there so nobody can sneak up behind you."

"Thank you."

She jogs away from me, her footfalls quiet, and within seconds, she disappears into the greenery as completely as Danika did.

I catch up to the Killer, who waits beneath the third archway. I expect to encounter impatience, but he is unsettlingly quiet.

"They are worthy of your pack," he says. His gaze pierces me as he adjusts his speech. "*Our* pack."

When I fought the Killer at Mother Lavinia's, he told me he wanted to destroy my father, conquer the forest, and make a new pack filled with strong supernaturals. He said that he and I could be two alphas leading a single pack for the first time.

I want what he wants, only I want it with Tristan. I'm aware of how complicated that will be. When Tristan is free, he must return to his pack. It's a startling truth that I have my own pack to care for now, too. No matter how I've tried to push them away, Iyana and Danika have shown me they will stand by my side. Not just as part of my pack, but as my friends.

Small pieces of my heart are starting to *feel* again, and it hurts.

There are things I wish for but might never have. Tristan and I both have packs we need to protect—but where is the room for us in that?

The irony is that if I were content to have Tristan's body without his mind, I would let the Killer remain in his place. The Killer would run beside me in this forest until his dying day. He has no other responsibilities. No other desires but to stand at my side and wreak darkness on the living. And, most probably, to sire a child so that he will live for another generation.

I shudder at the darkness he and I could create together—and at the possibility that my mother could be right. Will I start new wars? If I kill my father, will I become what he is? Standing at the head of an empire that is built on the pain and suffering of others?

The Killer's big hand curls around my shoulder, a firm grip. "Your friends are strong and aren't afraid of their rage. Cody Griffin was worthy, too." The Killer's lips curl up into a smile. "Tristan is the most worthy, which is a shame, because I must destroy him."

The Killer turns away from me, but I catch his arm. "Destroy Tristan?"

"Tristan fights my mind unlike any other host before him," the Killer says. "The others whose bodies I occupied faded away within days, but Tristan refuses to be controlled. I must destroy him completely so that my three minds can fully inhabit this body."

My hand closes more tightly around the Killer's arm. "How long will it take?" I ask, burying my fear beneath a mask of darkness.

"A matter of days. Maybe a week," the Killer says. "Then I will be in complete control."

Damn.

"Come. We have witches to kill," the Killer says, turning away.

I let him go, but my claws descend.

A matter of days.

Tristan deserves to be free to make his own choices and determine his own future. No matter what I have to do, I won't let the Killer succeed.

CHAPTER ELEVEN

The rain continues to drizzle down around us as I step through the final archway into Mother Zala's coven. The magical barrier makes my skin prickle.

I find myself at the edge of a lake of water about a hundred feet wide. Its surface is so glassy that it's impossible to tell how deep it is. Enormous trees rise up around its edges, breaking through the surface of the water. Similar to how it is in Mother Lavinia's territory, cabins are built into the tree trunks. The cabins sit on the lake's surface and they're so closely packed that they form a wall around the watery clearing in the middle.

The space is lit by bright lanterns that float above us and keep the encroaching dark at bay.

Two short tree stumps rest side by side on the right-hand side of the lake a few paces apart from each other. The top of each trunk sits about four feet above the water's surface and is jagged at the edges.

The area is quiet and still, as if the witches have gone, but I sense their power gathering, even if I can't yet pinpoint exactly where they're located.

I immediately remove my boots and roll up the bottom of my jeans. I'm prepared to strip down to my underwear and swim across the lake if I have to. After surviving a crashing ravine, this lake doesn't scare me.

The Killer hunches beside me. "Those are the pits where this coven holds its prisoners," he says, pointing at the hacked-off stumps. "That's where Mother Zala held Tristan."

My forehead creases. "Inside a tree trunk? How?"

"They're hollow," he says. "They go a long way down. The rain falls freely into them and gathers in the bottom. Tristan nearly drowned on the first night."

I shudder and squeeze my eyes closed, imagining Tristan lying injured and unable to stand in the bottom of the pit while the rain pooled around him. My rage at the witches in Mother Zala's coven increases. When I connected with Tristan in the Near-Apart Room at the Spire, it rained around us. I realized later that he had brought the rain with him.

Containing my anger, I gesture to the lake directly in front of us. "How deep is the water right here?"

"It changes," he says. "As deep as the mother witch makes it. They will have chosen a new leader already. Be careful, Tessa Dean. There are as many witches in this coven as in Mother Lavinia's."

About twenty then.

I brace at the first signs of movement on both sides of the lake.

Five witches emerge from the corners of the cabins where they must have been cloaked. They're all wearing dark-colored pants with button-up long-sleeved shirts that sit open at the collar to reveal the tops of multi-colored bras. Each of them has colored streaks in their hair and they all wear the same necklace. It's an oval amulet that glows aqua and appears to be filled with liquid.

They stride confidently toward us across the pool. With every step they take, a stone platform appears on the surface of the water so they don't step into the lake itself.

I wait for them to approach, comfortable in the knowledge that they can't harm me. Their black boots clunk on the rising stones until they come to a stop in an arrow formation.

The woman at the head of their number carries an ebony wand similar to Mother Zala's. Her long, brown hair is streaked with yellow like sunflowers and hangs loose across both of her shoulders. Her bangs are cut straight above her eyes and her jaw is square.

Her hands rest at her sides, but her shoulders are tense, ready to move when she needs to. "We saw what happened to Mother Lavinia's coven," she says. "Our scout reported what you did. We won't make the same mistakes. We're prepared to negotiate an alliance."

I glance at the Killer before I return my attention to the witch at the front. I arch my eyebrows at her. "You'd like to make an alliance with a man who was previously held prisoner here? What makes you believe we're interested in a truce?"

The woman throws back her shoulders. "As I said, we don't want to make the same mistakes as our dearly departed Mother Zala. My name is Suma. I am the new Mother here. You will negotiate with me."

"Oh, I will?" I ask. "Tell me first, Mother Suma, where are the other witches?"

She gives me a blank look. "What others?"

I glance again at the Killer. Either he was deceiving me about the number of witches in this coven—which is certainly possible—or Suma is lying to me now.

"You only have four sisters," I say. "Your coven can't really be this pitiful, can it?"

Suma flushes, but her expression is hard, her jaw clenching. "Only the strongest deserve to live."

"So you killed your sisters and syphoned off their power," I say, drawing conclusions from her statement.

As I speak, my gaze runs quickly over the other women from left to right. All of them meet my gaze with varying expressions of dislike, except for the final woman, who stands farthest to the back of the arrow formation on the right. Even though her shoulders are held back, a seemingly confident posture, her eyes are downcast, her cheeks are pale, and her lips are pressed together in a straight line. I suddenly notice that, unlike the others, she isn't wearing an amulet.

Her ash-colored hair is streaked with violet and is pulled forward across her right cheek. The edge of a yellowing bruise is visible along her jaw, not quite concealed by her hair.

I'm aware of the Killer's scrutiny of the same woman. He leans in, as if to nudge my cheek, and whispers in my ear, "One of these witches is not like her sisters."

I couldn't agree more.

Exhaling, I turn back to Suma. "If you planned to surrender, I wonder why you felt the need to make yourselves stronger?"

She bristles but replies smoothly. "We didn't think you would agree to a treaty with us if we were weak."

I shrug as if it doesn't matter. "Very well. We will negotiate terms."

She relaxes and a smile crosses her face, but before she can speak, I point to the witch with the violet streaks in her hair and the bruise across her cheek. "But we will only negotiate with her."

Suma stiffens. She sidesteps into my line of sight, her boots clunking onto a stone surface that rises up to meet her feet. Blocking my view of the violet-haired witch, she says, "Maeve is not worth your time."

"I'll make that judgment for myself," I say.

Remaining at the side of the lake isn't doing me any favors. Just now, when Suma sidestepped, I'm sure she didn't actively summon the stone to appear beneath her feet, which could mean that any movement above the lake's surface conjures a platform to stand on. It's worth taking a risk to test my theory—even if I end up plummeting beneath the surface.

Taking a breath in case I need it, I step toward her without looking down.

My foot meets a hard surface and all of the witches flinch.

I suppose they were hoping I wouldn't take a chance on stepping onto the lake.

Quickly, I cross the distance to Suma.

She braces as I approach, her grip tightening on her wand, but she doesn't budge from her position between me and Maeve.

I lower my voice to address her. "You're either incredibly brave or tremendously stupid to step between me and something that I want."

She gives me an unsettling smile. "I may be brave, but you're reckless to step onto our lake."

She snaps her fingers.

Water rushes up around me, rising on all sides. I manage to take a deep breath before a sphere of water closes around me. It's as if I dropped into the lake, except that the water came to me. I'm completely enclosed in liquid. The stone platform remains beneath me, but when I attempt to drop to a crouch, I only manage to stay there for a split second before I float upward.

Damn! I can repel magic, but I can't repel nature.

If their scout was watching my fight with Mother Lavinia's witches, then she will have seen that I can only break through magic that touches my body directly. Still, if they're using magic to contain the water, then I should be able to break through the outer shell of magic.

Paddling so I can turn inside the sphere, I find that the Killer is also enclosed in his own watery sphere behind me. Alarmingly, his sphere is elevated above the surface of the lake and floats toward me.

Outside the sphere, Suma and the three other dominant witches have split into groups of two—each group controlling a sphere. The amulets around their necks are glowing brightly and even through the water, I can sense the power in the amulets, some sort of stored magic.

Maeve has moved so that she stands on a stone platform even farther back, but her focus flicks from my sphere to the Killer's and back again.

I've held my breath for ten seconds now, and I won't be able to hold it forever. I drop to the stone platform, crouch on the stone, and propel myself forward, attempting to dive through the side of the sphere. The moment my outstretched hands reach the edge of the water, the sphere moves with me.

It means I can't reach the magical shell holding the water together to break through it.

No matter.

I float upright in the liquid for a moment, allowing my crimson vision to rise. My lips press into a hard line. My rage allows me to see that the power the witches are wielding glows directly from their amulets and isn't being drawn from their bodies. They've either stored up enough of their own power into the amulets over time or the necklaces contain another witch's power.

My hair swirls around me and my eyes glow so brightly that the water glitters ruby red. At the corner of my vision, the Killer is

79

removing his jeans—swimming up and out of them as he prepares to shift into his wolf form.

My deep rage rises and I don't clamp down on it.

I surge forward, swimming through the sphere as it moves with me above the surface of the lake, drawing closer to Suma and the witch beside her.

The witches poise on the balls of their booted feet, prepared to move.

Suma cries, "Sisters! Evade and contain them! We only need to wait for them to drown."

My focus flicks to Maeve, who has dropped to a crouch on the stone platform on which she stands. The air glows around her torso and head, a deep violet color that matches the streaks in her hair. It looks like she's drawing on her power, but I'm not sure who her target is. Right now, she's glaring at Suma's back.

I can't deny that I need to breathe. Desperately. But I use my growing panic as an energy source that twines through my rising darkness.

In the sphere beside mine, the Killer has shifted. His wolf is like Tristan's, except that his wolf's shoulders are as dangerously bunched as the Killer's always are, the curves of his furred body giving an air of perpetual violence.

I wait another heartbeat until I'm close to Suma's position—timing my attack for the exact moment before she decides to leap backward.

I release my wolf from my body in a burst of power.

My wolf's insubstantial form is as arctic blue as the hair of the fae we left behind. Her energy blurs within the water as she leaps through the outer shell and right through Suma. Her leap doesn't break the magic, but Suma screams and drops her wand, which clatters onto a new stone platform. The impact of my wolf's energy raging through her body forces her to her knees, where she gasps for breath, her eyes wide.

The other witch in charge of maintaining my sphere of water shouts and freezes, a moment of indecision that gives me all the time I need.

As Suma scrabbles for her wand, I push forward, taking the watery sphere with me and enclosing Suma in it alongside me.

I was hoping Suma's presence inside the sphere would break it immediately, but even so, the source of Suma's power is now within my reach.

Her head snaps up, her mouth closes as she appears to inhale water, and her hand closes around her wand.

Just as she raises her wand toward me, I grab the amulet, plant my feet on her chest, and propel myself backward.

The necklace snaps. I clutch the amulet securely in my hand while the sphere explodes around me and water sprays in every direction.

Oh, sweet oxygen.

I backflip away from Suma as stones form beneath me, my wet clothing slapping around me. Still gripping the amulet, I land securely on my feet. I quickly slip the amulet into my wet pocket, gratified to find that Silas's orb rests safely in my other pocket.

The Killer's wolf attacks at the same time. He leaps from stone to stone to gain speed before he surges forward, his claws breaking through the sphere's outer spell. The water explodes around him, droplets splashing outward from his leaping form.

His jaws clamp around the neck of the nearest witch, pulling her down. Within seconds, she lies still, but the stone platform on which she rests descends beneath the lake's surface, taking her with it.

Suma spins to my wolf, trying to keep both of my forms within her sight. She backs toward the remaining two dominant witches to stand clear of the Killer.

Suma points her wand at Maeve. "When we've killed these two, you're next, Maeve, you fucking useless, lying scout."

I'm not sure what Maeve lied about—but if she was the scout they sent out, then she clearly left a few things out in her report about what happened to Mother Lavinia's coven.

Maeve stands her ground, all alone on her tiny stone platform far to the right of the clearing. The violet glow around her continues to grow, sparks forming around her fingertips, but she has yet to let her power loose. I don't have time to consider her more carefully, but I'm suddenly intrigued that she isn't carrying a wand.

Suma and the other two witches spin to the Killer and me, demanding my attention again.

They scream in unison, the remaining two amulets glow, and new spheres of water rise up around me and the Killer.

Really? I shake my head at the group of witches.

Huddled together now, they're all nicely placed and ready to fall.

My wolf leaps at them, preparing to jump through all three of them at once.

I flinch as two shots ring out in quick succession.

Blood blossoms in the center of the foreheads of the witches who still wear amulets, both of them collapsing to the surface of the lake. Stone platforms appear under their fallen bodies, but only for a moment before the platforms lower into the water, taking the witches with them. Within seconds, their bodies disappear beneath the surface.

The water-filled spheres collapse around us as the witches' magic breaks, liquid splashing down around our bodies and cascading back into the lake, causing waves that ripple across its surface.

My wolf pulls up short and peers across the distance behind me, locating the source of the bullets. With her eyes, I don't need to turn to make out Danika's form in the branches above and beyond us. The distance would have made the shots difficult, but Danika's eyesight is second to none.

Danika tips her head to give my wolf a nod before adjusting her rifle slightly to aim it squarely at Suma. Danika took out the witches who wore amulets and were controlling the new spheres of water, but she left Suma alive.

My wolf prowls around Suma as she grips her wand.

Once again, my wolf prepares to jump.

A blast of violet magic hits the air in front of Suma, forcing her to leap backward. She manages to maintain her balance as she spins with a startled scream.

I also turn to Maeve, who speaks for the first time.

"Tessa Dean!" Maeve calls as violet light sparks even more brightly around her fingertips. "I understand I will die by your hand today. I won't fight you. I only ask that you leave Suma to me."

THIS CAGED WOLF

I'm surprised by Maeve's declaration, but I'm unwilling to get in her way. The bruise on her cheek didn't come from nowhere.

I incline my head and take a step back, drawing my wolf's energy to my body in a rush that fills me with warmth. "I won't interfere. Neither will the Killer."

He snarls at me, his teeth bared. His jeans have fallen onto a stone a few paces away, but he doesn't seem in any hurry to hide all of his naked glory.

"Fine," he says. "But if she fails, I will tear Suma apart myself. She's the one who collared me."

The Killer was held captive here for three days, during which time Mother Zala used him to win the entire northern territory. I don't doubt that the Killer welcomed the fights she created with the other three covens, but he also wore a collar around his neck that was used to hurt him.

Suma makes a hissing sound at Maeve. "You can't hurt me. You're a caged witch!"

Maeve lifts her chin, her hair falling back and revealing the extent of the bruise across her jaw and cheek. "I *was* a caged witch. But Silas is dead."

The blood drains from Suma's face. "What? But you said—"

"That Silas escaped with Ford and Brynjar. I know what I said." Maeve gestures to me. "I didn't tell you about Tessa Dean's wolf. I told you she took down every witch in Mother Lavinia's coven, but I didn't tell you how. Why would I tell you that the wizard who caged me is dead?"

Suma squares her shoulders. "It doesn't matter. You're weak."

Maeve's lips press together in a firm line. "I was made into a weapon, Suma."

The sphere of violet light around Maeve's hands continues to grow brighter.

Suma's wand shoots out, crackling power spearing from it. The electricity hits the air in front of Maeve's form, but her violet magic glistens around her, the electricity splashing and not hurting her.

I smile to myself. During our fight, she must have been quietly creating a shield around herself.

Taking firm steps across the surface of the lake, Maeve releases a bolt of violet light that rages across the distance. Suma attempts

83

to deflect it, but her magic disintegrates as soon as it touches Maeve's light.

The violet bolt hits Suma's chest and knocks her backward.

Maeve releases another bolt with every step she takes, hitting Suma across her shoulder, stomach, right thigh, and finally, across her heart. Every time Maeve releases her magic, I catch a flash across her palms of a dark substance and I'm not sure what it is.

Suma sinks to her knees, her lips twisted, a yellow glow building around her form. Her power gathers and hits Maeve at close range, but Maeve barely flinches.

She leans over Suma and takes hold of her shoulder. "I'm not your weapon anymore."

Suma's magic explodes, but Maeve's cuts through it, knocking Suma across the surface of the lake, where she lies still. Suma's feet dip into the water before the platform she's lying on descends beneath the surface, taking her with it.

CHAPTER TWELVE

Silence falls as Maeve rises to her feet. Her eyes are a beautiful shade of cedar brown that contrasts with her ash-colored hair.

"Who are you?" I ask. "Really."

"My name is Maeve. I was a gift to Mother Zala from your father. He killed the coven I was born into but kept me alive."

"Show me your hands," I command.

She lifts her palms, holding them out to me.

I gasp. The inside of each of her hands is coated with what looks like cedar wood, except that it must be malleable because it doesn't prevent her from closing her fists and using her fingers.

"What is that?" I demand to know.

"It's my wand," she says. "The dark wizard—Silas—who worked for your father molded my wand to my hands."

My eyes widen. To have a wand adhered to her hands would mean she would never be without access to her power. And yet...

"Suma said you were caged," I say, a question in my voice.

"Silas cast a spell to place a lock on my magic so I could only use my power if commanded. I couldn't free myself. I could only do what Mother Zala or one of her witches told me to do." Maeve holds herself upright. "When you killed Silas, you freed me from his spell. A fact I kept from Suma until just now."

I take a step toward her, impressed when she doesn't flinch.

She told me that she is prepared to die, but now I see that she was as caged as I was.

"Come with me," I say on impulse. "Join my pack."

She blinks at me, her gaze darting to the Killer. "I won't be tricked into trusting anyone again. Tristan Masters wears the Killer's face, and he's tainted by the Deceiver. Tristan warned me not to trust his minds. If I can't trust him right now, then I can't believe you, either."

"Then believe the hawk shifter in the trees," I say. "Or the vampire beyond the barrier. They'll tell you who I am."

Maeve narrows her eyes at me. I understand her caution. I also suddenly understand what Helen must have felt when she first met me, wanting to connect but unwilling to hurry or push, recognizing the need to give me space.

Maeve looks around at the four dead witches. "You've killed the witches, but they were your enemies. You allowed me to kill Suma, but again, any enemy might allow someone else to do their work for them…"

I'm not sure where she's going with her statements until she points to one of the tree stumps. "I will judge you by what you do with the woman in that pit," she says.

My eyes widen. Even with my crimson vision, I can't detect any life form within the stump or down beneath the surface of the lake. "What woman?"

"Mother Zala captured her a year ago. I don't know her name." Maeve watches me carefully. "The amulets the witches wore were filled with power syphoned from the woman in the pit."

Power over water.

I spin to cast a glare at the Killer. "Did you know there was another prisoner?"

He shrugs, nonchalant. "There are two pits. I can't sense anyone down there, but it stands to reason that the other pit is occupied."

I narrow my eyes at him. Maeve's right—the Deceiver lurks in the Killer's expression, an indefinable air of carelessness about him.

He could have known about the woman in the pit all along.

Not wasting another moment, I hurry across the lake to the enormous tree stump Maeve pointed out. Stones appear and disappear beneath my feet as I move.

The stump has a large enough diameter that a person could lie within it. The edge at the top is jagged and sharp—which I discover when I cut my palms on it. Ignoring the shallow wounds, I lean over the edge and peer into the darkness below.

Far, far below, I make out the shape of a person.

Releasing my wolf from my body, I send her across the air, where she hovers. She turns to look back at me while I look at her.

My human form is drenched, my hair plastered to my face and neck, my flannel shirt stuck to my curves and catching the increasingly cold breeze.

My wolf form drops from view, her energy plummeting.

Closing my human eyes, I allow my senses to fill with what my wolf form sees and feels.

It's cold—*freezing*—within the pit. The air smells like stale water. It's a long fall down that takes nearly half as long as the fall into the ravine yesterday. When I reach the bottom, my paws come to rest in several inches of water.

In the darkness, a female form sits with her back resting against the side of the pit, which is held together with mud and tree roots. Her head is tipped to one side and her eyes are closed. The water laps at her hips and legs.

She's wearing indigo armor that covers her body from her ankles to her neck. Her feet are bare, her toenails chipped where they poke up through the water.

I discern the faintest flicker of a pulse at her neck, but I don't dare touch her or my wolf's angry energy could kill her.

Her hair is lank, but I make out forest-green streaks in her brown tresses.

Based on her hair alone, I wouldn't be certain that she was fae, but she's wearing the same armor as the fae women I encountered today. It's disconcerting that I can't sense her, but it must be because these fae are pure elementals. Their power is so strong that it allows them to merge with their surroundings—water, stone, earth, air. They are part of the world around them so seamlessly that I can't detect them. I may as well try to sense the air around me.

Aboveground, I open my human eyes and pull my wolf's energy back to me.

"This woman is fae," I say to Maeve. "I'm certain she's the daughter of the Fae Queen, Calanthe. She needs to be returned to her people." I take a deep breath. "Will you use your power to lift her out of there?"

"How do I know you won't kill her once I do?" Maeve asks.

"Because I could have already," I say. "You've seen what my wolf can do."

Eyeing me with distrust, Maeve stands at the edge of the stump and holds her hands out over the edge. Closing her eyes, she murmurs quietly beneath her breath, a look of concentration settling on her face.

A long minute later, Calanthe's daughter rises above the edge of the stump, her arms hanging at her sides and her lank hair brushing across the top of the tree trunk.

She remains unconscious while Maeve carefully begins maneuvering her away from the pit.

"Killer!" I call, unable to take my eyes off the frail fae woman. "I need you to carry her."

The Killer races to my side, his hand coming to rest on my shoulder, a strong, firm touch. "I'm here, Tessa."

His voice is different, and he didn't call me *Tessa Dean*...

My head snaps up to meet Tristan's crisp, green eyes, flecked with amber. His presence beside me is suddenly so strong that I gasp and inhale the scent of his power, all the layers of bitter orange, nutmeg, and cedar. "Tristan?"

His touch is warm but brief before he releases me to reach for Calanthe's daughter.

"I'll carry her," he says to Maeve. "Can you bring her all the way clear of the pit?"

Maeve's expression softens as she looks at Tristan. "Welcome back, Tristan Masters. *You*, I trust."

Tristan has pulled his jeans back on, but he's as equally drenched as I am, water dripping from his black hair onto his shoulders.

He cautiously folds his arms around Calanthe's daughter after Maeve moves her closer, until he's supporting her head, arms, and legs against his chest.

"She's in bad shape," he says.

The fae woman is incredibly thin, her armor hanging loosely off her arms and legs.

"How much of her power did they syphon?" Tristan asks Maeve, an edge of rage creeping into his voice.

"Too much," Maeve says. "They stood out here and filled their four amulets until her power stopped flowing from the pit. I thought they'd killed her."

"Can you help her?" I ask Maeve.

She shakes her head, downcast. "Mother Zala used me to hurt and fight others. Healing spells are complex—you can do more harm than good. I was only beginning to learn about healing when my coven was killed. I don't have the skills for this."

"Then we need to get her to her mother," I say. "Queen Calanthe mentioned they have healers."

Tristan turns to Maeve. "Can you remove the protective barrier around the clearing so we can carry her out safely?"

Maeve nods, her eyes brightening. "I'm good at breaking things. I'll need to blast the archway apart, though. You should take cover."

I immediately gauge the distance from the archway to Danika, but I catch sight of her hawk in the distance angling expertly through the trees. She'll make sure Iyana is safe from the blast.

I step in front of the fae woman, facing Tristan. "I'll shield you."

The hard line of his lips softens as he catches a corner of my flannel shirt with a spare finger, urging me down into a crouch so we can both protect the fae with our bodies. I position myself curled across her upper torso, my arm wrapped firmly but gently around the top of her head while my legs tuck under her. Tristan kneels, gathering her legs up and leaning across her so that his cheek presses mine.

"Tessa," he murmurs. "I want you to know that I'm aware of much more now. The Killer and Coward can't block me out completely."

"You're fighting them," I say, pressing closer to him, the corner of my lips touching his. "The harder you fight, the more determined the Killer becomes to destroy you."

"Only because I've resolved to annihilate *him*." Tristan's response is growled so harshly that I have to check his eyes and his posture in case the Killer has returned.

I take a deep breath, sensing the rise and fall of his chest, matching my breathing to his. My shoulders relax when we breathe together, and I'm certain that he is himself.

I'm facing away from Maeve and the entrance now. As a violet glow builds behind me, I remain focused on Tristan. "Once the fae is safe, I'm going after my father." *I'm going after the book.*

"I'll be right beside you, Tessa."

Violet light explodes around us, reflected off the surface of the lake.

One explosion. Two. Then a third. Each one greater than the last.

At Mother Lavinia's, Helen destroyed the coven's protective boundaries with a single blast of her power, but she is one of the most powerful witches in existence.

Maeve's scream of effort reaches me a split second before there's a fourth burst of light and the archway finally explodes. Pieces of wood and leaves fly around us, splashing into the lake's surface and sinking beneath it, kicking up waves, a ripple of power breaking across the clearing as the boundary around the clearing shatters.

I sense another wave of debris, the shifting air, the imminent impact of wooden rubble across my back and head, and I brace, ready for the pain.

Maeve screams again and violet light washes across me.

I dare to glance up to see all of the wood and debris sucked in a rising tornado of power before the pieces splash harmlessly into the lake farther to my right.

Water sprays across us and silence settles again.

I crane my neck to look behind me where Maeve rests on one knee, facing us. Her shoulders are hunched over as she catches her breath, recovering.

She raises her head with a smile. "It's safe to carry her through now."

I pause for the briefest moment, trying to snatch every small moment between Tristan and me, to remember every heartbeat.

I'm about to rise when I sense the fae's stillness.

Her cheeks are far too pale.

Quickly lowering my cheek to hers and pressing my fingers gently to her neck, I discover her breathing is impossibly shallow.

"Her pulse is thready." My shoulders sink as I meet Tristan's eyes. "The ravine is at least an hour's run from here. She isn't going to make it home."

Tristan remains where he was, kneeling, supporting the woman while one of his arms tucks around my side, keeping us all close. "You can help her, Tessa."

"How?" I whisper. "I can't heal her."

"Your wolf can give her strength," he says. "You can keep her alive until we get her to safety."

My forehead creases in confusion, but he persists. "I saw what you did the day I brought the two injured girls to Helen at Hidden House. Your wolf's energy did more than calm Becca. Your wolf gave her physical strength."

I stiffen and draw back, but Tristan refuses to release me. I remember the moment he's talking about. It was the day he broke through the lock Helen placed on Hidden House. Tristan raced in with Becca and her older sister, Carly. Both had been badly injured in an attack perpetrated by Baxter Griffin and the man I thought was my half-brother—Dawson Nash. Becca was crying and my wolf's energy curled around her and calmed her.

"No," I say. "I can't do that anymore. I've changed. My wolf will kill her."

I continue to pull away, but Tristan holds me tightly. "Tessa. You can do this." His expression softens and for a moment, I'm terrified that I'm looking into the eyes of the Deceiver, but my breathing still matches his. He takes a deep breath and I sense the pull within my own chest, inhaling calming air the way Helen used to urge me.

Breathe in. Breathe out.

Tristan speaks quietly. "I never told you that I was grateful for what you did that day. I never told you how much your heart meant to me—"

"No," I whisper, breathing out the sudden pain in my chest. "I'm not that person anymore, Tristan. That woman—*that Tessa*—she's gone. I'm brittle on the inside. And angry." I squeeze my eyes closed against the burn of tears. "I'm fucking angry. It's taking all of my energy right now to restrain myself from unleashing hell on the world. The need to destroy everything beautiful is so… fucking difficult to deny. Too difficult to control. All I can do is channel my impulses and focus my anger on my father."

Tristan remains still and quiet. He's completely in control in the face of my admission. "The day might come—very soon, in fact—when I need you to be like steel. A necessary blade through my heart." His eyes pierce mine. "But not today. Not yet."

His jaw clenches, the intense determination in his gaze increasing even though his lips soften. "You aren't cold or unfeeling, Tessa. I fell in love with you that day at Hidden House—right in that moment when I was too stubborn, proud, and angry to admit that I needed you. That I need you," he says. "More than I've ever needed anyone."

He leans close, lifts his hand to my hammering heart, and rests his palm across my chest, a steady presence. "Your anger is a flame that can burn and destroy, but it can also warm."

His certainty compels me to believe him. "Use it to help her."

CHAPTER THIRTEEN

I shudder as I contemplate the dying fae woman. I don't know her. I'd never met her before today. I didn't know she existed, didn't come here to rescue her, don't even know her name. She is another broken body in the trail my father has left behind.

Yet she is the one who will prove to me whether or not any trace of humanity, compassion, or grace still exists in me. This stranger. This woman to whom I owe nothing. Whose life hangs on the extent to which my heart has been damaged.

I sink back to my knees, leaning across her, one arm remaining beneath her head, my other hand pressing to Tristan's bare chest, mirroring the way his palm rests over my heart.

Reaching deep for my power, I pull it upward.

My mind fills with the undeniable rage and hatred that my power brings, the thirst for blood and vengeance that will never be sated—not even if I fight a hundred wars.

I draw on my power without controlling how my wolf will appear, the way I didn't control her during my life before I met Tristan. The color of my wolf's fur, before I could regulate my power completely, was a reflection of my dominant emotion at any given point in time: sapphire for fear, black for strength, crimson for rage, and golden... *the color of Cody's wolf...* for sadness.

I don't know what she will look like this time.

I release my power slowly.

My wolf appears in a cautious influx of light, rippling through sapphire, ebony, crimson, and gold as she takes shape, an enormous, powerful wolf capable of tearing a person apart from the inside. As her light ebbs and flows through her head, shoulders, torso, and legs, she finally settles on a color that resembles the streaks in the fae's hair, the color of the forest.

I fight the sob rising inside me.

This forest is the place where I can run free.

Her fur is the color of freedom.

My wolf's body fits in the space between Tristan and me, her energy passing through the fae woman's torso. My wolf's tail curls across the woman's thighs while my wolf settles her head onto her paws on the woman's chest. Her snout rests gently beneath the fae's chin.

My wolf's eyes are still crimson, pure rage, and my heart stills. I sense Tristan's heart skip a beat at the same time as mine does, as affected as I am, but my rage is warm, a heat that spreads between us and glows across the woman's face.

She inhales a sudden, shuddering breath through her cracked lips, although her eyes remain closed.

I watch her carefully as, minute by long minute, the stiffness in her torso and shoulders eases and a hint of color returns to her lips and cheeks.

Finally, she breathes deeply and the pain in her face eases, her features smoothing out.

I'm suddenly aware of Tristan's gaze on my wolf. The way she's lying, one of her shoulders presses against his chest. Her forest-green fur brushes against his skin—becoming solid where she touches him. Tristan and my father are the only two supernaturals who have the power to cause my wolf to take form in flesh and blood. It's why we're all so dangerous to each other. We have the capacity to kill each other's wolves when nobody else can.

If Tristan lowered his head to my wolf right now, he could rest his cheek against hers.

"I can carry them both," Tristan says quietly, breaking the silence.

I tip my head, a little confused until he continues. "Your energy needs to remain with her to keep her warm and alive. I can carry her and your wolf."

The tips of Tristan's fingers rise to trail across my cheek. "You did it, Tessa."

He wraps his arms around the woman, and I allow my wolf's energy to remain with her, directing her to stay with Tristan.

We rise together and step apart, and I can't help but close my eyes and feel everything my wolf feels right now.

My energy, my power, my wolf... have never come into contact with Tristan before. Over the last few days, I've battled the possibility that I would have to use my wolf against him, a last possible effort to rip the three minds out of him. Somehow.

Now, my wolf rests beside his heart, keeping him warm.

My heart suddenly aches and I have to turn away from him before I reveal my pain. I find myself facing Iyana and Danika, who have joined Maeve and ventured across the lake to stand only a few paces away from us.

"Will she be okay?" Maeve asks.

"I hope so," I say. "She's stable, but we can't delay. We need to get her home quickly."

Danika peers into the water while Iyana hands me my boots. "Maeve rescued these from the blast," she says to me. "I know we need to get moving, but you're dripping wet. So is Tristan. Maeve and I will get you both some clean, dry clothes and gather supplies. We'll be quick."

Maeve is already moving. "This way."

Iyana gives Tristan a nod as she hurries past him. "Nice to see you again, Tristan."

He returns her nod with a grim smile before he moves up beside me, adjusting the fae woman in his arms. "Let's get her off the water," he says.

Danika falls in beside me as I follow Tristan across the lake, stones appearing and disappearing beneath our feet with every step we take until we reach the shattered opening.

Maeve's magic has destroyed the archway at the entrance, along with the next archway, but the surrounding trees appear unharmed.

Iyana and Maeve appear moments later, out of breath. Maeve is in the process of shoving bread and apples into a large bag at the bottom of which I also catch sight of a number of weapons—all enclosed blades.

Iyana's arms are full of clothing.

"This is what I could grab," she says, holding a pair of black jeans up for me while handing another pair to Tristan.

I take the long pants, rifle through the various shirts in her arms, and choose a gray T-shirt and soft black jacket that are both a little too large for me, but it's better than the too-small options. Without hesitation, I peel off my dripping clothing, strip to my underwear, and pull on the new garments, welcoming the warmth. I quickly retrieve the dark magic orb and the amulet and slip them into one of my new pockets.

Then I reach for the fae woman. "I'll take her while you change," I say to Tristan.

I brace for her weight, finding her impossibly light, severely undernourished. Even so, I sink to my knees so that I can hold her. My wolf remains with her, my wolf's body creating a buzzing energy beside me.

The other three women turn around the moment Tristan begins to remove his pants. He's dressed within seconds in a clean pair of black jeans and a soft-looking navy blue T-shirt.

Reaching for the fae woman and my wolf once more, he says, "Let's move."

Quickly pulling on my boots, I focus on the task ahead of us. "Iyana, I need you to continue watching our backs. Danika, I need you to scout ahead. There shouldn't be any witches remaining in this forest, but I don't want any surprises. Fly back if you spot anything unusual."

"We can do that," Iyana says, dropping behind us while Danika jogs ahead.

I fall back behind Tristan, but I touch his arm as I pass. "You set the pace," I say. "We'll keep up."

He promptly breaks into a jog.

Maeve falls into stride beside me.

As we run, I stay as close to Tristan as I can, keeping watch on my breathing. As long as I can sense that my breathing matches his, I'll know he's still with me. I need to be careful in case the

Killer—or one of his other minds—surfaces while he's carrying the fae. The Killer had no concern for her wellbeing back at the lake.

Maeve keeps pace with me, but she's quiet.

I wasn't sure what she would do when we left the clearing and I don't want to question her decision to join us, so I decide to let her control our conversation—or our continued silence, if that makes her feel more comfortable.

"You surprised me," she finally says.

Scanning the forest around us, keeping my breathing aligned with Tristan's, I keep my response casual. "How so?"

"I've lived the last three years of my life surrounded by darkness," she says. "I've learned to recognize it. There's darkness in you, Tessa. A darkness I've only felt once before."

"You've obviously met my father," I say with a wry arch of my eyebrows.

"That's why I couldn't trust you," she says. "But you're fighting your inner nature." Her forehead creases as her perceptive gaze falls across Tristan's back. "Tristan pulls you from the edge."

While the Killer pushes me toward it.

I return to something Maeve mentioned. "Was it three years ago that you were gifted to Mother Zala?" I ask.

"It was."

I can't stop the growl rising in my throat. "That was when the witches started fighting over the forest. My father gave a number of gifts at that time. One of them was a wolf shifter I know. All of his gifts were given to gain favors from the witches."

Cody's sister, Ella, was my father's gift to Mother Lavinia. It took Tristan a year to rescue her and in that time she was forced to fight other prisoners to win wagers that the witches made against each other. I shudder at how many other lives my father destroyed to gain favor with the witches.

"Why didn't Suma and the other four sisters syphon your power today and kill you like they killed the rest of the coven?" I ask, curious about Maeve's survival.

She stretches out her fingers while she jogs, turning her palms toward me to show me the wood molded to her skin. "My hands were my cage—but they're also my protection. My power can't be pulled from me because my wand forms a wall around it. It's a barrier of sorts."

I consider this for a moment. "If you could remove the wand from your hands, would you?"

She purses her lips in thought before she puffs out an exhale. "I am who I am now," she says. "I wouldn't have chosen this for myself if I'd had a say in it. For a long time, I thought my hands were ugly—my wand was like a horrible scar. A constant reminder that I was a prisoner. But now... This may be an imperfection, but it's *my* imperfection."

I allow myself to smile. "I have more than a few of those," I say. "Imperfections."

We run in silence after that.

The moon rises high above us, its crisp white light filtering through the canopy overhead until I hear the rushing waterfall again.

Danika waits for us up ahead through the trees, Iyana catches up to us, and Tristan slows his pace.

When we first came across the ravine, I stepped right into it. I can hear the water, but all around us, only trees are visible.

"It's close," Danika calls as we approach. "Do you want me to walk ahead? I won't be able to pass through the boundary."

After a glance at Tristan, I nod. "Yes, that's safest."

As much as I want to hurry, we walk slowly and carefully forward until Danika jolts and stops in place. She presses her palms against the air immediately in front of her.

"It's here," she says.

Unlike the unfortunate spot where I stepped over the edge, the trees are farther apart here, far enough for a person to stand, and I can make out the open space ahead: a moonlit chasm. If I didn't know it was there, my eyes would glaze over it.

"What is this place?" Maeve asks, stepping up beside Danika and pressing her palms to the air in front of her. Her eyes widen when her palms flatten against the barrier.

I'm surprised. "You've never come here?"

She shakes her head. "I grew up in the Cascades and I was taken directly to the coven. After that, I only went where Mother Zala took me. She never brought me anywhere near here." Maeve pats her hands against the barrier, testing it. "How can anything get through this?" Her fingers glow violet for a moment before her power recedes. "It repels my magic."

"Calanthe said it was created with the oldest of magic. Clearly, the fae can get through it or this woman would not have ventured out, but I don't think any other supernatural species except Tristan and me can get through."

I turn to him. "How will we get her down the ravine?"

He rests on one knee, his chest heaving with the effort of carrying Calanthe's daughter all of this way.

My wolf raises her nose to nudge his chin. "Are you okay?" she whispers.

He gives her a firm nod. "We need to find a way," he says, taking a deep breath before he rises to his feet again.

I spin back to the ravine. "I could call the thunderbirds."

My thoughts buzz as I try to remember how Myra had called the two birds earlier. I think it was two short whistles and then a longer one.

"Danika. Maeve. Step aside, please," I say.

They move apart, pressing themselves against the trunks of two trees facing each other.

I hope I get this right. Placing my fingers to my lips, I lean forward through the barrier, wincing as it scrapes across my skin and I teeter at the edge of the cliff.

Just as I complete the first two short whistles, Tristan shouts behind me.

At the same time, there's a shriek of rage.

I spin, but I've already seen what happened with my wolf's eyes.

The fae woman's eyes have flown open, a scream on her lips.

My wolf leaps up and away before her energy might react in a way that could hurt the fae. My wolf lands on a soft patch of ground, backing off as the fae thrashes to escape from Tristan's arms.

For a second, his muscles cord and I'm terrified that the Killer is about to make an appearance. The Killer is more likely to crush her than let her go.

Tristan growls, shakes his head, and reverts to himself, immediately releasing the woman, his palms up to show he won't hurt her.

As agile as my wolf, she lands on her feet a few paces from his position. Her chest rises far too rapidly and her steps wobble as she backs away from him, spinning between us. Her gaze darts to the open space between the trees and the sky over the ravine behind it. She must recognize how close she is to her home, but her panicked breathing and rapid movements tell me she thinks we're here to harm her.

Her voice is raspy, her vocal chords damaged, barely audible. "I won't be a prisoner again."

My eyes widen when she runs straight for the cliff. "No! Stop!"

I gesture wildly for the others to stay back as I remain in the fae's path, preparing to stop her from jumping to her death. She can control the water rushing through the ravine, but she won't survive the rocks.

Her brown hair flies behind her while her thin legs pump. Her eyes are determined, the rings under them stark and black as she prepares to tackle me.

I brace for the impact of her momentum, digging in my heels.

At the last possible moment, she sidesteps me, spinning to push me with all her might. Water splashes across my face, called by her magic, and in the time it takes me to blink through it, she darts like a bird toward the cliff.

My hand closes around the empty space beside her, trying to grab her but only succeeding in brushing her arm.

She leaps through the barrier as easily as through air, twisting so that she faces me, her back to the ravine.

Her eyes meet mine before she tips her head back and plummets.

CHAPTER FOURTEEN

"No!" With my heart in my throat, I push through the boundary, ignoring the pain, reaching out through space, teetering dangerously on the edge of the cliff.

A rush of wind billows up around me, blowing back my hair and buffeting around me. Lightning crackles in the air, racing across my skin like a caress.

The blue thunderbird rises up in front of me, her wings cracking as she beats them. The fae woman is safely caught on her back, leaning across her neck, resting her face in the bird's feathers.

She wobbles a little, incredibly weak but determined to rise to a sitting position on the bird's back. Her eyes fly wide when she sees me standing halfway through the barrier. "How have you passed through...?"

Before she can say another word, a new crackle of lightning breaks the midnight air around us, ruby electricity scorching the sky. The second thunderbird speeds toward us so fast that the sapphire bird ducks and rolls in an evasive maneuver. The fae drops to her bird's neck just in time, gripping with her arms and legs so she stays on her back.

With a shriek, the ruby bird soars up in front of me, her wings beating the air in aggressive cracks. She tosses her head at me and shrieks again, her wild eyes filled with anger.

I brace, preparing to leap away from the barrier and the fae

101

woman when the ruby bird makes a keening sound that tugs at my heart and stops me in my tracks.

She's unhappy and angry... but she's not trying to scare me away.

I purse my lips, my head tilted. "Why are you angry with me?"

The ruby bird tosses her head again, but her focus shifts to the sapphire bird, which rises up again on my left, coasting clear of the angry ruby creature.

The fae woman takes glances between the ruby bird and me, but her eyebrows quickly draw down as she turns on me.

"Who are you?" she asks, her voice scratchy, a shouted demand for answers.

"I'm Tessa Dean," I say, unwilling to take my eyes off the ruby bird.

"How has Lyra bonded with you?" the fae woman asks.

Bonded?

My tension eases. "Lyra," I say, reaching out toward the bird but not touching her, my palm still a long way from her neck. "Is that your name?"

The ruby bird tosses her head at me and it feels like an answering nod.

I allow a small smile to cross my face as I guess her feelings. "Then you're angry because I went away and... you were worried about me."

Lyra makes a keening sound again, her fierce eyes checking me over as if she's looking for wounds.

"Because you know I'll always run toward danger," I say to Lyra. "Like you would."

Casting the fae woman a certain glance, I say to her, "Lyra hasn't bonded with me. A creature this wild *chooses* to share her presence with someone—to care about them—but she will never belong to anyone."

The fae woman narrows her eyes at me. "What *are* you?" she asks.

"A war wolf."

Her thunderbird coasts in the air, drawing closer to me for a moment. "No," the fae says, peering at me. "War demands a thirst for blood and glory. You are wilder than that." Her focus flicks to

Lyra. "Only the wildest creature could form a connection with Lyra."

I don't doubt that.

"You are a wild wolf, and that is more dangerous." As the fae woman speaks, the starry night sky around us seems to move, streaks of starlight washing across the air around the thunderbirds, bright sparks glittering in between the crackles of their lightning. They're the same streaks of light that I thought I saw when Tristan and I fell from these cliffs.

I want to ask the fae what the streaks of light are, but she has slumped further toward her bird's neck, her strength waning. I can't make her trust me, but I can force her to end this conversation and seek the help she needs.

"You should return to your mother," I say to her. "My power sustained you for the journey here, but you will lose strength again soon. If you want to live, you need to forget about me and seek help."

She is pale. "Why did you rescue me?"

"Why wouldn't I?" I reply.

My response seems to unsettle her, but she slumps all the way to her bird's neck. "I wish you well, Tessa Dean."

I give her a nod and her bird banks to the side. The little streaks of light scatter from around her as her bird soars toward the waterfall. Several female forms have emerged from behind the waterfall far below. One of them could be her mother, but they're too far away to tell.

Lyra shrieks at me and cracks her wings, demanding my attention. The little streaks of light dance toward her, gathering around her form as her eyes pierce mine.

She seems to understand me when I speak—even though she can't speak back—so I dare to say, "I will never call on you, but I suspect you could leave this place if you want to. If you do, come find me, but be careful. The humans won't understand what you are. You need to stay hidden."

She tosses her head at me, scattering the dancing lights. I follow their path as they ebb and blur, skipping across the air between the thunderbird and me. One of them approaches hesitantly, a blur of light no bigger than my hand.

"What are you?" I whisper as the light plays around me, tracing a semi-circle back and forth. I hold up my hand to it under Lyra's watchful eye.

My eyes widen when the dancing light rests down on my palm. The contact is like electricity shooting through my arm into my chest. I gasp but force myself to remain still instead of pulling away.

This magic... I've felt it before... when I sat beneath the silver trees in Hidden House.

Pain strikes through my heart, the deepest pain that makes me want to scream because I can't go back to who I was.

Danika said I just needed a little glue to pull the pieces of my heart back together, but it will take more than that.

It will take my father's blood.

It's a seemingly impossible task to bring down a wolf who has survived through the centuries, who has defeated enemy after enemy, who is always two steps ahead of me.

My teeth clench as the little streak of light rises from my palm.

Lyra tosses her head at me, but this time, it feels like a promise. I don't know how, but she seems to understand why my heart is thudding hard.

As she banks and soars back to the misty sky above the waterfall, taking the little lights with her, I turn and step back into the forest.

Maeve and Danika have remained on either side of the gap between the trees, both in a crouched position, as if they contemplated throwing themselves at the boundary to get through to me.

Iyana hovers a few paces along the path close to Tristan.

He stands quietly beside my wolf, his palm resting on my wolf's head, his fingers running slowly back and forth in her fur, calming strokes, as if both he and she were prepared to hurtle through the barrier after me, and now they're taking a breath.

The magical barrier dulled my sense of what my wolf was seeing and feeling, but now awareness hits me hard... Tristan's hand on my head, his fingers stroking through my fur, my wolf's body pressed to his side because that's where I want to be, standing beside him, nothing between us.

Wherever he touches my wolf, she takes form, substantial. Real fur. Real flesh.

Closing my human eyes and immersing myself in my wolf, I look up at Tristan with my wolf's eyes.

I speak through her mouth. "I'm okay. The fae woman needed to know who I was, so I told her. She's safe now, and so am I."

Tristan's hand stills on my wolf's head. He slowly takes a knee in front of my wolf, his fingers running across her neck to rest on my shoulder, my wolf's body taking form where he touches me.

He presses his human forehead to my wolf's, his raven-black hair falling across my wolf's cheeks.

"She's alive because of you, Tessa," he says. "So am I."

Across the distance, I open my human eyes, the sensation of Tristan's touch overwhelming my senses in my human and wolf forms.

Nearby, Iyana gives me a quick nod before she exchanges glances with Maeve and Danika. They have both risen to their feet beside me.

"Well." Iyana clears her throat, glancing from Tristan to my human form. "The sun will be up in another few hours. We need to get some sleep. We'll set up camp that way." She points back the way we came. "You two probably have a lot to talk about. Come find us when you're ready."

Danika gives me a quick, silent hug as she passes me, her light brown hair soft against my neck. I accept the gesture, my arms rising, but I'm not quite fast enough to hug her back before she releases me.

She and Maeve join Iyana and stride quickly away.

"Thanks for not shooting me back at the coven," Maeve says to Danika as they leave.

I catch Danika's answering smile before they disappear into the moonlit forest.

Quietly crossing the distance to Tristan, I kneel beside him.

I can't quite comprehend that it's only been a week since we went to Baxter Griffin's home, determined to change the future. So much has happened since then. Too much.

Tristan lifts his head from my wolf and reaches for my human hand.

"Tessa?" The intense desire in his eyes makes me shiver, but he doesn't make a move to kiss me. "I know we don't have a lot of time, but I don't want to lose this chance to be with you right now. Will you explore the forest with me? As wolves?"

A thrill passes all the way to my toes. I lean forward to drop a light kiss on the edge of his lips, tasting the rain on his skin.

"Yes," I say.

CHAPTER FIFTEEN

*D*rawing back to my feet, I quietly peel off my boots and clothing, piece by piece, until I stand naked in the moonlight.

I call my wolf's energy back to my body just as quietly. Her emerald light glimmers across my torso as my power returns to me.

Tristan rises smoothly to his feet before removing his boots, shirt, and pants. I follow the lines of his body from his wolf's head tattoo with the deadly snake across his chiseled chest down to his powerful thighs. I nearly lose my resolve to wait—nearly close the gap between us—but he says, "It's painful to shift with a broken bond, but I want to try."

I catch my breath, my heart squeezing. Jace once told me that the reason he never shifts is because of his broken true mate bond with Ella. He can handle the pain as long as he doesn't take his wolf's form.

Tristan's expression is shadowed, his shoulders tense. The Killer chose to shift earlier today, and I suddenly wonder if the pain of that choice hurt Tristan when it happened.

He seems to follow my thoughts when he says, "The Killer's choice to shift brought me back to myself. The pain was like a lifeline—a path I could follow to the surface."

His lips press gently together, his gaze trailing across my face, my hair, following my flowing tresses to my waist and hips. He shifts as rapidly into his wolf form as if he were about to leap into a fight. His wolf lands only a pace away from me, standing as high as my waist, massive and sleek, its fur as black as his hair.

His wolf lowers its head and growls softly, a gentle hum that sounds more like a greeting than a warning.

He edges toward me, step by step. I hold my breath as his nose nudges my hip and his face brushes against my stomach. Lifting my arms slightly, I allow him to circle around me, his fur brushing against my hips, backside, and the back of my thighs as he presses up against me. He circles around in front of me, his body curling around the side of my hip before he raises his head to meet my eyes.

Everywhere his body comes into contact with mine, it feels like being worshipped, loved beyond words.

His scent envelops me, all of its many layers, and beneath them is a fire that burns for me.

I lower myself, remaining within the circle of his body, to kneel and press my cheek to his. Closing my eyes, I allow my power to fill the shape of a wolf, shifting completely.

My wolf stands as tall as his, my body more lithe, less bulky, but my fur is just as dark.

I inhale his scent with my wolf's senses, my heightened ability to discern all of the layers of want, determination, and hope that exist in him.

He draws back with a growl, and I return it.

I expect him to lead, but he doesn't, waiting for me to take the first steps. Cautiously, I raise my nose to sniff the air, sensing all of the small creatures—and not-so-small creatures—living in the forest around us. In the distance to my right, the thunderbirds are a vast presence. Much farther to my left, Iyana, Danika, and Maeve are making camp. With my heightened hearing, I make out their murmured conversation like whispers on the breeze.

My focus returns to Tristan, who waits patiently for me to be comfortable to move. With a final nudge of my cheek to his and a short, soft howl into the air, I break into a run, racing through the trees and following the edge of the ravine.

I needn't have worried about his ability to catch up.

He reaches my side quickly and then shoots past me, his wolf's body an agile blur as he darts between the trees and leaps over the underbrush. Inhaling the night air, I speed after him, determined to catch him, until we're running side by side and heading deeper into the forest.

We run for half an hour, exploring the forest together, our heartbeats steadily rising before he veers toward a clearing. With a burst of speed, I pounce on him, playfully knocking him off course. We tumble across the clearing, and I sense his power surge through his body a split second before he shifts back into his human form.

I match the speed of his shift, returning to my human form just as fast as he does so that we're both completely human before we come to a tangled stop on our sides in the thick bedding of leaves and moss.

My chest rises and falls rapidly, but my breathing syncs with his as I dart forward to press my lips to his, dragging in the scent of his skin, loving the sheen of sweat on his chest beneath my palms and the press of his thighs against mine. The moment that the tip of his tongue coaxes my lips apart, I moan against his mouth, hooking my upper leg around his hips.

My senses fill with the heady scent of his skin mingled with the musky forest floor, the moist leaves, as he eases me onto my back. He plants demanding kisses against my shoulder, the tops of my breasts, his tongue swirling against my sensitive skin, down to my stomach. Hooking his arms under each of my thighs, he draws back to lift my hips off the ground so that his tongue can swirl across my center. Moans pass my lips and my head swims as intense pleasure rides my body, my toes pointed and barely touching the ground. Shivers run the length of my body and every inch of my skin is alive to his touch.

When he plunges his tongue inside me, I'm lost.

Pure pleasure bursts through me, heightening my senses. His big hands tense around my hips and his tongue continues to move against me in a way that indicates he intends for me to come this way, but... orgasm eludes me. I whimper, the pleasure without release becoming agonizing.

Lowering me to the ground, he growls against my center, the vibration making me clench. He doesn't seem the slightest bit worried about the challenge that my body is posing tonight, even though it's confusing the hell out of me.

He growls against my skin. His incisors peek between his lips as he presses kisses against my inner thighs, across my lower stomach, up along my ribcage, and across both of my breasts as he moves up over me. The gentle scrape of his incisors is electrifying, not frightening, and he doesn't break my skin.

When he fits his body to mine, I hook my legs around his hips and moan at the first thrust, the ache inside me intensifying, building.

Tristan's eyes are dark, his breathing exactly matched to mine, hitching and increasing, easing and slowing in time with each thrust. The heat between us is unbearable, my body feeling like it's burning up.

"Tessa." Tristan's whisper is thick with need. "Your body wants more."

I gasp against his mouth. "What more could I want?"

With a growl, he bares his incisors again and lowers his mouth to my shoulder. I rock against him, a shiver of anticipation thrumming through me.

I've always refused his mark. Still refuse it. Will always deny it because I will never be owned.

"Trust me." He growls against my skin, his movements slowing, giving me the chance to control what happens next.

"I do," I whisper.

His lips, his teeth, hover above my shoulder as he starts to move again. I match his rhythm, drawing him deep inside me with each thrust, relaxing into him, losing myself to the power in his body, the flex of his muscles beneath my hands.

I catch the fierce look in his eyes, sense his strength and inhale the scent of his skin a second before his lips touch my shoulder.

His incisors scrape the soft skin at the edge of my shoulder.

It's the briefest contact.

Pleasure explodes through me. Release washes over me in wave after screaming wave.

Tristan lifts his mouth from my shoulder as the waves continue and he crashes with me on the next thrust.

Lifting me up off the ground, he pulls us both up so that we're kneeling together, our bodies still joined, still moving, still crashing, his arms wrapped around me and mine wrapped around him. His mouth claims mine and my body rocks against him, our hearts beating in unison.

I don't have to look at my shoulder to know that he didn't mark me. My skin is unbroken.

As we settle into each other's arms, I push the hair from his eyes, kiss his cheeks and his eyelids, make him growl and smile before I nestle my head against his neck.

"Fuck," he whispers, pressing kisses to my forehead. He runs his hands through my hair and down my back. "Tessa."

"Hmm?"

He's quiet, so I look up at him, trying to read his thoughts.

He gives me a little shake of his head. "Too fucking much," he says.

I growl against his throat, my body already aching for his again, but I force myself to remain still because I don't know the cause of the slight crease in his forehead.

"You're carrying too much responsibility," he finally says. "There's a weight on your shoulders and I want to lift it—"

"You can't," I reply softly, stroking his jaw, trying to ease his tension. "It's my weight to carry."

Pressing my hand across his heart, I check our breathing.

My heart falls and my stomach plummets when, suddenly, I can't... quite... sync with him.

His forehead creases more deeply.

He squeezes his eyes shut. Deep concentration passes across his face. "The fucking Deceiver is trying to take over," he whispers.

He shakes his head, suddenly urgent. "Don't ever tell me what you plan to do, Tessa. No matter what happens. You have to keep your secrets." He grips my shoulders. "Do you remember when I told you to command, order, rage if you have to, but never beg?"

"I remember." It was moments before he challenged Cody to fight—moments before I found out that Tristan was a descendant of Cerberus.

"Command the Killer," Tristan says. "Tell him what you want. Order him. Rage at him. He craves violence and strength. But never

111

trust him with your inner thoughts or your true plans. The Deceiver dominates all of us."

I meet Tristan's gaze without faltering, knowing that the Deceiver won't let him go until he gets what he wants.

I speak only half of the truth, keeping my truer intentions to myself. "But my plans are simple," I say. "Not a secret. My plans align with the Killer's goals. I will kill my father."

"How?" he asks, and this time, I'm sure of the discord in our breathing. He is not himself. "I tried to kill your father, Tessa," he says. "I couldn't. You saw me fall. You also must have tried already—"

Too many times.

I choose my response carefully. "The answer lies in the book of old magic, hidden in the library only two blocks from where your pack lives. Remember we spoke about it? My father told me it contains all of the secrets of creatures of old magic—including *his* secrets. I plan to get the book and use it against my father. It's the only way to end him."

I kiss Tristan before he can ask me another question, my mouth warm on his. Our breathing is still not quite in sync and I know that the Deceiver is still listening, so I say, "There's nothing to hide. But trust me when I tell you: I will never beg."

My tension eases as I sense my breathing finally aligning with Tristan's again. The clench of his muscles beneath my palms also lessens, and he is in control once more.

I dip my lips to his, a soft nudge before I take my time exploring his mouth. Trailing kisses down his throat, I brush my lips against his shoulder, bare my teeth, and press them gently to his skin without breaking it—the same way he did when he tipped me over the edge.

His eyes meet mine and all of his power makes my senses burn.

When I lift my lips from his shoulder, he tips me back onto the leafy ground, where we explore each other's bodies all over again.

∽

By the time we return to the place near the ravine where we left our clothing, the sun has risen and glitters through the canopy overhead.

We dress quickly—me into my black jeans, gray T-shirt and black jacket, and Tristan into his black jeans and navy-blue shirt. I check that the dark magic orb and the amulet are still safely contained in my pocket. For a second, I consider throwing the amulet through the shield into the nearby ravine, but Tristan brushes my arm before I step toward it, urging me in the direction of the camp our friends made.

We head back into the heart of the forest, following Iyana's trail until we find the spot where she and the others are sleeping.

They've chosen a dense part of the forest where very little light reaches the ground. It feels like it's still night here, but even so, Iyana has deployed her cloak. I'm surprised to see that the small umbrella has opened into a vast dome-like enclosure that stands as high as my shoulders and stretches from one side of the small clearing to the other, sealing at ground level. It's large enough for multiple adults to sleep beneath it.

Although I can't see through its opaque black material from the outside, I sense their breathing, deep and even, which tells me they're all peacefully asleep.

We find the opening—a glowing crack that seals itself once we crawl inside.

I catch my breath when I see that, inside, the enclosure appears even larger, a starry night sky glittering above us. It looks just like the glimpse of Iyana's room that I caught at Hidden House.

My heart aches again, a strong homesickness, a desperate wish to go back, to start over, to make different choices.

I wouldn't have all of this knowledge if I'd chosen to stay hidden, if I'd fought Tristan harder in the beginning, if I'd killed Baxter Griffin that night.

I know Tristan's heart now, and I trust him with my life.

I know that Cody wanted me in his den.

I know how I came to be and what I'm capable of.

Taking Tristan's hand, I draw him to the soft patch of ground between Iyana and Danika, creeping in quietly, not exactly piling on them, but squishing in.

It's the closest to a den that I might ever have.

CHAPTER SIXTEEN

We awake in the early evening and rifle through our food supplies to fill our hungry stomachs.

Tristan and I sit side by side, while Iyana, Danika, and Maeve find a spot facing us. Nobody seemed alarmed to wake up and find us squished in with them, although Iyana nearly bopped me on the nose when she stretched her arms.

During the meal, I take a deep breath and tell the women everything that happened after my father captured me. I tell them about Cody and the Spire, about my mother, and about the book. I leave out any information that Tristan's minds might use against me, including my plan to use the book of old magic to destroy his minds before I go after my father.

"You've destroyed the witches," Iyana says, turning the empty glass vial around in her hands from which she's just drunk a dose of mercury that she brought with her. "The forest is yours, but your father will have spent the last two days strengthening his alliances."

I nod. "He controls the Spire. He has at least fifty leopard shifters housed there, not to mention Brynjar, the ice jotunn, whom you should *not* engage in a fight under any circumstances." I give them all a hard look. "Brynjar is a creature of old magic like me and my father. He's the last of his kind. He follows my father because my father gave him purpose. There's a chance I can still turn

Brynjar to my side, but he is capable of killing you with a single touch."

I press my lips together and return to the subject of my father's alliances before my friends can question my conflicted feelings about Brynjar. "To the east, my father still has his alliances with Baxter Griffin and Peter Nash. For all I know, he could be allied with all of the other alphas in the Cascade Range."

Tristan is quiet beside me, but he nods. "I believe he is."

Iyana leans forward. "He could also be aligned with the demon Banta Sol, who operates a black market within Baxter Griffin's territory," she says. "Sol supplies weapons and drugs to the highest bidders. There are rings of demons throughout the Western United States all involved in black market trafficking of weapons and illegal substances. Their operations used to stretch into the eastern states also, but the eastern ring collapsed around two years ago when the head demon was assassinated."

She stops speaking and closes her hand around the vial as if she would crush it before she glances at Tristan.

I follow her gaze to him too. He considers Iyana quietly, but he doesn't speak.

I turn back to the dark-haired vampire. "Iyana?"

"I went after Banta Sol without backup," she says, her fingers twitching on the glass. "I thought I was prepared, but I barely got away alive. His men pursued me across the bridge into Tristan's territory. I don't remember much after that."

When I first met Iyana, she told me that it had taken six months for Helen to heal the damage that was done to her body and face, but she didn't tell me how she sustained the injuries.

She clears her throat before she raises her eyes to mine. "Sol is bound to supply all of your father's weapons."

I don't push her for more details about her past, only about her judgement of the present threat. "Are Sol's people likely to get involved in a fight between me and my father?"

"Only if you go after Sol directly," Iyana says.

I rub my chin in thought. "I'd like to take out the supplier of my father's weapons, but the book of old magic is my immediate concern. Something stopped my father from retrieving it before, but I don't know if it was a temporary hurdle. I can't take the risk that he'll get the book before me. I need to get to the library and find out more."

"We left an SUV parked a few miles from here," Danika says, brushing her hair behind her ear. "We'll need to trek through the main part of the forest to reach it, but we can take it to the library. I'll fly ahead and warn you if you're approaching trouble. If we leave now, we should reach the library before sunrise."

"Once we get there, I can help you get inside the library undetected," Maeve says, violet light glowing around her hands. "I haven't perfected as many spells as I would have liked, but Mother Zala often made me help her sneak in and out of places."

When I glance at Tristan, he looks around the group and shrugs. "I'm here to fuck up anyone who needs fucking up."

I break into a dark smile. We can't plan for every eventuality, but each of the people around me has a place in the path I'm about to walk.

"Okay, then," I say.

We pack up camp quickly and begin our trek through the forest.

A few times, my skin prickles the way it did before my mother appeared, and I'm reminded that there are assassins in this forest and that they can hide wherever they wish.

Danika draws closer to me at one point to murmur, "I sense we're being watched."

"Assassins," I say. "It has to be."

"Do you believe that Alexei Mason will remain true to his word and stay out of this fight?"

"His attitude toward me was surprising, but I don't have any reason to mistrust him. Not yet, anyway."

I don't believe that the assassins will attack us—but if they do, I will retaliate with full force.

Turning to peer between the trees where the moonlight is dappled, I can almost imagine a powerful, backlit silhouette standing quietly, observing our progress through the forest.

"Unless they choose to reveal themselves or pose a threat to us, I believe our best approach is to ignore them," I say.

In a strange sort of way, I'm comforted to know that they're there. I don't yet know if I'm leading my pack to their deaths. I need an independent group to be witnesses to tell my story if we don't make it out alive.

It takes us over an hour to reach the SUV, which is parked in a clearing at the end of a dirt road. When we reach it, we stop briefly to quench our thirst with the spare bottles of water stashed in the trunk. After that, Danika leaves her duffel bag with us so she can shift into her hawk form and fly ahead.

She rises into the air, maneuvers artfully between the branches overhead, and soars away into the sky.

Iyana and Tristan have a quiet standoff about who is going to drive. Iyana reaches for the driver side door, eyeing Tristan closely as she moves.

"I know the streets as well as you do," she says. "And I don't want the Killer making an appearance behind the wheel."

"Fair enough." He capitulates, nudges up against me, and slides into the back seat with me while Maeve rides in the front passenger seat.

I'm even more conscious now of the two objects of magic I'm carrying in my pockets—the dark magic orb and the amulet filled with elemental power. I'm about to carry them back into a populated area and I need to be careful that they remain in my possession.

By the time we navigate out of the vast forest and reach the city, midnight has passed and the cold light of dawn approaches.

The streets are nearly deserted, which allows us to pull up directly outside the library. It's a three-story Georgian style building with arched windows on the second level and arched doorways at street level.

We exit the vehicle quickly while Danika circles overhead.

I grab her duffel bag from the trunk, check that the street is empty, and hurry up the stairs behind the external arches to the shadowed entryway. Danika soars smartly into the shadows, shifts back to her human form, and pulls on the clothes I hold out for her as the others join us.

Iyana takes up the rear. Sunlight isn't yet spreading across the horizon, but she deploys her cloak, this time pressing it against her chest. It rapidly spreads across her body to form a black suit that covers her entirely except for her hands, booted feet, neck, and face

—and her weapons. When I cast her a worried look, she reassures me that the suit protects the parts of her body that are still visible—I just can't see it from the outside.

Danika quickly gives her report. "We need to be careful. There are supernaturals everywhere," she says. "Tristan's pack has patrols closer to the clock tower. The good news is that I didn't spot your father or the ice giant anywhere."

Maeve pauses in front of the doorway, eyeing the security bars in front of it. "I can translocate the door for a few moments, but we'll need to enter quickly. It's the best way to make sure there's no damage that might raise an alarm, but I can only hold the spell for a few moments."

Danika has finished dressing, Iyana has finished fitting a sound suppressor to her gun, and Tristan is poised beside me, my breathing matching his.

"Do it," I say to Maeve.

She closes her eyes, her shoulders relax, and violet light rises from her palms to curl around the security bars and the wooden door beyond them. The surfaces shimmer for a moment before they disappear.

"Quickly now," she says as we hurry around her.

She steps inside with us, the curling tendrils of her power fade, and the door reappears behind us.

Inside, the entrance is dark, but the arched windows allow enough light through to see that the front room is laid with mottled white marble. A wooden welcome desk sits to the left and a gleaming floor leads to a grand staircase.

I expand my senses, unhappily aware that if my father is here, I won't be able to detect his presence, but I also don't sense any other supernaturals. I doubt he'd come alone.

"Where to, Tessa?" Iyana asks, her blue eyes gleaming in the dark. Dark places don't faze her. Likewise, Danika's eyes are reflective, her hawk's vision in full operation. Maeve's hands glow faintly in the dark to light our way, and I harness my ability to see in dim places to make out our surroundings in more detail.

I turn in a circle. "If I wanted to hide a book in plain sight, where would I put it?"

"Upstairs," Maeve says, surprising me with how certain she

sounds. She points at the stairway. "Do you see the writing on the edge of each marble step?"

Striding closer, I peer carefully at them. What appears to be mottled lines at first glance are, on closer inspection, cunningly concealed inscriptions that run together.

"What does it say?" I ask Maeve.

She shakes her head. "I learned some rune language growing up and then Mother Zala taught me some basic runes, but these..." She runs her fingers across the marble. "I've never seen runes like these."

Iyana bends close on my left, her fingertips also passing along the runes.

She gives a sudden gasp and jolts away from them.

"This is the language of angels," Iyana says. Her hand tightens on her gun and I sense her anxiety. "I've heard of angels guarding libraries, but only the large, important ones. I wouldn't have expected angels to be here."

She turns swiftly, scrutinizing our surroundings again. Tristan and Danika respond by fanning out around me, taking up a protective formation.

"Angels!" The light glowing around Maeve's hands brightens. "If angels are guarding the book, then that would explain why your father had trouble retrieving it."

I eye my friends carefully. Having grown up in the closed environment of the Middle Highland pack, I've never encountered angels or been exposed to angel lore.

"Explain to me why we should be afraid of angels?" I ask.

Iyana lets out a harsh laugh. "Forget sweet white-feathered creatures who believe in goodness and rainbows. Angels are fierce, bloodthirsty warriors. They are especially merciless toward supernaturals they consider to be undeserving." She bares her fangs. "Vampires are at the top of their hit list."

I shiver. "They won't like me, either."

Taking a deep breath to calm myself, I grip Iyana's shoulder. "I want you to stay here. We need you on lookout in case my father turns up."

Iyana narrows her eyes at me as if she's about to protest, but I quickly continue. "Yes, I'm trying to protect you, even if it hurts

119

your pride. I won't endanger you unnecessarily. You're staying here. That's an order."

She meets my hard eyes and seems to reconsider whatever she was about to say. "Okay."

"Let's follow the runes and hope they lead us to the book," I say, taking the first step.

We ascend the marble staircase to the first landing from which a staircase rises perpendicularly on each side. We take the stairs on the right, following the breadcrumb trail of angelic runes to a balcony that extends around the second level. Multiple wooden arched doorways lead off from the balcony into other rooms.

Reaching the second doorway, Maeve pauses, her glowing fingertips running along the wooden frame up to the golden lettering on the plaque above it.

It reads, simply: *Periodicals*.

While Danika watches our backs, Maeve points to the narrow side of the doorframe and the faint gold runes etched down its vertical surface. "This has to be the place."

I step into the room first with Tristan close behind me, while Maeve and Danika bring up the rear.

Inside, the room is filled with rows and rows of bookcases. Beyond them, on the far side, I can make out the end of a table and some chairs—presumably a place to read once someone has chosen a book.

I sigh at the rows of bookcases. The book of old magic could be hidden among them or concealed out of sight.

"Spread out," I murmur. "Search for runes on any of the bookcases. I'll check out the far side in case there are any hidden compartments near the table and chairs."

I've nearly reached the last bookcase, with Tristan following close behind me, when his hand suddenly circles my arm, warm but firm. "Tessa. Stop."

I pause. At first, I'm not sure what has alarmed him.

Then, I notice the way the air shimmers above the table. It doesn't look like a barrier, more like a concentration of magic that glistens when I look at it from this angle and disappears when I tilt my head. "There's magic around the table. Heavily concealed."

He nods. "Go carefully."

I take a cautious step forward just as a glowing form takes shape standing at the end of the table directly ahead of us. The bright swirl of light stretches out in a rippling mass of energy that morphs into the form of the wolf whose existence triggers more violence in me than I can contain.

The white wolf—my father—snarls at me, his voice low and guttural, his teeth sharp. Deadly.

"Hello, little one," he says, as if we're meeting for the first time. As if he weren't responsible for breaking apart my humanity when he killed my beta, Cody.

"I was hoping you'd come," he says.

My claws descend and my power rises inside me, turning my vision crimson. Tristan can survive the white wolf, but my friends can't. My only instinct now is to protect them.

"Danika! Maeve!" I shout, catching sight of their tense forms from the corner of my vision when they hurry around the end of the bookcases they were inspecting.

Their eyes widen when they see the white wolf.

The violet light around Maeve's hand brightens as she begins to mutter a spell, and Danika looks like she's prepared to rip off her clothing and shift right where she stands.

I spin to them. "Get the fuck out of here!"

"Tessa?" Danika pauses while Maeve stops muttering.

"Now!" I roar.

The last thing I want is for my friends to be used as leverage against me. I can't and won't let that happen again. It's why I pushed them away to begin with.

"Get out of here!" I scream. "Don't come back!"

Danika's jaw tightens, but she grabs Maeve's arm and pulls her away through the door, after which I sense them break into a run.

Beside me, Tristan's claws have also descended. I'm not sure if the Killer will make an appearance, but my breathing is still in time with Tristan's, even if we're both breathing much faster, our hearts pumping now.

With every passing hour we've spent together, the melding bond we formed is healing and growing stronger. It allows us to move in unison toward the white wolf—and also to stop at the same time when my father's human form steps out from behind the farthest bookcase.

He's a tall man and his eyes are an indistinct shade of hazel green. He proved to me that he can change some aspects of his facial features to suit his circumstances, to appear more or less threatening according to his needs at any given time. He's wearing black pants and a black collared shirt but isn't carrying any weapons.

"I'm glad you brought Tristan with you," my father's human form says, his eyes cold and hard.

"Where's the book?" I demand to know.

"I don't have it. Not yet," he says. "What I omitted to tell you, Tessa, is that I can't retrieve it without both of you."

I narrow my eyes at him. "What are you talking about?"

"It's a failsafe mechanism," he says. "Three creatures of old magic must seek the book together. It's incredibly rare to find three of us these days, let alone for us to work together."

"You're lying," I say. "If it takes three of us, why not bring Brynjar and me here after you captured me?"

Ford sighs heavily. "Oh, little one. You may not seek the book unless you are truly yourself. You weren't yourself until you killed the witches. You couldn't have triggered the magic in this place before then. Sadly, that was also when I lost you."

"What about Tristan?" I ask. "How does he satisfy that test?"

Surely, he is not himself while the three minds play havoc with his body and soul.

My father rubs his chin. "I'll admit Tristan is a wild card. Is he himself with all three minds released? Or not? We'll know soon enough."

The space above the table that was previously glistening suddenly darkens. The first rays of dawn grow across the bookcases behind us, but at this end of the room, night is rapidly falling.

"Ah," my father says, waving his hand at the growing dark. "It seems that one way or another, we've passed the first threshold."

Beside me, Tristan is partially shifted, gripping my hand with his palm and thumb while his claws slowly extend. He won't hurt me, but I sense how hard he's working to keep his impulses under control. He has just as much reason as I do to end my father's violence.

"Three must try, but only one will make it through," Ford says, his voice descending into a growl while his wolf circles around us.

"Make it through what?" Tristan asks, his incisors bared, his eyes amber-flecked, his power simmering at the surface.

Ford points to the spot where the table is quickly disappearing, the darkness is growing, and three luminous silhouettes form.

"Them," he says.

CHAPTER SEVENTEEN

Three women step from the darkness.

They each wear high mahogany boots beneath knee-length flowing white dresses, the bodices of which are covered with mahogany leather breastplates. Their eyes are the color of spun gold while their blonde hair is braided back and pulled up into tight ponytails. The skin around their eyes and temples is painted with mahogany wings, although they haven't yet revealed whether or not they are hiding feathered wings beneath their armor.

They each hold a spear that is tipped with a large gold spearhead and they wear a band of flat gold about half an inch wide across their foreheads.

As they move, their silhouettes are backlit with dancing streaks of light that shift around them, reflecting off their weapons and their gleaming hair. I follow the path of the dancing lights as they play around the women's shoulders. I'm certain they're the same lights I saw in the ravine, glittering creatures that seem to appear whenever I face a new threat.

"We are the Sentinels." The women speak in unison. "Do you seek the book of old magic?"

"We do," Ford says. He calls his wolf form back to himself in a wash of energy that causes the dancing lights around the women to retreat.

"Be warned," says the Sentinel on the far right.

"Only one may take the book," says the one in the middle.

The Sentinel on the far left speaks last. "But all must come to us without lies, or you will face death at our hands."

My father grins, but I shiver.

My breathing is still in unison with Tristan's, but the Deceiver could surface at any moment.

The Deceiver can speak nothing but lies.

This is not a safe place for Tristan.

My hand clenches around his, but he cuts me off before I can speak. "You need this book, Tessa."

The certainty in his expression hurts my heart.

He winces, likely sensing my deep anxiety through the melding bond, but his grip is warm and firm.

His claws retract and his voice lowers. Calm. "I need you to have faith in me."

I inhale a shaky breath, focusing on the honesty in his eyes and the warmth of his hand around mine, remembering all of the moments of truth between us since he revealed the existence of Cerberus to me. The Killer, the Coward, and the Deceiver don't define him. He is a fighter, principled and deadly. And right now, *I* am his purpose.

"I do," I say, believing it with every part of my heart. "I have faith in you."

His expression softens, one corner of his mouth rising in a half-smile that has the power to make everything else around us—all of the danger—disappear.

His thumb brushes across mine in a reassuring sweep as we turn back to the Sentinels.

The middle Sentinel steps closer to me, her unsettling golden eyes piercing me. She taps the butt of her spear lightly on the floor and the dancing lights return to rest on her shoulders.

"Truth is difficult," she says, speaking quietly. "Even for those who claim to live by it. You must answer every question I ask you honestly, or I will kill you without remorse."

"If those are the rules, you should know that I'm not great at following orders," I say.

She tips her head to the side, the bottom of her ponytail sliding across her left shoulder. "That is indeed the truth."

As she speaks, Tristan's hand slips from mine.

"No!" I spin to him, but he has already disappeared.

So has every part of the library. I'm surrounded by endless darkness and only the Sentinel stands in front of me.

I back away from her, trying to see across the inky space, to find Tristan in the mire. My connection with him is gone. I can't sense his heartbeat or his breathing and it feels like I've been cast adrift.

"Where's Tristan?" I demand to know, spinning back to the Sentinel.

"His trial has begun," the Sentinel says. "Each of you must face the truth alone. Only one of you will reach the book." She shrugs. "If, indeed, any of you do."

"Ask whatever you want to know," I say, a growl on my lips.

She paces around me. "So impatient." She cocks her head to the side as she stops behind me, forcing me to twist to see her. "Are you always this impatient, Tessa Dean?"

"Only when I'm afraid for the people I care about," I say.

She narrows her eyes at me. "Do you often put your own safety in jeopardy for the sake of others?"

I grit my teeth as I push away all of the unwanted memories from the last week. "Fuck you."

She arches an eyebrow. "You must answer."

My fists clench, my claws scraping against my palms before they retract.

Tristan's pack. Cody. The three shifters my father held prisoner. Every woman at Hidden House. My closest friends.

"I'm a danger to everyone I know," I say.

"You must answer the ques—"

"Yes!" I shout, my shoulders hunching, my muscles tensing, the void of darkness rising up inside me. I narrow my eyes at her. "Yes, I put myself in danger. Are you satisfied with that answer?"

She appears unflustered by my anger. "I'm intrigued why you're so defensive about your capacity to love others, Tessa."

"Because I'm..."

I press my lips together. *Because I was taught from the moment I was born that I am not worthy of love in return.* Even Andreas Dean, who attempted to keep me safe... even he was unable to provide a place for me that was without danger. There was no such place. I spent the first twenty-three years of my life reminded daily that I was not wanted."

"Do you seek to be loved through acts of sacrifice, Tessa?" the Sentinel asks.

"Not anymore," I say. "I would rather be unloved, even hated, than risk losing any more of my heart. I've lost enough already."

"Hmm." She hums in the back of her throat. "That is the truth." She taps her spear on the ground as she circles me again. "But is it the whole truth?"

"Am I supposed to answer that?" I ask.

She studies me as she walks. "You continue to cage your power because of love, Tessa," she says.

I bare my teeth at her. "That's a judgement, not a question."

She shrugs. "Making judgements is my only purpose." She gestures at the dark space around us. "It's why we're here. To judge if you are worthy to hold the book of old magic, which we have kept safe since the time of the Bright Ones."

"The Bright Ones?" I ask.

Her answer is to gesture at the dancing lights that flit around her silhouette.

"What are they?" I ask.

"They are the purest form of old magic. It is our duty as creatures of the light—theirs and ours—to protect the most sacred knowledge of the old ones." She holds out her palm so that the dancing light can rest on the end of her fingertips. "You've seen them before?"

"In a hidden ravine in the forest."

"Ah," she says. "The last refuge of the ancient fae." She considers the dancing light quietly, her expression shifting with the weight of sadness. "How quickly power can be destroyed. I wonder, Tessa... What would you do if you had to choose between sacrificing your power to survive or holding on to your power, even though it means you will die?"

I stiffen. Cody made that choice. He chose to sacrifice his wolf in order to survive, but the loss of his wolf killed him slowly instead of quickly.

"I don't believe there is a choice between the two," I say. "Not when they are so intertwined that losing my power means dying anyway."

She levels her gaze with mine. "Your reply devalues the importance of time," she says. "Isn't another day of life worth the pain of survival?"

"No."

She arches her eyebrows at me. "So you would choose to die with your power intact, rather than seek another day of life?"

"I've already answered your question."

"Indeed." She gives me an acknowledging nod. "You believe you've spoken truthfully, but I'm not sure you're being honest with yourself."

She turns to me while she holds the dancing light. "Let me ask my question a different way. If someone you cared about needed you for another day, would it change your answer?"

I hesitate. Was that what Cody did? Did he choose to live without his wolf because he knew I would need him? Because otherwise, I would have been alone... without Tristan or Iyana or Danika...

Did he decide, even though he had fucked up any chance that I would ever really trust him, that I needed his presence so I could remember what it was like to be human? Since that was what he was in the end: *Human*.

My answer is faltering. "I... don't know..."

The Sentinel scrutinizes me, her golden eyes emotionless as the dancing light rises up out of her palm and floats toward me. A crease forms in the Sentinel's forehead as the orb of light bounces across the space in front of me, flitting back and forth as if it's skipping across stones in a pond. The other two dancing lights join it, swirling around each other.

"How curious," she says. "They recognize your essence. You must have come into contact with a pure form of old magic before."

I remain silent. After all, she didn't ask a question.

My mother said that my true nature was hidden when I was a baby by a woman who cloaked me in the purest of old magic to conceal my existence from my father.

"How is this possible?" the Sentinel asks.

I have no choice but to answer this time. "I'm told a creature of old magic protected me when I was a baby."

The crease in the Sentinel's forehead deepens. "That is truly intriguing, since there is only one woman who could have bestowed such magic on you, and she..." The Sentinel steps back, her head held high, reassessing me. Her gaze passes from my head to my toes and back to my face. "She should have been your enemy, not your protector."

"Are *you* my enemy?" I ask.

The Sentinel stiffens but doesn't answer my question. "What will you do with the book of old magic, Tessa?"

"I will use it to free Tristan and kill my father."

"You have a lot of faith that this book holds the answers you need."

"It will," I say. *It has to.*

The Sentinel leans forward. "What if I told you there is nothing in the book but a collection of meaningless stories?"

"Then I'd say you were lying. My father has a purpose in everything he does. He wouldn't have come here if he didn't believe—"

I pause, my lips pursed, a sudden warning instinct passing through me.

My father never says what he means.

He never reveals his true goal. He is a master manipulator, always winning the long game.

Rapidly, I sift through my memory of the moment he first told me about the book. We were walking around the clearing outside the Spire and he said... I close my eyes and try to remember... something about the book telling him how to end Cerberus once and for all.

Maybe he's here for the book. Or maybe... he's here to ensure the Sentinels kill us.

Maybe he's here for both.

My eyes fly open. "Do you have the power to kill me?"

The Sentinel taps her spear on the ground with a confident smile. "I might."

I spin, searching the darkness for Tristan. My search is wild. Increasingly desperate. I'm afraid I won't find him. Whatever magic has taken hold of me won't let me go.

It won't let *him* go.

"Does your Sentinel sister have the power to kill Tristan?" I ask.

The Sentinel taps her spear on the dark surface beneath our feet again. This time, the sound *cracks* in my hearing. "She might."

Fuck! It's a risk my father would consider worth taking. I believe my father genuinely wants the book, but by drawing Tristan and me here at the same time, he can achieve two purposes at once: Get the book and have the Sentinels take us out.

I grit my teeth as my heart tugs. "Did my father lure me here because he believes that you—the Sentinels—have the power to end Tristan and me?"

"I can't speak for your father's intentions." She takes a step forward. "But you can be assured my sister Sentinel will ask your father that exact question."

"That doesn't help me!"

"I'm not here to help you, Tessa. I'm here to guard the book."

I pace around in the darkness.

This darkness… it's another cage.

I stop in front of her. "Give me the book."

She arches an eyebrow at me. "You must answer all of my questions first."

"How many questions?" I ask. "When will you be satisfied that I'm worthy?"

She is silent while I prowl up to her. Her lips press together and her golden eyes are completely emotionless. Perfectly empty of any intention other than following her duty.

I give an angry laugh, my claws descending as I eye her weapon and take stock of her armor—her heeled boots, armored breastplate, gleaming spear, golden headband.

"Never," I whisper, answering my own question. "You will never stop asking me questions. You will never give me the book."

"It's my duty to guard the book—"

My fist snaps out. At the last moment, I open my clenched hand and allow my claws to extend so that I scratch her face, cutting through the mahogany wings painted around her eyes.

She screams and jolts to the side, half-crouched, clutching her face. She snarls up at me. "That was a bad move, Tessa."

I bare my teeth and advance on her. "I've made plenty of bad moves. I'll add this to the tally."

I aim a savage kick at her chest, but she twists, evades the hit, and retaliates with a thrust of her spear. I regain my balance just in time to leap back to avoid the weapon's sharp tip.

She goes on the attack, beating the spear at me, spinning and jabbing at me, but I grab the weapon, wrenching it to the side with my left hand while my right fist knocks against her chin. At the same time, I release my wolf in a bright blur of black fury. My wolf's energy collides with her body at the same time as I do. The Sentinel's head snaps back under the force of my fist, and we fall together.

Her spear hand hits the floor first and the weapon clatters across the ground.

The Sentinel screams as my wolf's energy fills the space around her chest and my human form straddles her, both at the same time.

"Where is the book?" I roar.

"No!" She claws at her chest, trying to dislodge my wolf's energy, but her hands sail right through my wolf's form.

"I am old magic," I roar at her. "I demand the book that belongs to me!"

Abandoning her fight against my wolf, she aims a sequence of punches at my chest and face. I take the hits, my power dulling the pain.

Instead of retaliating with my fists, I snatch at her headband. I've already cut through her painted wings and disarmed her. If I have to, I will tear her weapons apart piece by piece to draw the truth from her. The crescent pulls away—a half-circle that shines so brightly at my touch that I have to squint.

The Sentinel's eyes widen beyond the light. "No… My halo…"

Well, damn. Not a headband, after all.

The band seals itself before my eyes, the two ends curling toward each other and forming a complete circle the size of my fist. As soon as the two ends touch, the Sentinel's body glows brightly, golden light streaming upward from her chest. I throw my arm across my eyes, trying to protect my sight, attempting to keep her in view at the same time. A nearly impossible feat.

131

Within the pool of light forming above her chest, I suddenly make out the shape of a book.

It's large and appears leatherbound. Pure white.

It's right in front of me.

Quickly slipping the golden halo over my wrist, where the metal band settles around my arm like a bracelet, I grab the book from within the pool of light and leap away from the Sentinel, pulling my wolf's energy with me.

The light around her body fades. She struggles to rise, gripping her forehead where her halo used to rest.

"Take the book," she whispers. "But be warned, Tessa: The answers you seek will force you to make choices you won't want to make."

Her silhouette fades, but the brightness remains, washing over me until I find myself sitting in a beam of sunlight on one of the chairs that was situated at the end of the library room. I'm clutching the book against my chest.

The table is broken down the middle and the two pieces have been flipped to the far end of the room, ten paces away. All of the other chairs are splintered, scattered rods and planes of wood littering the floor around me.

My father kneels under the window to my left, holding his head in his hands, blood streaming down his face from his forehead. Only one eye is visible from beneath his hands, but he's glazed, slumped against the wall, appearing barely conscious.

I swivel to my right, where Tristan stood before the darkness consumed us.

He's not there.

CHAPTER EIGHTEEN

"Tristan!" Leaping from the chair, I search the debris wildly until I spot his foot protruding from behind one broken side of the table.

"Tristan!"

Gripping the book to my chest, I round the table and skid to a stop on my knees beside Tristan. His cheeks are pale, his navy shirt slashed open, and his breathing is shallow.

I scream at the mess of stab wounds across his chest.

"No! Tristan!" Dropping the book to the floor, I kneel on it in an effort to keep it safe while I work.

I rip his shirt open to reveal four stab wounds across his chest, all deep, although by some miracle, his lungs must not have been punctured because he's still breathing. A glance down tells me he also sustained a stab wound to his right thigh. All of his wounds are bleeding, a pool of blood growing beneath him.

My breath screams in and out of my chest as cold fear thrums through me, but fear is quickly followed by rage, the darkest rage that my power brings.

He is not going to die.

"I won't fucking let you!" I scream at him.

Tearing off my shirt, I rip it into two. The wound on his thigh is bleeding the most, so I attack it first, twisting and wadding up the central portion of my ripped shirt and wrapping the rest around his thigh to keep the wadding tight. The material is barely long enough to make it round his big thigh and my hands are shaking, but I manage to tie it off with the smallest knot.

Wadding up the second portion of my shirt, I press down on the wound at his side—the second-most vicious bleeder—applying as much pressure as I can to stem the flow of blood. His shirt is my only other option for wadding. Reaching one-handed for the base of it, I use my claws to tear off strips of material, awkwardly wadding them and pressing the bundle to a third wound.

He has two more wounds, and I don't have enough fucking hands.

Dear fuck. I'm sobbing now, but I need to release my fear and rage somehow. I need to figure out a way to get Tristan out of here, to get help. I told my friends to leave, but if I know them at all, they'll have stayed nearby. I just have to drag him far enough to reach them while somehow keeping up the pressure on his wounds—

A soft snarl meets my ears as my father looms up on the other side of the table. "You got the book."

My vision is blurry with tears, but they're as hot on my cheeks as my fury is in my heart.

"Unless you plan to help me, get the fuck away from me!" I shout at him, baring my teeth. "Or I'll tear you apart."

It's an empty threat and he knows it.

"You can't kill me," he says, wiping his bloody forehead on his sleeve. "My existence is essential to the balance of the world. It's been foretold that I will be alive when the world ends. I am the monstrous wolf. We'll have to find a way to live with each other, Tessa."

When I ignore him, he continues at a low snarl. "Give me the fucking book."

"Or what?" I ask, pressing hard against Tristan's wounds, considering whether I can somehow extend one of my elbows far enough across his chest to apply pressure to the nearest uncovered wound. "You can't kill me, either."

My father shrugs. "I'll grant Baxter Griffin the favor he wants."

I become still. When Baxter Griffin handed me over to my father, my father promised Baxter a favor.

"What favor?"

"Baxter wants me to annihilate Tristan's pack so Baxter can finally control the western lowland territory. It's what he's wanted all along—to control the largest territory. Once he does that, he will become the supreme alpha, feared by all," Ford says. "I'm inclined to grant his wish."

"Of course you are." I grit my teeth as I realize that I've come full circle. Tristan wanted me at his side to stop a war between shifters. He told Helen that I was the answer to prevent a conflict that would draw in other supernaturals, bounty hunters, and even assassins. Now, here I am, the daughter of an assassin, the daughter of a war wolf, standing at a precipice. I'm about to tempt my father to start a war because I refuse to hand over a book.

While my father prowls to the side of the table, stopping at Tristan's feet, a deep calm settles over me.

"Do it," I say, looking up at Ford, making him frown. "Go after Tristan's pack. But know this: I'll be right there waiting for you. Maybe we can't kill each other, but I can sure as fuck make your life miserable." My lips draw back in a snarl and my crimson vision rises, the gift of darkness that he gave to me. "I made a promise to you, Father, and I intend to keep it. You will have no peace from me."

The corners of his mouth turn down. His focus shifts to the book on which I'm deliberately sitting. I imagine him working through his next moves. He could punch me, knock me off the book, try to grab it. I picture myself retaliating by driving a claw into his throat.

"Let's go, Dad," I whisper, painfully aware that Tristan's blood continues to pool beneath him and my fucking father cares only for his own supremacy—cares only for beating me.

I press hard against Tristan's wounds as I shout at my father. "Come on! Start the fight you want to start! Fucking do it!"

Without a sound, Ford leaps at me, releasing his wolf at the same time. His animal crashes into me, knocking me toward the floor at Tristan's side, my legs sprawled across the book. The wolf's claws rake across my chest and neck as he leaps. My own claws shoot out in response, dragging across the wolf's side. My scream of pain mixes with his anguished howl as we both draw blood.

When his wolf attempts to slash at me again, I drop completely back against the floor and kick the animal right in the spot where I cut across his ribs. The impact forces the wolf aside, allowing me to leap to my feet with a surge of strength, but it also means the book is completely exposed.

Ford is already lunging for the book, but I'm faster, my power giving me speed that seems to take him by surprise.

My claws ascend as he descends.

They are perfectly aimed at his jugular. He freezes, half-leaning, impaled on my hand, a shout on his lips. Blood pours across my arm and splashes across the book's white surface, where Tristan's blood is also smeared.

"No peace," I whisper, ripping my claws through my father's throat.

Before I've even begun to cut his flesh, he wrenches his wolf's energy back to his body in a streak of bright white light.

The collision of his wolf with his human form drives him back off my claws and away from me before I can do any damage.

He shifts completely into his wolf form in the next instant.

His full wolf form hits the side of the table, tangles in his human clothing, slips the material, and deftly leaps to the side. Already, the wound across his neck is healing, just like I healed myself by shifting completely after I fell on the rocks in the ravine.

I drop back to Tristan, grabbing the wadding as fast as I can and pressing again, but my stomach sinks when I realize that my father isn't giving up.

Snarling at me, my father's wolf prowls toward me again.

Despair fills me, smothering my anger.

I can't save Tristan's life while my father is in the way. He wants the book, but I can't free Tristan from the minds without it.

The angel told me I'd have to make choices I don't want to make.

The book sits at my side, bloodied now.

I tell myself I'll get it back somehow.

I open my mouth, ready to tell my father to take the book, when a scream sounds from the doorway.

Maeve rages into the room and a bolt of violet light blasts from her hands straight at my father.

The magical onslaught knocks into his wolf's chest, propelling him off his feet and knocking him against the wall. The magic itself slides harmlessly off his fur, but the impact makes his wolf yelp.

Maeve runs across the room with another scream while Danika soars above her, fully shifted into her hawk form.

A sob of relief passes my lips as Maeve lets another bolt of magic loose at my father's wolf—a protective strike—that keeps him busy while Maeve runs toward me. At the same time, Danika soars straight toward him, distracting him for long enough that Maeve can reach my side.

"Tessa!" She's pale as she stares at the mess of Tristan's chest and all of the blood around us. She doesn't hesitate, ripping off her shirt, tearing it and wadding it up, pressing the wads to the two remaining wounds. It's no use asking her to heal him—regardless of her knowledge of spells, her magic won't work on Tristan, just like Helen's healing magic didn't work on me.

"We need to get him out of here!" she cries.

I'm too choked up to do anything other than nod.

Nearby, Danika's talons rip at the wolf's back and head while he snarls and snaps his jaws. Like me, he is not insubstantial in his full wolf form. He is able to be cut and hurt, although he heals instantly.

"I'll give you a week, Tessa!" he roars across at me, still trying to threaten me. "A week before I slaughter Tristan's pack. Give me the book and I'll leave them in peace."

Before I can tell him where he can shove his promise, he leaps up at Danika, his sharp teeth aimed for her left wing in an attempt to pull her from the air and savage her.

She shoots backward and out of his reach, nearly hitting the ceiling before she opens her beak and lets out an earsplitting shriek.

The shrill sound slams into me like a physical force, nearly sending me sprawling from Tristan's side. Maeve flies backward, tumbling across the floor and hitting the back wall before her hands shoot up. Her magic glows around us in a shield, wide enough that I can't touch and break it. The sound of Danika's scream reaches us, but we're protected from the impact.

Crawling back to me and Tristan, Maeve resumes her pressure on his wounds.

My father's wolf doesn't fare so well.

Under the force of Danika's shriek, he flies all the way back against the end of the nearest bookcase, nearly toppling the entire structure. With a yelp, he attempts to scramble to his feet, pressing down on his wolf's belly to crawl toward the door. His paws scratch at the floor as he fights the force of her continuing scream.

Danika's powerful wings spread as she coasts the air directly above him, following his path, her shriek becoming more shrill, more painful. My father's wolf manages to drag himself to the doorway, his chest heaving, panting with effort.

Danika pauses to draw in a new breath and scream again.

The moment that the room falls silent, my father's wolf leaps to his feet, shoots through the door—

A gunshot sounds and his wolf jolts.

Iyana!

I make out her fully-protected outstretched arm just beyond the doorway in the shadows, where she must have been waiting for her chance.

My father's reflexes are second to none.

His human form disengages from his wolf in the tiniest space of time that it takes for the bullet to reach him. The bullet sails through his now insubstantial wolf and chips the doorframe while his human form jumps safely to the side.

I can just make out his human shadow beyond the doorway, launching into a run at the same time that his wolf's energy disappears. I picture him drawing his energy back to his body while he sprints away.

Iyana runs into the room, holding a duffel bag. Danika drops to the floor, shifting mid-flight and landing lightly in her human form.

I don't waste another second. "Help me! Tristan's bleeding out! We need to get him out of here!"

What I'm struggling to understand is why Tristan's power isn't helping him heal—at least to some extent. Stopping the blood should have been an interim measure while he healed himself. I'm sure his ability to heal helped him survive the fall at the ravine. These wounds should have started sealing up—at least a little.

Now that the immediate danger from my father is over, I'm

aware of the way Maeve is watching me, a stillness in her body, even though she continues to press on Tristan's wounds.

"Tessa..." She speaks at a whisper. "I'm so sorry."

"Why?" I ask, sudden panic flooding me. "Why are you sorry?"

She lifts the wad she's pressing against Tristan's chest. "Do you see?"

I glance at the wound, swiping my tear-filled, sweat-filled eyes against my shoulder, trying to clear them. I look again. The edge of the wound is red and angry, but within it...

I am suddenly frozen.

A golden substance smears the inside of the wound.

"Did an angel do this?" Maeve asks, replacing the wad.

"A Sentinel," I say, feeling like I'm going numb. "With a golden spear."

Maeve glances up at Iyana and Danika as they round the table. Danika is hurriedly pulling on her clothes while Iyana sinks to her knees on Tristan's other side, dropping the duffel bag to the floor.

"Dear fuck," Iyana whispers.

"The angel's magic is coating the inside of Tristan's wounds," Maeve says to me, her voice barely above a whisper. "I don't know much about Tristan's ability to break through magic, but he should have been able to repel this magic already." She swallows as she shakes her head. "The fact that he hasn't means that for some reason, he can't."

My voice is strangled. "What is it doing to him?"

"It's like a deadly vine twining around a tree and cutting into it," she says. "If the blood loss doesn't kill him, then the angel's magic will."

My chest is heaving, my heart beating too fast. I hunch over him with a wail, my hands clenching against his chest. "Can you remove the angel's magic?" I ask Maeve, forcing myself to speak.

She's pale. "I'm sorry, Tessa. Angels control the strongest of light magic—second only to the ancient dragons. I don't have the power to remove it. If I try, I could drive the magic deeper. He needs a witch far more powerful than I."

"Helen," I whisper. "He needs Helen."

Opposite me, Iyana's jaw clenches. "Then we'll fucking keep him alive for long enough to reach her."

With rapid efficiency, she pulls several pieces of clothing from the bag, along with a roll of duct tape. She gives me a determined nod. "He's a fighter, Tessa. He'll make it."

I'm beyond words now. Working together as fast as we can, Iyana, Danika, and I wad up fresh shirts and tape them around Tristan's chest and thigh. While we're busy, Maeve hurries around the room, muttering spells to repair the furniture and clean up the blood so that the humans won't know we were here. The brightening sunlight shining through the windows tells me we won't have long before the library staff turn up for the day.

When Iyana presses the final wad of material to Tristan's leg so I can tape it in place, she says, "Tessa, you need to sustain him with your wolf's energy like you did with the fae."

"I can't," I whisper, unable to keep the frustration from my voice. "My power works differently on Tristan. I can't give him my energy."

My eyes burn with fresh tears. I'm filled with so much rage. Anger at myself. Anger at my father. Anger at the fucking book that will either save Tristan or be his end. My wolf's energy becomes hot and angry inside me, hellbent on destruction, my power glimmering at the edges, a danger to everyone around me.

I drag a ragged breath into my chest, trying to calm myself as I finish tying off the last strip of duct tape.

As if she knows what I need, Danika presses her hand briefly to my shoulder—a brave move while my power is so volatile. Maeve drops to a kneeling position beside me and rubs my other shoulder gently, also ignoring the imminent danger. I sense the warmth of the wooden wand molded to Maeve's skin and the spell she's trying to use to calm me. It slides over my skin and can't do its work.

Danika scoops up the book, deposits it into her duffel bag with a soft *thud*, and just as quickly removes the remaining clothing—handing Maeve and me new shirts. The shirt I pull on is a soft gray like the one I was wearing before but with a lower neckline.

Danika is insanely calm. "We'll get him there in time, Tessa."

I reach for Tristan's hand as my rage subsides under the force of my pack's calm and strength.

A worse emotion replaces my anger. Fear makes my heart race.

Tristan's skin is far too cold. We've stopped the flow of blood, but he's lost too much already.

I tell myself that Tristan can survive anything. That he'll survive these wounds, just as he'll survive whatever I have to do to free him from Cerberus.

Taking a deep breath and calming myself, I move to kneel beside his head, curling my arms under his shoulders and preparing to lift him.

Danika throws the duffel bag over her shoulder and quickly positions herself at Tristan's knees, hooking her arm under his legs, while Maeve slides her arms under Tristan's back. Iyana takes his feet.

"Ready to lift?" Danika asks.

Harnessing my power to give me extra physical strength, I say, "I'm ready."

We groan as we heave Tristan off the floor, our muscles straining to carry his weight. Shuffling as fast as we can, we head to the door, carry him along the balcony, and make it down the stairs with difficulty. Tristan is *not* a small person. We're sweating and our arms and legs are shaking with effort by the time we reach the bottom of the staircase and shuffle across the entryway to the door.

A glance through the nearby window tells me that the streets are still mostly deserted, but it won't be long before the humans begin going about their business for the day.

Sweat drips down Maeve's face as she takes a moment to concentrate and translocate the door for us. As soon as the door disappears, we shuffle toward the SUV as fast as we can.

Iyana unlocks it and opens the back passenger door so that I can climb in backward and maneuver Tristan head-first into the vehicle. Luckily, the walkway on either side of us is empty of humans right at that moment.

Heaving with all of my might, I pull Tristan up onto the back seat, collapsing beneath his head and torso while Danika quickly bends his knees so she can climb in and rest his calves and feet on her lap.

Maeve races to the front passenger seat while Iyana starts the engine.

Within seconds, we're back on the road.

Iyana drives with a focus that surprises me, putting her foot down as we speed around corners and along streets. She expertly controls the vehicle in a way that indicates she's had practice driving at high speeds. I pray a human police officer doesn't pull us over.

As the streets rush by, I have time to take a breath. My hands rest lightly across Tristan's jaw and shoulder. My knuckles are busted and bleeding. It's only now I realize just how fucking hard the angel's body was where I punched her. Her fists on my face and chest have left me hurting, a dull ache in every location where I'm beginning to bruise. My father's claws also raked across my chest, leaving red welts up to my neck. I could heal all of my wounds if I shifted into full wolf form, but that isn't possible right now.

I stroke Tristan's hair, my fingers trailing across his clammy forehead and down along his jaw. The angel's halo glints on my wrist and I consider the wisdom of walking around with it in full view. Quickly, I slip the halo into my left pocket beside the elemental amulet.

Only now do I have time to consider that taking Tristan to Hidden House is incredibly dangerous. Not for him, but for all the women who shelter there.

He's unconscious right now, but there are no guarantees that the Killer or the Deceiver won't surface if... I take a shuddering breath... *when* he wakes up. If any one of Cerberus's minds is in control when Tristan wakes, he could cause terrible damage.

My heart is beating faster, a heavy weight settling across my chest. I make a promise to myself that I won't allow Tristan's minds to hurt anyone at Hidden House.

I tell myself that I won't allow my own inner darkness to break anything while I'm there.

My fingers twitch, my hands clenching into fists.

I'm just as much a danger to those women as Tristan is.

CHAPTER NINETEEN

My voice is scratchy as I speak into the silence, addressing my pack. "I'll need your help if Tristan wakes up and one of his other minds is in control."

It's difficult for me to ask for help, but already, these three women have shown me that they're willing to face any danger with me.

I clear my throat, trying to bring moisture to my dry lips. "I'll also need your help if anything happens that triggers my anger. You must protect Hidden House—even if it means protecting it from Tristan or me."

Danika leans across to squeeze my arm while Maeve swivels in her seat and Iyana gives me a quick, firm nod in the rearview mirror.

"We understand," Danika says. "We took on your father. We'll take Tristan on too." She meets my eyes. "And you, if we have to." Her voice softens. "I don't believe it will come to that, Tessa. You aren't like your father. You will make different choices. Just like Tristan has."

I exhale an anxious breath as the SUV turns onto the leafy street on which Hidden House is situated. It's an immaculate home from the outside, nothing out of the ordinary about its appearance that would compromise its true nature.

The garage door opens on the right and Iyana drives the SUV smoothly down into the parking garage.

The roar of a motorcycle right behind us makes me freeze.

I rotate in my seat, trying to catch a glimpse of who's following us. The bike rider appears male, dressed all in black. He leans low as the motorcycle roars through the open garage door just before it closes.

"Fuck!" Iyana says. "Who is that?"

"I'll take care of him," Maeve replies, violet light growing around her body as she unclicks her seatbelt and prepares to leap from the SUV the moment Iyana screeches to a stop in a parking spot.

"Wait!" I call, stopping Maeve in her tracks.

There are only a handful of male supernaturals who can breach the protective spells around Hidden House. One of them lies unconscious in my lap. Another would be my father. But the third…

My senses buzz as the motorcycle pulls to a swift stop beside the SUV. The bike is a beast, sleek and black with an emblem painted on the side panel of a rose dripping with blood. It's the same image that is tattooed across the chest of Tristan's beta, Jace.

My breath catches painfully as he pulls off his helmet. His honey-blond hair is cut short and his eyes are as deep green as pine needles. It's been nearly a week since I saw Jace, and he looks a fuck sight more unshaven than the last time, dark shadows across his jaw as well as beneath his eyes. He never shifts, but his incisors are partially descended, a state that must be causing him pain.

Jumping off his parked bike, he wrenches the door open beside me before I can even reach for the handle. "Tessa, where the fuck have you been?"

His gaze falls on Tristan and he freezes.

I force myself to take a breath before I give in to the temptation to punch Jace in the nose. Between Tristan and Jace, Jace was always the more considerate and well-mannered one. A week without his alpha seems to have changed that.

"Explanations can wait," I say, allowing a growl to enter my voice and my vision to flood crimson for long enough that he backs off.

"Fuck." Despite my glare, he continues to meet my gaze. I'm impressed when he plants his feet, his concern for Tristan clearly visible in the anxious crease in his forehead and the tense press of his lips. I'm reminded that Jace chose to be Tristan's beta despite being strong enough to be an alpha in his own right.

"I need answers," he says, his fists unfurling. "But clearly, we need to get Tristan to Helen right away."

He takes a wary step forward, his focus remaining on me, another hint of his wolf appearing in his demeanor when he lowers his eyes in an apparent acknowledgement of my strength. "Will you let me carry him?"

I sense the collective sighs of relief from the women inside the vehicle, who are all poised with their hands on their respective doors, prepared to leap out in a hurry if they needed to.

"Yes," I say. "Let me slip out first."

Sliding from the vehicle, I stand clear while Jace tucks his arms under Tristan's shoulders and pulls him out, his muscles straining. I reach out quickly to support Tristan's back and legs.

Maeve and Danika exit the other side of the vehicle—Danika with the duffel bag firmly slung across her shoulder. The book of old magic is contained in it, and I need to make sure the bag doesn't leave my sight. Iyana's protective suit retracts as she slips from the driver's seat. She holsters the cloak at her waist again and hurries after us.

"What happened?" Jace asks as we proceed as fast as we can toward the elevator.

"Angel spear," I say, keeping my explanation short. "How did you know where we were?"

"I sensed Tristan's presence as soon as I woke up this morning." Jace's forehead is creased, his biceps flexed as he supports Tristan's weight. "I was up most of the night trying to hold the pack together. Without Tristan, they're falling apart. We couldn't sense him for days. You have no idea how much they love him."

I think I might.

My focus shifts to Tristan's face, the black strands of his hair plastered to his clammy forehead.

Iyana hurries ahead of us to call the elevator, but the doors open before she can press the button. Hidden House dampens the power of every supernatural living here, but even so, Helen's presence is strong. While I was my father's prisoner, I found out that Helen was once known as Mother Kadris, a witch who is hundreds of years old and once traded in souls. She has a dark history that I find difficult to reconcile with the woman running toward us now.

She races from the elevator, her dark hair pulled up into her characteristic topknot, messy-looking this morning. She's dressed in her usual soft-looking sweater and tight jeans, but they appear hurriedly pulled on, her sweater caught up at the side. Her cheeks are blotchy, her gray eyes bloodshot, and her lashes are wet.

She swipes at her face as she calls out. "Tessa! Quickly! Bring Tristan inside."

She waves us toward the elevator, where the doors remain open. I'm surprised to find that it's larger than last time—big enough for Jace and me to carry Tristan and continue to hold him as horizontal as we can, while Danika, Iyana, and Maeve squeeze in around the sides and offer their support on either side of him.

The elevator doors close after Helen steps in. She presses the button for the twentieth floor before turning to face all of us.

The last time I saw her, she looked on me with wary distrust, having just learned my true nature.

Now, she steps up in the gap between Danika and Iyana to hover her palm over Tristan's chest.

She gasps. "Angels!" Her eyes widen even further. "Not just any angels, but Sentinels. But... how?"

The other women glance my way, deferring explanations to me. After all, they don't know what happened after they left the library room. Jace also considers me, the need for information clear in his worried green eyes.

My grip on Tristan's legs tightens as I attempt to give them the most succinct explanation I can, parts of which Iyana, Danika, and Maeve already know. "We needed a book. The Sentinels were guarding it. I got past the Sentinel I faced, but Tristan didn't." I attempt to clear my throat, my speech sticking. "The Sentinels required honest answers, but the Deceiver must not have allowed Tristan to speak truthfully."

Jace's vehement growl strikes at my heart. "Fucking three-headed wolf."

I take a deep breath. "Tristan is fighting as hard as he can. He's present a lot of the time now, but the Killer, Coward, and Deceiver can take control without warning." I meet Helen's concerned gaze, knowing I have to be truthful. "By bringing Tristan here, I'm risking the life of every woman sheltering at Hidden House."

Jace growls his frustration, but Helen is calmer. "Can you control Cerberus's minds?" she asks.

"The Killer and I have a fragile truce," I say. "I can beat the Coward into submission, but I'm only now learning how to play the Deceiver's game."

Jace narrows his eyes at me, cynicism creeping into his voice. "You have a truce with the Killer? That fucker annihilated innocent members of my pack. You're telling me a truce is possible with him?"

I level my gaze with Jace's, allowing my crimson rage to rise again, reading his impulses. He's frustrated. Tired. I discern his exhaustion in the tension in his face, the shadows beneath his eyes. Beyond all that, he carries a bone-deep fear that the past is about to repeat itself.

It's a real fear, proven by history.

Shutting down my power, I answer him honestly, even though it startles him.

"The Killer and I are the same," I say. "I'm just as much a danger to the women here as Tristan is, but I will curb my inner nature."

I can only imagine how I look right now, my ruby red hair falling disheveled around my shoulders, my clothing smeared with blood.

I continue. "I will make sure Tristan's minds don't hurt anyone for as long as it takes to heal him and take him away from here. I'm sorry about your pack, but he can't return to them until the minds are defeated."

The elevator doors open. The warmly lit entrance room with fabric armchairs is both a familiar and a painful sight—my first memories of Hidden House were of coming to this floor to be healed after my fight with Cody and Dawson. It was a lifetime ago.

"Hurry," Helen says, stepping from the elevator.

We follow closely behind her, carrying Tristan along the corridor, but we stop abruptly when she does.

"This can't be right," she says, jolting outside the door that leads into the medical room. "Hidden House always does what is needed, but even so..." She turns in my direction. "I'm sorry, Tessa."

She heads inside and we reach the doorway to see what has unsettled her.

The medical room is as warmly lit as I remember it with a large window on the opposite side. The window is shielded by a dark screen that allows me to see the outlines of the city buildings beyond without letting the sunlight through. The medical examination table sits closer to the far side of the room. The walls are lined with cupboards, and Helen's wand floats in the air above the table. But between the door and the examination table, floor-to-ceiling metal bars have risen, broken only by a door also constructed out of vertical metal bars.

The House has turned the far side of the medical room into a cage.

A shiver runs down my spine and my heartrate speeds up so fast that my breathing becomes audibly rapid.

My incisors descend, my voice guttural as my darkness rises. "Heal him out here," I order Helen. "We don't belong in a fucking cage."

"I didn't choose this," Helen says. "The House is trying to protect everyone from Tristan."

My crimson vision rises hot while my voice lowers. "Don't make me repeat myself, Helen."

Her expression hardens. "A fight between us would not end well, Tessa. If you don't want to enter the cage, then the others can carry Tristan inside." She raises her chin, determined. "I won't heal him until I know it's safe for everyone who shelters here."

The tension rises between Helen and me. Everything inside me screams against putting Tristan in a cage, but it took us long enough already to reach Hidden House. Every second we delay now could cost Tristan his life.

"Open the fucking cage door," I say.

Helen waves her hand and the cage door swings wide. It won't lock with magic. I spy the reinforced hinges and the deadbolt in the door as we approach.

Iyana, Danika, and Maeve follow us in, their faces pale, their eyes wide as they take quick glances at me. I'm too angry to care that I'm scaring them. It's all I can do to contain the rage inside me. My wolf's energy is buzzing beneath my skin, begging to be unleashed. Fear and rage—so closely entwined inside me—could cause me to lash out at any of them right now.

I shudder as I pass through the cage door.

Jace watches me carefully while the others remain outside the cage, and we finally lift Tristan up onto the medical examination table.

My arms are shaking, my voice a snarl as I address Jace. "Get the fuck out unless you want to be locked in here with the dangerous animals."

He hesitates, the glint of anger rising in his own eyes. For a second, I think he's going to stay, but Helen hurries into the cage with a terse order. "Jace! Out! *Now*."

Jace bares his teeth at me. "I lived with the Killer for four years when Tristan's father was my alpha. The Killer and I have a score to settle."

With a final growl, he turns to leave, but I'm not done with him.

"If you're so determined to face your fears, then take that fucking bravado and go see your mate," I snarl. "You've abandoned Ella for long enough."

He stiffens. Misses a step. "You don't know what you're talking—"

"I know a hell of a lot more than you do," I say. I saw firsthand the place where she was imprisoned, felt the darkness that surrounded her, know the consequences of having my soul broken.

"Out!" Helen shouts at Jace. "Unless you want Tristan to die."

Jace backs out of the cage, directing a snarl squarely in my direction. I'm not afraid to be harsh with him. Ella needs him. Especially now that her brother is gone.

When Helen hurries to Tristan's side, the cage door clangs shut and the lock *clicks*, a sharp sound that grates on my already frayed nerves. I tense up before I exhale and attempt to ease out the stiffness in my shoulders.

Helen snatches her wand from the air, running it over Tristan's body from his head to his feet while I pace the length of the cage.

"We don't know why Tristan didn't repel the angel's magic," I say. "He should be able to break through it."

"The Sentinels are creatures apart," she says as she works. "They are born of light magic, but there are whispers that old magic was bestowed on them by the Bright Ones—their spears may be strengthened by it. I'll know soon enough."

She focuses on Tristan, murmuring beneath her breath as she carefully removes the makeshift medical patches we plastered across his chest and thigh. The five wounds are even more unsettling than they were when he was bleeding badly. His skin is angry and red, the wounds refusing to seal. His face is paler than I've ever seen it, but his chest continues to rise and fall, and I focus on the movement, the knowledge that he's alive. That he'll fight this.

Iyana, Danika, and Maeve gather just beyond the cage while Jace paces on the far side near the door. Iyana eyes him as she opens the nearest cupboard and retrieves bottles of water for everyone. She brings one to me, holding it through the bars.

When I shake my head at her—I can't swallow anything right now—she gives me a hard stare. "You need to stay hydrated."

Reluctantly, I take the water from her and try to drink. It's hard when my throat is constricted with an awful mix of anger and anxiety.

Helen works quickly. The cupboards open and close as she uses her magic to fetch fresh medical pads, bandages, and tape, but the materials halt in the air when a sudden crease forms in Helen's forehead.

I continue to pace from one side of the cage to the other, my free hand brushing against the metal bars, my claws clanking.

Back and forth. Back and forth.

My pacing becomes more intense as I wait for Helen to tell me what's going on. "Helen?"

She doesn't answer me, her mask of concentration so deep, she doesn't seem present. Her hands hover above Tristan's chest, practically frozen, her chest rising and falling faster than before.

"Helen?"

When she finally speaks, her voice is strained. "The angel's magic has been strengthened with old magic, intertwined, just as I feared. I should be able to remove it, but it's bound to his flesh, as if it's clinging to the lies he told. I can't seem to..." A pained moan passes her lips. "I can't..."

I advance on her. "You can!" I grab her shoulders. "You have to help him!"

She gasps for breath, wheezing as if she's struggling to breathe. "I... can't..."

With another moan, she slumps in my hold, her weight dropping so suddenly that she nearly takes us both down. I grab the edge of the table to keep us upright. Outside of the cage, my friends all dart forward, but the bars keep them separated from me.

"The angel's magic has adhered to Tristan's body," Helen says. "This is beyond my capabilities."

Tears slip down her cheeks as she looks up at me. "I'm sorry, Tessa. There's nothing anyone can do for him now."

CHAPTER TWENTY

I can't accept that I've come this far, only to lose Tristan now.

"No." My voice is in danger of breaking. "I won't accept that."

Helen wobbles to her feet, slowly drawing herself upright. "I can stabilize him using human medicine. I can replace the blood he lost, keep him hydrated, and sew up his wounds. But I can't remove the angel's magic. As long as the Deceiver remains a part of him, the angel's magic won't lift."

Then I have to get rid of the fucking Deceiver.

I raise my head. "How long does he have?"

"Any other supernatural would have died already." Helen gives me a frank stare. "But this is Tristan. The power of Cerberus is both dooming him and keeping him alive. With the help of human medicine, he could live another four days. Possibly five." Her expression softens, her eyes glistening with fresh tears. "Long enough to say goodbye."

I snarl quietly back at her. "I'm not done yet, Helen. Tell me one thing: If I free him from the three-headed wolf, will he heal?"

Helen nods. "Maybe. But Tessa, freeing Tristan from the wolf is impossible. Tristan fought for years to free his father. In the end, he had no choice but to kill him."

I back up against the cage wall before I turn to my friends.

"Danika," I say, reaching through the bars. "I need the book."

Danika immediately crouches to unzip the duffel bag before she brings me the book of old magic, slipping it between the bars. Tears fall down her cheeks as she steps back. Iyana and Maeve are also crying, too quietly to be obtrusive.

My hands shake as I draw the book to my chest. I can't give in to grief. Not yet. Not until I know I've done everything I can.

The book's white leather cover glimmers softly in the warm light—even the patches where it's smeared with blood.

Helen is pale when I turn back to her. "That's the book of old magic," she says. "Supernaturals have slaughtered each other across the centuries to find and control that book."

Her gaze drops across my body as if she's reassessing me. For a second, she focuses on my pockets. Hidden House should subdue the power of the dark magic orb, the elemental amulet, and the angel's halo. Even so, I brace for Helen's reaction, but if she senses them, she doesn't say anything.

They are each reminders of battles I've fought since I gave in to my true nature, and I'm not letting them go.

"This book has the answers," I say, hugging it to my chest. "But I don't know what I'll find inside its pages. I need a safe place to read it."

Helen considers me for another moment. "Take the stairs, Tessa. The House will provide a place for you to read that book. Don't open it until you get there. The pages are dangerous for any supernatural who is not protected by old magic."

The cage door clicks open behind me, but I pause.

Tristan is so silent and still. His dark hair falls across his face. His beautiful, broad chest is hurt. His mind must be hurting more. His real mind. I miss his growls, his snarls. I want to see the amber flecks in his eyes and feel the press of his teeth against my shoulder.

I refuse to say goodbye. He told me there would be no end for us and I'm determined to prove it true.

Spinning on my heel, I stride through the cage door, but I pause for a beat when I draw level with my pack, meeting their tear-filled eyes. I bite my lip before I join them, fighting the burn of tears. "You all need food and rest." *And clothing that isn't covered in blood. And a safe place where they aren't threatened by constant danger.* They deserve so much more. "Make sure you get it."

Iyana gives me a quiet nod. "We'll show Maeve around."

As I turn to leave, her hand snakes out. "We're here, Tessa. When you're ready, call us."

I give her a nod before I stride to the door, where I pause again. Jace stands there, his shoulders hunched.

"If I can help," he says, "tell me how."

I recognize the despair in his eyes. His anger at me and at the Killer hides years of pain.

"I will do everything I can," I say, knowing I have to take back my anger at him about Ella. "Your pack needs you right now, Jace. You should return to them. Keep them safe."

He gives me a nod before I stride away.

Returning to the start of the corridor, I find a set of stairs instead of the elevator—these steps leading upward. I ascend them while the temperature around me drops, my breath frosting in the air. Inhaling the scent of ice, I step out onto a glittering mountain.

I've been here before. On my last day at Hidden House.

Opposing rockfaces soar up on either side of me, leaving a treacherously slender path between them. Far above me, the sliver of a gap between the rockfaces allows the sunlight to glint off the crystalline surfaces.

Holding the book tightly, I step carefully along the pass, following it as it curves and twists more than I remember it doing last time until I finally see the clear sky ahead, a thread-like promise of open space.

The first time I walked this path, I understood the metaphor for my future, how boxed in I was, how shrouded my future was.

This time, the glittering surfaces on either side of me are jagged, sharp enough to cut my hand when I reach out to tentatively touch them. I leave a thin smear of blood on the rocks that quickly freezes over.

My journey to discovering my inner nature began with ice.

I shiver, but not from cold, pushing onward as fast as I can. I need to know what lies at the end of this path, even though I've seen it before—a battlefield below me where my father fought against the gods.

I approach the opening slowly, wary of stepping out into nothing, but a wide cliff's edge stretches out beyond the pass. Its surface is dusted with snow that reminds me of the flurries that would fall from Brynjar the ice jotunn's fingertips.

A breeze brushes the exposed skin of my hands and face, tugging at my shirt, but it's quiet around me, no sounds of bloody battle. When I venture toward the edge of the platform to peer down, the earth far below glitters with a carpet of silver.

I squint and try to see… silver vines and flowers like the ones in Hidden House's garden. They twine over protrusions of rock…

No. *Gravestones.*

My jaw clenches as I draw away from the edge and sit down in the middle of the snow-dusted ledge. Just like Brynjar's power, this snow isn't cold. It's old magic—of the glittering kind.

I run my palm over the cover of the book.

Taking a deep breath, I open it.

CHAPTER TWENTY-ONE

The book doesn't contain words.

Images leap out at me, moving across the parchment and rising off the page.

An enormous wolf steps from the pages, its teeth bared, head lowered, eyes glowing crimson. Its fur is like black coals, its claws sharply white.

It jumps to my left as I sense the air behind me shift. The clanking of metal meets my ears a split second before gleaming chains strike past me, making me flinch. The chains wrap around the wolf's neck and a roar of triumph washes across the air, also from behind me.

Just as I turn to see the wolf's attackers, multiple creatures race past me. Each of them is a glowing, powerful silhouette so bright, I can hardly look at them. They leap at the wolf, throwing more chains, shouting, and trying to subdue him, but he is just as big as they are.

The wolf tips his head back and howls, slashing at his attackers with his teeth and claws before throwing them off.

"New gods!" he snarls, his crimson eyes flashing with derision. "You are pitiful."

Tensing the muscles in his neck, the wolf causes the chain to snap.

Blood drips from his lips and it takes me a moment to realize it isn't his. His attackers back away, nursing their wounds, dragging their chains with them.

One of them—a male whose silhouette gleams with emerald light—shouts at the wolf. "Fenrir! All beasts loyal to the old ways must die!"

My father snarls back at him. "Not today."

He turns and races away into the night. I stay with him as he runs into a misty forest where the fog is so thick that his dark fur stands out. He changes color as he runs, turning pale and white, blending into the mist until he slows to sniff the ground, snarling at the earth beneath him.

Launching into a suddenly panicked run, he darts through the trees toward a cabin hidden among the foliage.

He shifts as he runs, resuming his human shape. His human features are younger—much younger—and his lips don't carry the same cruel twist that he wears now. He plucks a pair of pants from the floor of the little porch before he bursts through the door.

Inside, the cabin has been turned upside down. The fire in the hearth is cold, tiny wisps of smoke rising up from the dying coals.

My heart wrenches when I make out two cribs, both broken, baby blankets torn and strewn across the floor beside them. A woman's shawl is tangled among them.

My father snatches up the shawl. "No," he whispers, his eyes wide. "Eliande! My sons!"

With a howl of rage, he turns, casts the clothing aside, and races from the cabin, shifting into his wolf form again.

The image follows him, but only for a second before it drops so fast that my stomach remains behind. I shoot downward through moist earth, layers of dirt broken by tree roots, until the environment around me turns to layers of stone.

I try to catch my breath as the image finally slows and stops, until I'm looking down on a rocky cavern from above.

I'm submerged in overly warm air, my senses filling with the scent of burnt coal. It's hot, fiery, aromas that have lingered whenever I've inhaled Tristan's scent.

Below me, a man whose face and body are covered in a lion's skin is dragging a chained and unconscious beast along the rocky ground. The beast is as enormous as my father.

My breath catches as the beast's three heads come into view.

The Killer told me that the new gods stole him from the underworld and cast him into the world of the living, where he did not belong.

I peer at the man in the lion's skin. He doesn't glow like the gods who attacked my father. He's human. Maybe.

His muscles bunch as he drags Cerberus around the next corner of the rocky tunnel into a large cavern where a luminescent being waits. This goddess is female, judging by her curves, but she is just as bright as the others were.

She bends over a woman who lies unconscious on the rocky floor at the far side of the cavern.

The man shields his eyes when the goddess looks up. Her brightness fades so that her facial features become visible: high cheekbones, rose-colored lips, eyes that gleam like diamonds. Her hair glistens down her back.

"You've done well to bring me both Fenrir's wife and Cerberus," the goddess says to the man. "While my arrogant brothers try to end the old ways with force, I will end them with guile. I will take Cerberus's powers and use them to kill Fenrir. But first, I will kill Fenrir's wife and crush his soul. The monstrous wolf will not be our end as foretold."

She points to a spot on the rocky cavern floor where three concentric circles have been scratched, the outer circle no bigger than a dinner plate. "Place him on the rune. It will bind him to the spot should he wake up before I'm finished. He won't be able to get away."

The man's biceps and thighs bulge as he drags Cerberus to the center of the cavern, leaving the three-headed beast lying on the rune.

The goddess stares at the man, as if she is not yet pleased. "Did you bring the magical objects?"

He reaches into a pouch at his waist and opens his hand to reveal what look like four random objects: a silver feather, a tiny glass vial containing a single flame, an onyx gem, and a gold bracelet.

"One for each type of magic," he says.

My eyes widen to see the gold bracelet since it looks just like the angel's halo.

The goddess peers at the objects without touching them. "Did you take them by force like I asked?"

"Yes," he says. "The feather is old magic from a Valkyrie, the flame is elemental fire from a fae, the black gem contains dark magic belonging to a magician, and the bracelet..." He pauses, his shoulders hunching. "An angel who fought valiantly for her life."

"Good." The goddess beams. "Only with stolen magic can I steal Cerberus's power. Place them around him. Anywhere will do as long as they do not touch his skin directly."

The man's face remains shrouded beneath the lion's skin as he bends to place the objects at the four corners of a rough square shape around the unconscious beast.

When the man rises, he says, "I've done everything you asked. I want no further part in this."

"Then go," the goddess says with a dismissive wave, her focus shifting to Cerberus, but her eyes narrow before the man reaches the side of the cavern.

"Wait!" she calls. "What did you do with Fenrir's sons, Skoll and Hati?"

The man stiffens but doesn't turn back. "You don't need to worry about them."

She bares her teeth. "They're still alive?"

He rises up and squares his shoulders. "I've put them where they aren't a threat to you."

She purses her lips in thought. "Very well." A treacherous smile grows on her face. "You will be known throughout time for your daring feats."

"Bloodthirsty acts for arrogant gods," he says before he disappears into the dark.

The goddess continues to ignore Fenrir's wife, who lies only a few paces away, her forehead bleeding, while the goddess sweeps her skirt aside to straddle Cerberus where he lies on his side. She lowers herself down on top of him, resting her head on his shoulder, pressing her right hand to his heart.

Her hair falls across the beast's back as she takes a deep breath and lets it out slowly. The scene is laid out in front of me, but I'm still aghast at what I'm seeing.

She can't be... matching her breathing to his?

She can't be trying to meld with him?

"I will take your darkness," she whispers. "Your darkness will be mine."

I remember the way Tristan had lined our bodies up before we melded, his hips with mine, even the bend of our knees aligned before he asked me to place his hand over my heart and told me that we needed to breathe together. That our bodies and wolves needed to fall into the same rhythm.

We dragged each other's darkness to the surface, took it into ourselves, experienced the other's most violent, vulnerable feelings and then passed the darkness back.

The goddess's breathing finally falls into sync with Cerberus's labored breaths. His right paw twitches when she whispers, "I will take your minds. Your minds will be mine."

As if they're drawn to the energy growing around the goddess and Cerberus, the magical objects begin to glow, each one rising up off the stone floor, reacting to each other.

The goddess's forehead creases, her fingers curling against his heart, and her voice fills with pain. "I will take your deception. Your deception will be mine."

The dark magic gem suddenly sparks, its magic spearing across the space and exploding across the goddess. Cerberus twitches again and the goddess moans, "I will take your cowardice. Your cowardice will be mine."

Both the feather and the vial of fire burst into bright streams of light, also spearing across Cerberus and the goddess.

Her voice rises to a shriek. "I will take your violence! Your violence will be mine!"

The angel's halo finally bursts into light, all four magics glistening around them.

The beast opens his eyes, groggy. Then they flash wide.

He shifts from his beast form into human form so fast that I nearly miss it. In his human form, he has hair the color of a raven's feathers, his skin is bronzed, and his biceps bunch as he grabs the goddess. "Stop! You don't know what you're doing!"

"You're too late," she whispers with a triumphant smile. "I will take your minds. Your minds are mine."

The shapes of three wolves rise from Cerberus's chest, ghostly, each one lifted in the combined light of the four magics. The wolves are insubstantial, like my own power, but appear no less deadly. Their energy crackles across the air like lightning, a biting force that makes the hairs on my arms stand on end.

"You've lost your powers," the goddess says, rising up into a kneeling position, arching her back, her arms flung wide, ready to accept the power into her body. "Your powers are mine."

Smack!

The goddess screams as she flies to the side, knocked off Cerberus's chest.

Fenrir's wife rises up beside Cerberus, her fists clenched around a rock that bears the goddess's blood.

"Not. Fucking. Yet," she snarls.

Cerberus shouts a warning, trying to rise but bound to the ground. "Get back!"

Eliande's eyes widen as the ghostly wolves leap in her direction.

"No!" She stumbles back, but she isn't fast enough.

With a flash of darkness, the wolves rush into her chest.

She screams, thrashes, claws at her bodice. "No! Get out!"

The moment that the wolves enter her body, the rune flashes and Cerberus jumps to his feet, free again.

The goddess screams, rising up to advance on both of them, her silhouette brightening so much that she is like a burning sun.

Cerberus snatches Eliande into his arms, lifting her up as she screams and running with her through the rocky cavern and into the far tunnel.

They are a blur as the goddess cries with rage behind them, but she lets them go with a final curse. "You will never survive!"

Cerberus doesn't stop running until their surroundings change, the rocky tunnel becoming more earthy, tree roots tangling in the cave walls. Ahead of them, a spot of light beckons, but he places Fenrir's wife down on a rocky ledge, brushing the hair from her face, wiping the tears from her eyes.

His own cheeks are pale as he collapses against the rock beside her. "My minds were my only power. I won't live... much longer... You need to keep running."

She presses her palms to her temples as if she's trying to keep her head in one piece. "These minds... They're so loud... I can't think..."

"My powers were meant for me alone. The goddess could have controlled them, but you were meant to have only one mind..." Cerberus slumps, his voice losing its strength. "You can't go home. You can't go back to anyone you love. You will only hurt them." He exhales slowly, turning his face toward the distant light, the end of the cavern. "You must find a way to rid yourself of the minds. Unlike me, you have your own power. Get rid of the minds and you will survive. With them, you will only die..."

She reaches for him, but his eyes are becoming glassy.

"Cerberus?" she whispers.

"I'm sorry..." His head drops and he is still.

Jumping to her feet and backing away with a cry, Eliande strips off her clothing and shifts into her wolf form. She runs toward the light. With every step she takes, the shape of her wolf changes, morphing slowly until her eyes are hard and cold, her muscles bunched, and I sense her need for blood.

The Killer is in control of her now.

The images in front of me flash quickly through the years, snatches of time, mere glimpses. Eliande finds a new pack and has more children. She thinks she can control the minds, but when she can't, her children rise up against her. When she dies, the cycle continues. The strongest child becomes the Killer and the violence never ends...

I surface from the pages of the book, gasping for breath.

I'm still surrounded by glistening snow flurries, a beautiful crystalline environment that defies the blood and betrayal I've just witnessed.

Cerberus's minds were stolen. They were fucking stolen.

My breathing increases as I reach into my pockets to pull out the magical objects I've taken over the last two days.

I have three of them already... The dark magic orb, the amulet of elemental power, and the angel's halo of light magic.

I took them all by force from the supernaturals who controlled them.

I'm only missing one object—an object of old magic.

My jaw clenches with determination and a renewed sense of purpose.

If Cerberus's minds were taken once, they can be taken again.

CHAPTER TWENTY-TWO

I hurry back along the mountain pass, clutching the book to my chest, the three magical objects returned to my pockets. I consider slipping the halo over my wrist again but given the effect the angel's magic had on Tristan, I don't want to risk that the halo will harm others if they touch it. All I need now is an object of old magic—and this house must be full of them. After all, it's built on a foundation of old magic.

When I reach the stairs, I sway a little and clutch at the handrail, suddenly lightheaded. My stomach feels empty and my throat is parched. I've exerted a lot of energy since I last ate and I've been up all night *and* all morning.

I tell myself to get the fuck on with it.

I'll eat and sleep soon enough. I finally have the answer to freeing Tristan from Cerberus's minds and I only have a few days to do it. Five at most.

The Killer swore to destroy Tristan's mind within the week. It's the same time frame within which my father threatened to attack Tristan's pack. The same time frame within which Tristan will die if I don't help him.

The weight of responsibility squeezes my chest like iron shackles.

Hurrying back down the stairs to the medical wing, I pull up short to find myself in the garden instead. The House has the power to take me where I need to go with only one flight of steps, but it should have taken me to the medical wing. Not here.

The garden is a large space with a waterfall flowing down the entire left wall, while trees and flower bushes circle the courtyard in the middle. Women sit at the wooden tables positioned throughout the courtyard, some of the women talking quietly with each other while others eat silently. I recognize them all from my last stay, although the House continues to prevent me from sensing their supernatural status.

I'm momentarily disoriented by the night sky shining above me, since I'm sure it's still mid-morning. The trees are lit up along their branches with fairy lights that glow silver across the entire space. Then I spot Iyana at a table toward the middle of the courtyard. She's sitting with Danika, Maeve, and—my heart lifts a little—the card mage twins, Luna and Lydia.

This room always adjusts to night for Iyana's safety, so I don't think any more about the starry sky. For a moment, I consider joining my friends. As much as I want to, sharing a meal with my pack is an indulgence I can't afford right now.

I'm about to turn away and ascend the stairs again, determined to return to the medical wing, when I spy the silver flowers blooming on the vines that lightly encircle the branches of the farthest tree. I've always been drawn to them, my power rising when I was near them.

If they're old magic, then my search is already over. I'm not sure how I can apply force when I take one, but maybe I can rip the flower off the branch...?

I send a quick whispered *thank you* to the House for providing what I need like it always has. Not to mention an excuse to stop by my pack on the way.

Still gripping the book, my stomach grumbles loudly as I maneuver quietly between tables, avoiding bumping into anyone.

The first time I set foot in this place, nobody stared at me—the rules of Hidden House are that privacy is paramount—but I'm disconcerted to find that, despite my very quiet maneuvering, all of the women are looking my way.

The nearest women actively shrink away from me, their eyes wide, many of them visibly trembling. One woman has so much trouble putting down her fork that it clatters across her plate before she drops it.

She's fucking terrified and I don't understand why.

My steps slow, my hackles rising. *What the fuck have I done to draw their attention?*

When one woman can't stop staring at my stomach, I quickly check myself.

Oh, fuck.

My clothing is covered in Tristan's blood. Not only my shirt, but my jeans. And the book.

Damn and fuck.

Any reminder of violence would be triggering for most of the women here. Yet here I am walking among them with bloody violence on display.

More horrifying than stepping into this place covered in blood is my realization that I hardly thought about it. The scent of blood, the fact that it coats my skin, the fact that I'm bruised and bloodied… doesn't feel unnatural to me anymore, doesn't alarm, barely registers for me.

How far gone am I that battle feels natural to me now?

I back away from the garden as fast as I can, needing to disappear before I cause any more damage.

As the room falls silent, Iyana, Danika, and my other friends all look around, but even when Iyana jumps from her seat and calls my name, I continue to retreat.

I'll find an object of old magic somewhere else.

I bump right into Helen.

"Wait, Tessa," she says, reaching out to steady me. "You need to eat, too."

"I'll get food later," I say, attempting to pass her.

Her right hand clamps around my arm. "Tristan's condition is stable," she says. "He's safe—"

"For now," I say. "I need to get back to him."

Without releasing me, she calls out, "Iyana, Danika, please make sure everyone gets safely back to their rooms. If they haven't finished their meals, Ada will bring their plates to them in their rooms."

My forehead creases. "Dinner?"

It's not exactly the most important question, but Helen answers anyway.

"You've been gone all day," she says. "I've never opened one of the original four books of magic—never even seen one, actually—but apparently, they can steal whole days of your life. You were lucky it was only one."

That would explain my extreme hunger, but it only increases my anxiety. I've lost too many hours already.

I pull myself free of Helen's hold so I can stand clear of the women who are hurrying past me up the stairs. Now that they're occupying the staircase, I can't make a hasty retreat. I spin away from them, holding the book with its cleanest side out, crossing my arms around it. Hunching to hide the blood. "I don't have time for the luxury of food."

Helen's voice takes on a dangerous edge. "No time to look after yourself?"

"No. I need to return to Tristan—"

Again her hand grips my arm.

"Calm," she says firmly. It's the same moderated, controlled way she spoke to me before Tristan came to take me away from Hidden House.

My lips part, ready to argue when Iyana and Danika pause at my side. Helen inclines her head in a quick movement, indicating that they should keep going. They don't argue with her.

I exhale a frustrated breath. "*Calm* doesn't work for me anymore."

Before I left Hidden House, Helen attempted to teach me to control my anger and defensiveness. She nearly succeeded, but my father's entry into my life changed all of that.

Someone else pauses beside me and I'm surprised that it's Luna, one of the card mage twins. Her cheeks blush pink, a sign that she's accessing her power, as she carefully hands Helen a card. Her sister, Lydia, hovers behind her, but Luna doesn't give any indication that she wants Lydia to speak for her this time.

I can't see what's on the card, but it makes Helen sigh quietly before she slips it into her pocket and the twins retreat with the others.

Out in the courtyard, all of the tables except one slip backward into the surrounding trees, while the trees sprout new branches and leaves that knit together into a gleaming silver canopy overhead.

Helen gestures toward the table. "Please."

When I edge toward the stairs, she warns, "Until you accept your need to eat, the House will only bring you right back here."

With a sigh of defeat, I turn on my heel.

Reaching the table, I slide the book on top of it before I take a seat. A steaming bowl of soup sits in front of me and the scent makes my stomach growl painfully.

"It's broth," Helen says quietly as she slips into the seat opposite me. "I don't imagine you've eaten properly for the last few days. You need to go slowly."

She isn't wrong. I take a sip of the soup, grateful for the liquid warmth, but I shiver when the silver vines that are curling around the overhead branches begin to twine down like glittering strings to the ground, spreading across my feet. I bend to break off one of the flowers after it sprouts from the vine. It feels so fragile in my hand—too fragile to be what I need.

Helen begins to speak. "I won't ask what you saw in the book of old magic, but—"

"I need an object of old magic," I say, my fingers grazing across the flower petals. I can't sense the extent of the power in the blossom because of the House's dampening properties, but my instincts tell me it's not enough. The entire garden is a product of old magic—not a source of power like the halo or the amulet.

"If I ask you why, will you give me an answer?" Helen watches me place the flower carefully on top of the book.

Without answering her, I say, "I thought I might find one here, but now I'm not so sure."

Helen lowers her hands to the table while I take another slow sip of soup. Her gaze flicks from the flower to me. "Objects of old magic are rare. They come from the creature themselves. A part of their body: a bone, a feather, a claw. Or an object that has been fashioned out of such a body part."

I shudder at the idea of holding part of a creature's body in my hands, but I persist. "Other than trying to relieve my father of one of his claws, do you know where I might find an object like that?"

"Objects of old magic are very dangerous in the wrong hands," Helen says. "The bone of an old god was once fashioned into a wand. It was said that only a supernatural with a truly dark heart could wield it."

I lean forward in anticipation. "What happened to it?" *And how can I get it?*

She gives me a wary look. "A supernatural with a heart of rage took control of it. That wand is beyond anyone's reach now."

I slump a little before I dip my spoon again. "Are there any others?"

Helen exhales gently. A soft sigh. Instead of answering my question, she leans forward. "Why don't you let your power out," she suggests gently. "Let your wolf explore like you used to."

I pause as the spoon touches my lips before I force the liquid down. "Because I could hurt you."

"I don't believe you will."

I place the spoon back into the bowl. "You watched me slaughter an entire coven with only my wolf and a slender wand. I could end you within a heartbeat, Helen."

She is impossibly calm. "Yet Hidden House let you right in." She peers at me. "Despite all of the anger you keep caged up inside, you aren't a danger to me or anyone else here."

I pick up my spoon, tapping it on the side of my plate, only to put it down again. "You once told me that it's not physical pain that does the most damage," I say. "It's the psychological harm of being made powerless despite my strength."

She nods, slowly and carefully. "You couldn't kill your father."

"I tried—" I grip the table as my voice suddenly breaks. I hate the sudden rush of pain and frustration that fills me. My knuckles turn white around the table's edge. "I'm powerful enough to stroll into the Spire and rip his followers apart. I could rage through his allies—Baxter Griffin, Peter Nash, Dawson, even the demon he deals with—I could tear them all to pieces. But I still can't kill *him*."

"Why didn't you do it?" she whispers.

My forehead creases. "Didn't... do what?"

"Kill Baxter Griffin? Kill your father's followers?"

I close my eyes. Shake my head. "Who am I, if I do that? Am I bringing justice to their door? Or am I the new monster that everyone should fear—as my mother believes I am? How do I tell the difference between the two when the darkness my father gave me only wants blood?"

Helen reaches across the table to ease one of my white-knuckled fists off the edge of it, pulling my hand into hers.

"I was once feared," she says. "When you arrived this morning, in fact, I was mourning the actions of my past."

I remember her blotchy cheeks and glistening eyes when we arrived.

"I caused pain and suffering in the name of power," she says. "Glory was everything to me."

"They called you 'Mother Kadris.'"

She gives a short nod. "Mothers told stories about me to make their children behave. I was the shadow in the corner of the room, the wayward branch tapping the window in the middle of the night, the threat that hangs in the air when storm clouds roll over the sky. I walked the path that you now seek to avoid and I did it without regret."

Her expression is open and honest. Brutally so.

I struggle to reconcile the destructive person she's describing with the compassionate woman sitting opposite me now. Cody told me that Mother Kadris offered favors in exchange for a person's soul. My father said that Mother Kadris was once a member of Mother Serena's coven and that they used dark magic to rule the forest I've just purged of witches.

"What changed?" I ask.

"I made a choice that resulted in the near extinction of an entire race of supernatural creatures," she says. "Even when I saw what I'd set in motion, I didn't accept the blame. *I* wasn't the one killing them. Never mind that I'd given power to the one who slaughtered them. No… it wasn't until I had a child and then had to walk away from him because of who I had become…" She presses her lips together and swallows. "That's when everything changed for me."

Both Cody and my father said that Mother Kadris had lost someone she loved and after that, she disappeared.

"My mother walked away from me," I say. "I'm not sure I can forgive her for that or for the fact that she wants to kill me."

Helen doesn't lower her eyes, appearing resolute in her honesty.

"That is for her to atone for. As I atoned for my past actions. You can't control her choices, Tessa. She has to decide her own path." Helen grips my hand harder. "I'm going to ask you again: Why didn't you kill Baxter Griffin?"

"Because of Ella," I say, choosing the rawest, most basic truth. "I didn't know he was her father until that night. I watched Andreas Dean—the man who loved and raised me—die. I couldn't walk away from that party with Baxter's blood on my hands. Not without understanding more about Ella's past and her family."

"And what have you found out since?"

"That Baxter might have known all along that his daughter was alive. That he left her with the witches and told his family she was dead so he had an excuse to wage war against Tristan. That all along, all he wants is the prestige of controlling the entire eastern and western lowland."

Watching me, Helen appears to choose her speech carefully. "If you'd known all of that on the night of the party, would it have changed your decision to let him live?"

"Yes," I say, without any doubt in my mind. "I would have ended him without regret." My jaw clenches. "I thought I was protecting Ella, but instead, I failed her. Just like I failed her brother—"

"No." Helen's denial is short and sharp. "You acted out of love, Tessa. You didn't want to hurt Ella any more than she was already hurt. You did everything you could to keep Cody alive. To act out of love is never a weakness. It's never a failure."

Her hand is warm around mine, her gray eyes compelling me to listen and believe her.

"You gave up your freedom to protect Tristan's pack from Baxter's attacks. You did it again to keep Cody alive at the Spire," she says. "You're determined to free Tristan from his fate—and only the spirits know what you'll give up to do that. Love has many forms and you've experienced and *given* all of them."

She arrests my gaze, freezing me to the spot. "You have so much love to give, Tessa. You've proven that to everyone around you. That's why there's nothing you can do now that will frighten any of us away. And that's how I know you will never walk the same path as your father. You deserve love, Tessa."

I stare at her, shell-shocked, unable to respond to the sincerity of her claims. The Sentinel asked me if I often put my own safety in jeopardy for the sake of others. I'd taken it as a provocative question designed to make me question my motives, but maybe the Sentinel's intentions weren't as malicious as I first thought. She demanded to know if I thought I had to sacrifice myself to be worthy of love. Now Helen is reminding me of all the choices I've made that were because I cared about someone—not because I hated them.

"But my father—"

"Is he, though? Your father?" she asks. She continues to pierce my heart with her questions. "Fenrir has many names, but I'm not sure that 'father' accurately belongs among them. Perhaps a very long time ago, he was capable of love, but his actions now indicate he is not."

I have no response. The story I saw in the book showed me that he had sons in the ancient times, but he lost them. When he found out about me, he wanted to remove the barrier of my human soul—to make me like him, but only as long as I obeyed him.

"When you first arrived here, I told you I was sorry about what happened to Andreas Dean," Helen says. "You asked me what I knew about him. I wanted to tell you what I knew, but it would have only led to complicated questions—many to which I didn't know the answers. But I want to tell you now.

"I only knew about Andreas by reputation. I knew he was one of the most honorable alphas. I knew that Peter Nash could only have beaten him and taken over the alpha role through treachery. I knew that Andreas trained with assassins, who also follow a strict code of honor. I knew that Andreas was once..." She swallows. "He was once a good friend to the man I loved. I wish I'd known Andreas Dean better. So I wonder, Tessa. How much power do you give Fenrir over you by calling him your father?"

My lips part. Helen is quietly and gently stripping back all of my defenses and striking at the heart of my fears and vulnerabilities.

"I know you feel that you don't have a moment to spare. That time is running out for you and Tristan," Helen continues, "but if you don't take the time you need to regain your balance, to offer yourself the same protection you give others, you won't survive the choices that are ahead of you." Her eyes glisten with unshed tears. "I don't want to lose you, Tessa."

She pushes back her chair before she lifts her hands toward the canopy overhead. "I'm going to give you space now. Hidden House has everything that you need. It's time to show yourself a little kindness."

I stare into my soup, too many emotions rising inside me to separate them. I let them all happen, not trying to push them away. Cold fear. Burning rage. Empty despair. Crushing failure... Glimmering hope...

Helen gives me a gentle smile before she heads to the stairs, her footsteps quiet and calm.

"Wait," I call out, taking slow breaths to manage to speak through the storm of emotions warring inside me. "I have to know... What is on the card Luna gave you?"

Pausing at the base of the steps, Helen says, "There's something the House wants to show you. But it will only happen when you're ready."

She continues up the stairs.

I bow my head over my bowl of simple soup. The steam rises to dampen my cheeks, but it's the tears that really make them wet.

Beneath all of my layers and all of my walls and defenses, there is a quiet truth.

I am only one person.

When we ran together in the forest, Tristan quietly told me that there's a weight on my shoulders. He told me he wanted to lift it. He offered his help, but I told him he couldn't. Iyana and Danika asked me what I need, and I accepted their help for a time, but when my father turned up, I told them to leave. Asking for their help on the way here was hard, but I only asked for it when it involved protecting others from *me*. I can't seem to ask for help when it involves protecting myself.

My palm rests down on the book of old magic.

Some battles have to be fought alone.

Others... don't.

I exhale. Accept my emotions. All of them. I attempt to clear my head. Focus on eating. A simple act.

There is so much crowding my mind. My need to find an object of old magic. My need to save Tristan. My need to protect his pack. My need to protect the women in this house…

But right now, what I need is to be still. To eat. Maybe sleep.

"Fight tomorrow," I whisper to myself.

Even when I sat on the cliff and read the book of old magic, I didn't feel this peacefully alone.

When I finish eating, I sit back in my chair and tip my face up to the starlight glimmering between the branches overhead. I quietly release my power from the cage of my human body, my vision splitting between my wolf and my human form. Like I did so many times when I lived here, I close my human eyes to see the environment around me from my wolf's perspective. The new silver flowers spreading across the floor smell like the air right before it rains. The earth is soft beneath my paws as I explore the new growth, nudging my nose against the vines. The air is cool and fresh. My lungs empty as I exhale slowly, breathing out all of the savage emotions I've experienced in the last week.

Helen was right about my fear of time running out, the sense of urgency that tells me I can't afford to eat or sleep, that I shouldn't take care of myself, that everything else is more important.

My eyes open slowly as clarity about the path ahead of me builds. I calculate the days I have left: at least three to help Tristan, and at least five before my father makes good on his threat to attack Tristan's pack.

I have enough time to do what I need to do.

There's one person I haven't seen again at Hidden House yet, and I need to find her because her life, her past, and her present have been a constant influence on my decisions.

I need answers before I can move forward.

I need to see Ella.

CHAPTER TWENTY-THREE

*D*rawing my wolf form back to my human body and gathering up the book, I ascend the stairs from the garden.

This time, the House takes me where I want to go—the living quarters where my old bedroom is located.

I enter a room at the top of the steps that is low-lit and homely—a library of sorts with floor-to-ceiling bookshelves and lounge chairs with scattered well-loved cushions. The window on the far side glitters with the view of the city lights beyond it.

The corridor to the right is empty and the House continues to dampen my senses so that I can't sense the women living in the rooms I pass. I can't use my power to detect their movements, determine their supernatural status, or know the strength of their power. Only my human senses work. By living here, Helen herself hides the immensity of the power she controls.

I finally reach the door of the room that I used to share with Ella.

My hand hovers and I decide it's best to knock.

After two soft taps, the room remains silent inside.

Pushing the door open, my breath catches at the beauty of the bedroom in front of me. It's only been a short while since I left, but I was afraid it might have changed—that my side of the room might have disappeared at least.

My bed still sits on the left-hand side of the clearing, which is surrounded by endless forest. The scent of new leaves fills my chest, an achingly familiar fragrance. Our closets sit at the far end of each bed, while two enormous trees with doors carved into their trunks contain our bathrooms.

I immediately swivel to the plush armchair located at the base of Ella's bed on the right-hand side. Her favorite place.

It's empty.

A moment of indecision grips me. Ella wasn't in the garden at dinnertime. She wasn't in the library room at the end of the hall and she's not in her bedroom. When I lived here, she followed a well-defined routine. Toward the end of my stay, Ella started venturing out of our room to spend her mornings in the garden. Before lunch, we would walk silently back to our room, where I would shower after my training session with Iyana and she would slip into her bed to sleep off the effort of being outside.

According to what I know of her routine, she should be here.

I could go searching for her, but the House brought me here—just as it took me to the garden instead of back to Tristan. I fight the fear that rises inside me every time I think of him, but I remind myself that I need to trust Helen right now, that she's taking care of him for me.

I also remind myself: I am only one person.

Right now, I need to be here.

There's nothing to do but wait for Ella to return.

And clean myself up.

Opening the closet to find it contains all of the flannel shirts I could ever want as well as soft, stretchy jeans, I choose a set of clean clothing and underwear. Then I head to the bathroom.

The bath that sits on a bed of pebbles in the alcove to the right begins to fill immediately while the shower on the left turns on, filling the room with calming steam.

I carefully place the book and the three objects of magic on the side of the sink before I pull off my bloodied clothing.

Stepping into the gentle shower stream, I allow the water to run across my head, washing off the signs of my battle with my father and the Sentinel. My body doesn't wear the bruises and cuts that I had when I first came to Hidden House. I've already healed from today's fight. This time, my scars are invisible to the eye.

I let the water flow until the entire space is filled with steam. Then I cross to the bath and slide beneath the surface of the water. By the time I emerge, my eyelids are drooping. It's been twenty-four hours since I slept, and I can barely fight it.

Even so, when I find the bedroom still empty—still no Ella—I consider my options. I need to find a safe place to store the book and magical objects. The House has always provided for me, so I close my eyes for a moment and send a mental wish outward.

When I open my eyes, the first thing I see is a small wooden door built into the side of my closet. It's the size of a shoebox and positioned at eye height. Opening it, I'm grateful to find a compartment that's big enough to hold the book and objects. As soon as I close the little door, its outline disappears, undetectable again.

Now that the book is safe, my need to see Tristan rises again. I have to trust that Helen is taking care of him, but my heart pulls me in his direction. At the back of my mind is the fear that he could wake up when I'm not there.

With that thought in mind, I stumble, sleep-deprived, from the room, past the other closed doors, and make it all the way to the end of the corridor.

When I descend the stairs, I stop, staring at the library at the end of the living quarters again. The House hasn't allowed me to go anywhere. Ascending the stairs again, I exit once more into the same corridor.

I sigh as I grip the handrail at the side of the stairs.

The House really isn't allowing me to leave the living quarters. It's fucking serious about making me look after myself.

My heart tugs again, a painful sensation, the same breathlessness I felt when Tristan was in pain. Tears burn at the back of my eyes at the thought that he's alone right now, but also because the House is trying to force me to put my own needs first.

I'm barely upright by the time I make it back to my room.

Pushing open the door, I pull up short.

The configuration of the room has changed. The beds have receded, opening up the floorspace in the middle of the forest clearing, which is now covered in large cushions and blankets.

Iyana, Danika, and Maeve sit wrapped in blankets, speaking quietly while they nurse cups of what smells like hot chocolate.

They aren't alone.

My heart leaps to see the three shifters who were prisoners at the Spire, also wrapped up in blankets and hugging cups as they join in the quiet conversation. When I saw them last, I was afraid that the warlock Silas's dark magic had taken their power and sentenced them to slow deaths. Reya, the lion shifter, sits with her back to me, her golden flaxen hair streaked with pink highlights hanging loose down her back. The tattoo of a snarling lion across her upper arm peeks above the edge of the blanket that rests around her bronzed shoulders. Neve, the snow leopard with silver hair and pale blue eyes, sips her drink as she smiles at something Danika said.

Nalani, the panther shifter with olive skin and the darkest hair and eyes, sees me first, her lips curving into a smile. "She's here," she says quietly.

I sense someone—actually two someones—arrive behind me, and I turn to find Luna and Lydia waiting for me to go inside. Like the other women, their hair falls down their backs and they're wearing comfortable clothing. They sweep their tawny brown locks behind their ears, considering me quietly with their sage green eyes.

"It's about time," Lydia says with an arched eyebrow. She and her sister both struggle with time and space, evidenced by their close proximity to me, stepping into my space without blinking, although I'm certain Lydia's reference to time is deliberate.

Luna hooks her arm through mine, silently urging me inside the room, where Iyana stands up, her blanket falling to the floor as she hands me the cup of cocoa she was nursing.

"This one's for you," Iyana says with a warm smile that she follows up with a wink. "It may be laced with some kind of liqueur. I asked Ada for something with a little kick and this is what she gave me."

I bite my lip, gratitude welling inside me as I sink to a cushion between Maeve and Nalani. Luna and Lydia take up places nearby.

Maeve reaches across to wrap a blanket around my shoulders as I stare at them all. "How are you all here?"

THIS CAGED WOLF

"It was a long walk across the corridor," Danika says with a twinkle in her eye. "I wasn't sure if I'd make it, but Maeve pulled me through."

Maeve snorts, and I roll my eyes before I take a sip of the hot cocoa. My tongue warms with the taste of berries. There's definitely a kick in this drink.

When I look up, I meet Nalani's serious eyes. "We don't remember much after the fight with the witches," she says. "Except waking up two days ago in rooms that seemed to be made for us. I woke up in a tropical rainforest. Neve sleeps in a room that looks like the precipice of a snowy mountain. And Reya—"

"A hot desert," the lioness says, her amber eyes gleaming as she tips her head. "Where I can bask in the sun. Not that this forest is all that bad."

"I wasn't sure if Helen would be able to heal you," I say, focusing on my drink, afraid that if I lift my gaze, they'll see my pain. I'm trying to accept it, not push it away, but it's hard to share it. If Helen could heal these women, then she could have healed Cody. If I'd gotten him here in time.

"We don't know how Helen helped us," Neve says, her silver hair falling across her shoulders as she lowers her empty cup to the floor. "But we're happy to be alive."

"We're happy to be *here*," Reya adds.

I continue to consider my drink, then take another sip. "I'm glad you're okay."

My statement is met with silence, but it doesn't feel sharp or threatening. I blink to clear my eyes, compose my features, and take a deep breath before I look up.

Each of the women considers me with an open expression.

"We're here because of you, Tessa," Nalani says.

Reya tips her chin at me. "An alpha always looks after her pack. Am I right?"

My lips part in surprise. Especially when Lydia edges forward. "Your pack is growing, Tessa. We all want in."

"But..." I take a shaky breath, standing on the precipice of pushing them away.

I stop myself. I allow myself to feel the warmth in their smiles, the trust in their eyes. All of these beautiful, strong women. I might

179

struggle to accept their love, but I would fight to the death to protect each of them. "I'm honored."

Iyana grins at me across the way. "Put down your cups and bring it in, ladies. Even this vampire needs her beauty sleep."

I gulp the last of the warming liquid while all of the women begin bustling around me, gathering up the cups—mine last—and putting them off to the side. Then they choose cushions from what seems to be an endless supply all around the room and settle down onto the blankets in the center of the clearing, all of them piling in, staying close, as if the space were much smaller than it is.

Iyana treads lightly around them to make her way to me. Wrapping her arm around my shoulders, she drops a kiss to my forehead. "You're exhausted, sweetie."

She draws the blanket closer around my shoulders before I kick off my boots and we nudge our way in among the others.

Closing my eyes, I exhale the last of my fear.

Darkness burns inside me, but I'm not as afraid of it as I was. It felt like a rage that my father had inflicted on me, that he'd forced into existence, but now I wonder if it has layers.

As the light fades above us, the room responding to our need to sleep, I welcome the rush of rage inside myself. It's strong, burning, a violent need to act. I hold on to it, contain its wrath, and consider my power from a different angle.

How much of this rage could be driven by love?

The answer comes to me with shocking clarity.

As much as I fucking choose.

~

I wake after what feels like a full night's sleep, but I sense it's still very early morning.

A soft light glows beyond my closed eyelids, and I open them slowly to stare up at the small, hovering spark of light that dances across the air above me.

My eyes fly wide open. It's just like the Bright Ones who danced around the Sentinel and hovered in the air at the ravine.

"Where did you come from?" I whisper as it ebbs and glows, a glittering little orb no bigger than my thumb.

The dancing light hops from side to side as if it's impatient before it glides toward the door.

Around me, the room is silent and still. The deep breathing of my pack meets my ears. The women are all asleep—even Iyana, who must be suffering from some sort of vampire's jet lag, since she's normally awake all night.

Carefully extricating myself from the warm bodies around me, I creep across the room, leaving my boots behind in preference to the quiet of my bare feet.

The dancing light disappears through the closed door before I open it and follow the light's path down the corridor. The House is silently sleeping and the view from the library window sparkles even brighter as the city lights gleam in the distance.

The staircase that I turn to face leads upward and I'm suddenly filled with hope that the House will take me back to Tristan. When the orb of light heads up the stairs, I race past it, taking the steps two at a time to the first landing, but there, I stop.

A silver glow fills the air to my right and the next flight of stairs is bathed in vines so dense that I need to pick my way through them to ascend safely.

The orb flits past me, its dancing progress quicker this time. I follow it more cautiously, taking careful steps between the vines. I tell myself that I can handle whatever awaits me at the top of these steps.

Every other level of Hidden House opens into some sort of entry room with a corridor and other rooms leading off it, but not this one.

The stairs lead up into one large room.

I freeze on the last step, my breath catching at the beauty laid out in front of me. The ceiling gives way to a sky filled with stars, each one shedding light that is so pure, it's like looking up from the top of a mountain where the air is crisp and completely unpolluted. The floor is a wash of vines and flowers so thick, I'm not sure how I'll make my way through it.

In the center of the room, a woman sleeps on a pallet that could be made of stone, although it's hard to tell because it's also swathed in vines.

The moment I step into the room, the foliage covering the floor slides out of the way, clearing a path that directs me to the woman. The ground beneath sparkles like stone inlaid with millions of fine crystals.

The orb of light flits toward the woman, stopping above her, where it sways gently back and forth.

She doesn't move as I prowl toward her, my instincts suddenly on fire because I *know* her. Somehow. Some way. This woman is not a stranger to me.

As I draw nearer, her features become clear. Her hair is the purest white, so long that it flows to the floor on this side of the pallet, merging with the vines. Her skin glows as if it's lit from the inside and, while her eyes are closed, her lips are flush with life and her chest rises and falls as if she's in deep sleep. She's wearing a silver gown that reaches her ankles, while her hands are folded across her chest.

A curious weapon rests on the pallet on this side of her. Set at the top of a sturdy wooden pole that nearly reaches her height are two sharp-looking blades. One is shaped like a spike while the blade on the other side is large, curved, and carved with an emblem I don't recognize: a crescent on one side and outward spokes on the other.

"Who are you?" I whisper, even though I know I won't receive an answer.

With my next step toward her, I freeze again, because I can now see the floor on the other side of her. It's just as thickly covered in vines and flowers, but two figures lie on the vines close to the pallet.

My hand flies over my mouth and then I'm like stone, stuck to this spot, hovering at the edge of uncertainty.

The man lies facing upward, naked from the waist up, wearing long, black pants, his shoulders broad, his arms and thighs bulky while his waist is lean. His sandy blond hair is lighter than I remember, but that could be the glow from the vines swathed around his head, shoulders, arms, and legs.

The woman is curled up on her side facing him, her head on his shoulder, holding his hand, her eyes closed. Her white-blonde hair is not as pale as the locks of the woman lying on the pallet, but it's the shade of daisy petals, cascading across the floor. She's wearing a soft sweater and jeans, although her feet are bare.

Brother and sister.

Two people around whom my life has pivoted multiple times.

Cody and Ella Griffin.

CHAPTER TWENTY-FOUR

While Tristan has been an undeniable and unstoppable force in my life, Cody and Ella have been like jagged rocks in a raging river, changing my path at unexpected moments.

I want to reach for them, run to them, run *from* them.

Fuck, I don't know which.

I drop my head into my hands, trying to process their presence here.

"Life." Ella's whisper reaches me across the silence.

My head flies up.

Ella's eyes are open, although she remains with her head resting on Cody's shoulder. She considers me in her quiet way.

My lips press together, and my forehead creases, until I remember that I asked a question—one I didn't expect to be answered: *Who is this woman?*

Is Ella trying to tell me she's life? The purest form of old magic.

This woman—the woman lying here in the dark—has to be the one who hid me from my father.

Her magic also sustains this house, keeping us all safe.

My gaze follows the vine that trails from beneath the woman's hair, directly across her chest—right across the location of her heart—through her folded hands and down the other side of the pallet to twine across Cody's chest.

Walking carefully so I don't startle Ella, I make my way around the pallet to step between Cody and the woman. This time, the vines don't part for me and I find myself tiptoeing between the twisted ropes of them.

Kneeling beside Cody—between him and the pallet—I consider the glow along the vine that seems to connect him to the woman. I can't quite bring myself to look at his face or to study his torso, to consider the possibility that he might have survived.

Impossible. He died in front of me.

Ella's gaze follows my movements, but she remains silent. When I saw her last, she was only beginning to regain her speech and her ability to interact with people.

Now, her brown eyes are unexpectedly bright and intensely observant. She rises lithely to a sitting position, still holding her brother's hand, her white-blonde hair falling across her shoulder. A vine twists around her waist.

She takes a quiet breath.

"Helen told me you did everything you could for my brother."

I'm shaken by her fluent speech—more words than she's ever spoken to me before—but the magic in this room calms me. I have no doubt that this is where Helen brought the shifters who were struck down by Silas's dark magic to heal them. The purest of old magic—life itself—can restore what was lost.

My hands rest down on my knees, my head lowered.

"Helen told me you killed Mother Lavinia," Ella continues. "She was the witch who imprisoned me and forced me to kill others."

"I should have killed her sooner," I say, meeting Ella's eyes.

Her lips purse. "It's never soon enough," she says. "There is always space for regret."

Mother Lavinia kept Ella for over a year and forced her to fight and kill other prisoners. Lavinia's coven called Ella 'Daisy' because of the color of her hair, but she was apparently ruthless in a fight to the death.

I don't need my crimson vision to see the darkness in Ella's eyes now, a darkness she has been keeping in a cage. She may not have my power to separate from my wolf, but I recognize her strength of body and mind.

As if Ella follows my thoughts, she holds up her free hand and allows her claws to extend. Sharp, golden, but tipped in russet. The way the color of her claws shift from gold to bloody reminds me of the way Cody's wolf's legs looked like he'd waded through blood.

"I am a Griffin," she says. "Born from a long line of killers. My family has ruled the eastern lowland for countless generations by crushing any rebellion against us." Her incisors appear. "Now, I will be the rebellion."

I eye her warily. "What are you saying?"

"I'm saying thank you for not killing my father when you went to my home." She snarls. "Because that's *my* job."

I fight to remain calm in the face of her anger, even though the darkness inside me rises in response. I understand her pain and determination. I understand the protective way her hand tightens around her brother's palm.

"My father did this. To me and my brother." There's a metallic jangle as she shifts her arm. I spy a loop of the fine, gold bracelet she presses between their palms. One of the charms protrudes from between her fingers—a tiny canary. It's the bracelet Cody and I found while we were Mother's Lavinia's prisoners.

"What happened on the night you were taken?" I ask. "The night that Tristan promised to challenge his father?"

Ella's eyes gleam, her wolf revealing itself further in the way her irises change to a paler shade of caramel, flecked with gold in the way that Cody's eyes used to change.

"That night has repeated on me so many times." She exhales quietly and, for a moment, I see the cracks again, the fragility of her state of mind. "My father wouldn't let us enter the house. He stood on the steps with his guards behind him until Tristan took a knee—and then my father prowled around Tristan, trying to goad him into a fight. Jace was standing beside me, both of us watching Tristan's back. And I remember Cody..." Her gaze lowers to her brother, but I refuse to follow the line of her sight, refuse to find out if he's alive, because I'm not ready to know.

"Cody was standing to the side and he was really quiet. Really still," Ella says. "At the time, I thought he disapproved of my decision to join Tristan's pack—that he was judging me—but now I see it differently. He was worried, angry at me, feeling betrayed, afraid of what our father might do. All these complicated things."

She clears her throat. "When my father couldn't goad Tristan into a fight, he finally agreed that if Tristan could achieve the impossible—take over his pack that night—then an alliance would be formed. Tristan got back to his feet, I took a final look at my family home, and then we drove across town."

"What happened when Tristan confronted his father?"

"His father was in Coward mode," she says. "He was literally huddling in a corner of the meeting hall at the tower when we found him. He didn't put up a fight at all when Tristan challenged him. It seemed like a dream come true until we heard Tristan's mother screaming in the next room. That's when we discovered the real reason why Tristan's father was so afraid."

Ella stops speaking. Her claws retract and she reaches for her brother's arm, as if she's anchoring herself. I want to cross the distance between her and me, but the gap feels unreasonably far, the air too charged to move.

"I recognized Ford Vanguard because of his dealings with my father," Ella says. "He was holding Tristan's mother by her hair, a knife to her throat. I was slightly in front of Tristan and I started to run, to shift, but a power hit me from the side, and it—"

She gasps, clutching at her chest as if in remembered pain. "It was like being torn up from the inside. I found myself on the floor, screaming, just screaming, as I stared up into the eyes of a white wolf I'd never seen before. He was like no supernatural I'd come across, all light and shadow, pure energy. He leaped off me... I managed to turn... Tristan's mother was falling and Tristan was trying to stop the blood..."

She inhales a shaky breath. "I made it to my feet. Jace was coming for me, but Ford knocked into me first, snatched me up, wrenched me off my feet. Jace shifted and went right for him, but the white wolf attacked Jace in the same way he attacked me, and Jace was shouting for me, roaring my name, trying to get to me..."

Her lips draw back. "Ford dragged me out of there. I fought him. I shifted. I clawed and bit him. I nearly tore his hand off. All he did was laugh and tell me I was perfect for his plans. Then everything got cold and I blacked out."

"Brynjar," I say. "The ice jotunn must have taken hold of you."

"Yes," she says. "The ice giant was the perfect soldier."

Inwardly, I sigh. Brynjar is loyal to my father to a fault. A creature of old magic whose power overcame me multiple times.

"I woke up muzzled and hog-tied in the back of a van, but the doors were open, so I could see outside," Ella says. "My father was there."

My jaw clenches. Any remaining doubt I had about Baxter Griffin's motives and involvement in Ella's captivity disappear. "Cody was right. Your father knew you were alive all along."

"My father asked Ford what would happen to me. Ford told my father that I would never come home. My father could rest assured that he was safe from the threat of an alliance with Tristan that would weaken my father's position." Ella's eyes are hard again. "My father said, 'Good' and then he walked away."

Ella lowers her gaze to her brother, the charms on her bracelet clinking gently as she adjusts her position. "I think you've pieced together the rest."

I bite my lip, unsure how to ask the question about Ella that burns inside my mind now. "When I left, you were..."

"Broken," she says. "After Tristan found me, I broke all of the ties with my old life. I retreated completely, took deliberate steps to lose myself, to deconstruct every part of myself that still existed, because I couldn't reconcile what I became with who I used to be. I was once kind. Thoughtful. Compassionate." She shakes her head. "By the end, I killed without thought."

"You had no choice—"

"Didn't I?" She glares at me. "We all have a choice. It was me or them. That's the choice. Nobody chooses their own death. Except... *maybe*... you."

She pauses, her glare fading. "When Helen brought my brother to Hidden House, I was on my way to the garden and instead, the House brought me up here."

She tips her head back with a soft, sad laugh. "Oh, this house. It's hidden, but it's not for hiding in. It forces you to face what you don't want to face."

Ella inclines her head at the sleeping woman behind me. "*She* forces you to face your truths. The moment I stepped into this room, everything I had worked so hard to deconstruct started reforming in my mind. All the memories I wanted to forget. All the rage and pain. And now... here we both are. At the edge of leaping off the cliffs we've both dreaded."

I finally lower my gaze to Cody. My hand shakes uncontrollably as I hover my palm above his chest.

"Is Cody...?"

Alive?

Ella's expression hardens and her free hand snaps out. She grabs my hovering palm and forces it down onto Cody's chest above his heart—directly beneath the position of the vine that twines over him.

"You tell me," she says.

His chest is unmoving beneath my palm. Not rising. Not falling.

But... his skin is warm.

"I don't understand." Inhaling a shaky breath, I do the only thing I can, harnessing my crimson vision, searching for life signs. The glow of power streaming through the vine that runs across his chest is so bright, it nearly masks the faint flicker inside his heart. It's the smallest glow of power, not much bigger than a pinprick. It's the same glow I saw in his heart when he leaped at Silas and tried to stop him.

"He's alive," I whisper, my heart thudding painfully in my chest.

"But not awake," she says. "The three female shifters Helen brought back were healed within the first day of being surrounded by this woman's power. But not my brother."

She clamps her hand over her mouth to smother a sob. "He won't wake up." Her shoulders hunch. "I hoped that maybe if he heard your voice..."

I consider Cody carefully. "What about his wolf?"

"I don't know. I can't sense it."

Neither can I.

Exhaling my uncertainty, I lean over him.

I nudge my cheek to his like he did to me each morning we woke up together in the Spire. With my face inches from his, my jaw clenches and my vision turns crimson again, my darkness rising and my energy tingling beneath the surface of my skin like electricity. My power is seconds away from releasing from my body in the form of a wolf. Not calming or healing this time, but dangerous and deadly.

"What are you doing?" Ella's question is sharp. Alarmed.

Her arm snakes out again across the distance, attempting to push me away from her brother, but I snatch her hand into my fist, stopping and holding her with a threatening growl.

Claws form on my hand where I grip Cody's shoulder, digging into his skin as I return my focus to him.

I lower my cheek to his again, my power making my skin hot. The curtain of my hair falls to either side of his face.

"Cody Griffin," I growl into his ear. "I know you hate mornings, but *wake the fuck up.*"

CHAPTER TWENTY-FIVE

The glow inside Cody's heart flares like a struck match. Golden power strikes through his chest and shoulders, up his neck and into his head, burning so brightly that the breath stops in my chest. Ella jolts backward, out of my reach, where I let her go, allowing me to lower my palm to Cody's other shoulder.

His eyes fly open.

His pupils constrict, then widen, then constrict again. His hickory-brown irises are flecked with gold, but the flecks don't shift like they would if his wolf were present.

My crimson vision confirms for me that he is… completely human.

He focuses intently on my face, only inches from his now. His voice is scratchy. "Tessa?"

"Cody." I allow my crimson vision to fade. My voice drops to a whisper. "Welcome back."

He squints up at me. "What the hell happened?"

I allow myself to smile. "You tried to kill Silas, which was either really heroic or just fucking stupid. I haven't decided which."

He sucks in a breath. "The warlock! And the witches—?"

"Dead. All dead. You're safe. Completely safe. And somehow… healed."

"But you aren't," he says, studying me. "What's happened? What's wrong?"

"Don't worry about me." My eyes fill as I continue to lean over him, and I don't stop the tears before they drop from my cheeks to his. He follows the tear tracks down my face, but I quickly say, "New alpha rule, remember? Crying is allowed."

His forehead creases. "I don't know where the fuck I am, but once again, I find myself lying on my back and unable to move in your presence, Tessa Dean."

I attempt a smirk. "At least you're wearing pants this time."

Retracting my claws, I brush my fingers across his cheek. "How do you feel, Cody?"

His gaze becomes introspective. I wait patiently for him to answer, studying him intently.

"Stronger," he says, but his forehead creases. "Calmer."

"Maybe not as much of an asshole then," I say.

I finally sweep the curtain of my hair aside and rise back up into a kneeling position, allowing Cody to see the room around him.

His focus falls immediately on his sister. "Ella."

"Brother." Her lips tremble and she quickly presses them together, folding her hands and hunching her shoulders as if she's determined to contain her feelings.

Cody once again proves just how mobile he is, despite asserting otherwise, by lurching up into a sitting position and wrapping his arms around her.

"I thought you were dead," they say in unison.

"Fuck," Cody says, holding her tightly. "Ella, if I thought for a second you were alive, I would have come for you."

"The witches would have killed you," she says, tears slipping down her cheeks. "Only Tristan could get me out of there alive. It took him a year to find me because they kept moving me, but he never gave up." She grips Cody's shoulders hard. "Our father—"

"I know," he says, his expression hardening. "I know, Ella."

Her head sinks into the crook of his neck. "What are we going to do?"

Cody meets my eyes over the top of Ella's head. "First, we're going to heal," he says. "We're alive, and I won't ever take that for granted again."

I slip quietly to my feet. Cody and Ella have a lot to talk about and it's not my place to stay. I pause at the foot of the pallet to briefly contemplate the sleeping woman. She didn't stir or react in any way while I was here.

I hate myself a little when I undertake a visual check to see if she's wearing any jewelry or holding anything that could be an object of old magic. The weapon lying beside her is a possibility, but when I hover my hand over it... my instincts tell me it isn't what I need. It's not old magic.

"Tessa?" Cody draws my attention back to him and Ella before I can step away from the pallet.

"Yeah?"

"Am I still your beta?" he asks.

Cody wanted to be in my den, was prepared for me to be his alpha, but that was before he knew that his sister was alive.

I consider Ella for a moment—her expression is open, her eyes glistening, but she doesn't try to make any claim on her brother. I return my focus to Cody. "You're completely free to decide that for yourself whenever you choose. I think your family needs you right now."

As I pick my final steps through the wash of vines covering the floor, I glance around at this room that I'll probably never be allowed to enter again.

When I reach the landing, but before I turn the corner, I murmur aloud. "Okay, house. I've done what you wanted. I've eaten. I've slept. I've trusted. I can't be separated from Tristan for another moment."

I close my eyes and whisper, "I need him because *I* need *him*. Not because he needs me."

It's a truth that has been a long time dawning. Tristan has needed me right from the start. He needs me now, too. I've made a lot of choices based on what others need from me.

But now... I'm choosing for me because even with all of Tristan's mind-fuckery, he's the one who challenges, matches, and tames all of the darkness, shadows, and rage inside me. He's the one I want and this house had better not keep me from him any longer.

Rounding the corner to see what awaits me, I heave out a moan of relief.

The corridor to the medical wing is finally in front of me.

Racing down the steps, I'm vaguely aware of the first rays of sunlight breaking across the city visible through the window opposite the stairs.

My footsteps are whisper-quiet as I run directly into the room where I left him.

I pull up sharply. "Fuck!"

When I left this room, Tristan was lying on the medical examination table behind solid metal bars that turned that side of the room into a cage.

Now, the table lies on its side at an angle that allows me to see either side of it.

The cage door hangs ajar, its hinges broken.

Tristan is gone.

CHAPTER TWENTY-SIX

*D*ashing from the room, I scan the corridor again before I hurry along it, opening every door to check inside each room.

They're all empty.

He's not here.

If it weren't for the broken cage, I could imagine that Helen had moved him somewhere and hadn't told me yet, but the state of the room indicates either that he broke the cage on his own or that he fought his way free.

I shudder at the possibility that he could have hurt someone.

He could be anywhere inside the House now. Or he could have left already.

I take a deep breath because I'm determined not to let go of the calm I've found inside myself—the acceptance of anger and fear that I'm coming to terms with.

Accepting the hammer of my heartbeat in my chest, I stop in the middle of the corridor. Tristan once broke through the lock that Helen placed on Hidden House—or rather, he broke through the lock that Hidden House created around itself. I haven't tried forcing my own will against the House—and I don't want to—but maybe it will let me now that the safety of others is at risk.

Carefully, I harness my crimson vision, drawing on the deep dark inside me, controlling my power.

"Show me your secrets," I whisper.

I sense the House pushing back, the resistance as my power collides with its protective mechanisms—the protections that once afforded me the privacy and security that I needed.

"I need this," I say, my heart hurting. "I need to find Tristan. For *me*."

There's another moment of pause.... Then the walls burst into streams of light, the entire space responding to my wish by gleaming with magic, all of the pulses that knit together to form the building around me. It's more beautiful and powerful than I ever imagined, a glistening, living wash of starlight that thrums through me like energy coursing through my body.

After scanning the rooms around me, I lower my gaze to the floor, seeking the levels below me. I finally have a sense of the entire twenty floors of the House and—surprisingly—the different powers of its inhabitants. All of the women are bright streams of magic, though some are brighter than others.

I locate Helen in the garden, her power like a burning star—despite being muted within these walls. I see my pack and all of their various powers—all of them loyal and brave.

I choose not to look up to the level of the House above me where the woman in the dark lies, since I'm certain that her power will blind me.

But Tristan... *Where is he?*

I expand my scan of the House, but I don't see him anywhere.

Frustration rises inside me, but if Tristan can break into this place, he can also break out.

He's left the House, and I can't find him alone.

Shutting down my crimson vision, I race along the corridor, calling out, "Take me to my pack."

One flight of stairs down and I reach the living quarters again.

I keep my footsteps quiet as I race along the corridor. I don't want to alarm anyone else.

Stopping to take a breath, I push open my door.

The women of my pack are already awake, although the sky above the branches remains sunless for Iyana's safety. A table laden with toast, orange juice, and bottled water has appeared at the side of the clearing, but it doesn't look like they've touched it yet.

Reya—the lioness—and Maeve sit closest to me. Reya is braiding Maeve's ash-colored hair in a way that accentuates the violet streaks in it. On the far side, Danika is raiding my wardrobe, which suddenly seems to be full of everyone's favorite clothing—not just my flannel shirts and jeans.

Iyana and Neve—the snow leopard—are already dressed, while Nalani—the panther—has just taken a set of clothing from Danika and looks like she's about to head to the bathroom. On the other side of the room, Luna and Lydia are flicking cards into the air, controlling the flight of the cards so that they flit expertly between and around Iyana, Danika, Neve, and Nalani.

Neve proves her quick reflexes by snatching one of the cards out of the air, but she flicks it right back to Luna with a grin, as if this were part of the game. Luna deftly catches it, returns it to the pack of cards she's holding, and throws another into the air.

I take a moment as I hover in the shadow of the doorway, taking in the quiet scene. My heart aches in a way that I'm not familiar with. They are all safe and cared for here. Despite their short association, they seem to care for each other in a way I wasn't expecting.

I don't want to break their peace, but I need their help.

Asking is a new step for me. A hard step. It means being vulnerable, but I'm ready to try.

The moment I step into the room, the women look up and over at me, and the tug inside my chest grows stronger.

"I need your help," I say.

Maeve jumps to her feet with Reya beside her. "Of course. What do you need?"

At the same time, Iyana dashes forward with Neve close behind. They are such distinct opposites, Iyana's hair as black as coal while Neve's is silvery. Behind them, the other women quickly gather.

"What's wrong?" Iyana asks.

I have the attention of every woman in this room and the tug inside my chest becomes a strong pull. They seem to feel it too, all of them suddenly pausing, their foreheads creasing, some of them pressing their palms to their chests.

Only Danika moves. She steps forward in a way that indicates she seems to understand what we're all feeling.

"Damn," she whispers. "You're really our alpha now."

I press the heel of my hand against my heart. "What...?"

A smile breaks across her face, lighting up her hazel eyes. "We're bonded. Not like a mate bond. A pack bond."

Neve raises her eyebrows in a questioning look. "But... we're all different species. How can this happen?"

Danika gives a gentle shrug. "Anyone can be pack. Right, Tessa?"

I bite my lip. "That's right."

The tension in my shoulders eases, and I allow the sensation in my chest to build. Danika said I needed a little glue to put my heart back together, and it turns out these women have given me a shitload of it. I exhale quietly against the sense of responsibility I'm taking for their lives now.

"Tristan is missing," I say. "He's not at Hidden House. I need your help to find him."

Iyana is poised on her front foot, as if she were fighting her instinct to run after him right away. "Where is he likely to go?"

"If I had to guess—back to the forest," I say. "We were free there."

Maeve blows out an exhale. "Finding him in the forest will be impossible."

"What about his pack?" Danika asks. "Would he go back to them?"

I stiffen. It's a potentially horrifying thought. Tristan's father devastated the pack while he was under the sway of the three minds. As I cast my gaze over the trusting faces of the women around me, my stomach sinks with the realization that pack members are the easiest prey.

Luna steps forward, her cheeks fully flushed, and Lydia says, "We can help you find him. Will you let us try?"

"Of course," I say.

The other women step clear as Luna and Lydia turn to face each other. Taking a breath and focusing on the space between themselves, they throw the entire pack of cards they're each holding into the air. The cards scatter upward and then stop, suspended, each one spinning in place while Luna and Lydia turn their palms upward beneath the cards.

Danika draws closer to me while the sisters work. "This is one of the ways we attempted to find you when you disappeared," she says, keeping her voice low in the quiet room. "The twins' magic is strong, but it couldn't get through the old magic that was trapping you. If Tristan is anywhere in the city, they'll find him."

The cards begin to arrange themselves, some of them joining together while others separate. My eyes widen as the flurry of cards becomes so frenzied that it resembles a storm, the wind building around it, buffeting at Luna and Lydia, who stand firm. Within moments, all of the cards have pulled into the shape of a circle, spinning around in the air while a single card remains suspended in the center.

Luna steps beneath it and holds out her hand, palm up.

The card falls into her hand.

A second later, the other cards fly toward each sister, one by one, so fast that they come together in a cascade. The twins close their fists around their respective packs of cards.

They raise their eyes to me, the intense concentration on their faces fading.

Luna crosses the distance to press the single card she caught into my hand.

It depicts a glowing fireplace with a flame that flickers on the surface of the paper.

"It's the hearth card," Lydia says, communicating for her sister. "Tristan is trying to go home."

"To the clock tower," I murmur. "To his pack. We need to hurry." I turn to the women. "Get ready as fast as you can. Pack food and clothing. We don't know where this path will take us. Make sure you eat, too. You need to be strong."

After handing the card back to Luna and patting her shoulder in thanks, I hurry to the bathroom to splash my face and take a breath.

When I exit the bathroom, all of the women have finished dressing in various versions of jeans, T-shirts, and sweaters, and now they're standing around a duffel bag on the floor in the center of the room.

The bag is full of weapons—daggers and guns of all sizes—along with harnesses for each of the women. Danika crouches by the bag, handing out firearms and blades in between snatching bites of a piece of toast that she grips between her teeth to keep her hands free.

Iyana approaches me with two daggers, a weapon harness to loop around my waist, and two pieces of toast pressed together like a sandwich. "You can eat it faster this way," she says with a smile.

She also flips a plastic card into her hands to show me. It's a security pass into the clock tower where Tristan's pack lives.

I breathe a sigh of relief. "You kept it."

"Are you kidding? These passes are worth gold. Danika still has hers, too. We'll be able to access the garage under the building as well as the secure levels, including Tristan's penthouse."

Grateful that we'll be able to enter the building, I gobble the food Iyana brought me, drown the toast with quick gulps of orange juice, and multitask by strapping on the weapon harness.

Then I rummage in the bottom of my closet for a pouch to carry the objects of magic. I find a little velvet bag that looks like it once held jewelry. While my friends are occupied with getting ready, I quietly press my hand against the far side of the closet. The little door reappears at my touch, and I retrieve the magical objects from within the hidden compartment.

I leave the book of old magic where it is before I close the door, which promptly disappears again. I have what I need from its pages and now I can only trust that the House will keep it safe.

After tying the little bag to my weapon harness tightly enough that it won't bang against me when I move, I look up to find my pack waiting for me.

They're all dressed for battle, carrying varying combinations of guns and knives—except for Luna and Lydia, who slip their cards into pouches at their waist, and Maeve, whose hands are already weaponized.

Iyana activates her protective suit as I watch, and I'm grateful that she'll be able to come with us without fear of sunlight.

My heart swells that these women are prepared to back me up, even if it could mean going up against Tristan in his Killer mode.

"We're ready," Danika says.

"Okay, then." I stride ahead of my pack and they keep pace with me as we exit the room and hurry down the corridor.

The moment we turn the corner at the library room at the end of the hallway, I pull to an abrupt stop.

Ella pauses on the bottom step from the level above while Cody takes the final step into the library room slightly ahead of her.

It's the first time I've seen them standing side by side and I'm struck, not only by the family resemblance, but also by the way they both square their shoulders, both powerful in their own ways.

Fuck, we've come a long way since I first met them.

"You're leaving," Ella says, her perceptive brown eyes taking us all in. "In a hurry."

A quick glance at Iyana and Danika on my right, and Luna and Lydia on my left, tells me that they're already aware of Ella's healing progress, since none of them appear surprised to see her conversing with me right now.

"Tristan's gone," I say, keeping to the facts and forcing myself to be objective. "He's injured. Dying. He's headed back to his pack. We need to find him before he hurts anyone." My hand instinctively closes around the pouch at my waist.

Cody immediately steps forward. He's still wearing black jeans, but he's pulled on a T-shirt. "I'm coming with you, Tessa."

I shake my head. "That's incredibly dangerous—"

He levels his gaze with mine, immediately challenging my fear. "I realize that Tristan's pack will see me as a threat. It's time for me to atone for the conflict and pain that my father has caused. I can't do that from afar. I need to build the bridges that Tristan once tried to build." He takes a deep breath, his chest rising and falling. "No matter what it takes."

Before I can voice further concern, Cody turns to Ella and wraps her up in his arms. "You're safe here," he says to her. "It's time for us to make different choices for our future. When you're ready —whenever that is—I'll make sure there's a den waiting for you."

When Cody and I were trapped at the Spire, he told me that he, Ella, and other members of his pack had formed their own den, and that Ella had been the one who'd held them together. He said they'd fallen apart when she'd been gone. He wanted me in his den—he thought he could recreate what he'd lost. Now, it looks like he's determined to do just that.

Her head is bent to his shoulder, but when he pulls away, she grips his arms. "I'm coming with you, Cody."

"Now?" He pauses, searching her eyes. "Are you sure?"

She nods. "I can't stay hidden anymore. I have to make things right." Releasing him, she presses her palms together and worries at her lip. "I have to fix what I broke."

My forehead creases, slightly wary. I'm not sure what she's talking about. *She* is the broken one.

Cody considers her carefully, and I sense his worry, but he says, "I'll be right beside you. Every step. I promise."

Ella holds her head high before she takes a deep breath and places a determined expression on her face. "I hope you have enough vehicles to transport all of us, Tessa."

I sure as fuck don't, but Helen will.

I tip my head back and call out. "Helen! We need you!"

∽

Ten minutes later, all of the members of my pack are piling into three SUVs in the garage beneath Hidden House. Cody, Ella, Iyana, and Danika will ride with me. Luna and Lydia will go with Neve, while Maeve is traveling with Reya and Nalani.

Helen speaks privately with Ella at the side of the garage while we pack extra duffel bags of supplies and weapons into the trunk of each vehicle. Cody pauses at the rear of the SUV we'll travel in. He stays out of our way while he quietly observes the way my pack works together.

He hasn't officially met any of the women and there hasn't been time for introductions, but his focus falls most often on Danika. During the fight with the witches, she was positioned in the trees. She didn't make an appearance until after he was hurt. He hasn't met her before today.

Focused on her task beside me, Danika takes a quick inventory of the duffel bag containing her rifles before she zips up the bag and steps around the side of the vehicle. She stops before she collides with Cody.

"You're quiet," she says, tipping her head back to narrow her eyes at him. She's more than a head shorter than him, her tousled, light brown hair tied up in a loose topknot. The golden flecks in her hazel eyes grow brighter as she stares at him. When we were dressing this morning, she chose jeans that are ripped across the left calf and a short-sleeved T-shirt that reveals the lower half of the bird's wing tattoo stretching down her left bicep. It also leaves her scar on display.

He considers her tattoo and then her eyes. "You're a hawk?" he asks.

It's not a bad guess since the tattoo could indicate another sort of bird shifter—or any supernatural with wings.

"And you're human," she snaps, unusually combative. "I hope you know how to fight without your wolf."

She reaches for the door handle and he immediately steps out of her way, but he appears neither insulted nor provoked when she closes the door.

"Challenge accepted," I hear him murmur as he rounds the vehicle behind me to wait for Ella.

The rest of my pack is safely inside the vehicles when Ella finally heads toward us with Helen at her side.

Helen reaches for my hand before I can enter the front passenger side. I sense the sudden silence around us that indicates she has used her power to give us privacy. "Do you remember what I told you when you left this house last time, Tessa?"

I allow myself a small smile. I remember her final words to me like it was moments ago. "You told me to guard my heart and protect myself. To be calm. To stay in control."

"Also that these doors will always be open to you," Helen says. She drops my hand to take hold of both of my shoulders, leveling her gaze with mine. "Today, I want to tell you something more."

Her eyes are soft gray, hiding all the power she controls. "When you face the monstrous wolf, remember who your father really was." The corners of her mouth turn down and her eyes harden. "Give that monstrous wolf every fucking pain he deserves."

My lips part in surprise, but Helen grips me harder.

"You have all the strength you need, Tessa. Your future is yours. All you have to do is claim it."

Releasing me, she steps back and the silence breaks around us.

"I will," I say.

I have so many broken hopes, but this is a promise I intend to keep.

CHAPTER TWENTY-SEVEN

The three SUVs exit the garage into the early morning light. Iyana doesn't drive as recklessly as she did when we brought Tristan here, ensuring that we aren't separated from the other two vehicles following behind us.

My ears *pop* like the last time I left the House, all of the sensory input from the world outside rushing in.

I quickly twist in my seat to make sure Ella is okay. She has lived in the House for three years and will find the outside world a lot to deal with.

She sits with her eyes closed, taking deep breaths. She grips Danika's hand on her left and Cody's hand on her right while they lean in on either side of her in a way that will give her a sense of being anchored.

I decide not to speak, since any sudden sound could break her concentration.

The corner of Cody's mouth hitches up into a half-smile as he appraises me.

Cody saw me at my most vulnerable at the Spire, stood beside me while I locked wills with my—

I stop myself. *Not* my father.

While I locked wills with Ford Vanguard.

Cody didn't see what happened to me after the fight with

Mother Lavinia's coven, the consequences of the fear and pain I felt. The fact that Cody is alive at all is hard for me to comprehend. It's even harder for me to process how I reacted to losing him.

I slaughtered a coven of witches.

I shiver at what I would do if I lost Iyana... or Danika... or Ella... or any of the women in my pack. My friends.

Or Tristan.

My jaw clenches.

Fuck, no. I won't lose Tristan.

Lowering my gaze, I turn back to the front and focus on scanning the streets we pass. The twins weren't sure if Tristan had already reached his pack, only that he was going there. I appreciate that Iyana is taking the most direct route—the one Tristan would have taken on foot. The streets of Portland are waking up, filling with cars, the footpaths busier with every passing minute as we head into the heart of the city west of the river.

A half-naked man with a chest full of wounds would be sure to attract attention, but nothing appears out of the ordinary around us.

By the time we're close to the clock tower, I'm on edge, my senses at full swing. I'm wary of using my crimson vision in full view of humans—even from behind the SUV's tinted windows—so I expand my senses to their full extent instead.

The closer we get to the clock tower, the more my senses prickle, but I'm not entirely sure if it's because Tristan is near or for another reason. Rapidly scanning the shadows in the alleys we pass, I'm intensely conscious of the fact that this city is not only dominated by wolf shifters, but by assassins—assassins who can blur into their surroundings and make themselves invisible to the eye.

By the time we approach the garage under the clock tower, I'm intensely conscious of the black-clad shifters—members of Tristan's pack, I hope—who watch us carefully as we pass. Even from a distance, I can see how agitated they are, some huddled together, some pacing the street.

"Tristan must be here," I say.

Even if I didn't sense his presence like a punch to the head, the agitation of the shifters on the street tells me all is not right. If he's given them orders that they don't want to follow, it would explain why they're so unsettled.

"Be ready," I say.

Iyana scans her security pass the moment we turn off the street toward the garage door to the left at the base of the clock tower. As soon as the door opens, she drives through as fast as she can to allow the other two SUVs to follow us before the door closes.

The moment we pass through, the shifters on the street race toward the garage door, but it closes behind the third SUV before they reach it.

The lighting inside the garage is dim, but it's bright enough to see the scene near the elevator on the far side.

Jace stands in front of the elevator, blocking it, while Tristan prowls back and forth only a few paces away from him. Tristan's claws are fully descended and his back, shoulders, and biceps are pumped and corded.

Fuck.

Jace's chances of facing off with the Killer and surviving are low. Maybe he did it while Tristan's father was alive—I don't know—but the Killer in Tristan's body is undeniably strong. Pure violence and rage. The only saving grace is that it hurts the Killer to shift, so he's unlikely to take his wolf form, but he's dangerous enough in his human form.

Jace's focus shifts briefly to the vehicles and he jolts visibly.

I'm certain he will have sensed Ella's presence, since they once had a true mate bond.

The moment Jace is distracted, the Killer leaps forward, fist swinging. Jace barely manages to avoid the worst of the blow, the Killer's knuckles catching him at the edge of his jaw, knocking him off-balance. Before Jace can regain his feet, the Killer's claws spear through his shoulder, the Killer's other hand wraps around Jace's neck, and it looks like he's prepared to rip Jace's head off.

He killed Mother Lavinia in the same way.

"No!" My scream splits the silence inside the vehicle, but it's joined by Ella's shout.

"Jace!" She leaps across Cody's lap, elbowing him in the stomach in her panic to reach for the door handle on that side. I don't see what happens between them next because I'm already wrenching my door open.

"Tessa! Fuck!" Iyana shouts, unable to slam on the brakes while the other two vehicles follow so closely behind us or she'll cause a pile-up.

I fight the force of the car's momentum as I shove against the door. With a heave, I leap through before the door slams shut behind me and Iyana swerves into the nearest parking space.

I hit the pavement hard, roll, and leap to my feet, running straight at the next SUV. Vaulting across its hood as it screeches to a halt, I sprint toward the Killer and Jace.

I'm not alone.

Ella runs faster than I expected, several steps ahead of me because she exited from the side of the vehicle closer to the fight. Her hair flies out behind her and her arms pump, her muscles straining, her focus intense as I draw nearly level with her—more intense than I've ever seen her.

She reaches the fight first.

Throwing herself at the Killer, she knocks against his side using the full force of the side of her body—shoulder, hip, and thigh. Her leap is high enough that her elbow crunches into his jaw, a full body assault on him.

The Killer goes down, taking Jace with him, but the Killer's claws retract, releasing Jace from his hold. As the Killer hits the pavement on all fours, Jace wrenches free, stumbling backward, a shout on his lips. "Ella! No!"

Jace is right in front of me, blood streaming down his injured shoulder, while Ella and the Killer are on my right. Plowing toward Jace, I use my momentum to scoop my arm around his chest and propel him away from the fight.

"Stay clear!" I shout at him before I spin back to Ella and the Killer.

In the distance, my pack is running toward us, Cody and Danika at the front.

Directly in front of me, the Killer launches to his feet, attempting to tackle Ella, but she jumps upward and twists to the left. The moment he narrowly misses grabbing her, she drops her full body weight, driving her elbow into his spine and crashing

207

down on him. In the next second, she wrenches his outstretched arm backward, forcing him into a painful twist that exposes his upper chest, where she slashes him with her claws. All the while, she doesn't make a sound, her focus unwavering.

Holy fuck. She's merciless.

It's a side of Ella I've never seen. The witches kept her as their prime warrior—a winner of fights and spoils. I catch my breath, the quietest inhale, as I recognize the absence of emotion in her expression for what it is.

She's not really here.

She's back at the coven, fighting another prisoner, fighting for survival, and the violence doesn't belong to her. The violence belongs to… someone else.

"Ella!" Jace roars from behind me, ignoring my order to stay put as he lurches forward.

He steps into my fist as I spin toward him with a punch that knocks him backward.

"I said, *stay clear!*" I shout at him.

"No!" he roars. "She can't beat him. He'll kill her!"

I push at Jace again, fighting him as he struggles to get past me. "Trust me, Jace. I won't let that happen."

He meets my eyes for the second it takes for him to believe me. My heart is already in my throat and fear is tearing me to pieces. The longer I'm distracted, the more chances there are for the Killer to hurt Ella, no matter how hard she fights.

Spinning back to them, I find my pack surrounding the area, ready to jump in, just like Jace is. Cody is poised at the edge of the fight, while Danika is already removing her shirt, preparing to shift into her hawk form. Iyana races up behind them, her fangs descended, dagger held in her hand.

My darkness rises, my power streaming through my torso, arms, and legs as I harness my crimson vision.

"Stay clear!" I roar at my pack, my command so loud, so guttural that it makes them flinch.

The Killer jolts at the sound of my voice—but it doesn't stop him. As Ella aims a series of savage punches at his face, appearing to have the upper hand, he ignores the impact of her hits, wrapping his arms around her torso and lifting her off her feet.

She screams as his powerful arms squeeze so tightly around her that he could break her ribs, puncture her lungs...

I'm already running toward him, calculating the moments, the angle of his shoulders, the position of Ella's arms and chest within his hold.

I release my wolf, my fur dark, eyes glowing red. My wolf form leaps for the Killer's exposed side. My wolf's head becomes substantial the moment she touches him, her teeth piercing his jeans and sinking into his hip. My human form reaches him a split second later, my extended claws aimed precisely for the wound across his shoulder.

He seems oblivious to my wolf's teeth, but the moment my claw pierces the wound, he roars with pain, the blood draining from his face in a rush.

He drops Ella as the impact of my attack forces him—and me—away from her.

I retract my claws as fast as I can. My only purpose was to make him let Ella go, and I've achieved that. I pull my wolf back to my body in the same moment, merging with her again as I take advantage of the Killer's moment of agony to drive him to his knees. "Stay the fuck down!"

He prepares to rise, but I grab him. Dropping my body onto his, I wrap my legs around him, my arms around his chest. "You will stop!"

He struggles, attempting to stand, but I extend my claws with a snap and point them at his wound. *"You will stop!"*

His angry eyes meet mine, sharp, crisp, green, filled with rage.

And pain.

Half-risen, holding on to me while I hold on to him, he stumbles backward and bumps into the garage wall. The impact jars us both while my knees hit and scrape against the rough surface.

"Stop, Tristan," I whisper. "You don't want to do this."

He tries to find purchase against the wall with one hand but can't, sliding down toward the hard concrete pavement while I remain wrapped around him.

Sensing his resolve to continue fighting slip, I drop my center of gravity to urge him faster to the ground.

He ends up pressed against the wall, knees bent under himself.

He's wrapped in my arms, his face close to mine. He's partially turned to the side—far enough that I can see what's happening only a few paces away from us.

Ella fell to her knees when the Killer dropped her. She's gasping for breath, gripping her side where he must have bruised her. It's only been moments since I forced him to let her go and already her head snaps up to focus on him again.

With a scream that chills me, she throws herself at us, her claws descended.

My eyes fly wide. I prepare to defend myself when—

Thwack!

Jace tackles her from the side, lifting her off her feet, carrying her backward before he stops in the middle of the floor, holding her while my pack backs away to give them space.

Cody appears incredibly calm as his gaze passes from me to Ella, and I'm reminded of the way he picked me up when I panicked at the Spire—when I was afraid of what I was becoming. He looks at his sister in the same calm, accepting way now.

In the center of the floor, Ella struggles to free herself from Jace's hold, her focus still on the Killer.

She pummels at Jace with her fists, kicks with her legs. "I have to finish it!" she screams. "I have to finish him—"

"Or what?" Jace shouts. "What will happen if you don't?"

"I have to!" she screams.

"*Why?*" he roars. "*Why, Ella?*"

"Because…" Her chest heaves so hard that each breath is a shriek, but she focuses on him, so suddenly, so sharply, that it takes my breath away. She seems to see him for the first time since she jumped from the vehicle. "Because I'm a killer, Jace. Just like him."

Jace is like stone—frozen for seconds that stretch out painfully as she remains in his arms.

The entire space around us is deathly silent, nobody moving. Even Tristan is quiet where I continue to hold him.

The ferocity slowly drains from Ella's face as she continues to focus on Jace, her once-true-mate. Her lips press and un-press, her breathing shaky.

He allows her to slip to the ground, opening his arms to let her step away. Despite his open arms, she continues to lean into him, her face turned up, her hickory-brown eyes never leaving his face.

"Ella." His chest rises and falls, heaving in and out. He takes hold of her shoulders, pushing against her, as if he's trying to push her away from himself.

When she answers his push by finally stepping back, he winces. He presses his palm across his heart. He hunches his shoulders, a groan passing through his lips. It's such a painful sound that I feel it in my own body.

"I let you go," he says to her. "When Tristan found you and brought you back, you told me to walk away. So I walked away. You told me to let you go, so I let you go—"

"I'm sorry." Her voice is whisper-quiet, but it silences him.

Her eyes fill with tears. She reaches for him, her hands hovering in front of his torso, his shoulders, reaching for his face but not touching him.

"I'm sorry, Jace. I am... so sorry." Her voice breaks when his green eyes meet hers. "I'm sorry I broke our bond."

Slowly releasing the claws of her right hand, she rips at the left shoulder of her shirt, tearing away the material to expose her skin.

She reveals the crescent of Jace's mark. The true mate mark.

It's cut through with four downward scars.

Positioning the tips of her claws against the scars—a perfect fit—she draws them carefully down the broken flesh.

I'm frozen to the spot, my arms tight around Tristan, as I consider what this means.

When I asked Jace what it would take to break a true mate bond, he told me that only extended violence could do it—the kind that only a few supernaturals are capable of inflicting. I interpreted his answer to mean that his bond with Ella had been broken by the violence that was done to her, but now I'm seeing that *she* had chosen to break it herself.

The witches told me that Ella was unparalleled in a fight to the death. Cody himself told me that Ella should have been the alpha-in-training of their pack—that she was stronger than him—but his father wouldn't appoint a woman. Seconds ago, I glimpsed some of Ella's physical strength and resolve, and her determination to dominate her opponent.

211

I never imagined that she and I could be alike because of the darkness we hold inside.

Tears fall down her cheeks. "I couldn't be your mate, Jace. Not the monster I became. Not the woman who killed to keep herself alive. I hurt others who were just as frightened and trapped as I was..." She sobs out the words. "I wanted to free you from me and everything I became. I couldn't bring that darkness into your life."

She reaches out to brush his cheek, but her head bows. "You are the most loyal, the most generous man I've ever met. Please... please... Don't hurt anymore. Not because of me."

The silence is heavy as she waits for him to respond. The pained press of his lips eases as he reaches out to touch her cheek, too, mirroring her actions, both of them reaching out without closing the gap between their bodies.

His voice is low. Calm. "You were not responsible—"

"I was!" she cries, jolting but not stepping away. "I had a choice—"

"Between life and death."

"It was still a choice," she whispers.

He shakes his head, his jaw clenched. His focus on her is as unwavering as hers was during the fight, but his voice is quiet. Undeniable. "I don't see you that way," he says. "When I look at you, I see a woman with a heart that was torn out and savaged by monsters."

Taking a deep breath and a step forward, he slowly lowers his forehead to hers. The connection between them is so strong that it feels like a force ripping through me, tingling all the way to my fingers, all the way to my toes.

"*You* are not the monster, Ella," he says.

She leans into him, her head bent, tears falling directly to the ground.

"You are kind," he says. "Beautiful. Gracious." He lifts his head. Brushes the broken mark. Takes a breath. "Come back to me."

I sense him hold his breath, waiting for her response.

Ella's lips part. She doesn't pause. "I want what we once had."

Jace doesn't hesitate. He sweeps her up into his arms before he swings to me, looking directly at me with an expression as close to an alpha's as I've ever seen him wear.

"Ella and I need time," he says, his voice a soft growl. "I trust you to protect the pack, Tessa."

Without waiting for my response, he swings to the elevator, hits the button, and carries Ella inside.

She leans in close to him. A moment later, the elevator doors close, and they're gone.

CHAPTER TWENTY-EIGHT

I've barely taken a breath, barely pulled myself together, when Tristan groans, a sound of pain.

Now that the fight is over, I have the chance to check the state of his chest. Medical patches still cover some of the wounds, but two have been ripped off—including the one that was covering the wound I drove my claws into. The second visible wound cuts across the tattoo of the snake on his chest. The edges of the cut are exposed, angry, and red. It isn't bleeding, but the golden glow from inside it indicates that the angel's magic is still poisoning him.

I reposition myself so that I can check his eyes, trying to figure out which mind is in control right now. His eyes are half-closed. His breathing is more even, nearly syncing with mine, but it keeps hitching with every breath he takes, making it impossible to tell for sure. "Tristan?"

"Tessa." He winces. "What the fuck did I do?"

My voice softens as I think of Ella and Jace. "Maybe something good."

Tristan squints at me, trying to focus. Sweat beads on his forehead and when I press my cheek to his, I find his skin hotter than it should be.

My worry returns. "We need to get you back to the House—"

"I need to name my successor," he says, attempting to rise. "I came here because I can't leave my pack without an alpha. They need to hear it from me. They'll be lost if I die without choosing."

My jaw clenches. I could have helped him come here for that purpose, but he doesn't appear to be thinking straight. "You don't need a successor. You're not going to die."

A sudden light enters his eyes, but it's intense, his gaze unfocused. "You must have the book," he says.

I evade his statement, challenging him instead. "I'm your successor. Remember?"

"The three-headed wolf is dying with me," Tristan says, making my head spin with his rapid changes of subject. "He'll tell you what you're afraid to hear. Don't listen to him, Tessa. Don't fucking believe him."

Tristan can only be referring to Cerberus, but I'm not sure what exactly he's trying to warn me about—that the wolf will try to save himself? Stop me, maybe?

I'm suddenly aware of Cody and Danika approaching quietly on either side of me. Neither of them has reached for their weapons, but they both move at a cautious pace. A quick glance tells me that Iyana has remained with the other women, who look prepared to leap into a fight against Tristan if they have to.

"What do you need, Tessa?" Danika asks.

"Tristan has a fever," I say. "We need to get him back to Helen—"

"Fuck, no!" Tristan grabs my arms. "I won't die at the House. I need to be with my pack."

Cody kneels beside me. "You can't take him away from his pack now. He needs their energy. He'll be stronger if he's here."

Damn, there's still so much I don't understand about pack dynamics.

I press my hand against Tristan's forehead. He's definitely running a fever. I never thought I'd miss the Killer, but now that the three-headed wolf has retreated, Tristan's physical condition is much worse.

"Okay," I whisper. "Will you help me carry him to the elevator?"

Cody takes one of Tristan's arms, preparing to angle his shoulder to support him, but Tristan bares his teeth, growling a threat. "Cody Griffin. Step the fuck back if you know what's good for you."

Cody doesn't appear fazed, turning his hands palm-up. "Easy, Tristan. I'm not here to challenge you."

Tristan's incisors don't retract, but he slumps against the wall as he peers at Cody. "I thought you were dead."

"Death didn't know what to do with me." Cody's muscles bunch as he braces to support Tristan's weight while I maneuver around to the other side of him, hooking Tristan's other arm over my shoulders.

"Tessa destroyed an entire coven when you died," Tristan says to Cody, his speech slurring as he takes a wobbly step. "Don't you fucking leave her again."

"Imagine what she'd do if she lost you?" Cody replies smoothly. "You'd better fucking fight this, Tristan."

Tristan growls in response and my heart hurts a little.

I reach for Danika with my free hand. "Danika, can you get everyone inside the elevator?" I ask. "We'll need to cram in and head straight up to the twelfth floor. We can't risk Tristan's pack reacting badly to Cody's presence." *Not until Tristan is ready to handle the interaction himself.*

"On it." She hurries to the others, who quickly rush to grab their bags from the vehicles. Danika prepares to call the elevator while Cody and I shuffle toward it, supporting Tristan between us.

Tristan doesn't stop growling the entire walk, clearly hating being supported by anyone, let alone a "fucking Griffin."

Cody takes it in his stride. "Don't complain. You won't know what humility is until someone else has to put your pants on for you."

Tristan side-eyes Cody but stops grumbling at that point.

We shuffle in first with Danika, while the rest of my pack crams in after us and Iyana swipes the security card so we can access the twelfth floor. Danika ends up next to Cody while Reya and Maeve are closer to me. Each of them attempts not to fall over the bags stuffed between their feet.

Maeve's hands glow violet as she tries to wipe her palms across her jeans in the cramped space. I sense her anxiety about being confined so close to Tristan with nowhere to go. She trusts Tristan. She doesn't trust the Killer.

"You okay, Tessa?" Reya asks me, angled toward me, her hip pressing into mine.

"I'll be better once I can get Tristan some medication."

"Maybe one of us should go get Helen," Lydia calls quietly from the front of the elevator where she and Luna are crammed in with Nalani and Iyana.

Iyana gives me a nod to indicate she agrees. "Let's figure it out upstairs."

As soon as the elevator doors open into Tristan's apartment, we spill out with audible exclamations of relief. Iyana directs the others through to the kitchen, where they can deposit their bags while Cody and I help Tristan through to his room.

The apartment is just like I remember it. The elevator lets out directly into the lounge with a tiled kitchen farther back and the door to the right leading into the bedroom. The floor-to-ceiling windows to the left reveal the city, although the morning sunlight is obscured behind clouds. It looks like it's about to rain again.

The lounge area and kitchen are neat and tidy like we left them. So too, for once, is the bedroom. The burned charcoal scent of the Killer has become so prevalent in Tristan's body that the old scent of Tristan's room—his scent before the minds took control—grips me around my heart.

I shake my head, trying to dislodge the pain of lost moments. Focusing on Tristan in the here and now, I coordinate with Cody to lie Tristan down on his bed.

Tristan's eyes close the moment his head hits the pillow, and I lean over him in alarm. "Tristan?"

When he doesn't respond, I check his breathing, but it's even.

He's sleeping.

"Damn," I whisper. "He needed to take painkillers first."

Cody retreats a few paces away nearer to the door. "Can I do anything to help?"

"Not right now. Thank you. Tell the others I'll be out in a few minutes. Make sure they eat and rest." I glance at him. "Make sure *you* eat and rest."

The corner of his mouth rises. "I've had enough sleep, but I could do with some food. Call us if you need us."

As soon as he disappears into the lounge, I head to the bathroom off the side of Tristan's room. First, I hide the pouch that holds the objects inside one of the drawers beneath the sink. I'm lucky that Cerberus hasn't focused on the objects yet. Tristan's warning in the garage wasn't lost on me. He told me that the minds are aware I have the book. I briefly consider giving the pouch to one of my pack members to take away and guard, but if the Killer went after them, he could kill them. Hiding the objects here isn't a great option, but I don't have Hidden House to help me this time, and I can't endanger my pack.

I find cloths in the bathroom to soak in cold water. Folding one up, I return to Tristan to place the cloth across his forehead to cool him down. I use the others to wipe his face and chest, pausing around his wounds.

The moments before we faced the angels repeat on me.

Tristan asked me to have faith in him.

I told him that I did.

Reaching for his hand, I sink onto the bed beside him, lying down a few inches apart from him. I want him to know that I'm here, that I crave the nearness of his body, want to curl up against his side, but I can't add my body heat to his fever.

After a few minutes, I get up again to refresh the cloth across his forehead. I wipe him down again and whisper his name to see if he'll wake—until he wakes, we can't give him medicine—but he doesn't stir.

When Iyana quietly enters holding a glass of water and painkillers, I'm pacing by the side of the bed. "We need Helen. We need serious medicine. Maybe we should take him back to the House, after all..."

Iyana places the cup and tablets on the bedside table. She rests her hand on my shoulder. "You made the right decision to stay here. As much as Tristan's choice to come back here could have been powered by his fever, we can't ignore his instincts. He needs his pack."

She clears her throat and I sense her pushing at her own sadness. Tristan means a lot to her, too. "There's a limited supply of ice in the freezer. We'll go find more. We'll surround him with it if we have to. We'll bring the fever down."

She's gone from the bedroom within seconds, and I hear her

gathering the women in the lounge, dividing them into two groups —each with a security pass. She will lead one and Danika will lead the other. Moments later, they're gone and the penthouse suite is silent.

Cody is the only one who remains, which is just as well. I'm not sure how Tristan's pack will respond to Danika and Iyana hurrying around in search of medical supplies. They definitely wouldn't respond well to Cody—son of their enemy. Even without his wolf.

He pauses in the doorway, holding a cloth that's frosting on the outside and must be filled with ice cubes before he crosses the distance to hand the pack to me.

I bend to press it to Tristan's forehead, the cloth rapidly dampening as the ice melts.

Tears finally fall down my cheeks as I kneel beside the bed. "I need to help him, but I don't know how. This isn't a battle I know how to fight. My power is useless here."

Cody presses a hand to my shoulder. "You love him."

I nod, allowing my tears to fall. I can't begin to describe how complicated my love for Tristan is, but it's undeniable.

"It's impossible to watch someone you love experience pain," Cody says. "You feel it too."

When I look up at him, his gaze is piercing.

"You looked at me in the same way at the Spire," he says. "I was in pain and you felt it." Cody kneels beside me. "We've come a long way, you and I. You were forced to give up your humanity while I was forced to become more human. Neither of us will end up as anything other than ourselves."

I bite my lip so hard that I sense the skin break. "I know what I have to do to destroy Cerberus," I say, speaking more openly now that Tristan is asleep. "Once he's free of Cerberus, Tristan will be able to fight the angel's magic and heal himself. But I don't have all the pieces that I need to start—"

"Tell me what you need," Cody says.

It's a simple request, but I struggle with voicing my needs without telling Cody anything that could put him in danger. The knowledge in the book is dangerous. "I need an object of old magic, but they're incredibly rare."

He nods. "Because they're formed from the body parts of old magic creatures." He grimaces. "Claws, teeth, feathers, and bones."

"That's right," I say, surprised that he knows about it.

He exhales quietly. "Finding one is not as impossible as you think," he says. "Taking possession of it is another matter."

"You know where to find one?" I lean forward, hope rising within me.

He is quiet for a moment before he gives a nod. "Every assassin's ring is formed from old magic."

"What?" I'm stunned. "How do you know that?"

He grimaces for a second time. "I asked if I could join their ranks. They said *no*. When I pressed them for reasons, the Master Assassin himself told me that it's not safe for shifters to wear assassin's rings because the rings are made of old magic. The mix of my wolf's energy with the old magic would turn me into a monster. Different supernaturals react to old magic differently, but they don't take any chances. It's why all assassins are human."

My thoughts are in a storm. A fucking ironic storm. "I need an assassin's ring." Which my mother has. And I have to take it by force.

As if that won't be difficult.

"I have to caution you that the assassins won't let you walk away with one," Cody says. "Even if you manage to steal it, they'll hunt you down to get it back. You don't want that."

My memory returns to the moment that I met my mother, the way her ring drew me in, the death I felt in it. I'm not immune to old magic. Even *handling* a ring could kill me.

"It's a risk I have to take," I say. "Where is the boxing gym located?" Ford had pointed to the area on a map, but I don't know the exact location.

"Are you sure, Tessa?" Cody asks.

"I don't have a choice. If I have to fight the Master Assassin himself, then so be it."

Cody gives me an address not far from the bridges into Baxter's territory in downtown Portland. "What's your plan, Tessa?"

Over the last day, I've tested my ability to ask for help, to open myself up to the care of others, but this is one task I can't involve anyone else in.

"I have to do this alone," I say. "Tonight. After everyone is asleep. Don't tell anyone about this."

I give him my best alpha glare, complete with descending incisors to emphasize my command.

Cody is just as calm with me as he was with Tristan after the fight in the garage. His human self is the complete opposite of his former shifter self, who would have reacted with force.

"You're trying to protect everyone," he says, sounding more and more like Helen with every passing second. "I'll respect your wish because I know firsthand how dangerous the assassins are." He grips my shoulders. "But, Tessa, if you don't come back, we're all coming to find you."

I exhale slowly. "That's fair."

Tristan suddenly groans. His eyes are closed, but he lurches upward, trying to get off the bed.

I'm at his side in a heartbeat.

"It's okay, Tristan," I say, reaching for him right before he shoves the ice pack off his forehead. It hits the floor with a slap, spilling ice across the carpet. "You need to rest."

He squints at me from where he lies half-risen, half-turned, leaning on one elbow while the flat of my hands press against his chest, across his tattoo.

The corners of his mouth turn down and my heart sinks when his muscles cord. The Killer surfaces. A snarl leaves his mouth. "Fuck rest. There's an entire pack in this building that doesn't deserve to live." His lips twist. "Fucking weak shifters. They're only worthy of my entertainment."

I press harder against him, stopping him from rising further. The unnatural heat in his chest and shoulders warms my palms. He's still burning up. Still feverish.

A warning enters my voice. "You're not going anywhere."

"Do I have to fight you, Tessa Dean?" the Killer asks, his free hand darting out to wrap around the back of my neck. "I'd prefer to conquer you in this bed."

Cody darts forward from behind me, but I throw out my arm to stop him. "It's okay! I can handle this. I need you to leave us alone. If the others come back, keep them out of this room. I'll come out when the Killer's gone and it's safe again."

"Tessa. No. I don't trust him." Cody shakes his head, standing his ground while the Killer continues to snarl at me.

"Trust *me*, Cody," I say. "I know how the Killer's mind works. He won't hurt me. I promise I'll be okay."

With a frustrated exhale, Cody backs toward the door.

"Close the door, please," I say.

The corners of the Killer's mouth rise when Cody pauses with his hand on the doorknob.

"Your beta is wise to be concerned, Tessa Dean," the Killer says. "I've chosen to come on this journey with you until now, but all good things must come to an end."

"Cody." My voice doesn't allow for objection. An alpha's command. "Trust me."

Without another moment's hesitation, Cody swings the door closed, leaving me alone with the Killer.

The Killer's hand softens against the back of my neck, his stomach muscles bunching as he eases his way up into a sitting position, his chest only inches from mine where I perch on the edge of the bed.

"Tessa Dean," he says. "I think I've been patient enough."

The challenge in the Killer's green eyes is impossible to misinterpret.

Okay, you fucker. Let's see where this goes.

CHAPTER TWENTY-NINE

Taking charge, I move quickly to straddle the Killer's hips on the bed. I don't give the Killer a second to catch his breath before I speak.

"The Deceiver wants you to believe that I care about you," I say, meeting his heated eyes as I stroke my hands carefully around his wounds. "He wants you to believe that I'm weakened by my feelings."

The Killer grins at me, sudden and vicious, his incisors sharp. "You're not weak, Tessa Dean."

"Neither are you," I say. "Even now that you're injured, you're still fighting to stay alive." I lean in, my lips only an inch from his, inhaling the aroma of fire that smothers Tristan's true scent—the scent of bitter oranges that I crave. "You'll do anything to ensure that your minds continue, won't you?"

His hand tightens around the back of my neck, drawing me closer, his other palm resting across my ribs beneath my right breast. "I will survive, Tessa Dean. I've survived through centuries, passing from mind to mind, child to child—"

"Ah," I say. "But Tristan doesn't have any children." I dart forward to taste the corner of the Killer's lips, drawing out the contact, lingering as my lips tease his. "You need to do something about that now, don't you?"

The Killer's smile fades, but only for a moment before the gleam reenters his eyes. "I can promise you hours of pleasure, Tessa Dean, so much more than you've experienced with Tristan."

I shiver. The darkness inside me responds with a need I'm prepared for this time—the need to tempt danger and seek out the darker parts of my nature—but the power of my mind and heart is stronger now, fiercer than my darkness.

Tristan satisfies every part of me. Pure Tristan. Not the Killer, or the Coward, or the Deceiver. *Tristan*.

Pressing against the Killer's chest, ignoring the bandages and the wounds and the feverish heat of his skin, I draw him as close as I can, tasting his lips, settling against the hardness of his body between my legs.

Just as he groans and his arms close around me, I break the contact between our lips.

"I'll make you a deal," I whisper. "Keep Tristan alive for another day and I'll take you up on your offer. I'll give your minds the chance to live for another generation."

His eyes narrow at me. I have a second's warning before he reverses our positions, pushing me onto my back and looming over me with a possessive growl. Drawing up to kneel between my legs, he pushes up the base of my shirt to expose my stomach before he presses his palms across my bare skin above the waistband of my jeans. I'm very glad now that I hid the objects of magic in the bathroom and I'm not still wearing them at my waist.

When a look of intense concentration fills the Killer's face, I freeze for a different reason.

Is he... trying to sense my fertility?

I've lost track of my cycle since I first left Hidden House. It wouldn't do me any good to count days anyway because I've always been irregular, an odd mix between a human cycle of a month and a wolf shifter cycle of two months. All I know is that I haven't had a period since I first left the House.

His eyes rise to mine and I shiver.

"Today is viable. Tomorrow is guaranteed," he says. "I accept your deal."

I stare up at him, genuinely thrown by the certainty in his declaration. "How can you be so sure?"

He runs his forefinger up to the base of my neck, following the path between my breasts, then down to the top of my pelvis, his fingers skipping over my bunched-up shirt and coming to rest across the zipper of my jeans.

Bending his head to drop kisses across my stomach, he makes a satisfied sound in the back of his throat.

"Your power streams differently where new life could grow."

"Can Tristan sense this too?" I ask.

"Of course." A grin grows on the Killer's face. "He would never fuck you when you could conceive. He is determined to end me."

Contraception was the last thing on my mind when Tristan and I were together. My voice hardens. "You will keep him alive."

The Killer lifts his head from my stomach, but he doesn't move away from me. His hands stroke down my inner thighs from my knees to my pelvis before he moves upward, planting his hands on either side of my head as he looks down on me.

"I will keep this body alive long enough for it to sire a child, but then Tristan will die," the Killer says.

I don't close my eyes fast enough to hide the burn of tears. Angry tears. Determined tears.

The Killer drops a kiss to my lips that tastes like fire and lies. "Don't mourn a wolf who doesn't love you, Tessa Dean."

My eyes fly open, releasing a wayward tear. I curl my fingers into the bedding at my sides. It's the only way I can keep from lashing out. Gritting my teeth, I say, "You don't need to lie to me about Tristan's feelings. I've already agreed to give you what you want."

"It isn't a lie," the Killer says, dropping another kiss to my lips, each one more lingering than the last. "Each cut on Tristan's chest is the proof."

My forehead creases. "What are you talking about?"

"The Sentinel asked him if he loved you," the Killer says. "She struck him after that."

Pain spears through my chest. The angel would only strike Tristan if he'd lied. I try to force sound through my lips. "Tristan told the angel that he doesn't love me."

"No, Tessa." The Killer's lips twist. "He told her that he does."

The Killer's trying to make me believe that Tristan lied. That he told the Sentinel he loves me and she caught him in a lie. Staring up at the Killer's face, the twist to his lips, the light in his eyes, I suddenly realize…

I'm looking at the Deceiver.

The Deceiver has always been subtle, playing with Tristan's thoughts, but for the first time, he's showing his full face.

My hands fly upward. Pushing at the Deceiver's shoulders, I shove him onto his back with a snarl, reversing our positions once more.

He grips my hips, yanking me close. "Why wait until tomorrow, Tessa Dean?" he asks, running his hands up under my shirt to rest beneath my breasts. "Why not start now? Why not fuck all day and all night?"

I suddenly remember Tristan's exact warning when he surfaced in the garage. He said… *He'll tell you what you're afraid to hear. Don't fucking listen, Tessa. Don't fucking believe him.*

The Deceiver has discerned my greatest vulnerability: my fear of being unloved. More than that, he's trying to cut the heart out of Tristan's greatest need: for me to believe in him. To make me question Tristan's motives, to make me hate him.

With a controlled exhale, I relax every limb in my body, calm every combative instinct, because controlling the minds starts with defusing their anger.

"Why don't I want to fuck now?" I ask quietly, repeating the Deceiver's question back at him. "Because you're simple."

His forehead creases, a hint of confusion. The glint in his eyes grows sharper, the twist in his lips more distinct.

"You only have one purpose," I continue. "Your purpose is to manipulate. But Tristan? Oh. Tristan is complicated. And fucking imperfect. He has layers that I've only just begun to find. I plan to explore all of Tristan's imperfections and all of his complications for a fuck sight longer than a day and a night."

My palms soften as I lean down against the Deceiver's shoulders, the gentlest touch as the crease in his forehead grows deeper, the light in his eyes becomes more uncertain.

"I have faith in Tristan," I say. "I have faith in his pain and his convictions. I know that sounds trite, but I don't give a shit about how it sounds because it's true. And you… Deceiver… you don't even come close to everything that Tristan means to me."

He is silent beneath me. Quiet.

I stop talking, take a deep breath, and study the shadows that cross his face. I watch the way his eyes change, his lips soften, while the feverish sheen returns to his forehead.

I take another deep breath.

Tristan inhales at the same time as I do, matching his breathing with mine. All of the remaining tension drains out of me as his breathing is truly in time with mine again. Truly Tristan.

"Tessa?" he asks.

I allow myself to give a small smile, ease my fingers across his jaw to soothe his tension. "Yeah?"

"I fucking love you."

I draw a ragged breath and he does too, so in tune with me right now that his heartbeat hitches when mine does.

Slowly lowering my cheek to his, I nudge the corner of his mouth, inhaling his pure scent.

"This," I whisper. "This is not a lie."

His arms slide up to wrap around me, forming a warm circle that I'm a part of, a place of honesty and safety that I won't stop fighting for.

CHAPTER THIRTY

I rest my cheek against Tristan's jaw, a light press before I urge us onto our sides, trying not to push on his wounds more than I already have.

I attempt to arch back and reach for the painkillers and glass of water on the bedside table without breaking his embrace—nearly toppling the glass—but manage to bring them to him.

He doesn't immediately take them, giving me a heated look across the top of the glass. "If the Killer wasn't right about your fertility, I'd ask for something other than painkillers right now."

My cheeks heat. My body is in tune with his—responding to his need in a heady rush—but I'm acutely aware of the reality of our situation.

Pressing a light kiss to his lips, I urge him into a sitting position. I prop pillows behind him before I hand him the water and tablets. Slipping off the bed, I attempt to retrieve the ice pack, but the cloth is a soggy mess. Most of the ice has melted. I spin to the bathroom, intending to wash the cloth out, when Tristan catches my eye.

I pause in the intensity of his gaze. "Tristan?"

The corner of his mouth hitches up, but he seems to be having trouble finding words, a slight crease forming in his forehead. "You're looking after me."

"Of course."

His shoulders relax and the press of his lips eases. "Fuck, you're beautiful."

I'm both thrown and warmed by his declaration. He seems so surprised that I'm caring for him that it makes me wonder... if anybody has ever looked after him. Jace has always been there for Tristan, but from what I observed of Tristan's habits, he always spent his darkest hours in solitude, determined not to hurt anyone close to him.

I know all of his darkest secrets. I've seen the worst that the three-headed wolf can deliver. I've dived deep into Tristan's own darkness—not all of it caused by the wolf.

My lips part. I know how difficult it is to accept kindness when the darkness is so great, but he's accepting my help, not fighting it.

I return his smile, tipping my head. I cast my gaze across his face, his black hair, slick with sweat, the sheen on his bare chest.

I start to speak, but sudden voices outside the room make me jolt.

Danika's voice... others I don't recognize... but also Cody's growled response. He's closest to the door. I can only imagine the way he must be guarding the door right now—despite the fact that he probably wants to break it down.

"You need to get out there," Tristan says, and I appreciate that he's trusting me to defuse any situation that might be arising.

I wait for him to swallow the painkillers, his movements slower and his grip on the glass weaker than I hoped.

Then I stride across the room and swing the door inward.

The tension outside the room hits me like a mallet.

Cody's back is to the door, his muscles flexed, ready to move. He's standing far enough to the side that I can see past him. He's immediately aware of the open door and my presence, sending a quick warning glance in my direction as I pull up beside him.

Danika is poised closest to my left while three other women have stopped just outside the elevator in the clear space beside the lounge chairs. At their head is Bridget—Tristan's delta. She was the one who challenged me to a fight after Tristan first brought me here.

Beside her is Jemimah, the woman with the little girl who loved chewing on my hair. The third woman is much younger. I recognize her as Carly—the girl who was nearly killed by Baxter Griffin and Dawson Nash.

Bridget stands ahead of the others, her claws descended. "Cody Griffin!" She spits. "What the fuck are you doing here?"

Across the way, Danika steps between them, turning herself into a living barrier. I can't see her face, only her back, but I hear the soft determination in her voice and note the way she's holding her hands, palms up, urging calm. "You asked to see Tristan. I brought you here. You need to put the past behind you right now. There's been enough violence—"

Bridget's voice is a snarl. "Don't talk to me about violence after what Baxter Griffin has done to our pack. After what he did to Carly!"

Danika continues to stand her ground. "I understand your pain. I respect it. But there are no enemies in this room—"

"Get out of my way, hawk!" Bridget snaps. "He deserves to pay for what he's done."

Danika's back straightens and her hands lower, the change in her posture sudden and clear. "Cody Griffin is part of Tessa's pack. *I* am part of Tessa's pack. If you attempt to fight him, I will strike you down."

I remain where I am, my instincts telling me that Danika has the best chance of dealing with this situation right now.

Bridget growls, low in her throat, but something in Danika's face must make her pause—I picture the ferocity in Danika's hazel eyes right before she screamed Ford Vanguard into submission. Of all the members of my pack, Danika is possibly the toughest, the one who calls bullshit when she sees it, but she's also the one most determined to see past anger to the pain that lies beneath.

The defensiveness in Bridget's stance, the way she stands like a shield in front of Carly, isn't lost on me—and it's definitely not lost on Danika.

Right now, they're both protecting people who have been hurt by Baxter Griffin.

Beside me, Cody is subdued. His focus is—to my surprise—calmly on Danika and not on the others. Earlier today, she snapped at him. Now she's defending him.

He defers to me as the tension between Danika and Bridget rises, softly murmuring, "Tessa, with your permission?"

"Be careful," I say. "Remember, I have your back."

A small smile rests on his lips as he inclines his head toward Danika. "Apparently, you're not the only one."

Cody takes careful steps forward, his bare feet silent in the plush carpet as he draws level with Danika.

The moment that Bridget flinches at his approach, he stops. In a single fluid movement, he takes a knee and tips his head to the side, baring his neck, a submissive pose.

"My father has committed unspeakable crimes," he says. "Crimes of war. I can't atone for his actions, but I can fight for a better future. I've left my father's pack, and I plan to stand against him. I'm here as a member of Tessa's pack. As Ella's brother. As Tessa's beta. As a defender of Tristan's pack. If you'll accept me."

I hold my breath as the three women contemplate him.

Bridget appears ready to snap at him, but Carly reaches out, placing her hand on Bridget's shoulder.

When Tristan raced into Hidden House carrying Carly and her little sister, he said Carly was his last possible choice for an alpha-in-training. Carly is only fourteen years old, but the maturity in her eyes reflects the danger she's survived. Her hair is dark brown, her eyes even darker brown, and her skin is bronzed.

The way Bridget steps aside for her tells me that Carly has already taken a higher status in the pack. I can only guess that she has been working with Jace to keep the pack calm while Tristan was missing.

She steps right up to Cody, seeming to tower over him now that he's taken a knee. I stiffen when her claws snap down, but I relax when she draws them across her own chest, mimicking the wounds she suffered when she was attacked.

"Helen made sure I didn't scar," she says. "But I'll carry the memory always. It will drive me, but it won't define me."

I see now why Tristan would choose Carly as his alpha-in-training. She's young, which would have prevented him from making her his first choice, but she's strong.

She takes a knee in front of Cody, appearing unafraid of him. "We sensed your sister earlier. She and Jace will bond again." A perplexed expression descends across her face. "But you..." She tips her head to the side, deep in thought. "You don't have a wolf."

"My father's actions led to me losing my wolf," Cody replies. He glances up at Danika, who stands beside him. "It's a loss I can live with."

Carly tips her head. "How so?"

"It led me here," he says.

Carly considers him carefully, peering into his eyes. "I believe you."

She rises to her feet and Cody does the same. A silent moment passes between them before Carly says, "We'd like to see Tristan now. We're worried about him."

Cody immediately steps aside, and I read the relief in Danika's quickly relaxing posture as she meets his eyes across the space between them.

Bridget and Jemimah follow Carly toward me, but Carly stops in front of me. She was unconscious when I last saw her and didn't return to the pack until after I left.

"We've never officially met," she says, considering me with a wary light in her eyes. "In contrast to Cody, you have *too much* wolf."

I bare my teeth at her. "You would do well to remember it."

She gives me a disarming smile. "My little sister also tells me you're kind. She hasn't stopped talking about the way your wolf hugged her."

Carly arches an eyebrow at me, as if daring me to contradict her.

I incline my head toward Tristan's room, my expression remaining stern. "Tristan wants to see you, but I'll remain with you in case the three-headed wolf makes an appearance."

Carly's smile fades. "Thank you. Tristan won't want anything to happen to us because of him."

She strides into the room without hesitation. Bridget gives me a wary look—not surprising, given my new physical appearance—but Jemimah pauses at my side. She gives me a sudden hug that has me pedaling backward, but I quickly return it.

"I'm glad you're here, Tessa," she says. "We've lost too much already. We can't lose Tristan as well."

When I first met Jemimah, she told me that she lost her mate to the games Tristan's father used to play when the Killer held sway over him. "Our pack needs you," Jemimah says. She glances back to Danika and Cody. "All of you."

I remain in the doorway as the women hurry to Tristan's side. Behind me, Danika and Cody are quiet, but I catch their muted conversation.

"You didn't have to do that," Cody says to her.

She looks up at him. "We protect each other. No exceptions."

As soon as she catches me watching them, she clears her throat and hurries across to me. "Iyana should be here any second. They have a boatload of ice cubes, a thousand towels, and some hefty painkillers that should help."

"Thank you."

Half an hour later, the penthouse is filled with people again. My entire pack swarms around Tristan with buckets of ice. Since he doesn't have a bath, they turn his bed into a nest of cubes that are cooling his temperature significantly but also make him incredibly grumpy about submitting to the ministrations of so many women.

At some point, Iyana produces a waterproof sheet to put under him so that the melting ice doesn't soak into the mattress and ruin it.

Members of his pack visit him in twos and threes throughout the day, and I watch over the interactions carefully, alert for signs of the three-headed wolf that could threaten or hurt them.

By the time half of his pack has visited, he's barely keeping his eyes open, the painkillers taking full effect.

Carly remains in the penthouse for most of the day, but she finally declares that visiting hours are over, asking the final three pack members to tell the others they will need to see Tristan tomorrow. He needs to rest.

As the final visitors leave, I slip onto the bed to check Tristan's temperature, relieved to find his forehead, neck, and chest cool to touch, his breathing even and strong. Cerberus promised to keep him alive for another day—but only a day. Night will soon fall and that's when I need to act.

Carly approaches me before she leaves. "Tessa, can we talk?"

"Of course."

Over the course of the day, my pack pulled chairs into the bedroom. Carly draws one up, leaning her elbows on her knees, casting glances at Tristan's sleeping form.

"Baxter Griffin's pack has stayed on their side of the river ever since Tristan went missing," she says. "I'm told this is due to a deal you made with him that cost you a lot. I'm grateful, Tessa."

I give her a nod, sensing that she didn't ask to speak with me just to thank me.

"However, in the last few days, we've noticed other activity in our territory," she says. "Your half-brother has been sighted, along with his father and a mercenary we know only as Ford Vanguard."

I stiffen. My deal with Baxter only related to his pack. Ford has already threatened to attack. The fact that Dawson has been sighted isn't great, but that his father is also present in Tristan's territory doesn't bode well.

I worry at my lip as the voices of my pack filter through from the kitchen and lounge. They're currently eating and resting—and planning where they're all going to sleep tonight.

"That's not all," Carly says. "There's an unprecedented amount of movement from the other packs. We've had sightings of at least two other alphas traveling west with large numbers of their packs with them, including Sasha of the Lower Highland pack. As I'm sure you know, she has one of the most formidable female-dominated packs."

I growl in the back of my throat. Sasha was one of the alphas at the Conclave who voted for me to die. I still remember her calling out their reasons for wanting me dead because I was a fucking threat to them.

"It's as if they're having a Conclave somewhere, but our pack isn't invited," Carly continues.

"Have you had them followed to know where they're going?" I ask.

Carly shakes her head. "We don't have the resources. Protecting the pack here in the tower is all we can do. Jace and I were discussing sending out a small scouting party, but then you arrived."

"My pack can help us find out," I murmur.

Carly watches me as I slip from the bed. "Tessa?"

"Wait here," I say.

Ducking my head around the door, I call out softly. "Luna. Lydia. I need you."

The twins immediately put down their meals and hurry across the distance. Behind them, the rest of my pack is suddenly quiet and poised on their seats, their heads raised, casting questioning glances at me.

"Everything okay, sweetie?" Iyana asks from the lounge chair she's half-risen from.

I can't help my smile. Or the gratitude that I feel because my pack is ready to mobilize if I need them. "We'll see," I say.

Luna and Lydia enter the room, their skirts swishing, both of them so elegant that it's hard to picture them as the warrior-women who took on a coven of witches.

"What do you need?" Lydia asks.

"There are other alphas in Tristan's territory. Can you locate them?" I ask.

"We can try," Lydia says before she and Luna draw their packs of cards from their pockets and turn to face each other. As soon as they throw each of their packs into the air, the cards scatter and stop, suspended, before they start spinning in place.

I hold my breath, waiting for the cards to start arranging themselves, but the spinning intensifies, each card turning wildly on the spot. The twins' foreheads crease, their lips pressed with worry, the concentration on their faces intensifying before their gazes pass rapidly from one card to another. Their upheld arms begin to shake and then—

With a *whoomph* like a fire igniting, the cards burst outward and flutter to the floor in a mess.

Luna lowers her shaking arms, a bead of sweat trickling down her face. Her sister's gaze is downcast as she stares at the cards on the carpet.

"We're sorry, Tessa," Lydia says. "Wherever the alphas are, they're hiding themselves using powerful magic."

They both hold out their hands toward the dropped cards and the pieces fly in two cascades back up into the twins' hands.

"Should we keep trying?" Lydia asks, hovering.

"No, it's fine," I say. "We'll find them another way. Get yourselves some hydration and rest. You used up a lot of energy just now."

I follow them to the door, but I pause in its shadow, where I close my eyes.

There's one place to the west that is so shrouded in old magic that the twins' magic can't breach it. It's the place I was kept prisoner.

I'm certain now that the alphas are going to the Spire to join Ford Vanguard.

Tristan once feared that a war would begin.

Now Ford is gathering an army.

CHAPTER THIRTY-ONE

When night falls, my pack gathers in Tristan's room to eat a meal. They bring in the remaining chairs from the kitchen and the cushions from the lounge. Tristan is awake and intensely observant, watching my pack interact with me. He can't eat much, so instead, I ply him with hydration. Cody, too, sits slightly apart in the opposite corner of the room, remaining quiet and observant.

By the time we finish eating, Iyana is bleary-eyed, but she gives a groan of happiness when the last hint of sunlight disappears from the wide windows and she can finally remove her protective cloak.

Stretching out her neck and shoulders, she heaves a sigh. "We'll sleep on the ninth and tenth floors with the families tonight. Carly asked us to have a visible presence so the pack feels safe."

"What about Jace?" I ask.

Iyana gives me a rare smirk. "Apparently, nobody's expecting Jace and Ella to surface for some time. Not unless there's a disaster."

I smother my smile. Jace and Ella are a spark of happiness in an otherwise dire situation.

Iyana pins me with a blunt stare. "So what's the plan, Tessa?"

"What do you mean?"

"I mean that Tristan's dying and you're too fucking calm not to have a plan."

I study my hands, painfully aware that I can't tell them what I intend to do. But I also don't want to lie.

I start slowly. "You have all given me your trust. Your loyalty. Your friendship. I can't begin to tell you how much that means to me." I bite my lip to stop the tears that are trying to burn the back of my eyes. "The path ahead of me involves making choices that only I can make."

Looking up, I meet their serious eyes. "I need you to trust me when I say that I'm already doing everything I can."

Iyana's brow furrows. "In other words, you're not going to tell us anything."

"Yep," I say, popping the 'p' like she used to. "I need you to trust that I will ask for your help when I need it."

"Considering your history of not asking for help, that's going to take a lot of trust," Iyana says, her brow furrowed and her blue eyes piercing.

I don't have a comeback, searching for an honest answer and coming up empty. Tristan surprises me when he leans toward me. "This is the part when you tell them to get the fuck back to work."

His comment is met with narrowed eyes from the women around us, but he shrugs his broad shoulders. "Alphas will alpha," he says.

I clear my throat, resisting the urge to take his advice. "I need Danika and Cody to stay here tonight. The rest of you, I'd appreciate if you help Carly out as much as you can. We'll be fine here until morning."

Catching Iyana's arm before she leaves the room, I give her a hug. "Thank you for everything you've done for me."

She worries at her lip, searching my eyes. "That sounds scarily like a goodbye, Tessa."

"It's not," I lie. "I'll be right here in the morning." I clear my throat. "You should try to sleep in, get back into your routine."

She grimaces. "I have to admit, my body is pretty unhappy with me right now." She waves her hand at the now-dark windows. "Too much natural light."

I watch them all leave—Maeve with her violet-streaked hair still in conversation with Reya, their eyes alight as they remain in deep conversation. They've bonded like best friends or maybe... something more.

Neve and Nalani give me nods as they enter the elevator, both still more reserved around me than the women whom I originally met at Hidden House, but I sense the pack bond they have with me like a thread that connects us, spinning through all of us.

For the first time, I understand the pain Tristan felt at the prospect of losing a single member of his pack. To lose any of these women would be like snapping a rope and trying to knit the frayed ends together. Impossible to heal.

Lydia brushes my arm as she and Luna wait for the elevator to come back up. Her sage-green eyes are incredibly serious, her expression drawn. She surprises me when she hugs me tightly and, at the same time, Luna wraps her arms around me from the other side.

As I look between them, a shiver passes through me at the possibility that they can see my path as clearly as I can. If they can, they aren't sharing that information with anyone. Not yet.

"Thank you," I whisper.

"Remember that we love you, Tessa," Lydia says. "When the darkness becomes too much, look for us. We'll be there."

Finally, only Danika and Cody remain. We take turns showering while the other two watch over Tristan. I rush through my shower as fast as I can, worried about what could happen while I'm not there, but when I emerge, Tristan is fast asleep and all is calm.

When Danika and Cody retreat to the lounge, where I can hear them negotiating which couch they'll each take, I head to the bathroom to retrieve the pouch of magical objects. I debate leaving the objects behind, but I don't want to risk parting with them. I shove the pouch deep within my pocket where it rests against my hip, a reminder of the risk I'm taking in attempting to steal an assassin's ring tonight.

I lie down beside Tristan, waiting for Danika and Cody to fall asleep. I'm fully clothed in a fresh pair of jeans and a comfortable flannel shirt, my hair piled up on my head.

I trace the outline of Tristan's jaw, his face, the way the strands of his hair fall over his eyes, each curve of his muscular chest... memorizing every part of him.

His lips part. His voice is groggy. "I asked you not to tell me your plan, but I regret it now."

"You should be sleeping," I whisper.

"Tessa." He says my name like it's final. "A moment might come when you have to let me go."

He opens his eyes. Crisp, green, the most ruthless, fierce eyes. The most fucking fierce man.

My voice catches in my throat, a moment of fear too strong to speak.

"I keep replaying the moment that we met," he says. "I see it every time I close my eyes. You were standing in front of Peter Nash and you were bathed in power—a power that messed with my mind. You were fighting for your life. I was determined not to leave that place without you, but I convinced myself that my motives were about protecting my pack. Not about protecting you. Or about what I needed for myself. It was a lie I kept telling myself." He shakes his head. "I've lied to you too many times."

"I know," I say, a simple statement. "My favorite was when you told me that my life isn't worth as much as your pack's. I saw through that one."

"Fuck," he whispers, flinching. "It was one of the worst lies I've ever told. I failed to protect you, Tessa—"

"No," I say. "Acting out of love is never a failure. You needed to protect your pack."

"This magic is killing me." His voice is impossibly soft. His eyes begin to close, and I'm sure the medicine is pulling him under. "You need to be ready to let me go."

I rest my head on his shoulder.

"I'd rather crash with you," I whisper.

∼

Half an hour later, just when I think Danika and Cody are asleep, I hear Cody pacing around in the lounge room. He's quiet, but every time he passes by the window across the lounge, the light changes in the bedroom. For a moment, I regret asking him and Danika to stay, but I need them here with Tristan when I leave.

I hear Danika exhale quietly and picture her sitting up to rest her chin on the back of the lounge chair while she watches Cody pace.

"Are you okay?" she asks at a whisper.

"Yeah." His response is equally soft.

"All of the pacing indicates otherwise," she says.

He stops where I can see his silhouette against the backdrop of the window on the far side of the lounge. "It's a wolf thing."

I imagine her arched eyebrows, the hint of a challenge in her smile. "Try me."

He pauses. "I have trouble sleeping without someone beside me."

I know this to be true. Cody slept close to me at the Spire, giving me a wolfish greeting every morning that reestablished a connection between us. A sense of being pack. Despite losing his wolf, he seems to have maintained that trait.

Danika is quiet for a moment. Then she says, "There's room here with me if you're not afraid of falling off the edge."

He turns slightly so that his face is within the light. Just for a moment, I read the surprise in his slightly parted lips. "I trust you to catch me," he says.

I hear the sounds of material softly rustling as the two of them quietly maneuver around on the couch and rearrange blankets. Then silence again.

An hour later, I'm certain that it's time to leave.

I slip from Tristan's bed, reach for the security pass on his bedside table—the one Danika had—and creep from the room.

Pausing as I reach for my boots where they're set beside the elevator doors, I can't help but smile at Cody and Danika.

Of course, he's not on the edge at all. He presses against the back of the couch while Danika fits perfectly in his arms in front of him. They're both fast asleep.

I nudge the button for the elevator and tiptoe inside when the doors open. The last time I tried to creep from this penthouse, Tristan rushed after me, a disgruntled, half-asleep mountain of rage.

This time, the doors close without interruption.

My heart aches a little.

I take the elevator all of the way to the parking garage, where I

241

intend to slip out through the side door. Walking to the boxing gym isn't desirable, but I don't have much choice. I didn't have access to a vehicle growing up, so I never learned how to drive. The boxing gym is about five blocks from the bridges, so it shouldn't take me longer than an hour to walk there. It's only ten P.M.. I have plenty of time before the sun comes up.

The moment I step out of the elevator, my senses fire.

Iyana steps out of the shadows. She's dressed in fresh black jeans and a low-cut black T-shirt and is carrying two handguns and a dagger in a holster around her waist.

"I thought you might be headed out," she says.

"You can't fight this one with me."

She nods, breathing out a resigned sigh. "I know. Whatever battle you're headed into, I won't get involved unless you ask me to." She grins at me. "But I thought you might need a lift." She holds up a set of keys as well as a motorcycle helmet before she inclines her head toward Jace's sports motorcycle parked in the far bay.

"Jace gave you permission?" I ask, surprised.

She pulls a face. "Not exactly."

I don't give it another moment's thought. "I need a lift."

Iyana hands me the helmet as we stride to the bike. She retrieves the helmet sitting on top of the pillion seat. "Where are we going?"

I give her the address.

Her movements become slow as she processes my destination. "Are you sure about that?"

"Fucking sure."

"Okay, then." She doesn't ask me anything else. Swinging her leg over the bike as if she's ridden a hundred motorcycles before, she backs the bike out of the parking spot before she turns the key in the ignition and waits for me to slip onto the pillion seat behind her and find my footrests.

"Ready?" she calls over the purr of the bike's engine.

I lean into her back. "Ready."

The motorcycle leaps forward, but I'm prepared for the force of this beast. Iyana takes it easy up to the garage door until it opens, after which she expertly navigates the traffic outside, avoiding the hot spots where we know members of Tristan's pack will patrol.

We don't need them asking questions about why we have Jace's bike.

Within minutes, we're traveling across the Morrison Bridge, heading straight into Baxter Griffin's territory. I expand my senses, wary of any threat. Baxter is bound to have patrols along the river, but they won't follow us into the territory around the boxing gym.

Taking the expressway along the river and past the Convention Center, Iyana pays little attention to the speed limit. We'll only be safe from Baxter's pack once we approach the boxing gym. Then we'll face a different threat.

When we turn off onto the tree-lined street in downtown Portland, I sense Iyana's growing unease. The tension in her back increases even more than when we entered Baxter's territory. She slows the bike to a careful purr before she pulls off into a parking lot beside a neat-looking takeout restaurant.

I slip off the bike and remove my helmet after Iyana parks the motocycle in the shadows at the back of the lot.

"I can't go any closer than this," she says, taking up position beside the bike, her gaze darting around the area. "Fuck knows my name could be written in an assassin's ledger."

The back of my neck is prickling intensely, telling me that the place is crawling with assassins we can't see.

"Stay with the bike," I say. "If you're threatened, get out of here. Don't wait for me. I'll be fine."

Lifting her head and narrowing her eyes at the shadowy spaces around us, Iyana raises her voice a little, announcing into the darkness. "If anyone messes with you, they'll answer to me."

My heart warms because, despite Iyana's legitimate concern about her own safety, she's prepared to defend me.

I stride away through the neon lights projected from the restaurant. There's no point in trying to conceal my approach from unseen assailants. I walk right up to the door of the gym, not surprised to find it unlocked.

The truly powerful have no need to lock their doors.

I walk right in.

CHAPTER THIRTY-TWO

I pull in the familiar scent of leather bags, stepping through an entryway into a large training room.

All of the equipment appears surprisingly new. Somehow, I was expecting it to be beaten-up. The room is softly lit overhead with a long ceiling-to-floor mirror along a portion of the far right wall while rows of boxing bags hang from the ceiling along the back and far right sides. A boxing ring stands in the place of pride in the center of the room.

The space appears empty, but the sound of rapid thuds, fists against leather, comes from the far row of boxing bags. The boxer is hidden from sight behind the row of bags hanging in front. The familiar sound hits me as hard as the scent of leather. This is the gym where Andreas Dean trained.

The thudding stops, and I brace for an onslaught of men and women.

Instead, Alexei Mason steps into the light, carefully unstrapping his hands. He's naked from the waist up, wearing dark blue jeans, barefoot, sweat gleaming on his massive chest, his posture relaxed. Even from across the gym, it feels like he towers over me, a carefully controlled mountain of muscles.

"If you're here to kill your mother, you should know I won't let that happen," he says, still focusing on unwrapping his hands. "She's being dealt with under the Code."

THIS CAGED WOLF

"I'm not here to end her," I say.

He looks up. The impact of his gaze is no less intimidating across a boxing ring than it was when he was standing only a few paces away from me.

"Then why?" His question is direct, practically blunt.

"My mother has something I need," I say. "Without it, someone I love will die."

He drags out the silence while he finishes unstrapping his hands. Placing the wrapping on a table at the side, he scoops up a small towel and wipes the sweat from his face and chest as he strides around the boxing ring.

He's fast when he wants to be, but I stop myself before I backstep. Everyone is afraid of this man. I'm not entirely sure why, but I'd be stupid to ignore the fact that even Fenrir himself—a son of gods—fears Alexei Mason.

Once again, Alexei stops just outside of the reach of my fists. Whatever emotions he's feeling, he is completely unreadable. Unlike nearly every other person I've met, this man is a blank slate.

"Tell me what you need," he says, the towel gripped loosely in his fingertips. "I'll get it for you."

I'm stunned. *What?*

"You'll... get it for me?"

"The life of a loved one is worth more than any material object," he says. "Name the object and it's yours."

"I..."

Oh, fuck.

I came here expecting a fight. I was not expecting the Master Assassin to offer his help.

My speech is overly careful. "I'm afraid that what I need can't be given. It must be taken. By force."

He gives a heavy exhale. "That is unfortunate." He narrows his eyes at me, his gaze piercing in the way of someone who is reading my soul. "Will you at least tell me what it is?"

He has been so forthright with me that I take a breath and speak the truth. "I need an assassin's ring," I say. "Preferably my mother's, since force is required."

He glances at the onyx ring sitting on the forefinger of his left hand. The chunky red rubies catch the light. The faintest smile passes across his lips before it fades. All he says is, "Huh."

He turns his back on me, drops the towel at the side of the ring, and steps lithely up into it. Ducking under the ropes, he proceeds to the center of the ring, where he bounces on the balls of his feet and limbers up his shoulders. "Well, then, Tessa. Let's see what Andreas Dean taught you."

"I'm sorry?"

"Your mother is in the back room right now. She's been there for a couple of days now, drowning her wounded pride very successfully. Luckily, I didn't force her to give up her assassin's ring for the duration of her newest exile. If you can beat me, I'll let you pass."

A shiver runs to my toes, a combination of anticipation and dread. Fighting the Master Assassin is possibly one of the most reckless things I might do—or the smartest. I'll know when it's over.

Removing my boots, I roll up my sleeves, tie the bottom of my flannel shirt into a knot across my stomach, and ascend into the boxing ring. My hand brushes the pocket into which I pushed the pouch, checking that it's still secure. The objects bulge but they're less likely to slip out given how tightly they rest inside my pocket.

The non-slip canvas is spongy beneath my feet, soaking up my movements, but it's similar to the surface I trained on with Iyana at Hidden House, so I'm not totally unfamiliar with the sensation.

"No boxing gloves?" I ask.

Alexei gives me a crooked smile. "People like us don't need gloves," he says.

I don't disagree. I bounce a little on the balls of my feet and shake out my own shoulders. "You have an advantage—you're already warmed up."

He gives me an acknowledging nod. "I'll take it easy on you for a bit then."

I growl. "You'd better not."

Darting forward, I throw a loose combination of punches at him, making them deliberately sloppy. He evades each hit, bouncing back and around as lightly as if he were made of clouds.

He gives me a look. He knows I can do better.

I give him a smile.

I try again, this time a more serious combination of hits, which he again evades, but at the end of his evasive maneuver, I follow up with a little jab that lands right against his ribs.

He gives me an unexpected, but fleeting, grin.

I will get serious about my attack. Soon. I need to test him first. Despite our similar age, his broken-too-many-times nose tells me he has a hell of a lot more experience fighting in a ring than I have.

"I recommend that you don't try to use your power," he says as I dance around him. "Or you'll find out why Fenrir won't step foot anywhere near me."

"Well, now I'll definitely use my power." I give a soft laugh. "I'm incredibly curious about why everyone is so afraid of you."

I don't give him time to respond. I lash out with a set of serious punches, each one landing hard on his chest and shoulder but narrowly missing his jaw.

Damn-fuck! Connecting with his body is like hitting rock.

I nearly yelp, resisting the urge to nurse my hands as I bounce away from him.

This time, his grin is wide, a disarming smile that lights up his eyes. A dangerous light.

Then he attacks.

I duck and dance as fast as I can to avoid each powerful fist, bouncing back against the ropes, only narrowly getting away from the side of the ring so he doesn't trap me against it.

My fists are still smarting, and the agility of his movements, the power behind his punches, tells me I don't have a hope of beating him unless I harness my power. No matter that he's warned me not to.

Letting my strength flow through me, still ducking his punches, I spy an opening. I punch him squarely in the ribs in a two-hit combination that would break an ordinary man's bones.

He barely flinches.

I dart in again, aiming for his head, determined to knock him out, end this fight, and get to my mother. Allowing my power to flow through me, strengthening my fist, I aim it squarely for his chin.

Instead of evading me, he catches my hand, his stormy eyes meeting mine.

Suddenly, it's like I'm falling into an abyss.

All of the strength in my body fails, rushing from me. Rushing... toward his hand. Sucking out of me and I can't stop its flow. I may as well be made of water and I'm pouring into the darkness that builds around him, a vacuum that doesn't let up even when I feel like he's taken everything I have.

With a cry, I drop to my knees, unable to stand up, every limb in my body as weak as if my bones were made of feathers.

Alexei doesn't let me go, dropping to the canvas with me, maintaining my gaze.

"I warned you," he says.

For a horrifying second, his eyes glow crimson—just like mine—but when the glow fades, his expression is far from angry. He considers me with an unsettling amount of compassion.

I whimper. Gasp. "What did you do?"

"I drained your power," he says. "I don't keep hold of it. I can't store your power or use it for myself, but sometimes I feel what the power-holder feels. I caught a glimpse of your rage just now. I saw the world through your eyes. You battle internal darkness that is too great for one person, Tessa."

I let out a sob. I didn't expect him to understand me as well as he seems to. I can't sense my power anymore. Can't feel it, can't call it. I'm empty. Fucking empty.

"This is how you could kill Fenrir," I say.

"This is how I could kill a god," Alexei answers. "Like you, I didn't know or understand the full extent of my power until recently. It certainly would have helped me if I'd understood it sooner. I've had to learn quickly."

"Have I lost my power?" I ask, panic striking through me. "Have you taken it forever?"

He shakes his head. "Only for a time. The stronger the supernatural, the faster their power returns. But a mere second is all it takes for me to kill them while they're powerless." He pauses. "For you, however, I sense a quick recovery."

He's still holding my hand, but he lowers it between us, resting it on his knee, turning his palm so that my hand lies in his. The threat he poses to me is clear. Yet he remains quiet and still.

I hunch low, my shoulders sinking.

"You have to let me pass," I say. "I have to fight my mother and take her assassin's ring. If I don't... Tristan will die and this darkness you sense inside me... I won't be able to stop it."

Alexei inhales deeply. "Tristan Masters also fights inner demons." He considers me carefully. "Some warriors are forged in fire. Others in pain. Still others are forged in loss. Then there are those who are blessed to seek goodness despite never seeing the dark. They're the lucky ones."

His expression hardens. "We are not the lucky ones. Now, get back up and fight me or you'll never get what you need."

With a snarl, I leap away from him while he rises to his feet and squares his shoulders.

I can't use my power.

I have to fight like Andreas taught me.

Don't show your power, Andreas told me. *Your wolf will get you killed.*

Well, I guess he trained me for this moment.

Okay, seven-foot mountain. It's just your fists against mine.

With a shout of determination, I leap back into the fight, delivering a rapid sequence of punches designed to wind and knock him down. I'm satisfied to hear the air whoosh from his chest, but it seems he's done going easy on me, too.

I narrowly evade a thump to my face that would knock me out, taking the clip across my temple. The hit carries enough force to spin me backward. I use the momentum to my advantage, spinning and kicking his stomach hard enough to propel him back against the ropes. It's not technically boxing, but the kick seemed called for.

The damn assassin is too agile, evading nearly every hit until I leap and land a punch to his temple that splits his skin.

He falls to one knee.

Remorse is a hot burn inside me as I hesitate to follow through. I don't want to hurt him. Not at all.

He glares up at me.

"Is that all?" he asks. "Do you want to get past me or not, Tessa?"

With a scream, I attack with every combination I know, sacrificing my ribs so that I can get in closer even though he strikes back. Just as I set up a series of punches that should knock him out, a scream and a *crash* at the side of the boxing ring makes me spin.

My mother stands on that side of the room, her hair a mess, her blue eyes wide and watery, her cheeks blotchy. A bottle of alcohol lies smashed around her feet. The scent of spirits rises from the spilled liquid. She grips a shot glass in her left hand. The glass gleams and so does her assassin's ring.

"What are you doing here?" she asks, her speech slurring.

I'm surprised she can string two words together, given that she chose to run from the back room still gripping the means by which she has been drowning her pride. I doubt she planned on being separated from that bottle.

Alexei told me I had to get through him to get to my mother. Well, now she's right here.

With a quick, fierce glance at him, I throw myself beneath the rope at the side of the ring, sliding beneath it and shooting out the other side. I snatch up the small towel he was using as I race past it.

I risk gouging my feet open on the broken glass as I dash across to my mother while she gapes at me. Sprinting around the debris, I catch her arm and pull her sideways into the mirror on this side of the room.

Shoving one hand against her shoulder, I wrench her left arm to the side, catch the shot glass she's still gripping, and pitch it back at Alexei as he follows my footsteps, scarily fast.

He leaps to the side to avoid the projectile and it gives me the seconds I need to turn back to my mother.

She struggles, unsteady on her feet as I wrap the towel around her hand and knock her arm back against the mirror. I can't risk touching the ring directly in case my magic reacts with the old magic in the ring. I can only hope the towel will protect me.

Her eyes are glassy and unfocused, but her expression flits between emotions, her forehead creasing and easing, lips pursing and softening. Pursing again as if she wants to say something. "My daughter..."

"I guess we all have demons," I whisper.

Her assassin's ring slips off her finger and into the towel.

Bunching it in my fist, encasing it safely in the towel, I dart to the side.

Alexei plows toward me, but I dash out of his reach in the nick of time. Pelting across the room, I bend only to snatch up my shoes before I grab the door handle. I nearly drop my shoes, but I make it through the door.

Harnessing my power to give me speed, I plow down the footpath and don't stop. Up ahead, Iyana is waiting, the bike already growling its beautiful purr at the side of the street. She must have sensed my approach.

As soon as I launch myself onto the back of the bike, she takes off.

My heart is pumping. Once again, I nearly drop my boots, but I have the ring and I'm not letting it go.

CHAPTER THIRTY-THREE

*I*yana is paler than normal when we return to the parking garage beneath the clock tower. She drove like a maniac and we reached the safety of the garage in half the time it took us to get to the boxing gym.

She pulls off her helmet, her chest heaving. "What do I need to know?" she asks.

"They won't come after you," I say. My hand is turning numb from gripping the towel so hard. The curve of the ring and the sharp edges of the diamond at its center bite my palm through the soft material, but I welcome the sensation.

I have the object of old magic.

I have everything I need.

Quickly slipping on my boots, I retrieve the pouch from my pocket and carefully slide the ring inside it with the other objects.

Looking up, I find Iyana tense, her forehead creased and lips pressed together in an unhappy line. "Tessa—"

"I need you to return to the others now," I say, taking hold of her shoulders. "Whatever happens, don't come looking for me. It's very important that you don't come anywhere near me. Do you understand?"

I saw what happened when the goddess took Cerberus's minds and they passed into someone they shouldn't have. The minds won't just disappear. They will seek the nearest body to enter. It has to be me. Nobody else can be near us. I'll have one shot at taking them, and I can't fuck it up."

Iyana's eyes are wide. "You're scaring me, Tessa."

I try to soften my speech, but it's difficult. "You've been a true friend to me, Iyana. The best friend—"

Her jaw clenches. She grips my arms as hard as I'm holding her. "What are you planning?"

"I'm going to free Tristan and then I'm going to kill the wolf who sired me—along with anyone who stands beside him. I'm putting an end to this. Once and for all."

She stares at me as if I don't know her at all. "You expect me to sit out of this fight?"

"Not expect—*command* you not to get involved," I say, forcing her hands away from my arms. "As a member of my pack, I expect you to obey me. Stay away from me, Iyana. It's for your own safety."

Spinning on my heel, I walk away from her to slap the button to call the elevator.

It seems my position as her alpha and the pack bond between us still allows her to disagree with me, because she strides right after me. "No."

My reflexes are too fast—even for her. I grab her and propel her up against the nearest wall, my growl a deep order, a sound of rage. "*Stay the fuck away from me!*"

Releasing Iyana, I snatch the security card peeking from her pocket along with her dagger before I turn and run.

The card is the only way she can follow me to the twelfth floor.

She shouts as she regains her feet, chasing after me, but I skid into the open elevator a split second before the doors close. The moment I swipe the security pass and hit the button for the twelfth floor, the elevator begins to rise.

I press my hands across my eyes with a moan, backing into the handrail around the elevator walls.

Remorse, shame, guilt—all of the horrible feelings flow through me, but I can't let anyone follow me. If I have to make my pack hate me, then that's what I'll do.

The elevator doors open into Tristan's penthouse, but I don't step out, glancing at the quiet room to satisfy myself that nothing has happened before I press the button for the roof.

Once there, I exit the elevator into a small room with a transparent door and step beyond it for the first time. Outside, the wind howls around me and overhead the clouds are gathering, threatening rain.

A platform extends around the sides of the peak of the building that contains the clock. White stone balustrades rise up around the edge of the platform. They're high and sturdy enough to lean against. The platform itself is about seven paces deep—deep enough for what I need.

Returning to the door, I take a calculated two steps forward and one to my right. Then I crouch to the surface of the platform to find it tarred. Using Iyana's dagger, I scratch and gouge three concentric circles into that exact spot.

After that, I carefully place the magical objects around the balcony—one in each of the corners and then one at each side of the central peak, as if they are the corners of a rectangle. I'm taking a huge risk leaving them here. I can only pray they'll be safe.

Hurrying back to the elevator, I return to the twelfth floor. When the doors open, I prepare to creep through the lounge room to the bedroom, only to freeze.

Tristan stands in the doorway to his room, his silhouette shrouded in shadows. He takes a step forward when he sees me, but his focus shifts to Cody and Danika, who are still fast asleep on the couch.

My instincts are on full alert when Tristan makes a soft snarl, the sound of an angry, wounded animal looking for a target.

Quickly, I attempt to judge his posture. His shoulders are hunched like the Killer's, but his eyes are wide and green—the Coward's eyes—nearly human-looking, although they're partially hidden behind the strands of his raven hair. His lips—the lips I want to kiss when I tell him that everything will be okay—those lips are twisted into a snarl that tells me the Deceiver is also present.

My breath catches—and so does his, the quietest inhale, which should mean that he is himself. Yet... his body tells me that he is not.

I shiver as I realize that the closer he comes to death, the more his four minds seem to be merging. The Killer is ready to attack with his body, the Coward observes me through Tristan's eyes, the Deceiver will control his voice, but his heart...

Tristan's heart is mine.

I close my eyes for a moment, remembering the way he held me tonight. *This is not a lie.*

Opening my eyes, I reach out my hand toward him, silently urging him to come to me without waking Danika or Cody.

Tristan narrows his eyes at me, but he turns away from the sleeping couple and approaches me at a stealthy prowl, remaining quiet while I lean on the elevator door to keep it open.

I keep my movements calm, nothing sudden, as I take his hand and draw him inside and press the button for the roof.

"Why are we going to the roof, Tessa?" the Deceiver asks.

"For privacy," I answer truthfully.

He catches me in his arms. "But why?"

I tip my head back, my lips softening as my gaze follows the lines formed by the strands of his hair across his cheeks, studying the curve of his lips. I allow my speech to stumble. "I thought... maybe... If you have a taste of what you'll be missing, you might keep Tristan alive for longer...? After all, once he's gone, you can't have me again."

The Coward disappears from Tristan's eyes, the Deceiver ceases to twist his lips, and now the Killer takes over completely. "You will allow me to conquer you?"

"I will," I say.

His eyes narrow. "But only if I defy the angel's magic for as long as I can?"

"For me, yes," I whisper. "You're a creature of the gods. Surely, you can repel any magic you want—"

"We can't destroy pure magic," he says. "We can only corrupt it." With a growl, his lips descend to mine, a demanding press, his hands rising to rest beneath my breasts just as the elevator doors open.

I allow him to draw me out into the anteroom. The transparent door on the other side is so close, but the Killer stops right before it, pushing me up against the inner wall.

My body responds to his demanding kisses as if the darkness inside me were made for him, but it's my darkness that will give me the means to deceive even the Deceiver. I return his kiss, exploring his mouth with my tongue, running my hands up his arms to his shoulders.

Breaking the contact between our mouths with a heated gasp, I say, "Come out into the rain with me."

When he casts me a questioning glance, I persist.

"Remember the first time you showed me your face? It was raining in the Near-Apart Room," I say. "I want that again."

"I remember." He growls, easing up when I gently push against his chest so I can step toward the door.

Backing into it, I unbutton the top of my shirt to reveal the tops of my breasts before I find the door handle and push it open, stepping out into the rain.

The water falls in fat droplets onto my head and shoulders, quickly plastering my shirt to my curves.

Carefully, I step to the left. At the same time, I continue to unbutton my shirt until it's open to my stomach, keeping the Killer's focus above the ground. "Killer?"

He pauses in the doorway, still a step away from where I need him to be, his gaze lifting from my breasts to my face. "Our fates were always entwined, Tessa Dean," he says.

My chest rises and falls rapidly as the rain drips down my face and neck, a soft caress against my skin. My tongue darts between my lips as I hold out my hand to him, urging him to come to me.

He takes a step and my senses expand, focused on every tiny movement, every flex of his muscles as he lifts his arms, ready to wrap me in them. At the last possible moment—just as his hands brush my arms, sweeping around my sides—I take another step back out of his reach.

He jolts where he stands. Attempts to follow me. Confusion spreads across his face when he can't move.

He looks down. And freezes.

A growl rips out of him. "What have you done, Tessa Dean?"

I inhale the cold and the scent of rain, thick in the air. "You are a cage around Tristan's mind and body. I'm breaking you open."

His face transforms, deep rage passing across it. "We had a deal."

"Deception is in your nature," I say. "Yet you're surprised when someone else lies?"

His response is a snarl. "You've made a serious error, Tessa Dean."

"Why is that?" I ask as the rain continues to fall.

"I'm awake," he says, water dripping down his chest. "To take my minds, you must be in contact with my body." His claws descend and so do his incisors. "I will tear you apart."

A shiver runs down my spine, but I suppress it. "Will you, though?" I ask. "If you kill me, you'll have no chance of survival. My body is your future—whether in the form of a child I can give you or by giving *me* your minds."

He is a hulking mass of muscle and dangerous intent. "You are not the only woman in this building," he says, giving me pause. "There are several who would willingly bed Tristan if he approached them in the right way. I would not have to act with force. Only with deception. There is still time."

"Deception is just as wrong!" I snarl.

"Tessa, Tessa." He shakes his head at me, his lips twisting as the Deceiver takes the lead now. "Why won't you believe me when I tell you that Tristan doesn't love you?"

The Deceiver is playing on my fears again, trying to break open the layers of kindness under which I've buried my hurt and pain. He's trying to crack open the cage within which I've placed my worst nightmares.

I won't let him.

Daring him to hurt me, I step forward and slap my hand against his heart.

"I will take your minds," I whisper. "Your minds will be mine."

At the four corners of the platform, the objects of magic light up all at once. The angel's halo is a golden stream piercing the dark. The fae's power is a thread of glistening aqua. The dark magic orb is a creeping shadow, and the assassin's ring casts a silver line like steel. Each one shoots toward us, piercing the Killer's chest in front and behind.

"No!" His claws sharpen against my back, threatening to make good on his promise to tear me apart, but he pauses as the magic spreads across his skin. It makes him glow, every inch of his exposed skin a swirling mix of molten gold, glistening water, shivery shadows, and liquified silver. For a second, he is blank, as if he can't decide which mind will save him.

"I will take your deception," I say, trying to catch my breath as the magic flows across my hand and between my fingertips. "Your deception will be mine."

The Killer resurfaces, snarling again, but his lips lower to mine, hovering, threat dripping from every syllable. "I will kill you, Tessa Dean. In one form or another. I will disregard my feelings toward you and I will end you. It is inevitable."

A pushing sensation grows beneath my palm as the magic builds across his chest, the colors blurring before my eyes, casting a myriad of power up across the Killer's face.

"I will take your cowardice." I gasp for breath, my chest constricting. The darkness inside me rushes toward the surface, a violent defense against the power growing around me. "Your cowardice will be mine!"

The Killer searches my eyes—or maybe it's the Coward, or the Deceiver, I can't tell which now that the magic surrounds us and all I sense is his rage. The deep, undying rage of a creature whose minds were stolen—whose life was stolen from him.

His voice lowers and I don't know who he is when he says, "You will kill me by breaking my heart."

I press my lips to his, kissing him hard, tasting his anger, but also his fear. I want to tell him that everything broken can be put back together. Perhaps not the same. New and different. But his heart will survive. I'll make sure of it.

"I will take your violence!" I cry. "Your violence will be mine!"

All at once, his minds seem to merge and the pushing sensation beneath my palm and between our bodies becomes unbearable. I nearly scream as I lose my sense of where I end and he begins.

"You can't contain me," he says. "You won't be strong enough."

Beneath the pushing sensation is a tearing feeling, a horrible, sickening sense of being ripped apart on the inside. I can't tell where. Maybe he has finally torn open my back with his claws. Maybe my darkness is about to come apart. Maybe all the scaffolding I've built inside my mind to sustain myself through pain and even through happiness is about to come crashing down.

I tip my head back and scream. "I will take your minds!"

Above us, the sky is filled with thunder clouds. Lightning spears within the boiling mass overhead and down through the air around us. It's as if nature is sending a warning in the form of thunder and lightning because I am about to commit a crime against the natural order.

Sliding my hands and arms across Tristan's chest, through the mire of magic, the slick power, I hold on as tightly as I can.

My scream tears at my throat. *"Your minds are mine!"*

The tearing sensation bursts upward, through my torso, but at the same time, I recognize it as coming from outside me—coming from within Tristan.

He roars, a sound of pain so intense that I'm sobbing against his chest. His knees buckle and we both crash to the ground, the impact jarring up through my thighs.

His pain blasts through me and then I'm screaming. I'm sobbing and screaming and crying, and a shadow is growing between us that I can't deny. It splits into three and for a second the faces of the minds are visible in the lightning spearing around us.

The Killer, Coward, and Deceiver glower at me through the eyes of shadowy wolves with sharp teeth and sharper minds.

My voice is a wail of pain and fear as the shadows rush into me, disappearing beneath my rain-slicked skin. *"Your minds are mine!"*

I've taken them. Just as I intended.

The impact of their power knocks me backward, so hard and so fast that Tristan's arms open in a burst. My body flies into the balustrade. I nearly lose my balance, nearly topple over the edge before I drop safely to the ledge again.

The lightning continues to flicker above us, but the magic swirling around Tristan's head and torso fades, glittering particles disappearing and leaving bright spots in my vision.

Tristan kneels in the center of the rune while I slump against the balustrade. The magic should let him go now, but still, he doesn't move and fear grows within me.

The silence is heavy, broken only by the softly pattering rain that continues to fall.

Tristen's head is bowed, his arms loose at his sides.

His wounds... His wounds are still angry, the golden light within them faint but clinging...

Oh, please.

I close my eyes and pray. *Please, please...*

I have nothing left. No other way to save his life. This was it. This was all I had.

Please...

A light grows beyond me and my eyes fly open.

The glow within his exposed wounds flares, a series of soft bursts. Golden dust rises up out of the visible wounds like ash from a spent fire.

Tristan jolts. He shouts, a clear sound. A *strong* sound.

He rips wildly at the bandages over his other wounds, tearing them off, releasing the spent golden dust into the air to rise against gravity, traveling in the opposite direction to the rain.

Each of his exposed wounds begins to close, the angry red skin healing and calming.

His head snaps up and his eyes meet mine—fierce... *fucking fierce*... green eyes that are completely his own.

Finally all his own.

I sag against the balustrade as he leaps across the space between us, reaching for me, brushing the wet hair from my cheeks, checking my eyes, trying to gather me up.

"Tessa!" He wraps his arms around me. "Fuck! Tessa!"

I rest my head against his shoulder. For the very first time, I inhale his pure scent. All Tristan. All of the bitter, strong, imperfect, complicated, unexpectedly gentle, undeniably dangerous. All of him.

While he cries my name, a silence grows inside my mind.

A calm purpose.

The Killer rises inside me, together with the Coward and the Deceiver. Their voices are each unique, different skillsets that will protect me and give me what I need to kill my father and every person who enabled him, aided him, and hurt the people I love.

"Tessa?" Tristan's lips are hot and sweet, gentle and furious against mine.

"Talk to me," he orders. An alpha's order.

I'm calm as I meet his eyes. Completely at peace with what I've done and what I need to do.

"I'm here," I say. "I'm Tessa."

CHAPTER THIRTY-FOUR

I reach up to trail my fingertips along Tristan's jaw as he holds me. "You're free," I say. "And I have everything I need to beat my father now."

Tristan bends his head to mine with a groan. "You took the minds. For me."

"Yes," I say, as if it were the simplest thing in the world to contain the brutality growing inside my mind, the rising deception, along with the crippling fear. All of the power against which Tristan fought. I have an advantage that Tristan never had, and it's keeping the minds at bay—I have the ability to separate my power from my body and my mind, and I plan to use that skill to full effect.

"The three-headed wolf is mine," I say. "He belongs to me now."

Tristan strokes my cheek, pressing his forehead to mine, his fingers both rough and gentle. "You have to fight his power, Tessa. He'll take control—"

"He won't," I say.

Tristan leans back an inch to search my eyes. "You sound very certain."

"I am."

Carefully, I test the strength in my arms and legs, calculating my ability to make sudden movements, before I tip my head back and

261

cast my gaze up to the sky. The lightning, the thunder, it crackles in my hearing like an old friend.

A shape moves within the roiling clouds. A creature with the largest wings and gorgeous crimson feathers. I wonder how long the thunderbird has been following my movements, hiding within the ever-present cloud cover over Portland.

Drawing Tristan with me, I rise to my feet and wrap my arms around him. I press my cheek to his. "There's a war waiting for me and I won't lose another person I love fighting it. If there were another way, I would choose it."

Tristan's arms tighten around me. Cerberus is gone from his body and mind, but now, I sense his wolf returning and reasserting its dominance. His eyes partially shift, the amber flecks that I've missed reappear, and the deep growl in the back of his throat makes me shiver. I could listen to that sound forever. I could fucking fall asleep to that sound because he only makes that growl when he cares.

When he's angry.

Fucking angry that I'm about to walk into a fight against a wolf who has proven his ability to survive any assault.

"Cerberus was meant to die with me!" Tristan shouts. "*You* were meant to *live*." His arms squeeze painfully around me. "I need you to fucking live, Tessa."

My heart tugs painfully inside my chest. "It was never meant to be," I whisper. "I'm a creature alone, and alone I'll die."

Tristan's claws dig into my arms, scraping my back. "I'm not letting that happen. I'm not letting you fucking die, do you hear me? That's a fucking order, Tessa."

I bite my lip against the sob rising inside my chest. Far above me, I sense the thunderbird's agitation. Somehow, the minds are increasing the power of my senses a thousand times over. Every crackle of lightning thrumming through her wings tingles along my arms. I don't think she likes that Tristan's holding me so tightly.

"When have I ever obeyed orders?" I ask.

"Fucking never," he says, pressing his lips together, his brows drawn down. "Now is when you start!"

With great difficulty, I slip my hand between us and press it to his heart. The beat is like a terrified drum. His anger hides his fear. I press against him, sensing every ripple of muscle across his chest, the strength in his thighs, his arms, the ease with which he could throw me over his shoulder and run with me. Never stop running.

Tears slip down my cheeks, mingling with the rain. "You can't control this, Tristan."

"Like fuck I can't."

"Then come with me," I say.

He stares at me, his chest heaving. A perfectly healed chest.

I lower my voice. "Come with me to certain death—or stay and live for your pack. They need you, Tristan. They need you to be a good alpha, to help them heal. You can't leave them now."

He roars out his frustration. "How can I let you go?"

"Let it all crash," I whisper. "All the love and hope. Let it all break."

I sense the thunderbird's descent through the clouds from above, her rapid plummet toward the clock tower. She's done waiting for my call. Her gorgeous form soars down toward the far side of the tower before she sweeps around toward us. Her lightning is subdued now, so dark that she is a shadow in the rain.

Her wings are too wide for her to land safely without bashing them against the building, but I sense her approach around the clock tower at a level just below where we stand. She's too high to be seen through the twelfth-floor windows, but she's also too low for Tristan to see her.

Still, the way he twitches tells me he senses her presence, not as quickly as I did, but with just as much surprise.

Taking advantage of the diversion, I push against Tristan's arms and take a quick step back. "I will love you until I die, Tristan Masters."

Without another word, I spin, run, and leap from the edge of the building.

Sailing into the air, I stretch out for Lyra's wing, catch her wing joint in the nick of time, and pull myself up onto her back. She rights herself and ascends rapidly toward the clouds.

I used to feel pain that I can't bond like other wolves. Now I'm grateful because leaving Tristan is painful enough.

Below me, the clock tower grows smaller and Tristan grows smaller still.

"Lyra," I say, bending to the thunderbird's neck, burying my face and my tears in her feathers as we enter the cloud cover. "Take me to the Spire."

CHAPTER THIRTY-FIVE

The first rays of sunlight warm my face as we fly above the clouds. The light glints off Lyra's feathers when she cracks her wings. She seems to delight in the warmth of the sun as much as I do. My clothing was damp from the rain, and the wind made it freezing against my skin. Until the sun started to rise, I stayed low and close to Lyra's body so I didn't freeze.

Once we're clear of the city and the rain has stopped, Lyra swoops below the cloud cover and soars across the top of the forest. From this high up, I can see how vast the woodland is, how far it stretches north and south. An army of supernaturals could hide in it undetected for years, as the witches did.

Lyra heads across what was the neutral territory between the witches' covens and flies through the ravine where the ancient fae live. The magic that protects the ravine bites my skin when we enter on the eastern side, and then again as Lyra soars upward through the top of the shield. When I look down after we exit the shield, all I see is forest. No ravine. The fae's home is protected from detection by humans from every angle.

Heading due west, I know that the Spire will be equally well hidden. I won't be able to see it from the air. It's sheltered by strong magic—the same magic that protects the ravine—which is why Helen and the card mage twins couldn't find me when I was held captive there.

I'm sure there must be entrances and exits that allow other supernaturals to pass through—including from the air, since I first arrived in a helicopter—but finding them could be nearly impossible.

Like the ravine, the Spire is designed not to be found.

My heart sinks rapidly as I realize that I might not be able to find the Spire again. I was unconscious for both trips in and out of the hidden area. I don't know what the surrounding forest or the cliff faces look like from the air. I won't be able to recognize them. All I know is that the stone tower is located on the west coast. I asked Lyra to take me to the Spire because Queen Calanthe had said that her people used to live there, but that doesn't mean Lyra knows where it is.

My heart sinks further when Lyra flies all the way toward the cliffs at the edge of the ocean without stopping. The sparkling ocean is vast and choppy in the near distance. The air turns salty, moist on my tongue, and the sound of crashing waves grows louder.

I hold my breath, hoping the Spire will miraculously appear in front of me, but Lyra takes me all the way past the cliffs and dips toward the water. The savagery of the water below us takes my breath away. The waves crash white against the jagged cliffs, splashing upward before dragging back down.

I'm about to lean over Lyra's neck and ask her to turn around when she banks sharply to the right, soaring back toward the cliff—only about fifty feet above its edge.

Magic bites my skin in a sharp burst.

The breath catches in my throat as the Spire and its immediate surroundings suddenly appear. We sail neatly beneath the landing platform that juts from the left side of the Spire and over the top of the clearing around the Spire.

A group of leopard shifters is undertaking combat training in the square near the raised platform that sits at the front of the tower. They scatter, shouting, as Lyra soars over the top of them.

Clever Lyra. In the distance, patrols of shifters guard the forest side of the clearing. Approaching from the ocean side has given me the advantage of surprise.

"Don't land!" I call urgently to the thunderbird. "I'll jump from your back! You must fly to safety!"

She is free to make her own choices. She bounces her head, acknowledging my order, warily eyeing the leopard shifters. Many of them are armed. Several of them have dropped to a knee already and are lining up shots ahead of us.

"Thank you, friend," I cry as Lyra skims as close to the ground as she can without touching down.

I leap from her back, landing at a soft crouch before I duck and roll to absorb the impact without breaking my legs.

Gunshots sound from all directions and my heart leaps into my throat as Lyra soars away, rising rapidly and zigzagging to avoid the bullets. She makes it into the distance when her flying form suddenly blurs for a second before it's clear again. The moment that her silhouette was blurry must have been when she passed through the shield. I gauge the distance—much farther than I thought. That means a hell of a lot more supernaturals could shelter within the Spire's shield without detection from the outside.

As I rise to my feet, my back to the leopard women, a final bullet flies close to my shoulder.

I turn and pin the shooter with a glare as silence falls.

The women lower their weapons, shuffling where they stand.

It hasn't been so long since I was last here. They know who I am and what I'm capable of.

I can't see any wolf shifters among the women, but I can sense them. Hundreds of wolf shifters within the trees—possibly several packs. Maybe more. My expanded senses tell me they're all alert and merely waiting for a signal.

Up on the dais, Ford Vanguard sits in his customary morning location at the table with the map of his empire on it. He has half-risen from his seat and pushes his chair back as I stride the fifty paces it takes to approach the base of the raised platform.

Today, he's dressed in black pants and a gray collared shirt. His presence in human form is like a void in my senses. His hair is light brown and his eyes are a shade of hazel green, but as I approach, his features shift subtly, his eyes becoming more blue and his hair suddenly highlighted with red. The shadowed growth across his jaw and his perfectly curved lips don't change.

Behind him, Brynjar takes a step forward but doesn't approach me. Unlike Ford, his emotions are not hidden. His eyes are a piercing icy blue, his head cleanly shaved. Standing a full head taller than my father, he's dressed completely in black. His chest and silhouette are as muscular as Alexei Mason's. He looks at me with the same level of concern. Brynjar was the one who broke me. I froze in flurries of snow before I realized that his power was old magic like mine. I warned him that he would one day have to choose between me and my father. Today is that day.

Ford's lips curl in disdain. "I thought you'd be smart and bring me the book of old magic. But I see you're empty-handed."

I remain at the base of the platform—a good twenty paces away from it with space to move if I need to—even though it places me at a lower vantage point than him.

"I read the book," I say, without malice. "I'm sorry for what happened to your family."

He stiffens, then he recoils, as if my sympathy were repugnant to him. "You're a poor substitute for my sons. If I had ever found them, we would have torn apart the world together."

I sigh at his insult. "You can't stab me with words," I say. "I know that I'm loved."

"Loved!" he spits. "By whom? The woman who abandoned you or the one who rejected you?"

He's referring to my assassin mother and the wolf shifter whom I thought was my mother, but again, his verbal daggers roll off me. I'm done with my old fears and pain. There's an entire pack of women back at the clock tower who would lay down their lives for me. They're so willing to protect and stand beside me that, once again, I had to push them away to keep them safe.

My heart aches, but it's not grief or pain. There is no sorrow in protecting the ones I love. No failure in acting out of love.

I'm at peace with the choices I need to make.

"I'm here to challenge you, Fenrir," I say.

Behind Ford, Brynjar is tense, but my father is relaxed. He clicks his tongue at me before he draws out my name with scorn. "Tessa. You can't defeat me. I'm more powerful than you—"

"Prove it," I say. "Fight me. Just you and me. Nobody else has to die."

He lets out a laugh, a derisive sound. "That's very noble of you," he says. "But my pack has grown. There is no fighting me without fighting *them*."

Footfalls sound from within the tower of the Spire—multiple people descending the sapphire staircases at once.

All six alphas step out from the tower onto the platform behind Ford.

Baxter Griffin is the first to appear, his hair a darker blond than Cody's and Ella's and his eyes a faded brown. His chest bears the scars of former battles. He snarls at me as he takes up position on Ford's far left.

My former alpha, Peter Nash, follows, his hair shaved to his scalp on both sides and short on top. Like Baxter, he's naked from the waist up, the tattooed skeleton of a wolf's snarling head promising death. His neck and chest are thick. He's not as tall as Brynjar, but he's just as bulky.

They're followed by the female alpha, Sasha, who is dressed in black pants and a low-cut bodice that shows off the top of her tattoo, a wolf tipping back its head and howling. Like the night I first saw her, her blond ponytail is drawn up high and tight.

The physical appearance of the remaining three alphas is just as ferocious, each taller than average, chests chiseled and tattooed.

As they take up position behind my father, the leopard shifters behind me hurry away toward the back of the clearing, making space for the wolf shifters hidden in the trees to emerge. There are hundreds of them, both male and female, as I sensed.

They stride between the trees and spill out into the clearing, making their way toward me at a prowl. All of them are dressed for battle, the nearest revealing an array of daggers resting at their hips. Many of them partially shift to reveal their claws and teeth, but only the strongest maintain a partial shift for any substantial length of time. All but a few revert to their human form within seconds.

The threat is clear, though: They are here to tear me apart.

My father shakes his head at me. "I thought you'd arrive with an army at your back, Tessa. You're foolish to face us alone."

I turn slowly from side to side, contemplating the awful odds against me. As the packs close in around me, I recognize the distinctions between them. Sasha's pack is directly to my left—the leaders all women wearing leather bodices, their hair pulled up in tight ponytails like hers. Baxter's pack approaches from my right—I recognize some of the guards from the night I was taken. I quickly scan their faces for Cody and Ella's younger brother, Cameron. I'm relieved when I don't see him among them. Their brother is the only one I have a reason not to hurt.

Checking the approaching packs at my back with a glance cast over my right shoulder, I find Peter Nash's pack approaching faster than the others. At their head is Dawson Nash, my childhood tormentor. He's younger than me by two years, but he's as bulky as his father, his arms and legs thick with muscles. His head is shaved at the sides with sweeping lines forming a sharp pattern. His eyes are startlingly blue. The tattoo he wears across his chest is still an outline—he's still in training—but I have no doubt that he intends to prove himself today.

I inhale sharply when I recognize his mother prowling beside him. She is the one I once thought was *my* mother. Her hair is more orange than mine, her eyes the shade of blue that I once mirrored. She used to seem so large to me, a figure whose love I could never earn, but now I see her as just another wolf. She's dressed like the others, all in black, her claws extended.

She and Dawson stop ten paces from me, snarls on their lips.

Of course, they *would* be positioned where they can stab me in the back.

"I told you I'd break you again," Dawson says, his gaze raking up and down my body like claws.

Dawson's threat washes over me—as harmless as the breeze that brushes my face and arms. I catch the flash of uncertainty in his eyes when I ignore him and turn back to Ford.

I wonder if Ford has informed the alphas or their packs about the extent of my abilities. Or his own. Dawson is cruel, but he's not stupid. If he knew what he was up against, he wouldn't threaten me so openly. No. He'd attack from the shadows.

I inhale and exhale. Helen spent months trying to teach me the ability to be calm, and I've finally acquired it.

"You think I came alone," I say to my father. "You think I didn't bring an army."

I allow myself to smile, but it's reserved. Fighting him will be hard. Dangerous. I have no arrogance or certainty. Only determination.

The weapon he doesn't have against me this time is leverage. That simple, tactical weakness that he used against me time and time again. He wanted me to bring my friends. He wanted me to endanger them so he could use them to control me.

His real disappointment must be that this time, there's nobody here I care about.

"I brought an army," I say. "Just not the one you hoped I would bring."

My power rises inside me, and so do the minds of Cerberus.

They thrash at the cage within which I'm keeping them. It is the same broken cage that once contained my darkness—the cage that was so strong, it kept my true nature from me all of my life. My father cracked it open, but like all broken things, it mended, even stronger than before.

With a quiet exhale, I release my wolves from my body.

All four of them.

CHAPTER THIRTY-SIX

The Killer emerges first, an enormous, glistening, black beast who stands at my chest height. His teeth drip with crimson blood and his eyes are as black as Tristan's raven hair. His body is made of energy, streams of light that flicker in the early morning sunlight. His impulse is to attack, but I hold him back, containing his rage.

The Coward appears next, the smallest and wiliest, the one who will survive against all odds because he will always put himself first. His energy is a pale shade of gold, his claws gleaming yellow, his golden eyes wide, observing every threat and relaying it to me. He has already calculated the number of opponents in the trees and how fast my wolves can cut them down.

Third, the Deceiver slinks forward, his head low to the ground, a snarl on his lips that could be a smile, a beguiling light in his sea-green eyes that matches the aqua shade of his energy. While the other two strain forward, he prowls in a circle around me. He peers at Dawson and Dawson's mother before he creeps back to my side.

Like the other wolves, the Deceiver relays to me everything he senses: the unsettled jolt Dawson made, the nervous tick in Baxter's jaw, the tension in Peter's shoulders, and the bead of sweat suddenly dripping down Sasha's temple. The Deceiver has already isolated their physical weaknesses—just as he identified my emotional weaknesses—telling me where to attack each of them to take them down with the least effort needed.

Finally, my own wolf form bursts from me in a wash of rage, her fur as crimson as my growing fury, her eyes glowing red, her body as large as the Killer's. She gnashes her teeth as she stands at my back, daring anyone to attack from behind me. With her eyes, I can see everything at my back—including the way Dawson and his mother edge away toward the safety of their pack.

Up on the dais, my father is visibly shaken, his cheeks flushed with fury. "Those are Cerberus's minds. How the hell are you controlling them?"

"I took them," I say. "They're mine now."

I control them in a way that Tristan wasn't able to. His power—his wolf's energy—is assimilated with his human form, a relationship that is so close, there was no possible way for him to segment Cerberus's minds. My power can become external to me, allowing me to control them.

"Do you accept my challenge, Fenrir?" I ask. "Will you fight me without risking the lives of the packs you've brought here?"

Behind him, the six alphas shuffle a little, the smallest twitches that indicate they're smart enough to know I won't go down easily. It would be dangerous for them to fight me one-on-one. If I beat them without clearly defined consequences, I could claim control of their packs.

My father's jaw clenches as he descends from the platform, approaching me while keeping my wolves within his sight. I watch him carefully, not trusting that he won't try an underhanded move.

He stops within a few paces of the Killer.

He once told me that Cerberus is one of the few creatures who can kill him. I now control four wolves who can do just that—but I have no illusions that it will be easy.

He draws his shoulders back. "We are creatures of war, Tessa," he says. "It is in our nature to lead others into battle. I pity you for being born into the wrong age. You should have been at my side during the time of the gods. Instead, you were born into a world with machines and steel structures. I made you strong, but I didn't share my strategic knowledge—you don't have the tactical skills to win today."

"I'm not here to win," I say, quietly. "Winning means staying alive."

His eyes widen and then quickly narrow.

My wolves begin circling me and my father, forming a barrier between us and the shifters. My wolves and I move with the same mind. I feel their energy, their power—*my* power—flowing through me as if they were extensions of my own body, so connected that I don't need to send conscious commands to them. They snarl at the shifters, who edge toward us. The Killer bares his teeth at Dawson as he passes him, jumping forward with a deep growl that forces Dawson even farther back.

I raise my voice with a warning that I direct at the alphas since they will control what their packs do. "Anyone who tries to get past my wolves will experience crippling pain. This fight is between me and my father. If you try to interfere, I will respond without mercy."

Peter Nash and Baxter Griffin both take thudding steps forward, their fists clenched. They'll be the first to send their packs into a fight with me. Sasha doesn't react so boldly, but I sense she won't hold back, either. As the only female alpha, she can't be perceived to be weak. The other three alphas are more reserved. Other than the night they voted for me to die, I haven't interacted with them to understand their motivations. I won't discriminate between their packs if they choose to attack me.

The space within the circle is wide enough for Ford and me to prowl around each other now. He carefully removes his shirt, revealing a chest and back covered in intermingled tattoos, each one fitting seamlessly together like a story.

I'm surprised by some of them.

I recognize the face of his wife, Eliande, who was afflicted with Cerberus's minds. In the tattoo, she's holding two babies, one in the crook of each arm, her dark hair billowing across Fenrir's chest, the dark strands cascading past a moon under which a dark wolf tips its head back and howls. Intermingled between them are daggers, flames, and bones.

The tattoo that really surprises me is the half-shadowed face of a woman with red hair that sits across his bottom right rib. Whatever he claims about his ability to love, he had real feelings for these women.

I can't shift into my full wolf form unless I draw my energy back to myself, but I prepare for a shift anyway, quickly removing my shirt, slipping off my boots, and flipping open the top button of my jeans. All the while, my focus doesn't leave my father.

"Well, if you're determined to die," he says.

He's barely finished speaking when the white wolf manifests on my left side and leaps at me. The animal's claws slice the air, but my reflexes fire.

I drop and roll, finishing at a crouch.

Thud.

The Killer meets the white wolf in the air across my head, the two beasts colliding so hard that some of the surrounding shifters scream. The Killer's claws are a brutal blur while the white wolf attempts to defend himself, both animals landing and rolling in a tangle of claws and teeth. Snarling and clashing, they slash and tear at each other, every impact of their energy-filled bodies resulting in blood.

It's now up to my other three wolves to hold the line between me and the horde of shifters.

The Killer's thoughts stream back and forth between himself and me as if we were one creature. His fury is my fury. He won't give up until either he or the white wolf is dead.

His fleeting thought reaches me through his rage: *This fight can only end in death.*

A moment later, the Coward sends me a warning: *Watch out!*

I whirl back to my father's human form. His claws glint close to my cheek as he drives them at my neck.

Leaping back and twisting, I narrowly avoid the lethal blow.

He slashes at me again, anticipating my evasive maneuvers while I dance out of his path.

With every slash he makes, I watch the way he moves, the slight opening of his arms, the vulnerable parts of his body that he isn't protecting. I'm not the only one studying him. The Deceiver relays back to me Ford's every weakness—every miniscule imperfection in his skills, telling me exactly where to strike him to end this.

At the same time, the Coward calculates that I don't have long before the alphas will order their packs to swarm me—regardless of the damage their packs will suffer.

Ford attacks again and this time, I strike back.

Not in the way he would expect.

Dropping in a near-handstand, I twist and kick him. My foot cracks against his right ribs. The impact drives him back toward the waiting Deceiver, who abandons his post at my command and sinks his teeth into the back of Ford's right calf, tugging Ford's leg out from under him.

Ford drops to his other knee with a roar of pain as I race toward him. When he hits the ground, his arms fly wide, an involuntary movement for the split second it takes me to land a punch on his right shoulder. My hit forces his left shoulder further toward me.

My real target is his left wrist. My hand closes around it, clear of his claws.

Yanking his left arm away from his body, I land at a crouch, release the claws of my left hand, and drive them toward Ford's exposed ribs beneath his outstretched arm, right where the Deceiver told me he was vulnerable.

It's a perfect strike. My claws slip between Ford's bones.

His roar cuts short as he stares at me.

I've punctured his lungs.

He tries to breathe as the clearing falls silent.

I continue to grip his arm while I kneel beside him, my left arm punched against his side, my claws buried deep in his chest.

I've struck a fatal blow, but he won't die unless his wolf dies.

Sweat pours down his face, his eyes gleam, and I sense a thousand moments pass through his mind. I sense the speed of his thoughts, the flicker of his power, the way his gaze crosses to the white wolf and the Killer where they savage each other, evenly matched.

I sense him play out his next move.

He's going to let me rip my claws through his chest so that he can spin and slice open the throat of the Deceiver behind him. He knows it will take all three of Cerberus's wolves to kill the white wolf and if he takes out even one of them, he'll win. The second that he's free from the Deceiver's grip on his leg, he'll call the white wolf back to himself.

He'll shift, and he'll heal.

What's more, it will only take another few moments for the shifters to converge on me. Right now, my wolf form and the Coward are desperately trying to keep them back—to keep the knives and claws from my back.

The corner of Ford's mouth twitches upward. "I'll always survive," he whispers. "I'll always prevail."

I only have seconds to act. Less than seconds to make a deadly choice.

I don't waste them with final words.

My heartbeat slows, the wolf shifters and their alphas fade into the background, and every moment becomes crystal clear.

The Sentinel asked me what I would do if I had to choose between sacrificing my power to survive or holding on to my power, even though it would mean I would die. I knew the answer then, and I know it now.

My father spins to his right, dragging my claws through his own chest in a spray of blood so he can attack the Deceiver. Ford's claws spear toward the Deceiver's neck, but the Deceiver doesn't try to save himself, maintaining his hold on Ford's leg, keeping him there, just like I need him to.

The Deceiver's voice sounds inside my mind, an instant thought that takes no time to deliver: *We are glad to be free of this world, Tessa.* Perhaps his first truth.

At the very same moment, across the way, the Killer drives the white wolf to the ground with a final, dangerous thought: *Live your rage, Tessa Dean.*

He clamps his teeth firmly around the white wolf's upper shoulder to hold him down as the Coward leaps at the white wolf's upper hind leg. Together, they immobilize the white wolf. Despite the danger to himself, the Coward is trying to calculate the odds of my survival, but every strategy he projects into my mind results in my death.

His thoughts cut off abruptly.

The Killer's howl tears at my heart as the white wolf rips through the Killer's belly with his front claws.

The Coward's final scream fades as the white wolf tears open his throat with his hind claws.

Closer to me, the Deceiver falls as Ford slashes at his neck.

Ford's roar of triumph meets my ears at the same time the white wolf's crimson eyes gleam at me across the way.

My father was always two steps ahead of me, but this time... *this time*... he isn't watching his back.

I'm aware of Brynjar in the background, leaping off the platform, shoving shifters out of his way to reach me. He won't get here in time to stop me.

My right hand punches against the back of Ford's neck and my claws shoot out, slicing through muscle, sinew, and finally severing bone.

My father freezes, chokes, jolts toward his white wolf—tries to call his power back to himself—but my wolf has already closed her teeth around the back of the white wolf's neck.

I taste Fenrir's blood in her mouth, feel the warmth of his life surrounding my fist.

He tries to swivel. "Daughter..."

My claws cut through my father's neck at the same instant that my wolf rips out the white wolf's spine.

My father's deep blood splashes across the earth, the blood of a god.

Finally dead.

CHAPTER THIRTY-SEVEN

A savage silence falls around me, broken only by Brynjar's thudding steps, slowing as he reaches Ford and drops to his knees beside him. His hands shake as he reaches for Ford's face, checks his breathing, and then hunches silently over his body.

Shocked growls from the alphas reach me. The closest shifters retreat from me, casting urgent glances at the alphas, seeking instructions, but the alphas are still staring at Ford, their faces pale. I guess they didn't expect me to beat him. They will have to make decisions quickly now—do they call a truce, or do they attack?

The silence and stillness around me give me a moment to breathe. My wolf returns to my side, her energy moving so fast that she's a blur before she takes up a protective stance.

I drop to the ground, reaching for the Deceiver, who lies closest to me. His fur is soft, the color of the sea, his body very real now. The Killer, the Coward, and the white wolf all lie to my right. Death has turned them to flesh and bone, leaving their fur to lift in the breeze and their blood to stain the ground.

I don't have long to process my feelings about Cerberus's death. The three minds caused so much pain, dominating Tristan's life. I should hate them, but I also recognize that Cerberus's power was trapped where it didn't belong, corrupted by fate, and twisted over the course of hundreds of years. In the moments before the wolves died, I sensed Cerberus's true nature—as a guardian.

With my hand resting on the Deceiver's head, I seek Brynjar, who hunches within striking distance. I'm wary of the alphas and their packs, but Brynjar is the real threat to me.

Ford gave Brynjar's life meaning and purpose—even if it was a violent purpose. I told Brynjar he would have to choose, but I've taken the choice away.

The Coward's final warning rings loudly in my ears: *Your wolf must run. If her energy survives, you will survive.*

He wasn't wrong. My human body can suffer mortal wounds, but as long as I can call my energy back to me and shift completely, I'll heal. But... I didn't come here to kill my father and run from the consequences. I have to face them. All of them.

Drawing to my feet, I step toward Brynjar instead of away, casting a shadow across his hunched form. There's nothing I can say to ease the storm that must be growing inside him.

I wait for him to speak.

Finally, he looks up at me. "The death of an old god carries a cost," he says, drawing to his feet and squaring his broad shoulders, looking down on me now. "I can't let his death go unavenged."

My gaze flicks meaningfully to my wolf form. "I don't want to hurt you."

Brynjar's expression hardens while icicles form across his hands. "A fight between us is unavoidable now, Tessa."

I shake my head. "It doesn't have to be this way. You're free to choose a new path."

Slowly, I allow my claws to descend.

The ice giant narrows his frosty blue eyes, his power rising so sharply that my breath mists and ice spreads across the grass, turning it black all around us. His power washes across Ford and over Cerberus's wolves, covering their bodies with sparkling magic, freezing their blood.

The closest shifters leap agilely backward before the frost reaches their feet, but Baxter Griffin shouts from the platform, "Stand your ground! We don't leave until the bitch is dead!"

I guess the alphas have made their choice, too.

I lift my right hand slowly to my own chest while Brynjar watches my every move. A crease forms in his forehead, since it must seem strange that I'm pointing my claws at myself.

Gritting my teeth against the pain, I ram my foreclaw into my exposed left shoulder. Dragging my claw across the fleshy part of my shoulder in a single, diagonal cut, I draw my deep blood, allowing its scent to fill the air around me before it, too, freezes.

The wound I've cut is deep enough that the mark will remain—a necessary scar.

Helen told me my future is my own, if I'm willing to claim it.

Well, I'm claiming it.

I've marked myself.

My life belongs to me.

I will live, love, and die on my own terms.

CHAPTER THIRTY-EIGHT

*B*rynjar's jaw clenches. I told him he was free to choose a new path, but he says, "This is my only path."

Without another warning, his big fist snaps out, a blow that could crush my skull.

I leap backward, avoiding the hit. He proved to me in the past that he's strong enough to knock me out. I'm not immune to his power and my worst nightmare is that I'll lose consciousness in this place.

I dart into the clear space behind us, drawing Brynjar forward as my wolf leaps to my defense. Brynjar sidesteps most of her body, but she cuts through his shoulder, making him roar with pain. It doesn't deter him. His power continues to ice the air, making it difficult for me to breathe.

Fuck. He's turning the air into snow and it's clinging to my lips, my face, coating my throat with every breath. His magic once melted in my hands, but this is not a single snowflake.

I cough hard just as he runs at me. He bends, angling his shoulder, preparing to tackle and lift me off my feet. I somersault away from him—once, twice, gasping for air as I land in a crouch.

My wolf leaps again at his side, another attempt to deter him. This time, she tears through his torso, her energy like knives through his heart and lungs, ripping at every nerve.

Brynjar's face twists with pain as he thuds to his knees,

THIS CAGED WOLF

clutching his chest. He roars into the frosty air, but he's only down for a moment before he grits his teeth and forces himself to his feet.

Damn. He won't give up.

A heaviness settles in my chest. My hands are still covered in my father's blood. I don't want Brynjar's on them, too.

"Don't make me kill you," I shout, my chest heaving.

The ice jotunn shakes his head at me. "It would be an honorable way to die, Tessa," he says, making my eyes widen as he charges at me again.

I brace for impact, preparing to evade and use his own momentum against him to give my claws strength.

At the last moment, his eyes gleam.

A wash of snow blasts from his body, obscuring everything around me. I can't see Brynjar or the shifters or even the sky. My crimson vision rises, attempting to cut through the wash, but his magic is everywhere, a constant glow no matter which way I turn.

I spin to the side, trying to judge where his final steps toward me will take him so I can evade him. My wolf's view isn't faring any better. I can't even tell how far away from me she's located. Brynjar's magic is messing with all of my senses.

I whirl again, turning in the snow, the crystalline magic that fills the entire space making me cough and wheeze.

The Coward's voice repeats on me: *You must run.* But every instinct inside me tells me to stand my ground.

Mere heartbeats have passed since the snow descended.

Damn, damn... Where is he?

Shouts erupt all around me, the sounds of chaos rising, and I can only guess that Brynjar's power has enveloped half the clearing, making the shifters panic.

Just as the shouts intensify, Brynjar appears in front of me, his big fist closing around my neck as he wrenches me upward but not quite off my feet. The toes of my boots touch the ground as I call my wolf's magic to me—or attempt to. The snow between us is a barrier I can't get past, making it impossible to locate her energy.

I plant my hands against his chest, ready to fight, but he shocks me when he pulls my fist toward his chest, pressing it there.

"Release your claws," he commands. "The old ways must die." He lowers his eyes to mine while he grips my throat in a clutch that allows the barest slip of air to get through. Icicles shoot into my head, down my neck, through my chest.

I manage to whisper. "What...?" *What is he trying to tell me?*

"Cerberus is dead," he says. "We are the last of the old warriors. We must end it now or the shifters will make us their pawns."

"No." I gasp. "We belong to ourselves."

He shakes me. Hard. "The only way we achieve autonomy is to make them fear us. That was what your father did. You are not like him. You must choose to end this. It is inevitable, Tessa!"

I suck air into my chest in wheezing gulps. "There's another way. I have a pack who loves me for who I am, not because they fear me. I can give you a new purpose, Brynjar. I can give you a new life and a new home—"

"No!" he roars. "Power is corruptible!"

I attempt to exhale but can't. His grip has become too tight. I want to tell him that he's right. Power is hard and cold, but not with a pack like mine.

"Release your claws," he says. "My heart will beat long enough for me to make your death quick. Then we'll both be gone."

He's not giving me a choice. I lean against him, planting both of my fists against his chest. I'm sure I can take him down before he kills me.

My eyes fill with tears as I prepare to release my claws.

His hand tightens around my throat and then—

Whoomph!

A solid body hits Brynjar from the side. His attacker is a blur of black fur, gleaming claws, and sharp teeth.

The impact causes Brynjar's fist to clench harder around my throat, pulling me with him before we're forced apart. Released from his hold, I hit the ground, roll, and look up just in time to see both figures fly back through the white snow, the ice jotunn's power pouring around him while the silhouette of a wolf is momentarily clear.

The waft of the scent that remains nearly drowns me.

Every layer pierces my heart. Bitter orange, nutmeg, cedar...

Tristan!

But how?

Panic replaces my shock.

He can't fight the ice jotunn. I took Cerberus's minds from him. I took the old magic from him. He can't repel magic without it. He can't fight Brynjar without the minds. *He won't survive!*

I throw myself through the wash after them, reaching out, my hands coming up empty as I search the air.

There's a roar. A shout. But I can't see what happened.

A second later, the wash around me explodes outward, every miniscule crystalline fragment drawing together to form a million snowflakes that burst upward and then slowly drift down around my head and shoulders.

The air begins to clear.

Directly ahead of me, Brynjar drops to his knees, his arms loose at his sides, blood sliding from his neck and down his chest.

Tristan's wolf snarls opposite him, his lips drawn back, his teeth bloody, his head low to the ground.

"Yield," Tristan's wolf says, his voice as deep and violent as the Killer's always was. "Tessa doesn't want you to die."

Brynjar shakes his head. Slow. "My time is at an end."

"Then I'll make it quick." Tristan's wolf growls a final warning.

Brynjar lurches upward, bunching his fists, shoulders hunched, muscles flexing as he charges at Tristan's wolf, preparing to rip the wolf's head from his shoulders.

Tristan's wolf leaps to meet him, aiming a little to the side, dragging his claws across the ice jotunn's chest at the same time that Tristan shifts into his human form.

He lands on his knees beside Brynjar, who hunches over, also kneeling.

The claws of Tristan's now-human hand are buried so deep in the ice jotunn's chest that they must be curled around the giant's heart.

My own heart is in pieces. Tristan shouldn't be able to survive Brynjar's power, let alone beat him.

I run to Tristan's side, finally locating my wolf's energy and pulling her with me to stand beside us.

The two men are very still, but Tristan looks up at me as I pause beside them.

I'm suddenly cautious, but his eyes are just as crisply green and flecked with amber. My breath catches at the way his lips part a little, at the way my breathing immediately matches his.

Through the melding bond, I sense all of the emotions he's feeling and there are no walls between us. Warmth floods me at his relief to see me unhurt, then rage that he couldn't get to me sooner, then sadness as he considers Brynjar.

Quietly resting on my knees beside the ice jotunn, I lay my hand against Brynjar's cheek like I did when I began to understand my power. His chest rises with an indrawn breath.

A trickle of blood slides from his lips.

"Brynjar," I whisper. "I didn't want this."

The corner of Brynjar's mouth tugs up. His response is labored. "There's hope… for you… Tessa."

Tears slip down my cheeks as his head droops and his shoulders sag, his magic finally gone.

CHAPTER THIRTY-NINE

*T*ristan quietly removes his claws, holding Brynjar carefully and laying his body down on the blackened grass.

My father lies only a few paces away, along with Cerberus's wolves.

The final snowflakes fall to the earth, and I'm almost afraid to reach for Tristan. "How are you here?"

Tristan's gaze shifts beyond me. "Helen," he says. "She translocated us to the ravine. The fae led us to the Spire."

"The fae?"

Sound suddenly breaks through.

A great gust of wind washes over us as a giant ruby thunderbird shrieks past overhead.

Lyra!

Her wings carry away the final snow drifts, clearing the haze in the air so I can see everything around us. She's followed by a sapphire bird with a fae rider, both birds soaring toward the Spire. The shouting I heard before—and the reason for the shifter's panic —is suddenly clear.

To my left, the strongest shifters have gathered in rows, protecting the alphas, while a battle rages around me. To my right, an army of fae women dressed in indigo armor and wielding diamond-tipped spears fights hard against the shifters who are trying to regain ground.

My heart leaps with both joy and fear to see that my pack is with the fae. I make out Iyana, Danika, and Maeve fighting together, protecting each other's backs, while Reya, Neve, and Nalani fight alongside wolf shifters I recognize from Tristan's pack, including Carly and Bridget.

Farther back, I spot Luna and Lydia, their cards spinning in the air where they stand in a clear space. I make out the movement of their lips—they're speaking as they work. Essandra, the fae whose power can carry messages on the wind, is standing beside them, her gaze rapidly flicking around the fight. She's also speaking, but she's facing the battle.

"What are they doing...?"

"Reading the minds of shifters in the other packs and telling your pack where and how to attack," Tristan says. "They're keeping everyone alive."

A clear space exists around us, the battle circling us. It's a space that was filled with silence a moment ago. We can only be surrounded by some sort of protective sphere. "And this?"

"Helen," Tristan says. "She couldn't stop Brynjar's power, but she placed a protective sphere around you so the other packs can't get through." He pauses. "Translocating us and creating the shield around you has exhausted her, so she's remaining concealed within the trees."

My gaze flies around the battle. "I need to get out there!"

"Wait, Tessa." Tristan's palm lowers to my marked shoulder, and I inhale his power like it's a damn airborne drug, calming me and helping me take a breath.

My wolf watches the battle closely for me, relaying the way my pack has taken charge of the fight and how the fae are assisting them, working as one unit. They're keeping each other alive—and at the same time, the maneuvers they're pulling are keeping the damage to the other side to a minimum.

My wolf will warn me if I'm needed urgently.

I allow Tristan's palm to settle across my shoulder.

"Helen's shield allows us to see out, but the alphas can't see in,"

Tristan says. "Right now, they believe you're dead. You need to decide what you want—*now*, before you emerge."

His gaze arrests me and once again, he doesn't bury any of his feelings. He is completely open to me. My eyes burn as I realize that his mind is fully free now. He doesn't carry the burden of deception, or unwanted rage, or the desire to put his life above anyone else's.

His worry is his own and it's like a warm poultice drawing out all of my anguish. I twist my hands in my lap and swallow hard as I avoid looking at the death that surrounds me in this quiet clearing Helen created.

"You could claim your father's empire," Tristan says.

My lips part in surprise. "I want no part of it."

"What about the Spire?"

My incisors descend, sudden rage rising. "It's mine."

"And the forest?"

My fury increases. "Also mine."

"What about the other packs? If you challenge and kill the alphas today, their packs will be yours. Is that what you want?"

My rage subsides. My response is quiet. "I don't want that responsibility."

"Even if it means letting Baxter Griffin and Dawson Nash walk away today?" he asks.

I exhale the last of my anger. "Even then. I don't want to own their packs. Baxter and Dawson know what I'm capable of now. If they cross into territory that isn't their own, I will retaliate without mercy. If not, I will leave them be."

Tristan nods. "And me?" he asks. "What do you want from me?"

I read his question in both his heart and his mind. He needs to know where he stands with me. Our journey began with him claiming me, declaring me to be his. I won't ever forget the intense rage and desire in his eyes when he looked at me after he fought Peter Nash for the right to claim me. After that, I fought for my freedom, discovered that my goals aligned with Tristan's, only to have the foundations shift beneath me. I became an alpha like him. I found my strength... and I ended up taking his power.

Yet here he is, his raven-black hair just as wild as it was then across his amber-flecked eyes, his power filling my senses, just as strong... *stronger*... than he was before.

"I want you by my side," I say, my heart in my throat. "If you want me by yours."

He pulls me close, pressing his forehead to mine, nudging my lips with his. "I want nothing more."

I search his eyes, warmed by the depth of his belief, but there's one more question I need answered: I need to know the extent of Tristan's power now.

"How did you fight Brynjar?" I ask. "He's old magic... but I took the minds from you..."

Tristan squares his shoulders. "I was born with Cerberus's magic. The minds grew stronger as I did. They took over, but the old magic was always part of me. My father passed it to me. I will pass it to my children. I wanted to tell you," he says. "I wanted to tell you so many things, Tessa, but the Deceiver was always with me."

"Not anymore." I curl my hands into his hair, brushing his lips with mine. "It's time to get out there."

He gives me a determined nod. "It's time to end this."

Rising to my feet with Tristan beside me, I quickly scan the fight around us. Our friends have driven the wolf shifters back to either side of the Spire. Soon, the wolf shifters won't have anywhere to go. The alphas know it—and they don't look happy, pacing back and forth on the platform.

"You need pants," I whisper to Tristan with an arched eyebrow, failing to avert my gaze.

Shrugging, he gives me a grin. He shifts into his wolf form so fast that I miss the shift. His enormous wolf with its fierce, relentless green eyes looks up at me with a growl.

I stride forward, sending my wolf ahead.

My target is the alphas, and I'll clear a path to them any way that I can.

As soon as I touch the sphere, it breaks in a spectacular way. If Helen wanted us to make an impression when we emerged, then she succeeded. Magic blasts outward, a *boom* and a ripple that pulses in every direction. The surrounding fighters flinch and duck —even my friends, who might have been forewarned.

Above me in the sky, Lyra shrieks a greeting, soaring across the space above my head before sailing up to one of the Spire's landing platforms, where she casts a shadow across the nervous wolf shifters beneath her.

My pack quickly converges around me, forming a semi-circle so that I can continue moving forward. Iyana catches my eye and so does Danika. I read the relief on their faces to see me. I wish I had more time to reassure them, but I face forward, calling out to the wolf shifters, "If you don't want to experience crippling pain, get out of my way."

The strongest alphas remain in two rows in front of the platform, but the other wolf shifters scatter. Dawson and his mother have joined Peter Nash on the platform. Sasha and the other three alphas remain toward the back of the podium. But Baxter Griffin steps to the front.

"Tessa Dean!" he snarls. "You—"

I don't let him finish. "This fight is over," I shout. "I don't want your territories. I don't want to make deals or control your packs. This forest is mine. The Spire is mine. Leave now and I... *we*... will let you live."

Baxter's mouth snaps shut. He was clearly expecting me to come out raging.

His lips twist in a way that tells me he's preparing a retort, but Sasha strides past him, her boots thumping loudly on the platform. She holds her head high while the women of her pack in the front row look to her for instructions.

Without a word, she inclines her head sharply toward the forest and jumps from the platform. The shifters of her pack step back, turn, and stride after her.

The three other alphas also step forward, incline their heads for their packs to leave, and within minutes, they've all quietly but rapidly disappeared.

The only packs remaining belong to Baxter Griffin and Peter Nash. Only a single row of guards remains in front of them. I recognize many of them from the group of guards who were at Baxter's home on the night of the party.

"You might not baulk at slaughtering another alpha's pack," I say, addressing Baxter and Peter, my anger rising. "But do you really want to make a decision that results in the slaughter of your own?"

At the back of the platform, Dawson edges toward his father, his jaw tight. Dawson likes his victims weak. Never strong. He won't want any part of this fight if he believes he can't win it.

Peter snaps at him, saying something I can't hear. Dawson grabs his father's arm. Even Dawson's mother, Cora, her face pale, leans toward Peter, speaking rapidly and urgently. I could overhear them if I were to expand my senses, but I choose not to. Their argument is their own. The outcome is all that matters to me.

With a fierce growl, Peter says to Baxter, "You're on your own."

Peter, Dawson, and Cora jump from the platform while their pack—my old pack—crowds in behind them, following them as quickly as possible into the trees. Dawson throws a glance back at me—wary where he wasn't afraid before. He isn't alone. Other members of my old pack hesitate before disappearing into the forest. They used to know where they stood with me—over me, always above me—but I've turned the world around on them.

Still, Baxter Griffin hovers on the platform despite the urgent glances from his fighters who are standing guard and the remaining members of his pack. They have no backup now, except for the leopard shifters, who huddle at the side of the Spire, where my pack corralled them.

When Baxter narrows his eyes at the leopards, they shuffle farther back, eyes downcast. My father owned those leopards. He taught them to fear his power, just as they will fear mine. They won't go up against me.

Baxter's lips press together. I sense his rage, his determination not to lose this fight. He would rather sacrifice every member of his pack than swallow his fucking pride and walk away.

He takes a breath and prepares to speak, but a disturbance behind us interrupts him. Without taking my eyes off Baxter, I send my wolf to investigate. Through her eyes, I see the fae stepping aside, creating a path to me from the forest.

Ella and Cody stride along it with Jace close behind them. They are dressed for battle. Ella is wearing a bodice that isn't much more than a bra, along with a pair of very short shorts that don't have a top button. Her fair hair is tied back in a tight bun, and the scar across her left shoulder is fully visible.

Jace is dressed in regular jeans, low slung, but his top button is undone—the same way Tristan wears his jeans when he's prepared to shift. His tattooed wolf crushes a crimson rose between its teeth, the petals dripping like blood.

My eyes widen to realize that both Ella and Jace came prepared to shift.

Cody, on the other hand, is dressed in a protective suit that reminds me of the one my assassin mother was wearing. It conforms with the muscles of his chest and thighs, making him appear lean and formidable. He steps right up to my right side so that I'm flanked by both him and Tristan's wolf while Jace steps to the far side of the path, and Ella strides up between them.

Her pack's response to her presence hits me right in the heart. The wolf shifters' weight is suddenly on their front feet, as if they want to run to her despite the danger I pose to them. Her name is cried so loudly that all of their voices tug at my soul. The shifters standing guard echo the cry, edging toward her. "Ella!"

The bond between Ella and her pack is a palpable force that seems to draw them together.

It's a bond that is suddenly very clearly lacking between them and Baxter.

Damn. No wonder he wanted her gone. Cody said she was the glue that kept them all together. She must have been a threat to her father from day one. And by telling his pack that Tristan was the reason their beloved Ella had been killed… well… his pack would seek revenge with everything they had.

There are too many of them for Ella to acknowledge them all individually, but somehow, her gaze passes across them in a way that sees them. I sense the connection between them like the connection I have with my pack, an instinctive knowledge of where they are, whether they're hurt and need my help.

It's unspoken. Instant.

Her entire pack suddenly stands taller, their eyes bright, their focus sharp. Many of them begin looking to Baxter, as if they expect him to feel the same joy they do. Their brows furrow when his expression darkens and he remains on the platform instead of approaching her.

Nearer to me, Ella exhales a growl. The cries of her pack die down, becoming confused murmurings.

With deliberate movements, Ella turns to me and holds out her hand, a very clear gesture of friendship.

I step up to her side, place my hand on her shoulder, and return her brief, solemn smile. Tristan's wolf steps up with me and Cody remains a step behind but between me and Ella, while Jace stays on Ella's right, his palm pressed unobtrusively to her lower back, a physical connection between them.

Ella lifts her head and speaks. Quietly. Not a roar or a shout, but her voice carries power and command. "Shifters of the Eastern Lowland," she says, addressing them all. "Your alpha has lied to you. My *father* lied to you. But I will *not* lie to you."

Her jaw tightens. "On the night you saw me last, my father—your alpha—made a deal with Ford Vanguard to sell me to the witches. Ford Vanguard killed Tristan's mother and took me prisoner, the same way he took Tessa. For a year, I was beaten. Tortured. Forced to kill. I was humiliated, disrespected, and threatened daily with death."

The silence around us is so heavy with shock and rising anger that it could ignite.

Ella continues. "Tristan and Jace didn't stop searching until they found me. They took me away from all of that. But I couldn't return to you. I wanted to, but I was…" She draws a deep breath. Jace's hand presses to her back, circling her skin, and she calms again. "I was not the same person anymore."

She draws back her shoulders. "I come to you now as a daughter of this pack. I come to you with my brother's support, and with the support of my friends, including Tessa Dean."

Her voice rises. "I come to challenge my father."

Baxter leaps forward with a shout that makes the nearest pack members flinch. "You can't challenge me. I *am* the pack!"

Ella shakes her head. "*We* are the pack. That's what you never understood. If you lie to one of us, you lie to all of us. If you hurt one of us, you hurt all of us. This is not about you or your ambition or your pride. This is about *us*."

She steps toward him, the fury in her eyes growing. "I challenge you, Baxter Griffin, alpha of the Eastern Lowland pack. Do you accept my challenge?"

Baxter storms from the platform, his claws and incisors fully descended, while the shifters standing guard hurry to step aside. He doesn't seem to notice the way they bare their teeth at him as he passes.

Raging toward Ella, he roars, "You will regret the day you ever—"

With a scream that drains the blood from Baxter's face, Ella launches herself forward, the full fury of her rage and years of pain releasing in that single sound.

I saw her ferocity when she defended Jace against the Killer, but it's nothing compared to the breathtaking efficiency with which her fists fly now, her rapid punches landing on all of the vulnerable points of Baxter's chest, impacting his breathing and thumping against his heart.

He chokes as she leaps upward and kicks at a downward angle, sending him *smack* onto his back on the ground.

She lands on him, her wrists crossed. Her extended claws fly across his neck in opposite directions and outward, neatly slitting his throat.

Silence falls.

Her chest heaves. She stares down at him. Even though he can't hear her anymore, she says, "Just because I'm gentle doesn't mean I'm not also fucking fierce."

With a brief pat on my shoulder, Cody quickly moves to Ella's side. He kneels and closes his father's eyes, after which he remains by Ella's side for a long moment.

Beside me, Tristan shifts back into his human form, slipping his arm around my back, while I slide mine around his, our arms linked.

One of the shifter guards takes a knee where he stands. Very soon, the entire pack follows, all of them quiet until Ella lifts her head and addresses them.

"There will be no more blood today," she says. "Do not fear retaliation. We're among friends now."

She reaches out for Jace to stand by her side before she swivels to me and Tristan, then to my pack, then to the fae, tears sparkling in her eyes as she seeks our agreement.

Iyana and Danika step up beside me.

They're quickly joined by Maeve, Reya, Nalani, and Neve, along with the card mage twins.

Beside them, Tristan's pack gathers, headed up by Carly and Bridget. On their far side, Queen Calanthe stands tall and strong at the head of the fae army while the two thunderbirds remain perched up on the Spire's landing pads.

Tristan and I give Ella a firm nod that Calanthe mirrors.

We've finally ended the old wars.

CHAPTER FORTY

Tristan drops a kiss to the corner of my mouth, and I turn into his embrace. "You still need pants," I murmur, running my hands provocatively across his back.

"You could make use of me as I am," he suggests, the corner of his mouth twitching up as he gives a slight incline of his head toward the tower. The heat in his eyes tells me he's only half-joking.

I hum as I press my lips to his, but I end the kiss on a sigh. "Soon."

When I pull back, a sudden laugh bursts out of me because, in the distance, a pair of jeans is being pitched across the army at our backs from one person to another until they bounce from Carly to Danika and then to Jace, who brings them across to Tristan with a broad grin.

"Compliments of Danika's duffel bag," he says. "We have supplies back in the trees."

I check everyone around me while Tristan pulls on the jeans. I love that he deliberately leaves the top button undone. *Damn, I will definitely take him up on his offer.*

But first... Ella has her pack in hand and Calanthe is organizing the fae to clean up the battlefield of any dropped weapons and tend to any wounded, but the leopard shifters remain huddled beside the Spire.

Tristan is also aware of them. "Go," he murmurs. "I'll check on my pack."

The leopard shifters edge away from me as I approach. Perla used to stand at their head, but she escaped during my fight with Mother Lavinia.

I address them. "How many of you wish to leave?"

They cast glances at each other, and I sigh inwardly that they don't trust my motives for asking.

I try again. "This is not a trick. I don't play games like my father did. If you have somewhere you'd rather be, you're free to go. I don't want to see you again."

I sense the tension rise among them. They still don't believe me. One of them inches to the side, her shoulders hunched, her brown eyes wide and afraid, ready for me to attack her. It's the sort of power game my father would have played. She takes a visibly deep breath before she darts away, sprinting for her life across the clearing and into the trees.

"Go," I say to the others, glaring at them. "Don't come back."

Turning on my heel, I stalk away from them in case that helps them to believe me.

I head toward Iyana where she stands with her arms folded and a soft smile on her lips, but she gives me a quick warning glance.

I've already sensed the lone leopard following me.

I spin to the girl who is tiptoeing behind me.

She stops as abruptly as I turn.

She's younger than the others, might not be much older than sixteen, with wide eyes and unruly wisps of brown hair escaping from her ponytail. She hunches over like a frightened cat, as if she's preparing to leap backward.

"Why are you still here?" I demand to know.

"I don't have anywhere to go," she says, her fingers curling inward, her short claws digging into her palms. "My family is dead. I don't have another home."

The tightness in my jaw softens. With a flash of my crimson vision, I confirm the truth of her statement.

"Then stay," I say. "This is Iyana. She'll give you something useful to do."

Iyana arches an eyebrow at me. "Right after I give my stubborn alpha a hug."

She embraces me, and I wrap my arms around her, murmuring, "Thank you, friend."

"Always." Her expression becomes serious as she pulls back. "Helen needs to see you. She's at the back of the clearing."

I startle. "Is she okay?"

"She's recovering, but she asked for you as soon as possible. She needs to get back to the House."

I don't want to waste time, but I do pause beside each member of my pack, reaching for their hands, accepting and returning their hugs, allowing the warmth of their love to take away the sorrow I feel as I pass the area of blackened grass where Brynjar, my father, and Cerberus's wolves lie.

Death is hard, and it's final.

Calanthe hails me before I leave that spot, her voice quiet. She tucks her emerald-streaked hair behind her ear. "Tessa Dean," she says. "With your permission, we will build pyres for these fallen. It's the old way to say goodbye to creatures of old magic. No matter what they did in life, their magic must return to the earth."

I consider her carefully—and then the Spire where the thunderbirds have perched so naturally. "This is your home as much as it's mine," I say. "I won't be able to protect it on my own. I want the fae to come back, protect this place, restore it, and give it life again."

Calanthe's eyes sparkle with sudden tears. "We would be honored."

I give her a quiet nod, and she lets me go.

Hurrying all of the way to the back of the clearing, past the vehicle hangars, I find Helen leaning against a tree whose trunk is nearly as wide as the trees that surrounded Mother Zala's coven.

Helen is pale and her shoulders sag. "Tessa," she says, reaching for my hands with a weak smile. "Don't be alarmed. I'll be fine."

I guess she read the worry splashed all over my face.

Before I can respond, the back of my neck prickles and I stiffen, but Helen continues to hold my hands. "You've met Alexei."

The Master Assassin materializes beside Helen—right in front of me—his height forcing me to tip my head back to see his face.

"I certainly have," I say, edging toward Helen in a protective gesture, my tension growing. After my last encounter with Alexei, I was running away from him with my mother's assassin's ring. "If you're here for the ring, I can't give it back. Also, nobody else had anything to do with it. If you're angry about it, then I'm the one to blame."

Alexei is unusually relaxed, his hands flying up. "It's fine," he says, surprising me. "Don't worry about it. Your mother is happier without it. In fact, it was a burden she can do without. She has a lot to figure out, but she's taking the first steps. I also explained the situation to our Guardian, and she won't come after you, either."

"Guardian?" I ask, still pressed protectively to Helen's side, aware that there's a lot about the assassins I still don't know.

Alexei makes a humming sound in the back of his throat, tipping his head in a way that indicates he's simplifying things when he says, "She guards the rings."

I'm cautious. "If you're not here to retrieve the ring, why are you here?"

His expression falls blank again, the look of an assassin. "As you know, we couldn't interfere in this fight, but we came as witnesses to the events today."

"We?"

At my question, figures materialize all along the treeline at the edge of the clearing, nearly thirty of them, all dressed in protective suits. They stand so quietly between the trees that a shiver runs down my spine before they disappear again seamlessly into the shadows.

Dear fuck. They could kill us all without breaking a sweat.

Alexei leans down to me, but not in a way that makes me feel threatened. His stormy gray eyes are solemn. "I can now cross all three of Fenrir's names from my Ledger and record the circumstances of his death. His empire is in tatters. We are one step closer to a future where my son might be able to grow up in a world without the need for assassins."

I allow myself a small smile, but I'm curious. "You have a son?"

"He's six months old," Alexei says. "I'd like you to meet him, and my wife, when you're ready."

He told me a family was waiting for me when I needed them.

For the first time, I feel ready for the possibility that I have blood relatives who might welcome me into their lives.

"I'd like that," I say.

Alexei turns to Helen, placing his hand on her arm. "We can help you get home."

She gives him a small nod. "Give me a moment with Tessa?"

He inclines his head toward the shadows of the forest. "I'll be that way."

She nods as he disappears into the air again and my skin just keeps on prickling.

"You know each other," I say.

"For a little while now," she says. "Alexei Mason is believed to be human, but he isn't. He shouldn't be able to wear an assassin's ring, but he does. He defies every law of magic. He's a contradiction of nature itself."

"What is he?"

"I believe he is a rare Voidmancer. Possibly the first."

I peer at her, remaining calm. "Despite knowing him—and all about the assassins, apparently—you didn't tell me about the assassin's rings when I needed an object of old magic." Using my crimson vision on Helen to discern her motives is no use. Her power is too bright.

"Hmm." She considers me carefully. "If you recall, you wouldn't tell me why you needed it or what you were planning to do with it. Don't get me wrong. I understood your reasons for secrecy. In all honesty, I don't ever want to know what's in that book." She grimaces. "But assassin's rings are objects of death. Without knowing your intentions, I couldn't pass on that information. Of course, if you'd come to me again, I would have told you." A smile tugs at her mouth. "But it seems you found what you needed at the right time."

Her smile is so enigmatic that it makes me wonder how much she knows and doesn't let on.

Helen and her mysteries. There's still so much I don't understand about her past, and maybe that's for the best. It's time for me to focus on the future.

On impulse, I hug her. She is the closest to a mother that I've had.

She smiles as she turns away but pauses again. "Oh. I wanted to tell you. You left the book of old magic in your bedroom, but as you know, the woman in the dark powers Hidden House. Her magic has assimilated the book and buried it. I don't know where it is, but I want to reassure you that the book is safe."

She hobbles away into the shadows and I nearly go after her to help her since she looks so tired, but Alexei appears at her side and takes her arm to support her. She leans against him, and I know she's going to be okay.

I blink and they're gone.

~

Firelight flickers across the clearing in front of the Spire as night falls and the stars come out to play.

Seven pyres burn brightly in the center of the clearing, their flames controlled by the fae, who ensure the fires burn hot enough, but that the breeze carries the smoke up and away.

While the fae keep everyone else away from the immediate vicinity of the fires, I circle around each pyre. I'm barefoot, dressed in clean jeans and a sleeveless shirt that puts my mark on display. It caused a bit of a stir among Ella's pack when they first saw it, but her own mark is different, too, and I was impressed with how quickly their surprise turned to acceptance. Our hearts and minds have been forged in fires that mean we will never walk an ordinary path.

As my toes scrunch in the burned grass, I sense the magic rising into the air around me. Old magic. The foundation of everything. Its essence makes my skin tingle while all of the memories of its holders press in on my mind...

The wars my father fought with Brynjar by his side.

The way my father's heart turned to wrath and eventually became cold.

Brynjar's magic, primal and gorgeous, but corrupted over time.

Each mind of Cerberus, a guardian of the dead, wrenched from his place in the underworld into a world in which his power became poison.

Only Baxter's pyre is clear of old magic, but the cause of his death is equally heavy on my mind: a heart corrupted by power.

I don't try to stop the tears falling down my cheeks, my vision blurry as I suddenly inhale not the scent of smoke and magic, but Tristan's power.

The intensity of the old magic around me was too strong for me to sense his approach, but I welcome his arms as he wraps them around me from behind, his muscled chest pressing against my back, his biceps enveloping my shoulders.

He nudges my neck with his lips. "I feel it, too," he murmurs.

"Lost chances," I whisper, sliding my arms across his.

"We won't lose any more chances, Tessa." He growls, turning me in his arms. His lips brush mine, a gentle touch that is both soothing and tantalizing. And never enough.

Just as I lean in to him, wanting more from his kiss, he pulls back.

"You have things you need to sort out," he says, his green eyes burning me as intensely as the fire heats my back. "Come find me when you're ready."

His gaze tugs me like a rope—a fucking undeniable magnet—before he turns and disappears around the nearest pyre.

I stride after him, only to pause at the edge of the flames.

The three packs mingle quietly beyond the flames. Nalani and Neve took the leopard girl under their wing and set about making sure everyone was fed and hydrated, while Maeve and Reya helped the fae with those who needed medical attention. Members of Ella's pack stepped up and helped prepare food and find blankets, as did Carly and Bridget.

Now, they all sit with blankets around their shoulders, nursing cups of hot broth. What really takes my breath away is that there are no lines between them. My pack, Tristan's pack, Ella's pack. They're all talking with each other, getting to know each other for the first time.

My heart warms to see Maeve and Reya sharing a blanket, their heads together. Definitely something blossoming there. Luna and Lydia are showing their cards to a group of fae women, including Essandra, who are playing along by tugging at the cards with their power over air.

I catch sight of Danika at the edge of the group, leaning against the thick trunk of the nearest tree, and I'm worried that she's all alone until I follow her gaze to Cody. He's changed into jeans and a T-shirt that hugs his muscles. Danika gives him a nearly imperceptible tip of her chin. He rises from his conversation with Carly, casually extracting himself while Carly turns to the shifter beside her.

His focus is entirely on Danika, who arrests his attention before she turns and strides into the shadowed forest.

Cody disappears quietly after her.

I guess this means he has another good reason to stay with my pack.

I sense Ella's approach a moment later. Jace is by her side, both of them looking more tense than I expected, given the force of the connection between them. Their bond might not be the same as the one they had before, but it's stronger.

"We're looking for Tristan," Ella says, nervously picking at her nails. "We need to talk with him about the future."

"He knows," I say, reflecting inward, seeking Tristan through the melding bond, understanding his emotions as quickly as I understand my own. "Jace will join your pack as your true mate. Cody will join my pack as my beta. And Carly will be Tristan's new beta. Simple."

Ella blows out a quiet exhale. "Okay, then."

She smiles at me.

I smile back.

Turning to Jace, she tugs him toward the Spire and they also disappear into the dark.

My pack is safe—our *packs* are safe—and my need to see Tristan is undeniable now. I'm about to head toward the forest when I spot Iyana standing apart from everyone on the other side of the pyres. A shiver of worry runs through me at how still and pensive she is, her brow intensely furrowed. I hurry toward her and then slow my approach. I don't want to startle her out of her thoughts.

The tip of a fang is visible as she peers into the flames, watching them leap and rise. Her weapons rest around her hips. She's dressed for combat, always prepared.

I bump her arm with the gentlest touch. "You okay?"

She takes a deep breath. "Memories are hard," she says, watching the bright sparks. "The fire reminds me of someone…"

When she remains silent, I don't push her for information. This is a Hidden House moment. I have to trust that she will share more about her past when she's ready. If she's never ready, then I need to accept that, too.

She clears her throat, shaking out her shoulders. "I'm okay." She nods as if she's convinced herself. "I'll be fine." Her fangs disappear as she focusses on me. "I'll keep an eye on things here."

I wrap my arms around her, sensing some of the tension ease from her shoulders. "Love you, Iyana."

"Love you, too, Tessa."

Releasing her, I prowl across the clearing in the direction opposite to where the packs are settled. My senses expand, seeking Tristan's location, following the scent of bitter orange, nutmeg, notes of cedar…

Following Tristan's trail deep into the forest, I come upon a small clearing nestled between enormous trees, where the forest floor is covered in soft moss.

Tristan is on the far side, doing chin-ups using a low-hanging branch and his claws to grip it. He drops quietly to the ground, his torso gleaming, immediately focused on me.

"Tessa." He growls, his gaze running the length of me in an appreciative sweep.

"Mate," I greet him, freezing him mid-step.

"Mate?" he asks, regaining his momentum.

I wait for him to reach me, slipping my hand behind his neck as he pulls me close.

"Mate," I whisper. "For life."

His hungry lips graze my neck from beneath my earlobe to the curve at my shoulder before progressing outward. His mouth closes over the mark I gave myself.

It seems to drive him a little crazy. In a good way.

He growls at me when I interrupt him, but he gives me a heated look when I lift up my shirt and pull it over my head. My bra joins my shirt on the mossy forest floor before I undo my topknot to let my hair flow down my back.

"Are you sure about this, Tessa?" he asks, his lips brushing mine. "We could start a family if we do this now."

The Killer told me I could conceive today, but I'm not afraid of the possibility. There has been enough pain and enough sorrow. If a new life begins today, we will cherish it, love it, and raise our child to stand strong against the dark.

"I'm sure," I whisper.

Heat builds in my center as Tristan's mouth lingers over the soft curves of my breasts, tracing a path down to my stomach before he slides off my jeans and removes his own pants.

With a groan, he lifts me upward, guiding my legs around his hips before driving us back against the nearest tree. Desire burns deep in his eyes, amber flecks telling me his wolf is surfacing, the wolf whose energy I used to find foreign and now recognize as being more like me than I ever realized.

Tristan pauses, his body warm against mine, his lips whispering across my mark again before ascending to my mouth.

"For life," he says, a deep growl that echoes my commitment. A promise. His vow and mine. Through pain and sorrow, battle and hardship, joy and triumph, all the good and all the fucking challenging.

Gravity draws him deep inside me as our bodies join, driving the darkness away.

I meet the ferocity of each thrust, taking all of him, giving him all of me. Gripping his shoulders, I wrap my legs tightly around him, demanding every piece of him. Slapping my palm back against the tree, I meet his movements so sharply that I shove us away from the trunk. He responds by driving himself deeper inside me as we thud up against the tree again, intense pleasure striking through me. His claws rake down the wood at my side before they embed and grip the wood, giving him all the leverage that he wants. He's growling, I'm moaning, and every wild thrust is everything I need.

I tip my head back and scream, crashing so hard around him that I take him with me. Claiming his mouth, I inhale his growls, taste the sweat on his upper lip, and soak up the vibrations of his moans. When he draws me back to the ground, his hands and lips trail across every inch of my skin, his tongue branding me.

I soak up his touch, calm and warm.

When he returns to my mouth, the amber flecks in his eyes darken, but not with shadows. The shadows are gone.

"Run with me, Tessa," he murmurs, shifting into his wolf form. His animal's eyes are just as green, just as much Tristan. His wolf nudges my stomach and thighs, soft brushes that make me sigh.

Bending to him and shifting at the same time, my wolf nudges her face against his, inhaling the scent of his fierce power.

His breathing matches mine. His heart matches mine. And when I take off into the forest, my wolf's legs stretching, my power expanding, his strides match mine.

I am a wolf, and I am human.

I am an alpha, a friend, a daughter, and one day I'll be a mother. I am powerful and soft, forceful and gentle, angry and calm. I'm capable of love and joy, and I will give my hope to the future.

I am... me.

For life.

～

Read the next chapter in the Soul Bitten Shifter world with Iyana's story in *This Cruel Blood*.

Turn the page to find out how Everly Frost's book worlds are connected!

WHERE TO FROM HERE...

Did you know that many of my books are connected?

From the shadows of the assassin's realm to the bright world of fae warriors, and the fierce life of wolf shifters. Each series crosses over but can be read in any order.

If you'd like to read more about the Bright Ones and the enemies to lovers romance of human and fae champions, try the **complete Bright Wicked series**.

If you want to know all of the secrets of the assassins, check out the **complete Assassin's Magic world**. This includes Alexei Mason's story in **Assassin's Magic 5: Assassin's Match** (a quick read novella).

Follow that up with the darker **Assassin's Academy world**, where the lines between good and evil blur and the darkest heart is revealed.

For more about the battle between angels and dragon shifters, keep an eye out for Supernatural Legacy, starting with ***Hunt the Night.***

WHERE TO FROM HERE...

And if you'd like to know all about Iyana, check out her standalone story, **This Cruel Blood.**

Last but not least, thank you so much for the love and support you've shown the Soul Bitten Shifter series. It's a series that has pushed my comfort levels as an author with themes that have significance for me on a personal level, which are always the most challenging to write about.

Take care of yourself and the ones you love,

Everly

THIS CRUEL BLOOD: SOUL BITTEN SHIFTER 4

I am a vampire with a thirst for revenge.
Relentless. Fearless. Or so I thought...

I swore I'd never be pulled back into my old life.
I swore I was done... with him.

Aiden Brand. A pyromancer with hands of fire and a heart like ice.

Then he shows up asking for my help.
He's broken, beaten, and hell bent on seeking vengeance against the demon who hurt his family.

The same demon nearly killed me.

I thought I'd escaped the life of living in the dark spaces and fighting the monsters in the shadows.

Now my past is coming for me and there's no way out.

This cruel blood could be my end.

Content information: This is a dark urban fantasy romance, a fourth chapter in the Soul Bitten Shifter world with a HEA and NO cliffhanger. Recommended reading age is 17+ for sex scenes, mature themes, and language.

ALSO BY EVERLY FROST

SOUL BITTEN SHIFTER
(Dark Urban Fantasy Romance)
1. This Dark Wolf
2. This Broken Wolf
3. This Caged Wolf
4. This Cruel Blood

SUPERNATURAL LEGACY - Angels and Dragon Shifters coming soon!
1. Hunt the Night
2. Chase the Shadows
3. Slay the Dawn

BRIGHT WICKED - COMPLETE
(A Fantasy Romance)
1. Bright Wicked
2. Radiant Fierce
3. Infernal Dark

ASSASSIN'S MAGIC - COMPLETE
(Urban Fantasy Romance)
1. Assassin's Magic
2. Assassin's Mask
3. Assassin's Menace
4. Assassin's Maze
5. Assassin's Match

ASSASSIN'S ACADEMY - COMPLETE
(Dark Urban Fantasy Romance)
1. Rebels

2. Revenge

DEMON PACK
(Paranormal Romance)

1. Demon Pack
2. Title coming soon
3. Title coming soon

STORM PRINCESS - COMPLETE
(Fantasy Romance - Coauthored with Jaymin Eve)

Storm Princess Complete Set: Books 1 to 3 (with bonus scenes and a life after story)

1. The Princess Must Die
2. The Princess Must Strike
3. The Princess Must Reign

MORTALITY - COMPLETE
(Science-Fantasy Romance)

Mortality Complete Set: Books 1 to 4

1. Beyond the Ever Reach
2. Beneath the Guarding Stars
3. By the Icy Wild
4. Before the Raging Lion

Stand-alone fiction

The Crystal Prince (short story)

ABOUT THE AUTHOR

Everly Frost is the USA Today Bestselling and award-winning author of YA and New Adult urban fantasy and paranormal romance novels. She spent her childhood dreaming of other worlds and scribbling stories on the leftover blank pages at the back of school notebooks. She lives in Brisbane, Australia with her husband and two children.

- amazon.com/author/everlyfrost
- facebook.com/everlyfrost
- twitter.com/everlyfrost
- instagram.com/everlyfrost
- bookbub.com/authors/everly-frost

Printed in Great Britain
by Amazon